REDMAN

Finding the Man in the Maze

Deacon Hart

Three of We Press
Baltimore, Maryland

Cover design and artwork by Deacon Hart

ISBN: 978-0-692-05970-8
CreateSpace Independent Publishing Platform
North Charleston, South Carolina

To my boys—

Never forget

REDMAN

Finding the Man in the Maze

I will always remember the month that war nearly broke out in Arizona. I can record a video to show you if you like—a video of my memories that is. Nemy was with me the entire time. There's no denying that she's why I wound up at the center of it all.

I refer to Nemy as "she" because I named her after Mnemosyne, the Greek goddess of memory—and because we've developed a personal relationship over the years. Nemy knows more about me than I know about myself. At least she can show you things about me that I'm not even aware of—not consciously.

I prefer sharing with you the story of that fateful May the way I remember it without relying on a device to read my mind. There are some things I learned about myself I'd rather not share at all, but that was part of my problem. The whole time my world was falling apart, I thought I was in control. Until I admitted that I wasn't, I had been just wandering aimlessly through the maze of my life.

My name is Devi Patel—one more thing about myself I had to learn to accept.

1

☼ ☼ ☼

My canvas backpack looked out of place on the polished mahogany dining table. Even more out of place—the device inside can read minds.

That said, I should have known what Bren was thinking.

"David, for a brilliant neuroscientist, you don't have much common sense. Honey, that's the first piece of furniture we didn't get from a thrift store. Would you please put that thing on your desk?"

"Brilliant, huh?" I flashed a boyish grin. "Sorry, I stopped listening after that."

I knew this was the right time to give my beloved wife a playful kiss on the cheek and also the time to remove the tattered backpack from our new table.

"That 'thing' has a name, you know," I said as I returned from the first-floor bedroom I use as a makeshift office.

"I'm sorry, sweetheart. I appreciate how much you love...what's that adorable name you gave her? Fettuccini?"

I cleared my throat. "You know very well it's Mnemosyne. Since she's part of the family now, you have my permission to call her Nemy."

Brenda flashed a half-smile that I recognized as her signal to stop trying to be cute. "I don't want to come between you two, but with as much time as you spend together, I think she's more like my *nemeSISter.* I can be just a little jealous, can't I?" Bren pursed her lips and batted her straight black eyelashes.

Brenda nearly glowed when she pouted–one of the many reasons I fell in love with her back in grad school.

"Remember, she's the one who got us here. Your brilliant husband–research lead at the tender age of twenty-seven. At Fulton University no less." I feigned a dignified pose.

Fulton is a small but prestigious research institution near Chicago and a world leader in cognitive science investigation. The Department of Neurology secured a grant for my continued research using Nemy to transform human memories into video imagery.

"Thank God for that. I was afraid you'd have to accept that adjunct position at Nebraska and I'd become a Cornhusker."

"Just a Cornhusker's wife," I replied, "but you'll always be a *Wildcat* to me."

I pulled Bren close and tried my best at a sexy growl. The reference to her hometown team was laying it on a bit thick, but the threat of living in Nebraska deserved serious redemption. At least moving from the Arizona desert to Chicago was better than winding up on the prairie.

Bren could see right through my strategy–she always did–but she purred contentedly to play along.

"I don't know how you'll manage on your own while I'm in Amsterdam, Devi." She cooed my Hindu name motheringly as she considered me at arm's length. "I'll be away two whole weeks. No one will be here to find you matching socks."

"Excuse me," I replied with as much pomposity as I could muster, "but I answer to David now that I'm a highly respected Western scientist."

I paused to admire the tight smile that had formed on my wife's lustrous crimson lips. The way her short, dark hair framed her porcelain-smooth cheeks, the image of a Victorian doll flashed through my mind. The thought might have been what prompted me to affect an English accent.

"I do thank you for your consideration, Mrs. Patel, but I have already prepared for that contingency." Considering my Indian heritage, the irony of my mimicking British aristocracy was not lost on either of us. To recover, I pulled out the shopping bag I had dropped on the floor of the coat closet the night before and proudly displayed the half-dozen pairs of dress socks I bought at Target.

Bren replied mocking my feigned presumptuousness. "And I answer to Mrs. *Donovan*-Patel now that you've made an honest woman of me." She raised an eyebrow and added, "Don't forget who's the overlord in this Empire, my dear." Her pale skin blushed a light crimson at her pretense of cultural superiority.

Brenda returned to our small kitchen to retrieve the bagel she had been toasting. I glanced down at the morning paper she left lying open on the countertop and cringed. "Another article about Archie?" I commented. She just nodded and continued to butter her bagel. "It's been over a month. You'd think this would be old news by now."

"People don't get tired of stories about rich men who murder their mistresses," she said sardonically. "Especially when he's the son-in-law of a conservative governor."

"Well, I wish they would since he's also your brother-in-law."

"Archibald Trumble is *your* brother-in-law too," she reminded me. "When you married me, you married into all the drama that comes with the Donovan family," she added with a laugh.

"My life would be pretty boring otherwise, don't you think?"

Brenda grinned, but we both knew it was true. The academic world shuns the faintest appearance of drama.

"I really don't know what I'd do without you even for a day," I said as I folded my arms around her slender shoulders and pulled her close. "I love you, you know."

"We do make a rather good couple, wouldn't you say?"

Her kiss was proof enough.

Bren's face took on a more serious countenance. "You understand, I wouldn't leave if I didn't have to, but this is a real chance for me to make a difference. I might be at the conference as just the EPA recording secretary, but it's a step–a first step, at least." She looked earnestly at me. "Not a lot of people in this field get to take *any* steps these days, except maybe to the unemployment line."

"Yes, and I know how passionate you are about saving the environment. You may go with my blessing." I bowed gallantly and kissed her hand before breaking into a playful grin. "But knowing you, you'll wind up being more than just a secretary. God help them all."

Bren laughed, but she knew I was right. She was never one to take a back seat to anyone. Anyone except me, that is, that night two years ago during spring break. The pregnancy was a surprise, but we were elated, even if the timing was off. We had been planning to wait until we graduated and accepted the prestigious positions we dreamed of before announcing our engagement–and telling her father.

I was happy to forego the formal wedding, and Brenda really didn't mind either. We were very much in love and just wanted to be with each other. Her father, on the other hand, felt cheated out of hosting the social event of his career. Even worse, now he had a *macaca* for a son-in-law–not a vote-getting platform for Arizona politics.

Brenda retreated to our bedroom to retrieve her purse, and I grabbed some papers from my office and stuffed them in the backpack with Nemy.

"Hon, have you seen my wallet?" I called upstairs. That was a typical part of our morning routine. You'd think living in a small townhome would make it easier to find stuff, but it was quite the opposite, at least for me.

Before I could return to the kitchen, Bren was standing at the foot of the stairs again, holding the leather billfold in her outstretched hand.

"Did I say brilliant? I meant absent-minded. Here you go, professor."

I half smiled and slipped the wallet into the tweed jacket I'd just pulled on.

"And I must say," she added, "you look quite academic with those patched elbows and that goatee you're trying to grow. All you need to complete the stereotype is a pipe."

"Hmm." I stroked the black stubble accumulating on my chin. "That's a good idea. I should pick one up at 7-Eleven on my way home."

Bren grabbed my arm and squealed, “Don’t you dare! You'll be sleeping in the garage if you do. It was hard enough getting you to quit smoking. I'm sorry I even suggested the pipe thing.” She paused and grinned. “Besides, if you stop at 7-Eleven, you might wind up taking a job there.” Bren cocked her head derisively.

“My mother warned me I married a racist,” I teased. I gave my wife a peck on the cheek and slung the backpack over my shoulder.

“Here I thought I was just perceptive,” she said after she pulled me close and kissed me on my lips. “But you could pick up some tuna steaks from the fish market. I'll be home early, and it’s supposed to be nice out. We can grill on the patio.”

The long Chicago winter had given way to spring. The forsythia was in bloom, and it framed our tiny patio garden in gold. Bren enjoyed sitting under the budding red oaks that canopied the gentrified neighborhood of turn-of-the-century brownstone houses. She was happy to have escaped the gravel lawns and cactuses that define Arizona landscaping.

“All right. And no pipe. I promise.” I snatched the car keys from a dish on the kitchen counter and turned before opening the back door. We both mouthed the words *I love you* and blew air kisses as I left–a tradition we started back in college.

2

☼ ☼ ☼

"You got another message."

Marc didn't even wait for me to set down my backpack before delivering the news. We were getting used to the routine calls for interviews–and interrogations by Dean Krause.

"That thing of yours is causing quite a stir," he said as he tossed his blond ponytail over the back of the overstuffed chair in our small office.

"That's the second time this morning Nemy's been called a thing," I protested. "She has feelings, you know."

"All I know is that project of yours, or should I say *ours*, is either my ticket to a feature article in *SciAm* or the end of a very promising career." Marc ran his finger across the frame of one of his academic awards and grinned.

Marcus Anders was a top-notch research assistant from UC Berkeley, and I knew I was lucky to have him even if he was brash and cocky. In the cutthroat world of academic research, brash and cocky can be a good thing–even essential to survive.

"I can't do another interview. Not now. The semester is almost over, and I have twenty thesis papers to grade."

"You mean *I* have a twenty thesis papers to grade. Not that I mind. It's part of my job as your TA. Part of *your* job is to keep the funding coming in so I keep getting paid. Go out there and tell them how Nemy can change the world. That thing can read minds, for God's sake." Marc stood and bowed politely toward the backpack. "Sorry, babe. I shouldn't have objectified you like that."

"That *thing* is just a tool. We don't even know yet how reliable the readings are. I don't want to be making claims we can't support later. This could turn into another Segway–cute for mall cops, but life on the planet hasn't changed."

"There you go, selling your invention short again. You know what she can do. We both do. And she can do it better than any mall cop–or the CIA for that matter."

Marc was passionate about almost everything, and there was a touch of sincerity in his voice when he said that. He really believed we were working on something bigger than just our young careers.

"I'll talk to our public relations department. They're the ones who decide what I can say and when."

"Perfect. That's who the message is from. They said Krause wants you to meet with a reporter from the *Star* at noon." Marc plopped casually back into the chair. "Do you believe it? The *Chicago Star* wants to cover the story. You just shot past the academic papers and made the big time! A column right there between the financial pages and paparazzi photos of Miley Cyrus wearing crotchless panties."

"You really are just a dumb jock who got the wrong class schedule, aren't you?"

Marc winked and grinned.

"Can you at least pretend to get some work done before the entire day is wasted?" I slipped Nemy from her canvas case and started laying out her components on the lab table.

"Shouldn't you find your mistress more appropriate accommodations?" Marc whispered, pretending the hardware might overhear him. "Seriously, you haul around that multi-million-dollar invention in a flea market tote bag. She deserves at least an ostrich-skin briefcase."

"My brother gave me this pack. He brought it back from Afghanistan." I leaned in to zip the flap closed. The bag still held the smell of the desert or the PX or whatever it was that reminded me of Adam and the long first months after he got back from the battlefield. "We used this to smuggle Mom's Waterpik to the basement when we were scrounging together parts for our project."

"Now you're just pulling my leg–or maybe some other body part."

"No. I'm serious. We lived in India. We had to use parts from whatever we could get our hands on–an old game system, even alternator diodes from the '74 Jaguar he was trying to restore before he joined the Marine Corps."

"*Thus, from such humble beginnings, Mnemosyne was born.* Very touching. Make sure you toss that in at the interview. Nobody cares about the science. It's the human-interest angle that wins you a Nobel Prize."

Marc was totally Californian–he dreamed big and wanted results *now.* I probably should have been offended by his apparent lack of respect for me since I was his professor and team lead, but he was only a few years behind me and on the same career path. Soon, we'd be peers, and I looked forward to working with him in the future.

Marc pulled the six feet of his lanky frame up from the lounge chair he had "borrowed" from the bursar's office. "We seem to share a talent for appropriating materials," he observed as he patted the faux-leather upholstery.

"Let's talk about the trials," I said trying to redirect the conversation. "If we can start as soon as the school year is over, we have a better chance of enrolling some students before they take off for other jobs."

"You mean before they sign up for a study with the Human Sexuality Department. Bro, we can't compete with getting paid to masturbate." Marc paused and with a devilish grin, he glanced at his crotch. "But that gives me an idea how we can *earn* some money."

I rolled my eyes. "Thank you for the suggestion, but we were promised plenty of funding. Now that the IRB has given their blessing, everything is set except the schedule."

Approval from the Institutional Review Board can be the highest hurdle for any scholarly study, let alone one that requires subjects to divulge their memories. The critical argument had been over whether or not that was considered voluntary. We were fortunate that the board agreed to let us continue, under rigorous scrutiny of course.

"I say we offer tickets for a wild weekend on a party yacht off Navy Pier. I bet I can get every campus frat and sorority to sign up for that. Naturally, *I'd* need to be the cruise director–and I get to pick who gets into the study." Marc's hands outlined a sexy hourglass shape.

I could never tell when Marc was joking or seriously trying to play another one of his angles.

"The compensation has already been agreed to. Volunteers will receive one hundred dollars for each sixty-minute session. That should be sufficient."

"Well, at least think about switching from hypnosis to that new truth serum for putting our volunteers under. Promise them experimental drugs, and they'll line up like ants at a picnic."

"Seriously? We're not using any experimental drugs," I replied. "Maybe after cyclophaxolone gets approved by the FDA as safe, and then only if it works. For now, our subjects get a hundred dollars for an hour with Nemy."

Marc stroked the silver laptop lying on the lab table. "That's my little hooker." He turned to me and said, "That makes you her pimp, you know."

"Just get started on those research papers. I need some time to pull together this month's financial report for Krause before that interview."

Marc paused in the doorway on his way out. "Oh yeah. You're booked for lunch at Marchetti's. She must like Italian, which is probably good since you could pass for Mediterranean."

"She?"

"Yeah. The reporter interviewing you. Jill something. You're supposed to meet her there at twelve."

I rolled my eyes and sighed audibly.

"You gotta get your act together, bro. This is show time. Charm the panties off her." Marc already had a romantic lunch planned in his mind. Or at least a quickie. "But you can't show up looking like that."

"Like what? What's wrong with the way I look?" I asked.

Marc stepped back into the lab. "You look like a mannequin from Sears. The elbow patches are bad enough, but with a plaid shirt? Does your wife really let you leave the house dressed like that?"

He walked to the coat closet and yanked his black "date tie" off a hanger.

"This will help take the edge off. Or better yet, put an edge on."

He pulled me closer by my jacket lapels and draped the narrow silk tie around my neck, then deftly tied a perfect overhand knot.

"I bet your wife doesn't do *this* for you." He growled as he cinched the knot tight around my throat.

Marc patted my chest and stepped back. "Not bad. Kind of retro nerd. On you, it almost works.

3

☼ ☼ ☼

Aldo Marchetti's is only a mile away, just a couple of stops down on the campus shuttle route. I arrived a few minutes late. The semester was almost over, so students who had funds left for the year—and that excluded most of them—were either cramming for exams or finishing final papers over lunch. That made for an unusually light crowd.

"I'm meeting someone," I told the pimply teenage boy at the host station. "I don't know what she looks like."

The young man pointed to a corner booth near the window. "That must be the table you want. The lady with red hair said someone would be joining her."

I made my way past a long row of Formica tables to the window booth. A trim woman, probably in her late thirties, was texting while she nursed a Bloody Mary.

I cleared my throat. "Jill?"

The woman glanced up from her cell phone, which she immediately dropped into an oversized leather purse.

"Dr. Patel."

I shook her extended hand. Then she gestured for me to sit across from her.

"I apologize for sounding so familiar, but I didn't have your last name. And it's *Mr.* Patel, for now at least. I'm still just a doctoral candidate. The title comes later I hope. But please, call me David."

She tipped her head in acknowledgment. "I'm Jill Jackson, and Jill is just fine. I'm so happy you offered to meet with me."

"*Offered* might be an overstatement, but our dean thought it would be a good idea. I presume you want to talk about my research."

"Yes, of course." She glanced down at her handbag. "And other things. But first, let's order lunch. It's on me. Well, on DANG actually."

"Dang? I thought you reported for the *Chicago Star.*" I wasn't familiar with the name she offered.

"You haven't heard? The paper was bought by the Digital Access News Group. We're all DANG now. That's our new electronic news format. You have to offer online content for the masses to survive these days. Just keeping up with the times, so to speak." Jill giggled at her own unintended pun. "Don't worry. The *Star* gets to keep its traditional banner at least for a while."

A plump waitress appeared at our table and turned toward me.

"I'd like a Coke Zero with a slice of lime," I said.

Jill pursed her lips. "Without a shot of rum? What's the point?" She laughed. I smiled.

"And," I added, "a Greek salad."

The girl turned to Jill.

"The lunch lasagna for me. And bring us breadsticks." She tapped the empty glass in front of her, indicating she needed another Bloody Mary.

The waitress retreated to the kitchen.

"So, tell me about this project of yours," Jill said enthusiastically. "I read the article in last month's *FJCI.* It sounds like fascinating research."

The *Fulton Journal of Clinical Investigation* is a prestigious publication but with limited readership. Articles are intended to recruit students and generate funding. Seldom are they considered fascinating.

"Mnemosyne has consumed most of my attention for the past three years," I said.

Jill eagerly snatched the notepad from her bag. "Nee-moh-SEE-nee," she repeated slowly. "Is that someone you've been seeing?"

"Oh, no," I laughed. "Mnemosyne is the name my brother and I came up with for the device. She's the Titan Greek goddess of memory. The word *mnemonic* is derived from her name. We call her *Nemy* for short."

"Well, I imagine your wife will be happy to know that." Jill winked. "Although maybe not about the part that all your attention is being devoted to your work. Does she ever get to see you?"

"Research work is demanding, but we manage to have our moments together," I said and grinned. "Besides, she's busy getting her career started, or maybe I should say her *crusade.* She's been passionate about saving the environment from when she was little and her mother would take her on nature hikes in the desert."

"It sounds like you two have a dynamic relationship."

I tried to get the conversation back on topic. "So, what would you like to know about Nemy that you haven't already read?"

"I got the general idea of what you're working on—a way to unlock suppressed memories and display the images on a monitor so..."

"No, no." I stopped Jill in mid-sentence. "I don't want our memory research to sound like a video recorder for family vacations. The brain naturally stores our experiences in long-term memory, where they can linger for a lifetime. Nemy recalls these memories and moves them into short-term storage for access from the occipital lobe." I noticed Jill's eyes glaze over. I pointed to the pad of paper she was writing in. "You might mention that long-term memory is referred to as LTM. It's an opportunity to educate your readers."

Jill smiled and said, "I never miss an opportunity to inform. So, go on. LTM?"

"LTM isn't a recording of what we've seen or done—it's our perception of that experience."

"How do you mean?" she asked.

"Well, let's say your family had a pet beagle when you were two, and the dog nipped at you when you pulled its tail."

"We never had any pets, but go on."

"Right. That memory would have left a deep impression on you, and you might recall it often over your lifetime. The beagle would have been about your size when you were two, so each time you recall the event, you imagine a dog as big as you are, only now you've grown. By the time you're an adult, you're remembering being attacked by a hundred-pound killer canine. You refresh that memory and put it back in LTM."

"I see," she said. "I always wished we had a dog."

Jill resumed the interview. "Tell me how you came up with this idea for–Nesunami?"

"That's *m-n-e-m-o-s-y-n-e.*" I spelled the name as I gestured again to her notepad, which I noticed was still nearly blank.

"Oh, it rhymes with *schizophrenia,*" Jill commented matter-of-factly.

"Yes. I suppose so," I admitted, "if you drop the last syllable."

The waitress returned with a tray filled with food and drinks. She placed my salad and Coke in front of me and gave Jill a large plate of lasagna and another Bloody Mary.

"Let me know if you need anything else," she said, then disappeared into the kitchen.

Jill dipped a breadstick into the cup of marinara sauce. "Now, where were we? Oh yes, so where did it all start?"

"The idea? My brother and I were working on a project in our basement." I paused at the thought of the afternoon Adam and I first glimpsed a memory–*his* memory. If I hadn't switched the lead wires around by mistake, we might never have discovered what Nemy could do. I refocused and continued, "I was looking for a research theme for my dissertation, and we hit on this idea."

"So, you and your brother invented this–contraption? You must be close." Jill gazed into my eyes as though she were trying to read *my* mind.

"We were. Now, about the Mnemosyne research..."

Jill interrupted. "What will you be doing with your invention?"

"We haven't even started trials to see how well it works. That begins this summer. Then it will be at least a few years before any devices are approved."

"FDA, right? That must really grate on you, having to wait for their approval and all."

I laughed. "Yes, it does, but that's part of the process. It's better than just letting people put snake oil on the market."

I took a bite of my salad.

"OK, so after that. Where do you imagine this thing going?"

This was the third time today someone referred to Nemy as a *thing*, and I realized it bothered me. I pressed on. "A device like this could totally change how we treat mental illness. Schizophrenia, for example."

"Oh, just like the name sounds," Jill interjected, pleased with the connection she had made.

"Yes," I agreed absently. "What if we could actually view the experiences of alternate personalities?"

"I can only imagine what *The Three Faces of Eve* would have looked like using your footage." Jill laughed.

"Undoubtedly there would be commercial applications as well," I acknowledged.

"What about criminal investigations? I bet this could be used to solve serious crimes," she suggested.

I considered the possibility. "I imagine it could. If you had a witness at a crime scene or the victim of a traumatic assault, you could probe their memories."

Jill interrupted, "Or actually interrogate the suspect. It would be the ultimate confession, wouldn't it?"

Jill was moving in a direction I tried not to consider.

"I suppose so, but only if the suspect was willing to cooperate. Remember, memory isn't fact–it's simply our own reconstruction of our experiences."

Jill seemed to ignore my admonishment. "So, you can make movies of anyone's memories?" she asked.

"Anyone willing to undergo the treatment, yes." A tone of exasperation crept into my voice.

"Treatment?" Jill looked interested. "What kind of treatment?"

"After a subject agrees to participate–and the subject has to cooperate willingly–we conduct psychological and medical evaluations to reduce the risk of doing any harm."

Jill was attentive now. "People could be harmed by this *treatment*?"

"Well, yes. Potentially. That's true of any medical intervention–even taking aspirin. We want to know if the subject might experience a negative psychological reaction."

"Something like a bad acid trip," she joked.

"I guess you could say that," I conceded. "Enduring an emotional experience such as reliving a painful memory can be physically stressful. You want to have subjects with low risk of experiencing cardiovascular trauma."

"You're saying someone could have a heart attack undergoing your treatment?" Jill looked more shocked than quizzical.

"You could have a heart attack at any time if the conditions are right or, in this case, wrong."

"So, how do you get a subject to remember what you want to make movies of?"

"That's controlled through hypnotic suggestion. While the subject is under hypnosis, we simply ask him or her to recall the event."

"Hypnosis? I missed that part. You're a hypnotist too?"

"Yes, I hypnotize the subjects."

"Are you licensed to do that?" she asked.

"Actually, hypnotism isn't a regulated practice. There is no licensing, although there are some professional organizations that set standards. I've been experimenting with hypnotism ever since I was in my early teens."

"Is that something boys in India typically learn to do?"

"Not very often, although we'd see plenty of fakirs in the back alleys. However, the practice is closely related to shamanistic trances. A subject under hypnosis can recall events that the conscious self blocks out," I explained.

"You mean you can get someone to remember something they don't even know they remember? Did you ever have a subject remember a past life like maybe they used to live on the lost continent of Atlantis?" Jill bubbled with enthusiasm at the possibility.

"I'm sure if someone had lived on the continent of Atlantis, they'd remember it." I grimaced.

"I bet you're invited to a lot of parties." Jill flashed a big smile. "Have you ever put someone under who didn't snap out of it?" Jill seemed particularly interested now.

"No, I haven't. That rarely happens, and then only in subjects who are predisposed to psychotic breaks." I didn't mention the time I hypnotized my best friend's girlfriend at a party. It took several attempts before she recovered, and I was actually afraid she wouldn't come out of it. DANG readers didn't need to know that part of the story.

"And what about your wife?"

"What? Have I hypnotized my wife? No," I said emphatically.

Jill reached across the table and patted my hand. She smiled broadly. "I was just wondering how your wife is coping, what with you being away with your research so much of the time. This must be a difficult time for her, knowing her brother-in-law faces murder charges. Difficult for both of you, I imagine."

The reporter brushed her flame-red bangs from her eyes as she leaned back into the leather padding of the booth. She had the look of a cat about to pounce on an unsuspecting bird.

"Ms. Jackson," I said. "I came here to talk about my research, not about my personal life."

Jill tensed. "I apologize, David, but readers are always interested in the human angle of a story. You know, the personal touch. Your wife is the daughter of the governor of Arizona, so I'm sure you can understand their interest...as well as mine."

I folded my napkin and placed it on the table as I stood. "I think you have all the information you need for your readers. I look forward to seeing your article."

"I'm sure you do, Mr. Patel. I apologize if I offended you, but that's just part of doing my job."

"I'm sure it is." I pulled a ten-dollar bill from my wallet and laid it on the table. "Thank DANG for the offer, but I prefer paying for my own lunch."

4

☼ ☼ ☼

I decided to go straight home instead of back to the lab. I was in no mood to work on scheduling trials. The walk from Marchetti's to the parking lot gave me a chance to calm down after the interview and to text Marc that I was taking the rest of the day off.

"I can't believe I fell for that." I berated myself for letting Jill intrude on my personal life. She had no intention of writing a story about the research. The interview was just a ruse to publish a salacious article tied to Arizona politics. That dumb-bimbo routine was probably just an act to get to the juicy stuff she was really after.

I only hoped this wasn't going to be a black eye on the Neuroscience Department. Dean Krause relished publicity, but only when she could control the spin. Catherine was a good fundraiser, but she expected you to make compromises for the good of the program. "Poor research is better than *no* research," she would often say. Far too often for my liking.

Then there was Brenda. It had been hard enough for her to stand up to her father and tell him about us. Jack had always envisioned his youngest daughter marrying into a social dynasty or even just hooking up with a star quarterback–anyone to promote his political career. When her sister, Patsy, married Archie, I'm sure Jack was disappointed, but at least his daughter married money–big money. Money that ultimately poured into a campaign to reelect Jack Donovan to the highest office in state government. Look how that turned out. Arizona's most successful land developer and its governor's son-in-law and major campaign contributor now the prime suspect in a tabloid murder case.

Thoughts of when I met Bren's family flooded my brain: Her father's first words to me–*So you're the research scientist my daughter is going to have to marry.* Archie's condescending offer to help finance something *practical* I might come up with. Even Patsy suggesting that Brenda move in with them until I *got on my feet.*

Something I'd read about Albert Einstein randomly came to my mind. He had a closet laid out with seven identical outfits–white shirt, black suit and tie–so he could get dressed in the morning without having to decide what to wear. He didn't want anything to distract him from unraveling the mysteries of the universe. Well, I'm no Einstein, and Mnemosyne isn't the theory of relativity, but I could identify with his strategy. I'd just go home and try to refocus on my work from there.

It seemed as if I reached the faculty parking lot in just a few strides. Time and space are also relative when your mind is preoccupied. I bet Einstein hadn't considered that! I climbed into my yellow Mini and headed east on Addison. It was only one o'clock, so the drive home was relatively quick as well.

Bren would be home, so I tried talking through the interview fiasco to work it out of my system. She had enough on her mind preparing for her conference, and I didn't want to give her something new to worry about.

I was halfway down North Milwaukee when I noticed the yellow Post-It stuck to the dashboard. Bren had written a single word on the note before I left the house–*tuna.* I didn't want to have to explain why I was home early *and* forgot to pick up tuna steaks for supper, so I turned down Belmont and backtracked a couple of blocks to Binh Minh Market. We got our fish there because it was close to home, and Bren trusted that their catch was sustainable.

You wouldn't expect to find fresh fish in Arizona, but Brenda had grown up with only the finest. Jack was an ambitious man, and he had married into a wealthy family with roots deep into Arizona politics. The two Donovan girls were accustomed to having the best of everything. Brenda's mother, Evelyn, employed a family chef–not a cook, a professional chef–so the Donovans always ate very well. Bren was a junior in high school when her mother was killed in a suspected burglary of the Stillwell estate. That was a few months before Jack won the election and moved the girls into the governor's mansion. I don't know how Bren turned out to be so down-to-earth that she could fall in love with a homely guy like me. I didn't like reminding her how far she had fallen in status, so buying a couple of sustainable tuna steaks once in a while was a small price to pay.

When I left the Asian market, I realized how high a *small price* can be. A pound of ahi cost more than my food budget for an entire week while I was in grad school. The only tuna I ate for two years came in a can, and then only when it was on sale. But the price wasn't important now. I just wanted to get home and forget about the day.

We moved to Logan Square because it's halfway between Jefferson Park, home of the Fulton University campus, and the Loop, where Bren's office is. Our two-story brownstone is just a few blocks from the "L," and the Blue Line has a stop on Clark Street that lets out right in front of the EPA lab where she works. Bren doesn't mind walking to and from the station each day even in the bitter-cold Chicago winter, so we get by with just my Mini.

Rent is expensive even in this neighborhood of older homes, but Bren especially likes the mature trees and sense of history—two things you don't find in abundance in Arizona. Jack had wanted his daughter living in the Gold Coast neighborhood, and he offered to pay the difference for an apartment with a view of Lake Michigan, but we preferred doing this on our own.

Logan Square is just a couple miles from the fish market, so it didn't take long to get home. I turned down the alley behind our house and parked in the small brick garage in the back. When I opened the door to the space Bren calls our secret garden, I saw her sitting on the cast-iron bench, listening to the water trickling from the plug-in fountain tucked in a circle of deep-green hostas.

Bren looked up when I opened the garage door. She held a half-empty glass of iced tea in one hand and an Oreo in the other.

"Ah ha! Caught you," I said pointing accusingly at the half-eaten cookie.

"What?" Bren giggled with embarrassment. Oreos are her guilty pleasure—something you wouldn't find served in a governor's mansion. She held out the cookie sheepishly. "I only had one...or maybe two." She set her glass down. "And what are you doing home so early? Why didn't you call? Trying to catch me canoodling with that sexy young next-door neighbor?"

"All right. Where's he hiding?" I dipped my head to look under the patio table.

Bren stuffed the cookie into her mouth and stood to wrap her arms around my waist and give me a welcome-home kiss.

"Mmm. You taste like chocolate," I said as I licked my lips.

"And you remembered!" Bren took the package of fish from my hand. She would have been less surprised if I had forgotten.

"Why are you home so early?" she asked as she picked up the tumbler to get a refill.

"Because I knew you'd be home early, and you're cuter than Marc." That's all I needed to tell her.

"Why, that's the most romantic thing you ever said to me." She laughed and turned to put the tuna in the fridge.

I gallantly snatched the package of filets and the tumbler from her and said, "I'll do that, my lady. You just rest on your throne, and I'll return with fresh tea for you...and maybe something a bit stronger for myself."

Bren curtsied, then kissed me gently on the cheek. "Thank you, my prince."

I glanced over my shoulder as I headed up the back steps and realized I really had married a princess. My life was like a fairytale even if it would take more than a kiss to turn this frog into a handsome prince. I could only hope the *happily ever after* part would come true as well.

I tucked the tuna steaks in the refrigerator and dropped off my backpack–in my office this time. Then I poured another tea for Bren and made a gin and tonic for myself.

The day was perfect. Sunshine filtered through the budding oak tree that shaded the patio, and it painted her face with flecks of gold. I handed Bren her drink and sat in the patio chair across from her. Brenda stretched out her arms and threw her head back, eyes closed, soaking in the warmth.

"I do like it here," she said.

"You don't miss the desert?" I asked.

Bren's eyes shot open, and she leaned forward. "Are you kidding? As a girl, I always dreamed of climbing trees and playing in the snow."

I gave her a skeptical look. "Didn't your father have a treehouse built for you? And what about all those ski weekends in Aspen?"

Bren laughed. "It wasn't a treehouse–it was a plastic castle on stilts. And skiing Aspen was more work than pleasure. Patsy and I just wanted to play and be kids."

Bren loves her older sister, even if she can seem a bit shallow at times. Patsy was already married when their mother died, but she had managed to provide her little sis with the support she needed to get through the next year. Their mother's death, the political spotlight, her senior year in high school.... It must have been a difficult time even for a sixteen-year-old girl who had everything.

"Well, we can be kids now," I said as I lunged forward to tickle her under her ribs.

"Stop! Quit!" Bren squealed so loud I was sure neighbors' heads would start popping up over the board fence that enclosed us.

"Shhh." I held my fingers to her lips. "That boy next door might come over here to beat me up."

"He just might," she laughed as she pulled away. "Now grow up."

I wrapped my arms around her and pulled her close. We swayed in the spring breeze to the music of crickets and cardinals. We were in love.

After a couple of turns on the paving stones, Bren pulled back and asked, "So what's bothering you?"

"What do you mean? I just want to be home with my wife and hold her in my arms."

"Uh huh. I know you better than you think I do. Something's wrong. Did your experiment fail this morning?"

"No, no. Nothing like that." I was trapped, and Bren knows I'm a terrible liar. "I just had, uh, a meeting, and it didn't go the way I expected," I stammered.

"Obviously you don't want to talk about it, so I won't make your day any worse."

Bren took a step back. Not only does she know me, she always knows exactly the right thing to say.

"Would it make you feel better if we went inside for a nap?" She took the black silk tie in her hand and pulled it–and me–close to her chin. "Did you think I wouldn't notice that you're wearing a date tie? We wouldn't want it to go to waste now, would we?" She winked and started leading me toward the back door–and the bedroom.

☼ ☼ ☼

I actually did fall asleep for over an hour–afterward of course. Yes, we were definitely still in love.

Bren called from the kitchen, "Are you ready to start grilling the tuna? I thought we could eat in the garden before it gets dark."

I crawled out from under the white comforter and staggered naked into the kitchen.

Bren eyed me head to toe. "You might want to put on some pants first," she said. "On second thought, I like you just the way you are." Her devilish smirk let me know she meant it.

"What time is it?" I glanced at the microwave clock. "5:20? You shouldn't have let me sleep this long."

"Oh, you earned it," she purred.

Bren pulled out some greens from the refrigerator and set them next to the oil and vinegar carafes on the counter. "I'll toss the salad while you season the steaks. Oh, and no pants allowed." Bren wrapped a small apron around my waist and tied it behind me, so the apron strings were perfectly in line, and not just with each other.

She stooped to reach between my legs and pull the colander from the cabinet drawer, a task that took longer than necessary. I didn't offer to move out of her way. As she rinsed the salad greens under cold water, she said casually, "So, who did you have lunch with?"

I knew it! The interrogation hadn't ended with a bedroom call.

"They better watch out at the conference. You won't let anyone get away with any bullshit." A slight smile crossed her lips, but more to express impatience than amusement. "So how did you know?"

"The borrowed tie? Coming home early? The marinara stain on your shirt?"

Of course. Done in by a breadstick.

"So, who is she?"

I couldn't tell if Bren was just exercising her investigative skills or genuinely jealous.

"I had lunch with a reporter," I admitted.

"A pretty redhead?" Bren asked.

"No, she had mousy brown hair, and she was a frump." I lied. "And what makes you think it was a *she*?"

Bren reached into her blouse pocket and pulled out a ten-inch flame-red hair, which she held between her thumb and index finger like a dead mouse. She cocked her head and raised an eyebrow indicating I actually might be in trouble.

"OK, she had red hair." I was going to add, *but she was homely*, but I'd already dug a hole deep enough. "And she was pretty...for an older woman." That's the best I could come up with.

Bren eyed me over once more. Then she dropped the hair into the trash can and stepped closer to wrap her arms around my neck. She half-whispered in my ear, "You know I trust you, don't you?" and kissed me firmly on the lips. Then she pushed me away and added, "Don't give me a reason not to."

Bren resumed tossing the salad. "So why didn't you tell me? Is that why you came home in a bad mood?"

"I'll tell you about it over supper." I set down the salt grinder. "I'll get those pants on first," I said as I turned for the bedroom.

Bren pulled me back by the apron strings, letting the small square of fabric drop to the floor. "Oh no you don't. I haven't punished you for lying to me. You're going to serve me supper just the way you are."

I looked down at my exposed brown flesh and blushed. "But the neighbors...."

"They'll just have to peer through a knothole if they're that interested. Tonight, you're all mine."

This was one punishment I was sure I wouldn't mind.

☼ ☼ ☼

I finished searing the ahi as Bren brought out plates of salad and tall glasses of chardonnay and arranged them on the glass-top table. I slid the hot tuna steaks onto the plates and pulled out one of the patio chairs for her. I realized how cool the evening was becoming when my bare backside landed on the cast iron chair across from my beautiful wife. The chill was a bit exciting.

Bren took a bite of her tuna and smiled contentedly. “You Indians certainly know how to handle your fish.” She slipped off a sandal and rubbed her bare foot across my naked thigh.

“Thank you, kindly, Mrs. Pa... *Donovan*-Patel,” I replied obligingly.

“Now, about that lunch date?”

She hadn’t forgotten. Bren never lets go once she’s sunk her teeth in.

“Oh, that. Dean Krause wanted me to talk with a reporter from the *Star*,” I began.

“The *Chicago Star*! Honey, that’s wonderful. Your research is finally getting the recognition it deserves.” Bren was thrilled that a major newspaper was going to cover the story. “Why didn’t you want to tell me?”

“Because it wasn’t about my research. Not really. I think the reporter just used that as a way to get a story on Archie.”

Bren’s face froze, and she set her fork down slowly. “That man is nothing but trouble.”

Bren never liked Archie, and she tried to discourage her sister from marrying him. But Archie was charming and definitely rich, and their father accepted him. The two men even had business deals together. Still, Archie was a member of Arizona’s nouveau riche—not that any of Arizona’s upper class isn’t. He bore the trappings of sophistication but none of the substance. The girls’ mother was raised with money and the social responsibility that came with having it. Archie was not. Nothing seemed to matter to him more than having more money, but he was good to Patsy for the most part. They seemed to be happy together. Happy until he was charged with murder that is.

"When's the last time you talked to your sister?" I asked.

"Oh, a couple of nights ago. She's doing OK I suppose," Bren said. "She's loyal to her man. I guess that's good."

Patsy stood at Archie's side at the arraignment hearing, mostly for the news cameras, playing the role of the dutiful wife. That was probably Larry's idea. Larry Berman had been the Donovan family lawyer for years, and he took on representing Archie. He's the best trial lawyer in the state–best in the country if you asked Larry. If anyone could get Archie off, Larry could.

Bren muttered half to herself, "I can understand Patsy giving Archie the benefit of a doubt that he didn't murder his secretary, but not after the man admitted he was having an affair with her. If I were my sister, there'd be more than one murderer in that family."

Bren made an effort to regain her composure. She looked me straight in the eyes. "That goes for you too, mister," she said and then laughed. Bren took another bite of tuna, but I could tell that would be her last for the evening. Her long sip of wine would not, however.

I reached across the table and took her hands in mine. "I know how much you love your sister, and we'll do whatever we can to support her," I said. There wasn't much we could offer other than our sympathy, but maybe that was enough.

Bren stood to clear the table of my empty plate and the piece of tuna left on hers. "I'll save mine for a salad tomorrow," she said and hurried into the kitchen, wine glass in hand. I expected she'd want some time alone, so I sat naked on the cold cast iron chair and took in the chill of the evening air.

5

☼ ☼ ☼

"Bro, you've been DANGed."

"Good morning to you too, Marcus."

I peeled off my backpack and set Nemy in her place of honor on the lab table.

"Seriously, don't you read the paper?" Marc held up his iPad.

"That's a personal device, not a newspaper. And it's still the *Chicago Star*. DANG is just the corporate name."

"Whatever. You made top clicks–in the Style section, no less."

"You mean the Science section, right?"

Marc extended the screen again with *Style* in the banner. "Already three thousand likes, and it was posted this morning. You've gone viral. That's awesome!"

I wasn't comprehending the scope of what Marc was suggesting. Danged?

Marc continued reading. "'Fulton neuroscientist taps memories, by Jill Jackson.' She says, 'Soon, researchers may be able not only to read your mind but also make movies of your deepest and darkest memories.'"

"That's like something off the Syfy channel," I said.

"Wait. It gets better." Marc continued reading. "She goes on to say your device might be used to solve crimes by extracting 'irrefutable confessions.'"

"I never suggested any such thing. Where did she come up with that?"

"Maybe the same place she came up with the term *hypnoforensics*." Marc looked up from the small screen. "Is that something you coined? It's pretty catchy," he proposed.

"I certainly did not. Nemy isn't some Dick Tracy decoder ring. It can't just go around solving crimes."

"Well, Jill Jackson says different. 'With the potential to extract irrefutable confessions, Dr. Patel's device could revolutionize criminal science.'" Marc looked up again, this time accusingly. "*Dr.* Patel?"

"I made it clear I'm just a doctoral candidate. And I certainly didn't say anything about Nemy solving crimes."

"How about getting your brother-in-law off a murder charge?" Marc cocked his head. "Really? Your brother-in-law is a murderer? You never told me that."

I grabbed the iPad from Marc's hand and started reading the article. "David Patel may have a particular interest in testing hypnoforensics on his brother-in-law, Arizona land developer and investment tycoon Archibald Trumble, who faces criminal charges for the murder of his secretary and confessed mistress, Lauren Watson."

"That bitch!" I shouted. "She made all that up. She must have written that story before we even met."

"Yeah? Well, explain that to Krause. Her secretary called to schedule a meeting with you Monday, as soon as she gets back from the Philly conference."

Marc took his iPad back. "Bro, you could be in deep shit," he said. "And you didn't even fuck her." He paused. "Did you?"

Marc seemed more concerned about my romantic conquests than about the possibility of losing our jobs.

"Look, I'm sure this will all blow over," I said without the least bit of confidence. "By tomorrow, no one will remember they heard of Mnemosyne or hypnoforensics. We just have to get past today's news cycle."

I only wished I believed my own words.

☼ ☼ ☼

I managed to finish the April financials and comment on some student papers. Other than that, the rest of the day was mostly a waste. Bren had a full schedule of EPA meetings and wouldn't be home until late. I needed to be there when she found out about the story, and I didn't want to take the chance that she'd hear about it from someone in her office. She doesn't like to be disturbed while she's working, but I texted her a few times anyway.

It was three o'clock when I got a reply. All she said was, GET HOME NOW. That was enough for me know that she'd heard the news and that I was in deep shit, as Marc had proposed.

I answered, ON MY WAY.

I was ahead of the Friday rush-hour traffic, so I decided to take the expressway back instead of waiting for traffic lights by coming down Milwaukee. The route is longer, but it got me back to Logan Square before four. As I drove past our row of brownstones on my way to the alley, I noticed an expensive black Cadillac sedan parked by the curb. I squeezed the Mini into our garage and made my way across the patio to our back door. Through the small curtained window, I could see Bren sitting at the dining room table. In the chair across from her sat a tall, dark-haired man. From the back of his head, I immediately recognized the meticulously coifed silver-tipped curls, and my body tensed.

"Hello, Larry," I said as soon as I cleared the kitchen threshold.

The silver head turned to face me, and the six-foot-three-inch frame of the man beneath it rose and extended a manicured hand, which I ignored.

"What brings you to Chicago, Larry? Social visit?" I asked coldly. I already knew his answer.

Larry Berman withdrew his extended hand. "David! It's really great to see you. You're looking well. You must be enjoying the academic life. Bren tells me..."

"Cut the crap, Larry. What do you want?"

Larry knew I don't like him, and I'm sure the feeling was mutual. Still, he managed a façade of civility, the mark of every successful attorney.

"Actually, I do have business in Chicago...well, Milwaukee. But this is as close to Milwaukee as I care to come. Why anyone would actually choose to live in Milwaukee is beyond me."

"Milwaukee is on the other side of the airport, Larry–and you were just passing through?"

Bren had had enough of the verbal sparring. She stood and waved her hands. "Enough, you two. Just get down to business."

I could tell that Larry had already talked with Brenda about his reason for coming. She didn't like the family's lawyer any more than I did but she appreciated his skill for making the guilty appear innocent.

"Larry called me at work to let me know he was in town and wanted to talk to you about your research project," Bren said. Then she headed to the kitchen to pour herself a glass of tea.

"Sit down, David." Larry gestured toward the chair Bren had vacated.

I slipped off my backpack and set it in the doorway as I sat. "OK, Larry. Talk."

"Look, David, I know you don't like me, and that's your right, but I'm trying my best to convince you I'm on your side."

"Really? Like you were when my father-in-law sent you to buy me off so I wouldn't marry his daughter? And how you threatened to have my student visa revoked if I ever saw her again? Tell me, how did that work out for you and Jack?"

"You have a right to be angry about that. I hope you understand I was just looking out for the best interests of Governor Donovan–and his daughter. We didn't know you then. Jack figured you were just another immigrant looking for a ticket to stay in America." Larry paused. "I suppose that didn't come out quite right."

"Oh, I'm sure it came out exactly right. Only now this towel-head *immigrant* is part of the family unless you've come to disinherit Brenda. Just doing your job, I'm sure."

"David, please. You have it all wrong." Larry looked genuinely hurt. I imagined that was just part of the act. "I'm here to ask for your help."

Brenda returned from the kitchen stirring a packet of stevia into her iced tea. She looked directly at me and slowly nodded. I received her message, and it was clear.

"What can I do for you, Larry?" I asked.

"Jack read about your research project. He was very impressed."

Bren took the seat at the end of the table. "I was impressed too, dear. I learned an awful lot about Nemy this morning."

Her gaze seared into me like a red-hot poker.

"You know I'm defending Archie on this trumped-up murder charge. It's not just to save Archie's life–it could save Jack's career. The Governor called me this morning to see if we could get you to help prove Archie is innocent." Larry leaned his trim physique back in the dining chair and waited for my response.

"I don't understand," I said weakly. "I don't know what you or Jack or Archie expect me to do."

Larry reached into the silk pocket of his perfectly pressed silver Armani suit and produced a clipping from the morning edition of *USA Today*. Jill's article for DANG had been immediately syndicated. Jack must have read it while he was dining on eggs Benedict for breakfast.

"That..." I snatched the article from Larry's hand and clenched it in my fist like it was a live snake. "That's bullshit!" I said more forcefully than I would have preferred. "That reporter completely misrepresented my research."

"Then you didn't say, 'If you had a witness at a crime scene or the victim of a traumatic assault, you could probe their memories'?" It was no surprise that Larry had memorized the parts of the article that supported his case.

"Well, yes. I might have said that. But that's a far cry from calling Nemy a 'hypnoforensics' tool." I wasn't sure if I was helping my case or hurting it, but in Larry's hands, I knew how it was likely to turn out.

Larry nearly pleaded now. "David, Archie didn't do it. I'm convinced of that. You see what we need you to do, don't you?

Use your hypnoforensics thing either to prove Archie is innocent or someone else is guilty."

Bren leaned across the table and looked steadily into my eyes. "It's not so much for Archie, David. Patsy has gone through so much. I just want this to be over for her."

I stood and paced the floor a bit. "Even if Mnemosyne could do what you think she can, I can't leave my work now. We're about to start trials." I turned and stared directly into Larry's eyes, "Trials that are needed so we can learn exactly how much this 'thing' can and cannot actually do."

"Then start the trails with Archie," Larry proposed. "No one will blame you if it doesn't work. Just give it a try."

"You really don't understand research, do you? Clinical trials are highly regulated and scrutinized. I already signed contracts committing me to adhering to IRB guidelines. If I walk out now, the project would be terminated, the university would lose funding, and I'd lose my job–probably my entire career."

Brenda lowered her head and sighed as she rose. She stepped closer to me and took my hand. "You're right, dear. That's too much to ask just to gamble on a long shot. I thought it might help Patsy, but it really isn't likely to make that much of a difference."

She turned to Larry and said, "Tell Daddy we're sorry, but it just can't be done. Not now."

I stooped slightly to address Larry eye-to-eye. "This wouldn't turn out the way you think it would," I said calmly. "Tell Patsy I'm sorry too."

Larry rose and stepped toward the front door. He turned and said half to himself, "Jack isn't going to like your answer." He shook his head and walked back to his limo, supposedly to drive to Milwaukee.

Bren put her hands on my waist and said, “I’m sorry, sweetheart. I thought for a minute maybe we could do something to help my sister. I should have known once Larry got involved it wasn’t going to work out.”

She buried her head in my chest and did her best to control her tears.

☼ ☼ ☼

After Larry left, Bren and I took a walk through the neighborhood. It was comforting just to stroll hand-in-hand past the modest homes along Logan Boulevard. We stopped to sit on a wooden bench in Logan Park. The area is mostly a grassy field used for local concerts and art fairs. The festivals in the park were part of why we chose to live in this diverse community.

A shadow fell across our feet, cast by the giant wings of the limestone eagle perched at the top of the Illinois Centennial Monument. Bren turned to me and said, “I’m sorry I ambushed you with Larry like that.”

I told her I understood. Then I apologized for their family matters appearing in the tabloids.

She said she understood, but I had my doubts.

Bren noticed that trash had collected across the street in the community garden. On weekends, she volunteered to tend the rows of vegetables and flowers on the tiny plot of land. She said it helped her remember how much her mother loved working in their backyard garden. I picked up a large plastic shopping bag that had blown up against the monument pedestal, and we used that to collect the debris that littered the garden area. Doing something for the community and for the environment at the same time was good therapy for Bren, and since I had gotten out of shape after a long winter of nonstop work, even a little bit of bending was healthy exercise for me.

It was getting late, and we walked a block up Kedzie to a tapas restaurant Bren especially likes. The sun hadn't set yet, so we asked for a table outdoors by the sidewalk. There wasn't much of a view, just the metro station across the street, but we both enjoyed watching the eclectic mix of people in our neighborhood pass by.

Bren pointed at a long-haired skateboarder who rolled past. The boy nearly fell off his board trying to do a three-sixty in the intersection–then it was his baggy shorts that nearly fell off. The skater stumbled clutching at a belt loop and tumbled to the curb. Bren laughed so hard she almost knocked over the glass of wine the waiter had brought.

I pulled her hand down to the table. "Sweetheart, that was heartless." Then I laughed too. "I didn't know you had such an evil streak."

Only the kid's pride was hurt, and he continued skating down Kedzie pretending nothing had happened. I silently thanked him for breaking the dark mood that had settled over us.

"I have an idea," I said as we waited for our tapas plates to arrive. "This is the last weekend we'll have together for a while once you leave for Amsterdam. Let's get away."

I expected Bren to argue that she had too much work to do getting ready for the conference, but she instantly agreed. I, on the other hand, really did have too much work to do, but spending time together was more important.

"Yes, let's do that," Bren said. "Let's find a bed-and-breakfast place in the country and just cuddle for the weekend."

"Cuddle?" I raised an eyebrow as I said that. "Is that what you want to do on our last weekend together? Just *cuddle*?"

Bren blushed. “Maybe we could do some shopping too?” She giggled. “Besides, I’m just going to be gone two weeks.”

“Two weeks apart from you will seem like an eternity to me.” I wanted that to sound romantic, but we both burst out laughing.

I pulled out my Android and searched for B&Bs. “There’s a place in Milwaukee,” I suggested.

“No-o-o,” Bren moaned. “That’s where Larry will be.”

“How about a farm near Beloit?”

“A farmhouse might be nice,” she said.

“Not a farm *house*–an actual farm!” I showed her the picture of the hog snout on their home page.

“Uh, I don’t think so. Too smelly.”

“For you?” I laughed. “But that’s nature.” The gentle kick under the table let me know to keep searching.

“Well, it’s a bit of drive, but there are lots of B&Bs in Galena, near the Iowa border. Nice restaurants...and even *shopping*.”

Bren looked at a few of the promotional photos and immediately fell in love with the small historic town. She put her finger on a picture of one of the B&Bs listed.

“How about that one?”

I pulled up the site for the Prince George Guest House and booked us in the Queen Anne room.

Neither of us slept well that night, so we got up early and tossed some toiletries into an overnight case. We were both looking forward to spending the weekend away together. Bren added a nightgown, which I immediately pulled from the bag. "You won't be needing that this weekend, Mrs. Patel," I said.

She smiled and removed a pair of my cotton briefs from the suitcase. "No? Then I suppose you won't be needing these either." She flung my underpants over her shoulder and latched the case closed.

We stopped at Starbucks for coffee and a roll on the way out of town. Soon we were on the Kennedy Expressway heading west on our first road trip in almost a year.

It took half an hour to get past O'Hare. Bren had already fallen asleep by then, so I took in the countryside vistas alone.

The Illinois hills were already green with sprouting corn. The farms here reminded me of my life in India, although there's little resemblance other than an abundance of pastured cows.

Having grown up in a Hindu family, my brother and I never tasted cow until we lived in the States. Even now, I have tinges of guilt when I eat a hamburger—or at least feelings of guilty pleasure.

Adam was an American citizen. He was born at Boston General while our parents were on sabbatical teaching at MIT. They moved back to Mumbai before I was born, but Adam grew up embracing his U.S. citizenship and American culture. When he was sixteen, he informed the family that he wanted to be called Adam instead of by his Hindu name, Adamya. My father refused, but I admired my brother's willingness to throw off tradition and called him by his chosen name, at least when it was just the two of us. As an American citizen, Adam was eligible to enter the U.S. military, so he left India to join the Marine Corps when he turned eighteen. I, on the other hand, had to come to the United States on a student visa.

I was proud of my older brother. He would show up on the doorstep of our middle-class home on the university campus wearing his dress uniform so all the neighbors would see. It made our father especially proud to show the world he had fathered an elite soldier. Since our parents were academics, they were proud of me too, but for a different reason. I was top in my studies and easily accepted into the Computer Science program at India Institute of Technology, the country's most prestigious technical university. Still, I wouldn't have gotten in if my parents hadn't both been tenured teachers there, and our family certainly could not have afforded the tuition otherwise.

Adam and I were a little over two years apart in age. We fought occasionally but, for the most part, we were very close. We shared the same bedroom, although not the same interests. Adam loved the outdoors and sports and roughhousing with the neighborhood boys. I was the bookish one, which made me admire his masculinity even more. When he'd sneak a new porn magazine into the house, we'd lock ourselves in the bathroom and masturbate to pictures of sleazy Bollywood starlets. For Hindu boys, repressing sexual desire is the norm. Masturbation is the expected form of sexual release for young Indian men until they marry, even if the subject is never discussed.

A gold Camry pulled over suddenly into my lane, and I had to tap on the brakes to slow down. Bren woke up, startled and disoriented. "Did we hit something?" she said as she clutched the dashboard.

"No. Just some idiot cut us off. That's all. Go back to sleep."

"Sorry, sweetie. I didn't mean to doze off like that." She rubbed her eyes. "Are you OK driving?"

"I'm fine. It's all right, you didn't get much sleep last night. You kept tossing and turning."

"That means you didn't get much sleep either. Are you sure you're OK?"

"It's only a three-hour drive, and we're more than halfway there already."

Bren glanced at the speedometer. "At this rate, we'll be there in half an hour. Don't you think you should ease up on the gas so we don't get stopped?"

I slowed the car to seventy-five. "There. Now we're not the fastest ones on the road." I glanced over and smiled.

"Yes, that's better. Thank you. Besides, I'm in no hurry to get there." Bren turned and pressed her face up to the window. "The scenery is so beautiful."

"Nothing like Arizona, huh?" I asked.

"And nothing like India either, I suppose," she replied.

"Yeah, a lot different. I was just thinking about that."

My face must have reflected the melancholy I felt at that moment. Bren placed her hand on my thigh. "You still think about him, don't you?" she said knowingly.

"Yes, a lot."

Adam lost an arm to an IED while on patrol in Afghanistan. He was shipped back to the United States, where doctors at Walter Reed Hospital fitted him for a robotic prosthetic limb. The arm was experimental and state of the art–Adam was lucky to be selected for a trial version. It took him a couple of months to master controlling the movements of the mechanical limb with just his thoughts. The prosthesis functioned with remarkable agility, and its thought-driven control inspired me to apply some of the same principles to create the device that became Mnemosyne.

The Marines awarded Staff Sergeant Adamya Patel a Purple Heart and medical retirement from service with full disability. Adam chose to ship back to Mumbai and try to pick up the pieces of his life with family. That's when we began experimenting with memory for my research project–and that's when Adam chose to end his own life.

Bren left me to my thoughts for a few moments and then said, "I wish I could have met him."

"I wish he could have met you too."

We drove the rest of the way to Galena mostly in silence, me thinking about my brother and Bren about her sister. Then there was the episode with Larry. Neither of us wanted to think about that.

We arrived at the Prince George Guest House around noon. Our room hadn't been occupied the previous night, so our hosts offered to let us settle in right away.

The room was small but charming. Bren loved how the light filtered through the lace curtain and spilled onto the tatted quilt covering the four-poster bed that occupied most of the space. I laid the overnight bag on the side table, and Bren removed her chambray blouse and tossed it onto the armchair. I could tell we were going to have a late lunch.

I stripped off my T-shirt and khakis and kicked them under the bed. Without saying a word, Bren removed the rest of her clothing, as well as mine. We climbed under the covers naked and just held each other for almost an hour. I understood, and I felt that might have been the most romantic hour of my life.

I was nearly asleep when there was a knock at the door. I sat bolt upright in bed and instinctively pulled the covers to my chin.

Bren just responded, "Thank you."

The owner of the guest house apparently realized she had interrupted us. She left the extra pillow I had requested outside our door before quietly slipping back downstairs.

Bren and I looked at each other and giggled. We got up and dressed to explore the historic town. The springtime air was cool as we strolled down the steep, shady hillside to downtown Galena. The region is crowded in summer with tourists, but since we were there in the off-season, the town felt nearly deserted. After eating the double-dip gelato cones we called lunch, we visited each of the local shops and boutiques. We tried on silly hats and too-expensive jewelry, and we laughed like we used to when we were in school together.

In the leather shop, Bren held up a pair of assless chaps. "Here. Try these on," she ordered. The clerk glanced up and smiled while the two older women looking for graduation gifts for their grandsons hurried back onto the sidewalk. I started unbuckling my pants, which made Bren screech and pull me out of the shop as well.

"I was just doing what you told me," I said and slapped her backside. "You're a naughty little girl, aren't you?"

She grabbed me by my ears and pulled my face closer so she could kiss me. "I can be," she whispered.

The shops started to close before it was dark, so we found an Italian place around the corner for an early supper. Antonio's sounded fancier than the interior décor could support. We took a seat at one of the square tables near a display case of shop-worn promotional gear. At one time, someone must have envisioned franchising the now run-down establishment. We ordered a pepperoni and mushroom pizza and a carafe of their finest boxed wine. After a teenage couple, probably locals, left their booth, we had the entire dining room to ourselves.

"This is just like Roxy's in Boston," Bren whispered.

I noticed the faded travel posters on the walls and the curled green and red linoleum floor tiles. I had to agree.

"That's where we went after our first date," I said, the memory still vivid in my mind.

"Yes, after you took me to a Woody Allen movie. Very romantic."

"I thought *Blue Jasmine* was a chick flick and I'd impress you with how sensitive I am. Besides, how was I to know you prefer slasher movies?"

Bren kicked my shin lightly. "Not slasher movies, silly—horror films. There's a difference."

"I stand corrected. It turns out the girl of my dreams likes Freddy Kruger." This time, her kick was quite a bit harder.

Bren completed her undergraduate degree in Environmental Engineering the same year I finished my Ph.D. requirements with the Department of Brain and Cognitive Sciences. Brenda's love of nature was instilled in her by her mother. At an early age, Bren determined she would devote her life to protecting the environment.

Brenda Donovan had been a straight-A student in high school, and she graduated salutatorian of her class. As a female seeking admission to an engineering program and with her family's money and connections, Brenda could have gotten into any university of her choosing. She decided on MIT as much because it was about as far from Arizona as she could get as she did for the school's stellar reputation. My graduate project at India Institute of Technology–the one Adam and I stumbled upon–along with my parents' continued connections after teaching two years at MIT–got me a full scholarship and a student visa.

"Remember when we met?" Bren asked.

"How could I forget? My roommate dragged me along to his girlfriend's birthday party, and you were there."

Bren nodded. "And what were your first words to me?" She laid down the challenge. I had to respond.

"As I recall," I said, "'You don't know anything about me.'"

"Exactly right. I was a little drunk, and I started grilling you about..."

"...about 'third-world countries poisoning the planet through irresponsible industrialization.' Yes, I will never forget that. What a turn-on it was."

"What you didn't know was that I was fixating on your jet-black hair and your steamy dark eyes, and I told myself, *I have to meet that Indian boy.* Then it all came out wrong."

"That's an understatement. But it worked. I couldn't stop thinking about you after that night."

"I think it was the next day you called and asked if I *did* want to get to know you. Thus, movie night."

"You have no idea how traumatic asking a girl out is for a Hindu boy. Especially a pretty, WASPy girl like you. And I didn't even know then how smart you really are or about your family being all famous. If I had, I never would have made that call."

"I'm kind of glad you did."

"Kind of?!" This time I was the one doing the kicking under the table.

Our server arrived and set a limp-looking pizza on the red-and-white checkered vinyl tablecloth. I dabbed at the pools of oil that shimmered over the rubbery cheese topping. Bren and I looked at each other and broke out laughing. "Yes, exactly like Roxy's," I said.

It was dusk by the time we left Antonio's. I paid the bill, and we stepped out into the chilly evening air. A spring breeze had picked up, and we still needed to walk several blocks to return to the guest house.

I pulled Bren back into the now-patronless establishment. "I'll be right back," I told her.

She smiled probably thinking I was headed to the men's room. Instead, I walked to the young man clearing our table and pointed to the glass display case. I met him at the cash register and paid for the items I requested. Brenda's smile grew into a grin when I wrapped a pizza-slice shaped scarf around her neck and pulled a red ballcap embroidered with *Antonio's* down on my forehead.

"Now I'll never forget this place," she beamed.

"I know I won't," I replied.

"Never forget," we said in unison as we pointed to each other and laughed. I draped my arm across her shoulders, and we stepped back into the frigid night air.

As we strolled hand-in-hand past the now-shuttered shops, I couldn't help staring at my wife and admiring at how beautiful she looked.

"What?" she giggled. "Do I have pepperoni stuck in my teeth?"

"Your teeth are perfect, just like you," I said with complete sincerity.

Bren squeezed my hand, and we climbed the tier of concrete steps back to the tree-lined boulevard where our B&B was located. Bren and I sat on a wooden bench that overlooked the expanse of nineteenth-century brick buildings below us. A row of carriage lights bathed the narrow main street in a warm glow, and we huddled against the evening chill.

After several minutes of silence, I said softly, "Are you ready to try again for a family?" Losing the baby was a painful memory for Bren–for me too. But that was over a year ago, and the next day was Mother's Day. I knew the memory would be fresh on her mind, and this seemed like a good time to talk about moving forward.

"We'll see," was all she said.

We watched as the last of the street lights came on and then returned to the tatted quilt that awaited us.

7

☼ ☼ ☼

Our weekend in Galena was over much too quickly. We drove back Sunday afternoon snacking on chunks of fresh almond bark along the way. A light rain started falling, so I slowed the Mini to a more manageable speed.

About the time we arrived at the O'Hare exit, my Android pinged with an email invitation. Bren picked up my phone and read the message.

"MEETING WITH DEAN KRAUSE AT 9:00? What's that about."

The specific topic of my meeting with Catherine wasn't stated, so I didn't have to lie. "Oh, she just wants to get together after the Philly conference." I wasn't going to explain that I was pretty sure I knew what prompted the invitation.

"Certainly she's heard about the *Star* interview. How upset do you think she'll be?"

This time, I decided to lie. "You know how she loves publicity. Like they say, even bad press is better than no press. She might want to manage the follow-up. That's all."

Bren just turned her head and gazed out the window. I figured she caught me again.

☼ ☼ ☼

Monday morning, we had coffee on the patio. Bren stirred stevia into her mug as she sat across from me at the glass-top table.

"You have your meeting with Dean Krause this morning," she reminded me.

"Yes, I suppose I should leave a little early," I replied.

Brenda could tell I was apprehensive about the potential topic of discussion. She was probably concerned too. "It'll be fine," she reassured me. "Catherine has to appreciate how much you've brought to the Neuroscience Department. You've done so many wonderful things for the school." She took a sip of her coffee and rolled her dark eyes up at me. "Besides, you have lots of good karma on your side," she said smiling.

We kissed and headed for our respective jobs. Bren would use this week to prepare for her trip to Amsterdam. I, on the other hand, didn't know what to expect.

I arrived at Dean Krause's office a few minutes early. She was usually quite punctual, and I didn't want to start off on the wrong foot. Her receptionist, Cheryl, instructed me to take a seat in the small waiting area. The morning papers were neatly stacked on the coffee table, and the Tech section of the *Wall Street Journal* was conspicuously on top. I thumbed through the pages and came to the Privacy & Security news. There, in the first column, circled in blue ink I read, "Fulton neuroscientist makes big claims." I suspected in this case, no news would have been better than bad news.

Before I had a chance to read the article, Cheryl's intercom beeped. "Dean Krause will see you now," she announced.

I set the paper down and walked to the paneled door that separated the dean's office from the reception area. I felt like I had been sent to the principal's office and, in fact, I had been.

"Mr. Patel. Sit down." The words passed Catherine's lips even before I entered the room. She gestured toward the straight-back chair directly across from her.

I complied.

"How was the conference?" I began. The glare from above her amber cat-eye glasses was answer enough. I leaned back in the chair.

"Mr. Patel, I see you've been busy the few days I've been gone. Would you care to fill me in on what's happened?"

"Certainly." I cleared my throat. "I finished last month's financial report and submitted the IRB signature papers."

"Anything else that was *significant*?" She carefully enunciated the last word.

"Well, Marc and I started scheduling trials for Mnemosyne."

Catherine held up one finger, which slowly rotated downward to point directly at me. "That might be a bit premature," she said. "First, tell me about your interview with the *Chicago Star*."

I was sure there was nothing she didn't already know, and I panicked. "Dean Krause, the reporter ambushed me. She had her story already written before we even met." I took a deep breath and leaned back in the chair again.

"Really?" Catherine reached into her desk drawer and pulled out a marked-up copy of the paper.

"So, you didn't compare your research apparatus to 'a video recorder for family vacations'?"

"Well, yes, in a way. I said it was nothing like that."

She continued to scan the article. "It says here you named the project to sound like 'schizophrenia,' and you said, 'It's better than putting snake oil on the market'?" Catherine lowered the paper and looked directly at me.

"Mr. Patel. I'm sure you're aware that this institution has a reputation to protect. A very *valuable* reputation. Comparing your research project to home videos and snake oil, even in jest, does not reflect a favorable light on what we do here."

"Yes, of course, Dean Krause. I certainly respect that."

"Do you? Then exactly why do you..." she looked back down at the article, "'resent the FDA approval process'?"

"Mr. Patel, we're a research university. Much of our funding depends on FDA approval for clinical trials. If we lose that, we lose the support of the pharmaceutical companies that fund their research through us. Do you think an international conglomerate is going to trust research conducted by scientists who," she glanced down to her notes again, "'...started practicing hypnotism in India, conforming to Hindu shamanistic tradition'?"

"That was all taken out of context," I protested.

Dean Krause looked sternly at me. "Ms. Jackson's readers don't know that. Neither do the millions of people who follow the newspapers, journals, blogs, and possibly soon the network news outlets."

I felt it was best to remain silent at this point.

Catherine took a breath. "All this," she poked at the news article, "is a lot of media hype that could easily be forgotten by tomorrow. But right now, we have the world's attention, and we can take advantage of that."

Ah-ha! There it is. The bad-news-is-better-than-no-news argument.

"What concerns me more, however...."

However? That can't be good.

"What concerns me more is that you may have opened this department to criminal action."

I didn't see that coming. "What...what do you mean?" I stammered.

Catherine began reading again. "'Dr. Patel admitted some people could be harmed by this treatment with an experience comparable to a bad acid trip.'"

I sat upright, my eyes wide.

"Wait. It gets worse."

Worse? How could it be any worse?

"'Dr. Patel warned that subjects in his research could have heart attacks if the conditions were right.'" Dean Krause set the paper down and leaned back in her chair. "Mr. Patel," she said, "this department strongly believes that your research is important and that you are a brilliant young researcher."

I sensed another *however* coming up.

"I think it's best that we put your research on hold while the university conducts a thorough review."

I shot up from the chair and leaned hard on her desk. "But trials are scheduled to start in two weeks."

"Then unschedule them." She looked down and began shuffling through the papers that were neatly arranged on her desk.

"What am I supposed to do in the meantime?" I asked.

"Mr. Patel, I don't really care what you do, so long as you don't talk to the press about your research or to anyone else for that matter. Consider yourself on sabbatical for the summer, with pay of course."

I opened the office door to leave when I remembered Marc had scheduled his summer around the research trials. I turned to Catherine and said tentatively, "What about my research assistant, Marc?"

Dean Krause looked up. "Marcus Anders? That boy has a lot of potential. We wouldn't want to lose him. You may have him assist you with whatever other project the two of you dream up."

As I turned to leave she added, "One more thing. You probably should keep confidential the accounts of your subjects who," she looked down at the news article again, "'remember a past life as a resident of the lost continent of Atlantis.'" She leaned on her desk and said coldly, "Mr. Patel, I expect not to hear from or about you until September."

I closed the door behind me when I left. "So much for good karma," I muttered to myself.

Marc was waiting for me when I got to the lab.

"So, how did it go?"

"Pack your bags. We're flying to Phoenix."

8

The week passed quickly. I finished grading my students' term papers, and Bren stayed late at work preparing charts and spreadsheets for her EPA team.

Marc went back to Los Angeles for the week. He had promised he'd be home for his sister's high school graduation. Instead of flying back to Chicago, Marc changed his return ticket to Phoenix. He was arriving Saturday, and Bren didn't leave for Amsterdam until Sunday, so I told him to book us a room and a car, and I'd join him there.

Dinners were mostly carryout since Brenda and I were too tired in the evening to cook. Not too tired for bedroom calls, however–and not all of those were in the bedroom.

Sunday morning rolled around, and we packed for our respective trips–hers to catered lobster dinners and mine to drive-through burger specials. The department kept Marc and me on the payroll, but our travel budget was cut drastically.

Bren and I both had afternoon flights. The Blue Line terminates at the airport. For Bren, taking the commuter train is the environmentally responsible way to travel–for me, it's just cheaper. We rolled our bags the three blocks to the tapas restaurant for brunch. Then we walked across Logan Park to the CTA station. As we waited in the subway for the next train to arrive, Bren pushed up the brim of my Antonio's cap so she could kiss me. Then she flung the tip of the pizza scarf over her shoulder and laughed.

"Never forget," we said together–a new tradition inspired by our Galena weekend.

The northbound Blue Line pulled in a minute later, and we rolled our bags onto the commuter train. For most of the half-hour ride to O'Hare, Brenda texted her coworkers, and I browsed for information about Phoenix. We got off at the airport station. Bren needed to take a shuttle to terminal five, for international flights. I helped her with her bags, and we gave each other a quick kiss. As her bus pulled away, I thought, "Look at us. We're like an old married couple."

My nonstop flight from O'Hare to Sky Harbor Airport was uneventful. I had texted Marc that my plane was scheduled to land at 6:20 p.m. and to pick me up at arrivals by six thirty. We got in a few minutes early, and I made my way to the baggage claim area. I pulled my suitcase from the carousel and stepped outside into the uncomfortably warm desert air.

Marc hadn't arrived yet. That was to be expected. I texted him again to tell him I was waiting by the curb. A minute later he pinged his reply: OMW. I slipped off my backpack and sat down on the large roller bag I had brought along. It was packed with forty-nine pounds of textbooks and a change of clothes to get me through the two weeks we planned to be in Phoenix.

I pulled out my cell phone again and texted Bren. She should be over Nova Scotia about now, I thought. At least a message would be waiting when she landed to remind her how much I loved her. It was another ten minutes before Marc rolled up in a red Jeep Wrangler with the top removed. His smooth bare chest was already pink from the sun, and he had a red bandanna tied around his head to keep his shoulder-length California-blond hair from blowing in his face. I felt like I was hopping in next to Mad Max.

"Nice ballcap," he said. "What are you, the pizza boy now?" Then he added, "And you're early."

"No. You're late," I replied coolly. "But by your reckoning, I suppose that would make me early."

Marc ignored the comment and proceeded to our hotel room. North Scottsdale, where Archie and Patsy have what Brenda calls their Spanish villa in the exclusive DC Ranch community, was a two-hour drive north. Instead, we headed toward downtown Phoenix to the Festiva Inn. Marc said that was the only place where he could get a suite within our budget. I was pretty sure it was because the University of Arizona College of Medicine was within walking distance, and Marc has a thing for nurses.

We drove through Wendy's on the way, and I picked up a chicken sandwich and a Diet Coke. The hotel was nicer than I expected until we stepped into our ground-floor suite.

"You've been here twenty-four hours, and you have the place looking like this?" I was astonished by the number of empty beer cans and articles of clothing strewn around the small studio suite. The detritus included Coors Light and blue panties. I assumed at least the latter weren't his.

"Oh yeah. We kind of had a party last night. I got most of it cleaned up." Marc kicked a stack of pizza boxes aside to clear a spot for me to set my suitcase.

I peered through the closed glass French doors into the small bedroom. "Even your bed is a disaster," I observed. "Where's my room?"

"Your room? On our budget? Sorry, bro, this is the best I could come up with. But there's a pull-out couch if you don't want to bunk with me."

I pushed aside the tank top on the sofa and sat down. The cushion springs groaned and gave way to swallow my frame. "I guess I'll settle for the couch," I conceded reluctantly.

"What? You didn't have brothers when you grew up?" Marc asked half accusingly.

"Yes, I had one brother," I answered in a measured tone.

"Yeah, me too. We slept in the same bed until I was in high school. And that was a single. But whatever. It's your choice."

Immediately, I remembered sleeping in the double bed with my brother when I was twelve and the first morning I woke up with an erection. He ripped the covers off us and laughed. When he saw I was mortified, he stroked himself until he was hard too. We lay there in bed, stroking ourselves and sizing each other up. Adam assured me that's what it meant to be a man. After that, we sported morning wood with pride.

I removed the complimentary newspaper from the writing desk and placed the backpack there. "This area is reserved for Nemy," I said firmly.

"Yes, sir," Marc replied half sarcastically. "Only the best for the lady."

Marc lifted my suitcase so he could pull another beer from the small room refrigerator. "What do you have in here?" he groaned. "Books?"

"Yes, as a matter of fact, I do." I felt I needed to defend my decision to bring along reference materials. "We're on a research trip, remember?"

"Right," Marc replied. "Well, I plan to do a lot of my research poolside."

"And I plan to get some sleep. I was up most of last night getting ready for the trip."

"Uh huh. Getting ready as in a booty call to last you two weeks." Marc grinned. He wasn't wrong about that, however.

"Well, if you're going to crash early," Marc said, "I think I'll walk over to the campus library for some late-night study." Marc pulled on a white tank top and took out a slip of paper from his shorts pocket.

"What? You hooked up with someone already?"

"Bro, it's day two for me. Of course I did. With a nurse no less." Marc reached for the doorknob. "I'll try to not wake you when I get in."

☼ ☼ ☼

The next morning, I regretted choosing the couch. My body had conformed to a crescent shape, and I slouched around the apartment for an hour before I could fully straighten up. I looked through the glass doors and could see Marc sprawled across the king-size bed, fast asleep. I might renegotiate sleeping arrangements, I thought.

I slipped into some khaki shorts and headed to the lobby, where they served a buffet breakfast until nine. Mostly cold cereal and bananas. At least those were the menu items I went for–that and a Styrofoam cup of coffee.

I sat at one of the café tables near a window and pulled out my cell phone. I better let Archie know I'm here, I thought. I had emailed him the week before that I was planning to come down, but I had been avoiding talking to him.

My brother-in-law was the kind of guy you wouldn't buy a used car from. Or maybe you would and then regret it the next day. He moved from Las Vegas to Scottsdale in the nineties, just before the construction boom hit Central Arizona. Phoenix was a shimmering diamond in the desert then. Now, the valley looks more like a scrapheap of recycled glass.

Archie was proud of his start in construction as a blaster helping to expand the aqueduct system from Lake Meade to Las Vegas. He was only seventeen when he hired on to the crew using a fake ID. By the time Arch was in his mid-twenties, he had started his own company pouring concrete foundations for the casinos going up along the Strip. He sold the company at a sizable profit and moved operations to Scottsdale. Before he turned forty, Archibald Trumble made the list of Arizona's ten wealthiest residents, and now he was closing in on number one.

Southwest Enterprise was one of the few construction companies to survive the housing market crash of 2008. Archie had diversified into trucking and other building-related businesses. He even managed to buy out several of his competitors who faced bankruptcy. That put him in a position to build his financial empire during the recovery. It had long appeared to me that Patsy was just another strategic acquisition for him, but I kept that sentiment to myself.

Someone with a Hispanic accent answered the phone, "The Trumble Residence." A minute later I was talking to my brother-in-law. I told him we'd come over after lunch.

9

☼ ☼ ☼

"Look, David, don't get me wrong. I'm glad you came down to help me out. That shows real family loyalty, and I respect loyalty. At first, I thought our father-in-law was blowing smoke up my ass suggesting you could help, but maybe there is something you can do with that...that gizmo of yours."

Gizmo? At least he didn't refer to Nemy as a thing.

"See, I have enemies who are out to get me. Well, not so much enemies as hostile business associates who are jealous of my success." Archie's upper lip curled as he considered the perceived threat. "These guys have been trying to take over my trucking routes for years. I was skeptical when Larry informed me he planned to recruit your services, but the more I thought about it, I came up with a way maybe you can help."

Archie's eyes darted across the patio before he continued.

"So, this thing of yours..."

There it was.

"...it can really tell what someone's thinking, like a lie detector or something?"

Marc eagerly volunteered, "Not just tell you. Nemy *shows* you what someone is thinking."

I clarified, "What they remember, actually. The technique doesn't really tell what's true, just how someone remembers it. That can make a big difference."

"Sure. Whatever. But that could be just what I need."

The sound of the patio door sliding open interrupted our conversation. We all looked up to notice the long, tan legs that supported the fashion-model frame of Brenda's older sister, Patsy. I could see that Marc's eyes didn't make it past the small black bikini bottom tied on with silver laces.

"Archie, why didn't you tell me David was here?"

Patsy tossed back her auburn curls as her cork-heeled sandals carried her silently over to Archie's side. The ice cubes in the tall drink she carried clinked when she leaned over to kiss her husband's balding forehead.

"What? You couldn't bring drinks for all of us?" Archie complained. He leaned toward the veranda and yelled to the Hispanic houseboy who had met us at the door. "Hey, Zeus. Bring us a round of mojitos." Arch made a circle in the air with his finger and smirked at what he thought was a clever twist on the young man's Spanish name.

Patsy's green eyes fixed on Marc.

"David, you didn't mention you were bringing a friend."

Patsy eased herself into the Spanish-style lounge chair next to Archie and crossed her shapely legs.

"Patsy, it's nice to see you." I rose to greet my sister-in-law, then gestured toward Marc. "This is my research assistant, Marcus Anders."

Marc leaned in to take hold of her extended hand and to get a closer look. "Just call me Marc."

"Oh, I will, Marc," she said as she raised her left hand to stroke her temple, shooting a pointed glance in Archie's direction at the same time.

"I was just talking to David about how he might be able to help with my case," Archie interrupted.

"Would that have anything to do with the Paganos?" Patsy extended her lower lip on the last syllable.

"You know as well as I do they're behind setting me up. Maybe David can prove it."

"And Marc," Patsy added, turning her eyes in his direction.

"Yeah, whatever it takes."

"Well, I'll leave you boys to work it out. Heaven knows, Arch needs all the help he can get."

Patsy lifted herself from the padded chair cushion and retreated to the house. "I'll have Jesus make those doubles," she said before disappearing into the studio.

Archie leaned close to me and said, half to himself, "She hasn't totally forgiven me for that thing with my secretary."

"Lauren Watson? I've been reading up on the case," I said.

"Yeah. I guess I don't blame her, but she'll get over it." Archie picked up his drink and resumed his relaxed posture. "I just need to get over these bogus charges first."

So, he didn't do it. Of course, he would say that. I just wanted to get whatever it was Arch or Jack or Larry thought I could do to help over with.

Marc asked, "Who are the Paganos? Why did they set you up?"

"They set me up because they want to take over my trucking business. Pauly's been after that for almost a decade."

"Pauly?" I asked.

"Yeah. He's the head of the Milwaukee family, and he wants my trucks to run his drugs north. Now that the wall has the border sealed off at Nogales, the trade has become much more lucrative."

"Drugs?" You're running drugs?" I was incredulous, but I immediately realized I should not have said that out loud.

Archie slammed his fist on the glass tabletop and rose deliberately, exaggerating the height of his five-foot-six frame. "No, I don't run drugs." His tone was defensive as he trained his gaze in my direction.

Just as suddenly, he relaxed and said with a half-smile, "Although there's no way I can control what someone else hauls when they rent a rig from me. That's their business, but I like to keep my own enterprise clean. I have a good reputation as an honest businessman I need to protect."

I nodded in what could be interpreted as agreement.

Archie paced to the back of his chair. Then he said with a note of pride, "I built that wall, you know. Nobody crosses the Arizona border without having to go through *my* wall." Arch returned to his seat and leaned hard on his elbows. "Pauly has tried buying out my business, he's threatened me, he even offered me membership in the family."

This time Marc couldn't contain his astonishment. "You're being threatened by a drug lord? Wow! That's intense."

Archie laughed. "Yeah. You could call it that. But I have my connections, and Pauly doesn't worry me. At least he didn't until this."

"So, you think the Paganos blew up the office trailer and...." This time I stopped short.

"And killed my mistress?" Arch finished for me. "You can say it. We all know what happened. For Christ's sake, I'm fifty-six years old and rich—of course I had a mistress. Who doesn't? Patsy gets it. She might not be happy about it, but she gets it."

Marc changed the topic, "So why aren't the police after the Paganos?"

"The family's not dumb," Archie said. "You don't keep a business running for decades by being dumb. Pauly had this all planned out to make me look guilty. He knew about me and Lauren. I'm not going to score any points with public opinion arranging a romantic rendezvous with my secretary, now am I?" Archie looked directly at me when he said that. "It makes sense making it look like I set up a date with her at the company mobile office so I could stage an accident."

"Accident?" I interrupted. "I read that in addition to blowing up the trailer, almost ten acres of Native American burial grounds were destroyed by the explosion. How can that look like an accident?"

"Diabolical, right? Yeah, Pauly had this figured out from every angle. Not only might I want my girlfriend out of the way—and eventually, who doesn't, right?—I've been in a legal battle for two years with the Pima Indians—or Papago Indians, or whatever the hell it is they call themselves—for drilling rights on that land. I offered to relocate the *sacred remains of their ancestors* to an even nicer spot." Archie looked into the near distance imagining the proposed location. His hand swept through the air as he spoke. "A hillside overlooking the Santa Cruz. Some shade trees since there's a spring up there. I even offered to put up a wrought iron fence." The vision vanished, and Arch resumed the conversation. "Wrought iron, mind you. Not that cheap aluminum shit they put up now. They wouldn't go for it. I was giving them prime real estate in exchange for some dried-up plateau along the border. What better way to push the deal through than to just blow up the whole damn thing?"

Jesus arrived with a tray of mojitos and handed Marc and me each a frosty glass.

"You don't have an alibi?" I asked after a long sip of the perfectly crafted drink.

"Oh, sure. My alibi is that I should have been in the trailer when it blew. I texted Lauren to meet me there half an hour earlier. She was on time. Typical. But not me. I was stuck on the side of the road waiting for a tow truck."

"Then the towing company must have a record that you weren't there," Marc observed. "That you couldn't have blown up the trailer."

"You'd think, huh? But from the time I called until they showed up, I could have driven to the trailer twice. That makes me look even more guilty. 'Yes, officers, I was on my way to the crime scene, but my car broke down.'"

"That does sound a little fishy," Marc conceded.

"What's really fishy is why I had to call for a tow. I hit a javelina pig, that's why. It tore up the front end of the car and ripped a hole in the radiator." Archie leaned in and almost whispered, "So how did Pauly arrange that, huh? He sent out a hit pig for me?"

"That is weird," Marc agreed. He had already drained his glass and was chewing on an ice chip.

"So, if I hadn't hit the pig, I would have been there when he blew the trailer." Archie looked me straight in the eyes. "He wanted *me* dead too."

Marc turned to me and said quietly, "I think we're in some pretty deep shit." He set his empty glass on the table.

I sighed and couldn't help rolling my eyes. "So, what can we do about it?" I asked.

"You can get me off this murder rap, that's what," Archie said as he leaned in and poked a finger in my chest. "You can get a confession from the guy who did it."

For the first time, Archie actually sounded sincere.

"You mean Pauly?" Marc blurted.

"No, of course not Pauly. He's too smart to get involved like that. He just gives the orders. And I know who he gave the orders to."

"You realize," I said, "that Nemy doesn't work if someone isn't willing to be questioned. You'd have to get the suspect to let us wire him up and then submit to hypnosis. You can't force someone to do that."

"Oh, I think I can," Archie said with a sneer. "You just leave that to me. Set up your shit here tomorrow morning and plan to get a confession."

Marc and I exchanged puzzled looks.

"All right," I said. "You produce a willing subject, and we'll conduct the interview."

"That's all I'm asking," Archie said. "Be here by eleven o'clock. Get this over with, and then stay for lunch and spend some time in the pool. Jesus can give you boys full-body massages." Archie pronounced his Hispanic servant's name with a hard J sound. "His hands can perform miracles." Then he laughed at his attempt to make a crude joke.

Marc brightened at the idea, but I just finished my drink and grunted. "We'll be here by eleven," I promised as I stood to leave. "Don't trouble yourself with lunch."

10

☼ ☼ ☼

Jesus ushered us to the Jeep and swung the massive front gate open as we drove out. When Marc reached the end of the long driveway, I saw a silver Lexus pull away from the curb and disappear around the corner of Camelback Road.

"I think that's the same car I saw when we pulled out of the hotel," I said to Marc.

"Right. Like there wouldn't be another Lexus in this neighborhood. This drug deal business really has you spooked," he said.

"So, you're an expert on drug deals, I suppose?"

Marc just smiled and kept his eyes on the road.

I pulled out my cell phone and texted Bren. It must be about suppertime there, I thought as I poked at the phone. MET WITH PATSY AND ARCH. DON'T KNOW WHAT HE EXPECTS BUT WILL DO WHAT WE CAN. CALL TONIGHT?

It was almost a two-hour drive back to the hotel. When we got to Phoenix, we stopped at a strip mall to pick up supplies. Marc's beer, mostly. We ordered a couple of Subway sandwiches and took them back to the room. Marc plopped himself in the overstuffed side chair to consume his meatball sub. Two beers were perched on the end table to wash it down. He took the remote and switched on the TV mounted above a small entertainment center.

Scenes of Native Americans chanting and waving signs flashed on the screen. "Last night, members of the Tohono O'odham tribe, known locally as Papago Indians, were joined by more than two dozen members of neighboring tribes to protest the destruction of what they claim to be ancient sacred burial grounds," the voice-over announced. "The protest is now in its second week. National Guard troops have been placed on standby status for activation by Governor Jack Donovan to assure...."

Marc started to flip through the channels when I told him to go back to the news story. "That's the site of the bombing," I said.

"So?"

"So, that's the reason Patsy's husband is facing murder charges."

"But the Cubs are playing at home." Marc seemed incredulous that I asked him to change the channel, but he did reluctantly.

"...more than twenty people now occupy the site, with dozens more pledging to join the protest by Memorial Day weekend." An elderly Native American man appeared on the screen with a microphone thrust up to his mouth. "The O'odham have called this land home for a thousand years. We survived the Spanish invaders. We survived the American resettlement. We will survive this tragedy as well. Our ancestors are crying out for peace as much as for justice." The old man's statement sounded sincere, and the band of supporters seemed committed to the cause, whatever that cause might be.

"OK, you can switch to WGN," I said. "There's nothing on the news that helps."

I set up my laptop on the writing table in the small living area and worked on next year's budget. Marc watched the final three innings of the game. The Cubs lost, but that never seemed to get him down. He pulled out the last bottle from the six-pack and headed to the bedroom. Marc peeled off the loud Hawaiian shirt he'd been wearing and sprawled across the mound of pillows on the king-size bed.

"What's the Wi-Fi code?" I asked, but Marc was already asleep. I reached for the phone to call the front desk when I noticed the used condom behind the table lamp. *It's going to be a very long two weeks.*

My research on the O'odham people turned up a wealth of historical information but nothing that seemed to help Archie's case. There are two main O'odham tribes–the Akimal, south of Phoenix and the Tohono, on either side of the U.S.-Mexico border. When the Spaniards first met the indigenous inhabitants, they asked what the name of their tribe was, and the Akimal O'odham replied in their own language the equivalent of, "What are you trying to say?" To the Spaniards, the phrase sounded like *pima.* The name these people gave to their southern brothers sounded like *papago.* The derogatory term meant "bean eaters," but Europeans came to call the aboriginal peoples of southern Arizona the Pima and Papago Indians. To this day, the O'odham reservation is located primarily in Pima County. That and Maricopa County, infamous for police profiling and white-supremacist oppression in this century.

Since I didn't find anything helpful for our meeting tomorrow, I concentrated on researching the latest papers published on topics related to neuroscience. I really am getting boring, I told myself.

It was after six before I realized I had spent the entire afternoon reading papers about research in cognitive science. *What a geek.* Marc was still sleeping off too much alcohol and sun, so I decided to don my cap and find the nearest bar for happy hour. That was Casa Verde, about a quarter mile down the road. It turned out to be an upscale Mexican restaurant. I found a stool at one of the small tables in the bar area and checked out the happy hour specials. I opted for the handmade guacamole and a margarita. The waiter came back with a large glass filled mostly with ice, but I didn't mind–it was hot, and I didn't want a lot to drink.

I munched on tortilla chips while I waited for the side dish to arrive. From over my shoulder, I heard a familiar voice.

"Why, David. What a surprise to find you here."

I spun around on my stool to see Jill. She was fashionably attired in a chic white blouse and khaki culottes.

"What are you doing here?" My tone was more accusatory than asking.

"Oh, I just happened to be in the neighborhood," she purred.

"You! That was *you* in the silver Lexus. You've been stalking me," I nearly shouted.

"Stalking is a rather strong word, David. I think *investigating* would be more appropriate." Jill laughed at her perceived cleverness. "I found out you were on sabbatical in Arizona, and I thought that was an odd coincidence since this is where your brother-in-law lives."

"I'm just down here to support my wife's sister. That's all." I tried to sound convincing, but it came across more like sarcasm.

"Really? Then why did you bring your research assistant? No, I think you're here for more than that." Jill waved to the waiter and held up two fingers while she pointed to my drink. "I think you know something about the murder, and I want to help you."

"Help me? Like you help educate your readers? Or you help promote my research? No, you're here to help yourself to a salacious news story."

"David, how cynical. Although you're not entirely wrong. Yes, this story has all the makings of a runaway viral hit, but I really do have more altruistic motives. Please, just hear me out."

The waiter with the guacamole arrived and began mashing away at the green flesh of the soft fruit. I intentionally ignored Jill and concentrated on the onion and jalapeño accouterments being added to the dip.

"I'm sure I'll regret this, but I'm listening," I finally said.

"I knew you were inquisitive," Jill began. Then she leaned in and reached for my arm, which I abruptly pulled away. "You see, I've been following Arizona politics for quite a while, ever since they started walling off the state from Mexico. There's a bigger story here than you're aware of, and I think your brother-in-law is part of it. I'm sure he is, actually."

Jill leaned back on her bar stool just in time for the waiter to return with our drinks.

"I'm really not concerned about Arizona politics," I said. "In fact, I'm not all that concerned about politics in general." I took a salty gulp of my margarita.

"Maybe you should be," she said. "Maybe you should be concerned about the fate of the Indians."

"I know they have their sit-in going, and I sympathize with them. But what are you going to do? If the oil companies want your land, they're going to get it one way or another."

"Those aren't the Indians I was talking about," she said. Jill fixed her eyes on the dish I had ordered and reached for a tortilla chip. "I love fresh guac. May I?"

Without waiting for me to answer, she scooped up a large portion from the bowl and navigated it to her mouth.

"So, you're referring to *real* Indians?" I said. "Like me, I mean?"

"Exactly. You realize that the plight of the Native Americans is your plight as well, don't you?"

Jill's assessment was perplexing but intriguing.

"Go on," I said. "You have two minutes of my time."

Jill sighed heavily. "Don't you see? You really don't get it, do you?" The O'odham Indians–you Calcutta Indians..."

"Mumbai," I corrected her.

"It's all the same. You're all pawns in a giant game of political chess." Jill took another poke at the guacamole and washed it down with a cold sip.

"I'm a successful neuroscientist married to the daughter of a United States governor. I'm not making much of a connection here." I leaned back on my stool with a smug look on my face.

"Really? What about that student visa you had to get to come here? Yes, you've married yourself into the family of U.S. citizens, but have you ever felt entirely accepted? No, I don't think so."

The image of Adam in his Marine dress blues flashed through my head. He was born in the States and I wasn't, and that made all the difference. She was right, I never did feel entirely accepted.

Jill leaned in conspiratorially. "This country has always been about pushing out brown people. First, it was the Native

Americans, herding them onto reservations. Now, it's mass deportations. Your brother-in-law is a player in this. So is your wife's father."

"You sound like a radicalized liberal. No wonder the press is accused of bias."

"I sound like I'm going to blow the lid off their egocentric scheme, but I need your help."

"Look, Arch is my sister-in-law's husband, and I'm here to help her. I don't really care what happens to Archie Trumble, and I especially don't care what happens to you and this quest you're on."

I started to leave the table when Jill grabbed my arm. "Maybe you don't care today, but you will. Someday, you will."

Jill reached into her handbag and pulled out a business card. "Here," she said, stuffing the card into my shirt pocket. "You call me when you're ready." She snapped her purse closed, then looked deep into my eyes. "But don't take too long."

I scooped out the last of the guac as I stood to leave. "This time I'll let *you* pick up the check," I said and popped the chip into my mouth.

The evening air gave some relief to the sweltering afternoon heat. I unbuttoned my polo shirt to let the breeze blow across my chest while I walked back to the hotel. There was something gratifying about confronting the *Star's* muckraking reporter–no, *DANG* did sound more appropriate. Did she really think I'd fall for that pathetic appeal to my ethnicity? And why track me down in Phoenix? Was I that important to her story?

My cell phone interrupted my thoughts. "Bren? Hi. I was really hoping you'd call. I've missed you so much it hurts."

"You're laying it on a bit thick, aren't you?" Her response was predictable, including the delightful laugh that followed.

"Well, I do miss you. Are you settled in?"

"Settled in? We've already had a grueling day of pre-meetings. Those are the meeting you have to discuss what you're going to say at the meeting you're going to have."

"Ah, the music of bureaucracy. I know how much you love it. Have they put you in charge yet?" I half expected her to answer yes.

"No, silly. I'm still just the errand girl around here. But I'll have my chance."

"I'm sure you will, and then they'll all realize how fortunate they are to have you on their side." I wished she could see the grin that engulfed my face.

I leaned against a live oak tree at the edge of a small park while we talked about her trip and Amsterdam and the boutique hotel she was staying in. For someone not raised in opulent excess, this would have been a fairytale come true, but it was second nature for Brenda. I knew she would not only survive in that environment–she would thrive. It was a world we might never share, but at least I could indulge her continuing membership in that exclusive club.

Bren went on to tell me about meeting with people I'd never heard of but who were obviously living icons for her. It made me happy to hear her enthusiasm and utter joy over being part of this influential international cadre and all for a cause she sincerely believed in.

After several minutes, she turned the conversation to me.

"How are you and Marc getting on? Have you seen Patsy?" she asked.

"Oh, we saw Patsy, all right. Marc actually saw more of her than I did since I nearly had to pry his face out of her cleavage." I wondered as soon as I said it if that was an appropriate thing to say about my sister-in-law. Fortunately, Bren just laughed.

"Patsy will never change. I'm glad Marc is enjoying her *hospitality*."

"I'm more worried about Archie showing us some hospitality of his own. He doesn't seem to be the sort of guy who'd share his trophy wife with other men. Especially not when they're less than half his age."

"Don't you worry about Arch. Patsy can handle him. You need to worry about Marc!"

We both laughed.

"We'll find out tomorrow," I said. "Archie has an appointment set up with Nemy in the morning. He invited us for lunch and time in their pool. I declined, but somehow I think Marc will override me on this one."

"That's my loving husband," she said. "Always concerned about everybody else's feelings. Well, I hope you two enjoy yourselves."

"I promise I'll be nice, even if I don't particularly enjoy Archie's company. After all, he is my brother-in-law."

"So, nothing else exciting happened while you've been there?" Bren asked.

I fingered Jill's business card in my pocket. *She knows. That was twenty minutes ago, and she already knows?* I realized I had to be honest with Bren, not just because it was the right thing to do, but because she was sure to find out anyway.

"Well, there's one thing that was a little strange," I began. Silence on the other end didn't ease my mounting anxiety. "You remember that *Chicago Star* reporter, the one who trapped me into an interview to get a story about Archie? She followed me here."

More silence.

"Bren?"

"I'm listening. Did you two meet?"

"Sort of. She ambushed me while I was having a drink."

"I see."

For a moment, I thought she actually could.

"Did you tell her anything...new?" Bren asked.

"No. She did most of the talking. She seems to think this story is bigger than a murder charge," I said.

"What do you think?"

I paused as I ran my finger across the brim of my cap. I hadn't stopped to seriously consider Jill's warning. "I don't know," I finally said. "It's all sort of strange I suppose. But I chalk that up to Archie. He's pretty strange."

"Are you meeting with her again?"

"Again? I didn't meet with her this time." My defensiveness didn't work in my favor, and I knew I shouldn't have said that.

"No? Well, if you don't meet with her again, just promise me you'll be careful. I grew up in a world where the press will stab you in the back at the first opportunity."

"I promise I won't meet with her. And I'll be sure to watch my back." This time I hoped I had said the right thing.

"I know you will. You know I trust you, don't you?"

I could tell she meant it, and that made all the difference. "I know you do. I won't let you down," I said.

11

☼ ☼ ☼

I was dreaming that I was about to be crushed by a massive printing press when the phone rang. I reached for the receiver on the nightstand and pressed Talk. The digitized voice reminded me that I had requested a seven-a.m. wake-up call. Warm sunshine sliced through the crack between the drapes and seared a thin line across the bedspread.

Marc was out last night when I got back to the hotel, so I decided to claim the bed rather than suffer through another evening on the couch. Apparently, he got back late, because I didn't notice that instead of taking the hint and spending the night in the studio, he slipped in next to me and was sprawled out across the sheet. I guessed he was also trashed when he got in because he was still wearing his tank and floral-print board shorts.

I decided not to wake him and just got up to shower. We didn't need to be at Archie's place until eleven to meet his mystery guest.

After grabbing a cup of coffee and a stale muffin from the free hotel breakfast bar, I flipped open my laptop and started to do some research before the interview. I like to know some background information about my subjects before I hook them up to Nemy. All I knew about this person was that he worked for Archie's company, and even that wasn't much help. Archie had essentially built up an Arizona empire for his construction businesses all under the innocuous banner of Southwest Enterprise, so I started with searches about his company.

A 2018 article in the *Phoenix Business Daily* led with a photo of Archie at a ground-breaking ceremony. Naturally, my father-in-law was front and center, grinning into the camera as he pretended to lean into the ceremonial silver-plated shovel. Jack never missed a photo op. The article announced the start of Arizona's most ambitious public works venture since the 1968 Central Arizona Project, a three-hundred-mile aqueduct to siphon off water from the Colorado River. Southwest Enterprise had just been awarded the contract to build the final section of the concrete barricade separating Arizona from the Mexican state of Sonora. The massive project was hailed as a critical link in the U.S.-Mexico border wall.

The story went on to list the businesses operating under the Southwest Enterprise name: civil engineering, excavation, a cement company, warehousing, a steel roller mill, and Arizona's second-largest trucking operation. That didn't help much in narrowing down who Nemy's next subject might be.

It was almost eight thirty when I returned to the room, and I could hear Marc snoring in the bedroom. I went in and nudged him awake.

"Time to get some work done," I said.

Marc snorted and pulled a pillow close to his face. I resorted to a trick my brother used to play on me. The washcloth I soaked in cold water dripped into Marc's ear until he flailed his arms and shot bolt upright in the bed.

"Fuck!" he shouted. "What'd you do that for?" Marc swiped at his ear and then hurled the drenched pillow in my direction.

"Twenty minutes and we're leaving," is all I said in reply. Adam would have been proud.

We rolled up to the gated entrance of the sprawling hacienda five minutes early.

"We're here to work, not party," I reminded Marc.

"Yeah, whatever," he acknowledged grudgingly.

Marc left the keys in the ignition so Jesus could move the Jeep if he needed to.

"Right on time. I appreciate punctuality," Arch said as he greeted us in the Spanish-style courtyard. He eyed my laptop case and the bag Nemy was stuffed in and nodded. "I see you brought your gear. Good. You can set up in here."

Arch ushered us into a large, darkened room lined with massive rough-hewn bookshelves. "We call this the library," he said, oblivious to the obviousness of the name. I thought this would be a good place for you college boys." Arch laughed, "God knows, it hardly gets any other use."

Archie started to leave. "I'll have Jesus bring in some cold drinks. Just let him know if you need anything else. Our *guest* will be arriving in a few minutes."

"Just who is the person we'll be interviewing?" I asked.

"Oh, one of my truck drivers," Arch said. "He's been hauling for me for a couple of years. He thinks I don't know he works for the Milwaukee mob, but I figured it would be smart to keep him close so I can see what they're up to." He added confidentially, "We all know what that is now."

Arch headed for the pool while Marc set up the laptop computer on a natural pine coffee table in the library and I pulled Nemy from the faded backpack. We had gone through so many trials that we had the setup routine down to just a few minutes.

A flood of sunlight rushed into the darkened room when the massive front door across the foyer swung open to admit who we assumed to be our subject. Jesus hurried to the pool to alert his boss while one of Archie's hulking bodyguards ushered a stocky middle-aged man to the center of the terrazzo-tiled foyer.

Archie stepped in casually, now wearing a white terrycloth robe that exposed his smooth tanned chest and still-wet sky-blue Speedo. He gestured toward Marc and me to join him in the foyer.

The escort nodded to Arch as he released a firm grip on the shoulder of the man's sweat-darkened pocket T-shirt. With sudden and utterly fake cordiality, Arch grabbed the fat hand of the dark-haired man who stood before him. "Ted, I'm glad you could meet with me." He chuckled. "Don't worry, you can bill this time to the company."

Turning to Marc and me he said, "Let me introduce you to my brother-in-law and his associate."

The last word sounded almost sinister, and Marc furrowed his brow in response.

"They're college boys, and they'd like to run you through an experiment."

Ted's eyes darted toward the heavy carved door he entered through and then to me.

Arch continued with a tight sneer. "I told them you were just the person to volunteer to help them out." Arch's expression turned serious. "You don't have a problem with that, do you?"

Ted gulped. "What kind of experiment?" he asked.

I started to answer, but Archie interrupted.

"Oh, some research project David is working on. He just wants to ask you a few questions. I said you were a very smart man, and you'd be happy to talk to him." Archie looked deep into Ted's eyes. "I was right about that, wasn't I?" The question sounded more like a threat.

"And if I don't want to?" Ted tried to sound defiant.

Archie turned and took a few steps toward the library. "Of course it's entirely up to you." His head rotated slowly in Ted's direction. "But I know you have some friends who'd be disappointed to learn you've been holding back on some of your deliveries for them, and you've been doing it for years." Arch paced back to within inches of the larger man. "But you haven't ripped me off...as far as I know. I suppose how you handle your customers' shipments could be left for you and them to work out."

Ted sighed audibly and looked over at me. "Sure," he grumbled. "I got nothing to hide."

"Oh, you're right about that," Arch said. "Gentlemen," he nodded in our direction, "you have a volunteer."

The bodyguard clamped a hand on Ted's shoulder, and the two men followed Marc and me into the library.

"Take a seat over there," I instructed our subject, gesturing toward a dark leather armchair.

"Have you ever been hypnotized?" I asked.

Ted muttered as he settled into the overstuffed seat, "You mean like hocus-pocus shit?"

Marc interjected, "Yes, like hocus-pocus shit." He gave me a sideways glance.

"Something like that," I said and explained that I was going to help him get into a state of deep relaxation and then ask him some questions about the night of the explosion.

Arch had stepped into the room. "I have a few questions of my own," he said looking in my direction.

I picked up the headgear that was lying on the coffee table. "I'm going to put this on your head. It monitors your brainwaves to display what you're thinking about on the monitor Marc is hooking up now. Are you alright with that?"

Ted scowled at Archie. "Yeah, let's just get this over with."

After I fitted Ted with the cap, Marc calibrated the settings on the laptop.

I instructed Ted to try to relax and focus on the back of his hands.

"I'm going to start counting backward from ten," I said. "With each number I say, I want you to take a deep breath and find an even deeper state of relaxation. By the time I reach one, I want you to hear and respond only to my voice."

Archie interrupted gruffly, "And if you don't, I'll be asking the questions my way."

I raised a finger to my lips and turned to Arch, shaking my head.

"Just concentrate on the back of your hands," I repeated and proceeded to slowly walk Ted back into a hypnotic state.

"...and one," I said softly. I looked over to Marc, who glanced down at the monitor and then nodded. I motioned for Archie to view the screen. A shadowy shape resolved into the image of the backs of two large hands.

"That's what you told him to concentrate on, right?" Archie looked genuinely impressed.

"Yes. And we should be able to see whatever he's remembering when I suggest something to him."

"So, start asking him about the explosion. See if he did it or if he knows who did."

"We can do that, but in a round-about way," I explained. "I'll need to work up to it."

Archie nodded and stepped back.

I returned my attention to my subject. After a few innocuous questions, I determined that Ted was in a deep hypnotic state. The video feed from Nemy confirmed that Ted's thoughts were being converted into images. Arch was surprised he could even make out the label on the beer Ted remembered drinking the night before. I assured him that even if we couldn't, image enhancement in post-processing would be able to pull out details that the subject might not be consciously aware of.

Finally, I had Ted recall the night of the explosion. I had done enough research about the case that I felt I could lead Ted to remember the events of that night.

"It's a Saturday afternoon in March. March seventh. There was a rainstorm earlier in the week. Everything is green, and flowers are starting to bloom on the cactuses. The Phoenix Suns scored 155 points the night before. Do you remember that day?" I asked.

Ted nodded his head and said, "I remember."

Images of shop windows started to appear on the monitor. I began describing what I was seeing.

"You're walking down a street past some shops," I said, trying to reinforce Ted's memory. "Are you with someone?"

Ted's head drooped. Suddenly the smiling face of a young girl appeared. She was licking an ice cream cone.

"I'm with my niece, Nicole," he said. "I bought her a rocky road. She just turned eleven." Ted smiled broadly.

The images of Ted and his niece played out on the monitor. They stopped at a small shop where the girl picked out a pink polka-dot backpack. We could see Ted handing a twenty-dollar bill to the cashier.

"Where are you and your niece, Ted?" I asked.

"Tempe," is all he said.

With more probing, Ted revealed that he had taken his niece to a cheerleading competition that morning and then spent the rest of the day shopping and visiting the children's museum there. At six that evening, they were sharing a pepperoni pizza at Picazzo's.

"He wasn't there," Marc said shaking his head.

Archie appeared agitated. "No," he moaned. "He had to at least know about what was going down." He turned to me. "Find out if he ordered the hit. He had to know about it."

"What exactly do you want to know, Archie? I have to be able to set up a scene for him to relive." I was growing exasperated. I had already compromised the integrity of our research, and now Archie wanted me to play Sherlock Holmes.

"There had to be a call. Make him remember setting up the contract."

Marc looked at me and shrugged.

"OK, then." I turned my attention to Ted and asked him bluntly. "Who do you call when you want something illegal done?"

Ted shifted on the leather cushion. His head lolled back. Marc pointed to the monitor, where two faces started to resolve, one dark skinned with his hair tied back in a bun and a taller man with close-cut bleached blond hair. The men looked like they were in their twenties.

Arch blurted out, "Ask him if they're his hitmen."

I obliged, tiring of this cat-and-mouse game. "The two young men—are they hitmen?"

Ted nodded.

"I knew it!" Archie almost cheered.

"Ted, I want you to remember the last time you talked to these men," I suggested.

After a few moments, the image on the monitor shifted to the cab of a truck. The steering wheel and shifter were clearly in view. We could see Ted's thick fingers punching a number into his cell phone.

"What are you calling them about?" I asked.

"They need to scrub the scene," he said.

Archie wanted to know who told him to call the hitmen. Ted's answer was simple. "Angelo."

Archie threw up his hands. "That fucking bastard," he said. "I knew he was behind this."

He turned to me. "I've heard enough. This prick didn't do it. He was just a middleman. But he gets his orders from a Milwaukee boss, and Angelo is Pauly's second."

Marc looked surprised. "I thought you said you already knew that."

"Yeah," Arch said. "Knew. Suspected. Whatever. Larry was right. Those bastards are coming after my operation."

Archie slammed a fist into the bodyguard's shoulder. "Get him out of here," he said motioning to Ted as he stormed out of the library.

I held up a hand to wave the husky man off and told him that I needed to ease the subject back into consciousness.

After a few minutes, Ted was alert and listening to me explain that he would only remember that he had helped with a science experiment. Ted looked back vacantly at Marc and me as the bodyguard led him back to the black Hummer they arrived in.

On their way out, the two men brushed past Patsy, whose arms were heavy with shopping bags.

"Did I miss something?" she asked as she dropped her packages at the foot of the curved staircase.

"Yeah," Marc replied. "I'm just not sure what."

Patsy took us by our elbows and dragged us into the sunshine by the pool.

"Was that why you're here? Why Archie wanted you to come to the house?"

"I suppose so," I said. "I'm not sure he got what he was expecting though."

Patsy sat us in the poolside lounge chairs. She wanted to know everything about what happened with Ted. I explained that Arch thought Ted had blown up the trailer and getting a confession would get the prosecutor off his back.

"Well, he didn't," she said.

Marc and I looked at each other. "How did you know that?" I asked.

"Because I was there," she answered.

12

☼ ☼ ☼

Patsy picked up her designer straw bag and called up the cantilevered staircase to Archie, "I'm taking the boys out to lunch."

We heard a faintly audible grunt in the distance.

"Well, grab your gear," she ordered. "We have things to talk about."

Patsy slipped on oversized dark glasses and slid into the driver's seat of the lipstick-pink Porsche convertible parked by the front door. She motioned for us to get in.

Patsy cranked up Lady Gaga as we sped down the canyon highway. The desert wind blow through her long auburn hair. About ten minutes later, we pulled into the dirt parking area in front of a dingy Mexican bar. The neon sign in the window spelled out "Pool," underscored by a flashing tan pool cue.

"Grab your sacks, boys," Patsy instructed as she opened the car door. "You don't want your equipment to overheat in the sun." She grinned as she tossed the door closed behind her.

Marc hopped out of the car without waiting for me to open the passenger door. "Really?" he said. "This is lunch?"

"It's a favorite of mine," Patsy replied as we followed her into the brightly lit cantina. We cleared a tiled tabletop near the back door and sat down.

Patsy pushed the paper menus aside and said, "You want the menudo. It's the best you'll ever have."

A teenage girl took our order and returned almost immediately with a pitcher of margaritas and a basket of fresh tortilla chips. Marc squeezed a large slice of lime into the Mason jar of ice set in front of him and sloshed the yellow-green liquid to the top.

Patsy smiled as I poured drinks for the two of us.

"So why here," I asked, "other than great menudo?"

"We can talk," she said. Then she leaned in and added, "and there's no one to overhear us."

While we waited for our soups to arrive, Marc and I recounted the morning's events.

"You said you were there. I'm not going to ask why, but do you know who did it?" I hoped I wasn't prying too hard.

"I do," she said. "But I can't tell you."

Marc leaned hard against the chrome tubing of his chair and remarked, "That sounds mysterious."

"No, really," Patsy replied. "I got a good look at the man who did it and the truck he drove away in. I just don't remember the details."

I drained the rest of my glass jar and poured myself a refill. "So, do you want to tell us what you do remember?"

"Look, you need to know that Archie and I have been, shall we say, distant, for a long time now. I knew about the slut he was seeing. She wasn't the first, but I really didn't care. That kept him happy and out of my hair, and it gave me a chance to concentrate on my photography."

Marc looked away trying to avoid the conversation.

"But this time, I could tell Arch was getting serious–or at least she was." Patsy glanced around the noisy cantina. "I saw a text on his cell phone saying he'd meet her at the trailer that night. I decided to take my camera equipment and see if I could document their rendezvous."

"Document it? But why?" I asked.

"Because I suspect Archie is looking for an excuse to divorce me. That's why. Larry drew up a prenup when we were engaged, and if we divorce, I walk away with essentially nothing. On the other hand, if I outlive him, I get everything."

Marc suddenly was paying attention again. "You probably shouldn't mention that part," he said. "Someone might think *you* tried to blow him up." Marc started to laugh and then realized the serious implications of what he just said.

"Believe me, I thought about doing that more than once." Patsy laughed too. "No, seriously, I did. But I just figured he'd screw up somewhere along the way, and I wouldn't have to."

"So, Archie was there that night?" I asked.

Patsy rolled her eyes. "No, he never showed up. His excuse that the SUV broke down could be true. So instead of getting killed with his girlfriend, he gets charged with her murder. At least there's some justice in this world," she added.

Marc interjected, "But if Archie gets convicted, doesn't the state claim his assets for a victims' fund or something like that?"

"Yes, especially after a bill Daddy pushed through last year," Patsy said. "And that's not what I want to see happen either."

Three steaming bowls of menudo were placed on the table while we talked. Marc pointed to the empty pitcher to get it refilled.

"Dig in, boys," Patsy ordered. "You won't get tripe like this north of Phoenix."

Mark poked a fork at the spongy white meat floating in the dark broth. "Tripe? Isn't that like intestines or something?"

Patsy laughed. "Don't be silly." Then she stabbed a piece of the flesh with her fork and shoved it in Marc's mouth. "Delicious, isn't it?"

Marc swallowed hard and admitted it wasn't too bad.

"Not too bad?" Patsy echoed. "Cow stomach doesn't get any more tender than this!"

Marc grabbed the refilled pitcher from the waitress's hands and swallowed a large gulp of margarita.

Patsy took another spoonful of her soup and continued the conversation.

"I don't want to sound greedy, but it really is all about the money, and it isn't so much for me. There's enough in the Stillwell family trust fund to keep me comfortable while I try to get my photography career going, but Daddy needs the money for his campaign for Senate next year."

"So, he's definitely going to run?" I asked.

"Oh, he'll run. He's been campaigning his entire life. That's like crack for him, and he's relied on Archie's largess along the way. Why do you think he ever supported our marriage? I was young and thought I was rebelling–instead, I was just playing into his hand." Patsy looked away for a moment. "But I still love him.

If Archie goes to jail, the money is gone. If we divorce, the money is gone."

Marc interrupted brightly. "So, your only options are to stay with him or kill him."

Patsy laid her hand on Marc's arm and said, "Exactly."

Marc weighed the possibilities in his mind. "I can see why you wouldn't want to be caught at the site of the murder."

Patsy turned to me. "Nobody else knows I was there, and I'd like to keep it that way."

"So why are you telling us?" I asked.

"Because I think your gadget could be the key to finding the real killer."

At least calling Nemy a gadget was better than *thing*. "How's that?"

"Like I said, I saw the person who blew up the trailer. I was there, in my car watching–waiting for Archie to show up. I thought I could get some photos of him shacking up with his secretary, and I could use them if he tried to leave me."

Marc asked, "How close were you?"

"Oh, I parked off the road in a small grove of mesquite about three hundred yards away. I was using my telephoto lens, so I had a good view."

"Of what?" Marc said. "Archie wasn't even there."

"The killer was," she said. "I even got pictures of him and the pickup he pulled up in."

I asked if she recognized him. She said she didn't, but she could describe the scene.

"It was about six thirty and getting dark. This beat-up gray pickup truck pulled up in front of the trailer, kicking up a cloud of dust. A rather short man wearing a jeans jacket and dark felt hat got out of the truck and went to the back, where he pulled out a large red gas can. That's when I started taking pictures."

Marc gave me a questioning glance.

"It looked like the guy was dousing the base of the trailer with gasoline when..."

"What?" Marc said. "He set it on fire?"

"No, he didn't get a chance to. That's when the explosion happened. It knocked him back on his ass and shook the ground all the way back to where I was. Dirt and rubble were raining down on him, but I think he was knocked out or something. He just lay there for a few minutes. What was left of the trailer was in flames, and I thought the man must be dead."

"He wasn't?" I asked.

"Apparently not. After a few minutes, he pulled himself up, leapt back into the truck, and sped down the road."

"And you got pictures of all this," I confirmed.

"Most of it, yes," Patsy said.

Marc piped up, "Then you can identify the truck. Even if you don't know who the guy was, you have his license plate in the pictures."

"Yeah, you'd think so, right? I was even focusing on the back of the vehicle after the explosion went off, but I checked the pictures, and the plates are covered in a cloud of dust. By the time my head cleared after the explosion, the truck was too far down the road to get a clear shot."

Marc tossed his head back. "I suppose there are a lot of beat-up gray pickup trucks in this part of the country. So how do we find the guy?"

"Oh, I think his tag number will lead us to him," Patsy said.

"But," I interjected, "you didn't get a picture of his license plate."

"No, but I saw it. I even focused on it through the telephoto lens."

Marc's mouth dropped open. "Wait. Are you thinking what I'm thinking?"

Patsy looked him squarely in his eyes. "I can't remember what the tag number was, but maybe your device can look into my memory and pull it out."

I sighed and leaned back on the ripped vinyl cushion of the dining chair. "So, you want me to hypnotize you, right?"

Patsy smiled broadly. "We can do it right here," she said. "They have a back room for Friday-night poker games. I can talk them into letting you set up there."

Marc and I looked at each other. We knew the decision had already been made.

We picked up the gear and carried our jars of cold margaritas with us as we made our way past the old jukebox and through a wooden door with peeling bright-yellow paint. Patsy had rented the private room for an hour, which would be enough time for us to hook her up to Nemy. There was a cushioned wingback chair that looked like it would be comfortable enough for Patsy to relax in.

In just a few minutes, I had her fitted with the headgear, and Marc set up the laptop so it was ready to record her memories.

"You know what's going to happen?" I asked.

Patsy nodded. "Just limit your travelogue through my mind to that night, please. There are certain things I'd rather not share with my brother-in-law." She flashed a guilty looking smile.

"I promise," I said. Then I proceeded to ease her into a deep hypnotic state.

Marc nodded when the images on the monitor started to resolve. Patsy's recollections of that night revealed a late-model

Ford pickup truck pulling up to the trailer site. The man who got out was just as Patsy described–dressed like a cowboy, down to his snakeskin boots. His hair was long and black, and it looked like he might be in his late thirties.

"You're focusing on the truck through your camera now," I suggested.

Patsy's eyebrows arched, but her eyes remained shut. In a moment, the back of the truck seemed to enlarge on the monitor.

"You see the license plate number clearly," I continued.

In an instant, the image of an Arizona license plate filled the screen. Marc pulled a pen from the laptop case and wrote down what was clearly displayed on the tag–*REDMAN*.

Marc looked up at me. "She said that's all she wanted us to look for. We better shut down," he said.

After I returned Patsy to awareness, Marc told her what we saw.

"Then let's find out who REDMAN is," she said. "That will be easy."

Patsy picked up her designer handbag and headed through the dining room to the dirt parking lot. Marc and I stowed our gear and followed close behind. When we got outside, we saw Patsy rummaging through a pile of rubble next to the corner of the adobe building. She picked out a broken brick and walked over to the back of the Porsche.

Marc looked at me. "What's she doing?"

Patsy knelt next to the bumper and dragged a ragged edge of the brick from the taillight to the rear wheel. Marc and I just stared.

Patsy tossed the brick aside as she stood. With a broad smile she said, "There, that should do it." She gestured to us as we stared with our mouths gaping. "Come on. Get in."

Marc shrugged, and we climbed back into the car.

"What was that all about?" I asked as the convertible rolled past the fence posts that marked the cantina entrance.

"We need to know who owns REDMAN, right? Well, Archie has connections. He can pull the DOT records and find out for us. I just need to give him a good reason to do that."

"By scratching your car?" Marc said.

"If I tell Arch someone backed into us in the parking lot and then drove off, I'm sure he'll want to find out who did it." Patsy tossed back her auburn hair in the wind and laughed.

13

☼ ☼ ☼

The slice of sunshine through the bedroom drapes woke me early. As I lay in bed next to Marc, I picked up my cell phone from the nightstand.

SORRY I MISSED YOUR CALL. LATE-NIGHT PLANNING SESSION.

I tried phoning Bren after we left Archie's place, but she didn't answer. I texted back that I missed her, along with a suggestive comment about wanting to get hold of her. The thought of doing just that seemed even more appealing this morning.

I slipped out of bed and pulled on a pair of loose shorts and a T-shirt and headed to the lobby for coffee. The Wi-Fi connection was better from the narrow ledge that the hotel had labeled Business Center. I pulled up a mesh office chair and popped open my laptop. I could catch up on emails and do some research from there while we waited to hear back from Patsy.

A selfie of Brenda and me in Galena filled the screen while icons populated the desktop. That trip was just over a week ago, but I knew the memory would stay vivid no matter how old we get.

I answered a few emails and deleted most of the rest. A quick check of the news reinforced my gloom about the direction my adopted homeland was taking.

> Hispanic families crowd detention center. Trade war with China heats up. Estonia withdraws from NATO. Record high temps for sixth consecutive year. Russian military advisors arrive in Mexico. N. Korea threatens nuclear attack on Japan. Native American protest intensifies.

The headlines changed day to day, but the tone remained the same. Life in India had started to seem more normal than in the surreal world of bathroom laws and deportations the U.S. had devolved into.

I forced myself to focus on neuroscience and my research. The morning hours sailed past as I immersed myself in esoteric debates on recently published papers. Bren was right to label me a science nerd. I just hoped she'd find that trait as endearing twenty years from now as she said she did today.

"Dude, you let me sleep till noon." Marc's voice drifted over my shoulder. "Not that I'm complaining, mind you."

Marc poured himself a cup of coffee and took the other seat at the computer bar.

"Especially since you didn't get in until two," I pointed out. "Another wild night out with your nurse?"

Marc grinned. "You know it. I tried not to wake you."

"Well, try harder next time." I knew it was petty, but the thought of returning to dorm life haunted me.

Marc looked hurt. "I don't know why you didn't take Archie up on his offer for us to shack up at his place—and by *shack up*, I'm talking private suites with a balcony overlooking an infinity pool. Not the kind of shack you probably grew up in." Marc got in a dig about what he presumed was my upbringing.

"The reason we aren't staying there, nice as it might be, is I don't want to be taking anything from Archie. He and Patsy didn't exactly welcome me into the family with open arms. They were as worried about having a green-card in-law as Larry was."

"Right. I can see how that might have left some raw feelings. And, hey, I'm sorry about that *shack* crack." Marc glanced away and then added, "You didn't really grow up in a shack, did you?"

"Sorry. Not everyone in India lives like that, despite what you saw in *Slumdog*."

Marc laughed and grabbed my shoulder. "And not everyone in LA snorts crack and has sex every night."

I gave him a sideways look. "I know that could be at least half true."

My phone started to chirp, and I saw the call was from Patsy.

"Dude, you really need to get a different ringtone," Marc said as I turned to talk to her.

The conversation took just a couple of minutes. Patsy said Arch had called the dispatcher at his trucking company to run the plates, and he came back with an answer within an hour.

I clicked the phone off and turned to Marc. "I think we found REDMAN."

"What, already?"

"All it takes is one call from Archie, and the man gets what he wants."

"So, who's the dude with the rude tag? We're gonna check it out, right?"

Marc acted like we were about to start playing some real-life version of *Grand Theft Auto.*

"No, we're not checking anyone or anything out. You realize this guy could be a murderer, don't you? I'll let Larry know what we found out, and he can take it from there."

I should have known better than to tell Marc what to do or, in this case, what not to do. He automatically went into gamer mode and played a rational strategy.

"Oh, that should go really well for Patsy," he argued. "Let's let Larry tell her gangster husband that his wife saw the murderer because she was spying on him in case they get a divorce. I'm sure he'll be understanding."

I just sighed. "Well, there has to be a better way to go about it than simply finding the truck and telling the guy driving it he's under citizen's arrest."

"You never really learned how to play games, did you?" Marc was being sarcastic, but it was true.

"OK, what do you suggest we do?"

Marc had the opening he was waiting for, and he quickly laid out a rough strategy. When he was done, he cocked his head and asked, "So, who's the dude and where do we find him?"

"The dude," I said, "is Zacchaeus Redman, and we go to the Indian reservation where his truck is registered."

Marc was almost giddy with excitement. "Awesome! I'll grab my Air Jordans."

"Now? You want to just pick up and go?"

"Why not? You have something else scheduled?" Marc acted surprised that I even asked.

"Well, no. I just thought..."

"Right. You just thought. So, stop thinking and let's just do it."

Marc was headed back to the room before I could even respond. I packed up my laptop, tossed on my Antonio's cap, and followed him.

☼ ☼ ☼

Siri said it's a two-and-a-half-hour drive to Sells, Arizona, the capital of the Tohono O'odham Nation–three if you go through Tucson. Marc drove, so he opted for the longer route since it's mostly interstate. I was happy with that decision, especially after I discovered from surfing the web that the reservation is almost twice the size of Delaware, and the shorter route would have taken us nearly all the way across Indian territory.

I chuckled at the thought of traveling through an Indian nation.

"What's so funny?" Marc yelled over the noise of the hot wind blowing in our faces.

I smiled and shouted back, "I realized I just might be more at home in Pima County than I am in Chicago."

Marc either missed the irony of what I said, or he just didn't make the connection.

"Let's pull in at the next stop and get some lunch," he said. "Besides, I have to pee."

I nodded in agreement, trying to keep my ballcap from flying off in the wind.

Marc pulled the Jeep onto an exit ramp somewhere between Phoenix and Tucson. There was an Arby's in a new truck stop at the intersection, but he spied a place down the road where he thought he could order a cold Modelo.

The Wrangler rolled to a stop in a cloud of red dust as we pulled up to the pink adobe building. Marc pushed on the once-chrome handle of the plate-glass door to let us in. The sign on the window that read *Cool Inside* was partly right–at least it was cooler than the noon heat outside. I fanned myself with my cap, and Marc wiped his brow with the blue bandana that had been holding down his blond ponytail.

We mounted a couple of torn vinyl bar stools, and Marc called to the bartender, "A real cold one, please."

The man looked up from his cell phone and tossed an equally long gray ponytail off his shoulder. "You're fine, but your friend can't sit here," he said with what sounded like a low growl.

Marc looked at me, and his mouth dropped open slightly.

I poked a finger in my chest. "I can't be here?" I said. "And that's because...?"

"We don't serve Injuns." The bartender straightened his frame to its full six feet and puffed out his chest to almost his belly size. He pointed to a hand-printed sign taped to the cracked bar mirror. *American and Proud.*

Marc stood, suddenly defensive. "But he's not...." Then he considered what he was about to say. "I mean, he's not that kind of...." Again, his words failed him.

"Forget it, Marc," I said and pulled the red cap down on my head as I stood. "Let's just go."

The bartender smirked. "Yea, that's probably a good idea."

"Wait!" Marc shouted. I wasn't sure if it was directed at me or the bartender or even to himself. "You can't do that. You can't just tell people you won't serve them a beer because their skin's a different color."

The gray-haired man leaned hard on the bar and looked Marc straight in his eyes. "I can do whatever I damn well want," he said. "Haven't you heard? Americans like me have the law on our side for a change. Honest businessmen don't have to do shit for anybody who threatens our lives, our families, or our beliefs. And you better believe I believe in Americans first."

By now the three other patrons who had been shooting pool started to come over to the bar brandishing their cue sticks like katanas.

I grabbed Marc's elbow. "I said, *Let's go!*"

Knowing Marc's tendency to ignore the odds when they're against him, I dragged him back outside and shoved him into the Jeep. "Drive," I demanded. Reluctantly, he did.

Stones flew from the Wrangler's back tires in a spray of gravel and red dust as Marc lunged the Jeep back onto the highway. I knew he wasn't trying to get away–just leaving his calling card. Both of us looked straight ahead as we sped down I-10 in silence, the hot wind searing our faces.

We were on the interstate just a few minutes when Marc pulled the Jeep to an abrupt stop on the shoulder. He turned to me and grinned, "I still have to pee." We both broke out laughing, and he jumped out and took a couple of strides away from traffic.

While Marc relieved himself, practically in full view of any passersby–mostly truckers–an almost forgotten memory of my brother and me flashed through my head.

Adam was seventeen, and he had just gotten his permit to ride the family motorbike. Dad bought a small Suzuki for making runs to the market or when he didn't want to wait for the campus shuttle. Mumbai traffic can be terrifying, at least by Western standards, but IIT was basically a closed and tightly regulated community, so Mom was OK with him on our neighborhood streets so long as he wore a helmet.

I had just come home from school–I must have been fourteen at the time. Adam was on the bike in front of our small bungalow waiting for me. He told me to drop off my books and then hop on because Mom wanted him to pick up yogurt at the market. When

I came out of the house, he handed me a helmet and said, "Put this on, at least until we're out of sight." I did, and we took off down the shaded street toward the neighborhood banya, several blocks away. Instead of stopping, Adam looked back at me, grinned, and continued driving. We passed the campus entrance and rode under a busy highway overpass to find ourselves on the edge of the city. Afternoon traffic brought us to a stop without even enough room for our small bike to get through.

I was scared mostly of what our parents would do to us if they found out. Adam laughed as he managed to maneuver the bike to a narrow alley next to a convenience store. There he dropped the kickstand and hopped off.

"Wait here," he said as he handed me his helmet and went into the shop. After a few minutes, he came out with a small sack–yogurt for Mom and a Snicker's bar for us to share. Adam let me take the first bite. The thought of getting caught not just going to the city but eating an expensive American chocolate bar was as thrilling as it was terrifying, and I savored the sweet taste.

"Don't eat it all!" he ordered. Then he laughed again and said, "Give me a second. I have to pee."

Right there in the middle of afternoon traffic, Adam turned to face the stucco wall of the banya and let loose a heavy stream of yellow liquid. The thrill of danger intensified in me. Public urination isn't all that uncommon in India, even though it's illegal, but you didn't do it in a middle-class neighborhood like this, and you didn't do it if you were raised by strict Hindu parents with respectable positions in the community. After that day, Adam was not just my brother, he became my hero and my friend.

The honk of a passing semi made me aware of the I-10 traffic just a few feet away. A dark pool had formed in the dirt around

Marc's feet, and I could see he was shaking off the final drops. Marc took off his Hawaiian shirt and climbed back into the Jeep.

"Much better," he said as he flipped off the blinkers. "I traced the bartender's face in the sand with my piss," he snorted.

14

☼ ☼ ☼

We reached Tucson just after noon. Marc pulled in for a quick lunch at a Wendy's, and this time no one questioned our right to be served. The girl behind the counter just took my money without even looking up.

We sat down to a plastic tray of burgers and fries. Marc unwrapped his Dave's triple and took a bite, staring out the window the entire time. Without looking in my direction, he said, "Does that happen a lot?"

"What? Getting harassed by jerks who don't like the color of my skin? What do you think?" Now I was staring out the window too.

We finished our meals in silence. After he drained the last of his blueberry chiller, Marc stood and cleared the table. "I'll go fill up the tank," he said. "I don't want to run out of gas where we're going."

I headed the other direction to find the men's room. Maybe I'd add a few more shots of my own to the Neanderthal face Marc had traced in the sand.

When I got to the Jeep, the pump was clicking away. Marc dragged a thumb across his cell phone, where I saw he'd pulled up a Google map of our destination. "There. I just left us a trail of breadcrumbs."

I looked at Marc quizzically.

"The map. I saved it offline. Don't expect a cell tower nearby where we're going."

Marc topped off the tank and climbed back behind the wheel, shirtless again. "You ready for this?" he said flashing a giant grin in my direction.

"I don't even know what *this* is–or why I'm going along with it." I tried to sound annoyed, but the thrill of tracking down a possible killer distorted my droll delivery.

Marc pulled the Wrangler out of the parking lot and made it to the on-ramp before breaking into a hearty laugh.

"That's nervous laughter," I said. "Right?"

"No, dude. It's YOU. You're, like, so uptight. I bet you never had your butt kicked before, am I right?"

I just looked out the window at the passing billboards. Yes, I'd had my butt kicked–and it bruised more than my brown skin. It shook my self-confidence for years to come. I'd tried to forget the memory of that day Adam and I rode our bikes to the park to kick around a soccer ball. My brother took sports seriously, and I didn't want to be left out, even if I'd rather be down at the pond collecting frogs. I knew his classmates would probably be there, and that had me a bit on edge. They could be pretty cruel, especially to underclassmen. But I also knew my big brother would stand up for me, and I liked the idea of having a champion.

As we approached the gate in the wire fence that enclosed the field, Adam caught sight of Rachit, his best friend and the varsity team's star goalkeeper. Adam grinned and raised his arm in a casual salute as we headed across the field to the group of boys he was standing with. That's when things turned strange. The two larger boys stepped in front of Adam's friend and stood cross-armed like bodyguards. Adam shot a look in Rachit's direction. One of the boys that faced my brother declared, "We know about you."

Adam's bewilderment quickly turned to rage. He dropped his head and charged the line that had formed a few feet away. The boys in front were about my brother's size, but they were no match for his strength. Arms flailed as Adam landed a torrent of sincerely dealt blows. Rachit stepped back and just watched the scene, his mouth slightly agape. The fourth boy in the group fixed his eyes on me and lunged. He was smaller than his companions, but he still outweighed me by ten kilos, and he took advantage of an easy target.

Adam drove off his teammates and watched as they disappeared through the fence gate. He turned and noticed the smaller boy, who had pinned me down and was pummeling my head and chest. Adam let out a roar as he lunged at my assailant and sent him flying across the soccer field. My brother knelt next to me on the muddy patch of ground where I lay balled up tight with my arms clutching my face.

"They're gone," was all he said. He lifted me to my feet and pulled a soccer flag from his pocket to wipe my bloodied nose. "They won't be back."

We walked home in silence—a silence that was never entirely broken.

Marc intentionally swerved the Jeep into the empty lane next to us, enough to make me bang my head against the roll bar.

"What was that for?" I said, rubbing my forehead.

"So you'd stop pouting."

I cocked my head and shot him a questioning look.

"Over that crack about not getting your butt kicked. It's no big deal. You're Indian. I get it. You're into all that passive resistance shit."

"Thank you very much for your cultural sensitivity," I smirked. "Yeah, I guess I was feeling like a wimp."

"Dork's probably a better word, but they say acceptance is the first step. We might make a man of you yet."

We were in South Tucson now, on I-19 headed toward Nogales.

"Our exit is just ahead," Marc announced. "It's after noon. That should be about supper time for your lady, right? This might be a good time to give her a call before we run out of cell coverage."

I exaggerated shouting "Hello" over the sound of the deafening wind.

"Oh, right." The Jeep was on the long exit ramp to Ajo Way, the road that would take us to our destination. "We can put the top up when we get off the highway. Besides, I want to pick up a couple of Cokes."

"Sounds good, but make mine a tea, please."

Marc gave me a wink. "Naturally. You can take the boy out of India..."

Ajo Way is the part of Highway 86 that announced we had officially departed the relative wealth of Tucson. The level vacant lots that greeted us seemed to be pining to host one of the manicured establishments still visible on the other side of the interstate.

Marc pulled into a run-down Valero station. "Shit!" he exclaimed as he stopped the Jeep by the side of the building.

"What?" I gave him a worried look.

Marc laughed. "That's just what I have to do. I hope they'll give me a key." He got out and headed for the front door. "I'll get the drinks. You put up the top. Maybe you can get some of that red dirt off the windshield while you're at it." He jiggled the handle of the locked bathroom door on his way.

I stepped out of the Jeep to put up the canvas top. The sun was blistering hot now. When I grabbed the door frame to install the side rail, it scorched the palm of my hand. I recoiled in pain and just hoped the AC worked once we got back on the road.

There was a water pump on the other side of the cracked concrete parking pad. A plastic pail with a dried-out rag draped over the edge was sitting next to the women's bathroom. I picked up the pail and headed to the pump. While the bucket filled, I let the stream of cold water flow over my stinging hand to ease the pain.

From the corner of my eye, I noticed something dart across the barren stretch of land behind the gas station. A yellow dog was chasing something. *Not a dog*, I realized as I peered into the sun. *That's a coyote!* It wasn't more than fifty yards from me, indifferent to the presence of a human spectator. The animal it was chasing down seemed to be waddling more than running away. From this distance, it looked like a brown basketball dribbling slowly downcourt. *A badger?* I wondered. *In the desert?* The coyote was rapidly gaining on the loping creature, which was headed for a small outcropping of low shrubs. *That must be its burrow.* When the lumbering animal reached the shaded entrance, it turned and crouched, facing its pursuer. I could make out the shape of the badger's gaping jaws as it stood its ground, preparing to back into the safety of its desert lair. The coyote pulled up abruptly and sized up the uncooperative prey. The badger lunged and snapped menacingly at the wary canine. Then it quickly backed into the brush and down the hole.

Nature. You eat or get eaten, I thought.

I carried the filled bucket to the Jeep and sloshed water across the windshield with the dirty rag. Rivers of red mud streaked across the hood and down the front fenders. At least we'd be able to look out through more than just the two half-moon shapes scraped out by the wiper blades.

I took the wet rag and draped it over the metal frame to cool it down before continuing to put up the soft top. I was snapping down the last latch when Marc returned. Along with the drinks he went in for, he brought back a can of Pringles and a cold six-pack of Coronas. "I thought we'd need reinforcements," he said and set the carton of beer in arm's reach behind us.

"Just crank up the air and let's get this over with," I said as we pulled back onto 86.

I flipped open my cell phone and started to tap in Bren's number. Marc reached for the radio knob, then thought better of it when he realized I was already on the phone. He grabbed one of the bottles of gold from the back instead. I shot him a disapproving look, but Bren's phone was already ringing. When she answered, she said was having dinner with her team, so I kept our conversation short.

"Yes, of course I miss you," I said. "You have no idea how much."

We said our goodbyes and made our traditional kissing sounds—complete with exploding fingers. The signal was already down to one bar, so it was good that we didn't try to talk longer.

After I hung up, Marc turned on the radio and found a Tucson station that played progressive rock. Neither of us expected the signal to last long, but there'd always be Country. You can't escape it in this part of the world. That and radio evangelists.

An inconspicuous highway sign announced that we had entered the Tohono O'odham Reservation.

I remarked on the irony of this indigenous people being labeled with not just one but two erroneous monikers—*Papago* and *Indian.* "Pretty insulting, don't you think?"

"Whatever," Marc replied. "It's a lot easier than saying *Tohono O'odham,* but I suppose that's the politically correct name to call them."

I wondered, are these people just *them*? These Native Americans, now a conquered minority. A *them.* I realized I was only another one of *them* too.

"The highway goes through their territory. They're a sovereign nation, right?" I asked.

"Sovereign until eminent domain plows over the border. They's in Murica now." Marc applied his best redneck accent to the last phrase.

"You're kind of a pig," I said. "You know that, don't you? Lovable, but still a pig."

Marc grinned like he'd won an award. "Oink."

More serious now, Marc attempted to defend himself. "Look, just because I'm blond and I'm Berkeley doesn't make me a snowflake. We're just who we are, and that includes the baggage of *what* we are."

"Deep," I said.

The landscape was a desolate blanket of sand dotted with scrubby mesquite trees. Low mountain peaks surrounded us like a ring of sentinels. It reminded me of the foothills on our family outings to visit my mother's parents in Punjab for spring breaks. The mountains bordering Pakistan are lush and green, like an emerald island rising from a desert sea. I looked forward to those visits about as much as I was dreading this one.

"Where are all the cactuses?" I asked. "I was expecting to see giant prickly plants with their arms raised in the air."

"Uh huh. You grew up on Roadrunner cartoons, didn't you?"

I rolled my eyes. "Well, at least I've seen a few. Roadrunners that is. I didn't expect that."

"What, the state bird? Why would you think they wouldn't be around?"

I relented. "Maybe I expected the coyote finally caught them all."

After half an hour, the rock station was producing more static than music, so Marc turned off the radio. He handed me his cell phone. "Here, check the map. I think we're getting close."

I glanced at his screensaver–a skull with crossed guitars. "How mature," I said. "And you need to sign in." I held up the phone so it could identify his face. The satellite map he saved was already up.

"So, where are we?" I asked.

"We passed a trading post about ten minutes ago."

"I see it. That was about five miles past the turnoff for the Kitt Peak Observatory." I reflected for a moment. "You didn't know this, but if I hadn't gone into neuroscience, I probably would have been an astronomer. There are lots of sites around Mumbai just for star gazing. My brother and I would go to the peak before dawn and then watch the sun rise." I was feeling a little homesick.

I went back to scrolling over the map. "I think I found it. Could that trading post be like the only building between here and Tucson? So, you should be coming up on Schuk Toak District. The map shows a district office there–but no building."

"That makes sense. But there was a sign for that about a mile back."

"Then it could be the next turnoff. Look for some houses on the right." I peered down the road directly into the afternoon sun. Ahead, I could make out a small compound of trailer homes. The brush was lower here, so there was nothing to block the view.

"There. With that cluster of telephone poles. I think that could be it." A part of me hoped it wasn't.

15

☼ ☼ ☼

Marc slowed the Jeep and drove past the side road I pointed to.

"You just passed it!" I exclaimed.

"So, what were you planning? We go up and knock on the door and ask if there's a murderer home?"

Marc pulled the Jeep off to the hard-dirt shoulder. He was right. I hadn't considered what we'd do next. What *were* we doing here, I wondered? What was *I* doing here?

A small shrub partially obscured the Jeep.

"You see that blue trailer?" Marc said, turning around in his seat and pointing. "What does it look like parked under that tin awning?"

I peered through the light-green foliage and saw a beat-up gray pickup truck. "You think that's it?"

"This is as close as we can get to an address, and that truck looks like the one Patsy saw."

"But the license plate said REDMAN. Do you think we should..."

"Of course we should," Marc insisted. I could sense his adrenaline level rising. "So, let's take a look." Marc gestured toward the small blue trailer home. "After you."

"What if someone sees us pulled over here?" I was starting to panic.

"They'll think we stopped to piss, which is exactly what I'm going to do. I wouldn't want to disappoint anyone."

Marc strode to the shrub and pulled down the elastic band of his nylon basketball shorts. Over his shoulder, he said, "You walk toward the house like you're going to smoke or something. Get close enough to read the tag."

I pulled the brim of my cap down so it rested on my sunglasses and walked casually in the direction of the blue trailer. I felt the sweat pour from my body–more than just the sweat of the hundred-degree afternoon. I was genuinely scared. The feeling terrified and thrilled me at the same time. I kicked at a couple of rocks with my leather sandal and wandered in the direction of the carport while Marc relieved himself. Blinds covered the windows on the front of the trailer, which was probably a good thing. Three pairs of jeans and cotton underwear hung on a line attached to the front porch to dry. In this heat, that would take only a few minutes, and I hoped no one would be coming out to collect them. I stepped to the other side of the bush where Marc was peeing and could make out the plate on the back of the truck–REDMAN. We'd found what we were looking for. Now what?

I rounded the shrub as Marc was shaking off the last drops of Corona. "Let's get back in the Jeep," he said. "It's hot out here!"

We pulled the doors of the Wrangler closed, and Marc started the engine. "I'll turn the air back on," he said. "I can feel the sunburn on my chest." He pulled out a couple of Coronas and offered me one. They were still cool, and I gladly accepted.

"So, what do we do next?" I asked.

"We wait. We see if someone gets in the truck and drives off."

"And then what?" I realized I already knew the answer to that question. Marc planned to follow him. He just smiled.

"This is crazy, you know. It's like a dog chasing a car. What does he do if he catches it?"

Marc replied without really thinking, "He lets your brother-in-law know who the dude is, so he can get out of that murder rap." The distorted metaphor put a smile on his face. "Besides, you can't get this kind of excitement sitting in the patio of your comfortable Logan Square bungalow."

"If I want excitement, I can always go to Six Flags. What we're doing is...well, it's dangerous." I pondered the implications of my assessment. "I have someone in that bungalow I'd like to come home to."

Marc felt the sting of my implied commentary on his dedication to remaining unattached. We both looked away and settled into the silence of what could be a long stakeout.

After several minutes, a sour smell wafted to our noses.

"Is that a skunk?" I asked.

"I don't think so. Not out here, anyway."

That's when Marc noticed the temperature gauge. He quickly turned off the engine just as a blanket of white fog started rolling over the hood.

"Shit!" he exploded. "We overheated."

Marc leaped out and flung open the hood. A geyser of greenish-white steam shot into the air. Yes, we had overheated.

"Now what do we do?" My question was more rhetorical than constructive. This was his adventure, and I just hoped he had a backup plan.

Frustrated, Marc reached into the back of the Jeep and pulled out the last bottle of Corona. He gazed at the mountains in the distance as he downed the contents in one long gulp.

Marc belched, then turned to me and said, "We get help."

"Here? At the murderer's house? Are you insane?" I turned my back and picked at a tooth.

"You have a better idea? We don't have a phone. It's over a hundred degrees out."

"And you just drank the last beer," I added.

"Look, either we knock on the door and say we broke down, or we go back to one of the other trailers and explain why we didn't knock on *this* door instead."

It made sense in a damned-if-we-do, damned-if-we-don't kind of way. Besides, we'd been waiting for the guy to come out of the trailer. Maybe he wasn't even home.

"All right," I said. "But we need a good story for why we're here in the first place. What do you suggest?"

Marc thought for a moment. "You wanted to be an astronomer, right? Well, here's your chance. Say we're working at Kitt and decided to explore the area. You're a doctor. You should be able to come up with something smart."

"Almost a doctor," I corrected him. "OK, let's do this," I said reluctantly. "They have telephone lines around here. Someone should be able to call for a truck or something."

Marc nodded. He reached for the aloha shirt he had tossed on the back seat and gingerly put it on. Then he locked the Jeep doors.

"Do you really think that's necessary?" I pointed out as I took the lead walking to the blue trailer.

We stepped onto the shipping pallet that served as the porch just as the front door creaked open. The widening shadow of the dark interior revealed not the murderer, but a tiny old woman. She wore a long skirt and white blouse, and a green scarf was wrapped tightly around her silver-white hair.

The surprise left me speechless, so Marc introduced us. "Good afternoon, uh, ma'am." Marc tapped his forehead. "My friend and I broke down on the road, and we were..."

The woman raised a gnarled finger to her lips, and with her other hand, she motioned for us to come in.

The darkened room seemed utterly black after stepping in from the bright sun. I removed my sunglasses and blinked slowly. After a few moments, images of an overstuffed couch and a simple dining table and chairs resolved. The woman was gesturing toward the table, where two tall glasses of ice water were waiting apparently for us.

"Sit," she said.

Marc nodded and looked at me as though waiting for approval.

We pulled out the two rickety wooden chairs and sat down. The old woman took a seat in the bentwood rocking chair, which straddled the kitchen and living room areas.

I thanked the woman and started to explain our situation. "We're astronomers working at the Kitt Observatory, and we think last night's meteor shower might have deposited a fragment near here. While we were..."

The woman grinned and interrupted my story. "Really? How interesting."

Marc picked up from there. "Yes, I think our Jeep overheated and now..."

"I know," she said. "I wondered how long you could sit out there in the heat before that would happen. You lasted longer than I expected." She rose from the chair and took two steps to open one of the kitchen cabinets, leaving Marc and me with our mouths gaping. We both took a swallow of water at the same time.

"Yes, ma'am," I said. "I was checking my maps..."

"You won't be going anywhere today," she said ominously while preparing a plate of biscuits. "The sun is starting to set. My grandson returns in the morning. He's the mechanic for the casino, so he gets in very late. He has a room where he works, but he likes to check in on me when he can. He'll have the parts you need to get you going tomorrow." She set the platter of cookie-like objects between us. "Here. Eat. It is O'odham himdag to serve guests."

"Thank you, ma'am, for your hospitality, but if we can just use your phone to call for a tow truck..."

"I don't have a phone," she said, with an old black rotary telephone in plain sight on the end table. She registered my look of skepticism and added, "Not a working one. It was disconnected years ago."

"Then maybe a neighbor?" Marc offered.

"No neighbors. The other kis have been empty for a few years now. It's just me here. Besides, did you check your rental agreement? No one will come for you." She paused. "You wait for my grandson. He'll take care of you."

The old woman picked up a woven basket and headed for the front door. "I need to bring in my grandson's clothes," she said and closed the door behind her.

Marc looked at me. "This is like out of a slasher movie," he said. There was an incongruous gleam in his eyes.

"Except this isn't a movie," I whispered. "This is real life, and I'm starting to worry that our lives might not be all that real before this night is over."

"Chill," Marc said. "She's a harmless old lady. She's just showing us *himdag*. That's all. It'll be fine."

"Really? And how fine do you think that murderous grandson of hers will be?"

The old woman returned with the basket piled with jeans, T-shirts, and briefs. She deposited the laundry in one of the two bedrooms in the small trailer and came back to the kitchen to refill our glasses with chilled water. Then she opened the small avocado-green refrigerator and removed two very cold Heinekens and set them on the table. "I think you'd rather have these, but after you rehydrate," she said gesturing toward our water glasses. "I'll make supper for you now."

"No, please," I said. "Don't go to any trouble."

The woman stopped and turned. "Serving guests is no trouble. It's an honor." Then she instructed us to sit in the living room and read any of her grandson's books or journals on the bookshelf in the corner.

Marc and I drained our water glasses and carried the cold brews the few steps to the living area. We found coasters, apparently from the casino, and placed them under our beer bottles on a coffee table hewn from a large tree root.

Marc asked in a loud voice, "Is it alright if I turn on a light?"

"Of course," the woman answered. "We don't live in the nineteenth century, you know," she said with a wry laugh.

The orange ginger-jar lamp emitted a mellow golden glow through the dried skin of some animal. I pulled a couple of books off the bookshelf–three painted boards suspended across stacked cement blocks.

"Kafka? Heidegger?" My eyes grew wide as I turned to Marc.

Perusing other titles on the shelves, we knew we were dealing with someone special. Whoever he was, he didn't fit the stereotype of *them*.

Marc picked up a copy of a book written in 1949 about American expansionism. "Listen to this," he said. "It's a quote from a British officer to the Indians after England lost the Revolutionary War. '...yet you are not to believe, or even think that by the Line which has been described, it was meant to deprive you of an extent of country.'" Marc looked up. "It gets better. 'Neither can I harbour an idea that the United States will act so unjustly or impolitically as to endeavour to deprive you of any part of your country under the pretext of having conquered it.'"

Marc set the book on the coffee table. "Ouch."

"That's the same British that took over India after *conquering* my country in the name of the Crown?"

The next book I picked up took me by even greater surprise. The *Mahabharata*.

Marc noticed the astonished look on my face. He pulled the hardbound copy from my hands and glanced at the colorful dust jacket. "Is this some Hindu shit?" he asked.

"Yes," I hissed. "It's some Hindu shit. Two-thousand-year-old Hindu shit. Shit every college freshman has to read, in Sanskrit, of course. All 198 chapters. It's epic history, philosophy, religious dogma shit."

"Dude," Marc pulled back. "It's just a book."

"To you, maybe. But for an Indian boy, it's like a cattle prod to keep you in lock-step with traditions that defy reason."

"So, you Indians have your Hindu shit, and these Indians have their himdag," Marc observed. "You can't escape it, dude. That's how the world rolls." Marc put the thick volume back on the shelf. "But what do you suppose this guy is doing reading it?"

Before I could ponder an explanation, the old woman stepped into the living room to announce that supper was on the table. The savory aroma of beans and potatoes had already filled the small apartment.

The table had been properly set with a mismatched assortment of flatware and Melamine plates. A cast-iron pot rested on a wooden trivet in the center. A glass of red wine was positioned above each knife. The old woman motioned for us to sit as she proudly lifted the kettle lid and stirred the contents with a steel ladle. Large chunks of meat and potatoes rose to the top.

"Do you like rattlesnake?" she asked. The woman waited for our unspoken responses. "Well, this is chicken," she said with a disturbing cackle and served a heaping portion to each of us. We responded with uneasy laughter.

"This is really good," Marc said after swallowing a large mouthful. The surprise in his voice reinforced his sincerity. I concurred.

We both ate the chicken dish hungrily, and the old woman refilled our wine glasses.

Marc broke the silence. "You've been such a gracious host, and we don't even know your name."

"For O'odham, it's customary that the man introduces himself first," the old woman said.

I dropped my head, a bit embarrassed. That was part of my culture as well. I apologized and introduced Marc and me.

"Call me Ga'ga," was all she said.

After another sip of wine, I continued my story about searching for the fallen meteor.

Ga'ga smiled and shook her head slightly. "You aren't from the observatory, and you didn't stop to find a meteor," she said calmly.

I started to protest, but she held up her hand to stop me. "If you were from Kitt, you would have said you were looking for a *meteorite*. And there was no meteor shower last night. But I know why you are really here," she said.

Marc's eyes grew even wider than mine as we peered across the table at each other. The woman continued, "Even if you don't know yet why you are here."

With that, she stood and began clearing the table.

16

☼ ☼ ☼

Marc offered to help Ga'ga with the dishes, but our host insisted that it was her obligation to make us feel at home. She suggested we step onto the porch now that the night breeze had eased the scorch of day.

The evening air was still warm but refreshing.

"What do you think she meant by that?" I asked.

"What? The 'even if you don't know yet' part?" Marc mimicked.

"Yes. Exactly. It's kind of spooky." A light wind made me shiver—at least I attributed it to the wind.

"That's just part of the mumbo jumbo. You know about those snake charmers back in India. It's all part of the mystical showmanship."

"I suppose so," I admitted. "I guess everyone has to believe in something. If you don't understand science, then it's religion."

"Or maybe both," Marc said cryptically.

"So, if her grandson is at work, why is his truck still parked here?" I thought aloud.

"Beats me," Marc said. "Maybe he caught a ride or drove one of the casino's vehicles."

"Yeah, maybe."

Marc walked to the Jeep and placed the palm of his hand over the engine and nodded. "It's cooled down now," he said. "We might be able to start it up."

He pulled out the key to unlock the door.

"No," I said. "We can't leave without saying thank you. That's customary for *my* people."

"You're so not American," Marc moaned, and we headed back to the trailer.

We approached Ga'ga at the kitchen sink while she was washing the dishes.

"We want to thank you for your hospitality..."

"And for that fantastic stew," Marc interjected.

"But the Jeep seems to have cooled down enough for us to head back to town."

Ga'ga turned from the sink, her hands wet and soapy. "You won't get far," she said.

Marc and I exchanged looks.

"Your radiator hose–it ruptured."

Marc broke in, "But how do you know that?"

"That spray of coolant wasn't just steam. It shot up like a fountain. You have a ruptured hose–the upper one. From how your Jeep is covered with red clay, I suspect the radiator is clogged with dust." The woman could see incredulity on Marc's face. "Now that the engine has cooled down feel along the surface of the hose on top. You'll find that the rubber is cracked."

I looked at Marc and shrugged. Then I turned to our host and said, "It looks like we'll be taking you up on your offer to stay the night–if we're still welcome here, that is."

"Of course you are still welcome here," she replied. "You have always been welcome here." She led us to the living room.

The woman pulled a pillow and some towels from a cedar chest and pointed us toward the bedroom. "This is my grandson's room. He won't get in until after dawn so you can sleep in his bed. You'll want to cool off with a shower first," she added pointing to the bathroom door.

"You have been so kind to us," I said. "You remind me of my own mother. May I give you a hug?"

Ga'ga nodded and opened her arms to let me embrace her. I felt a warmth in her that was almost spiritual.

She looked me in the eyes and said, "You can know a lot about a man from his touch. Now, I know more about you."

Ga'ga returned to the kitchen to finish washing the last of the dishes. She hung up the dish towel and said, "I'll be sitting in the backyard for a while. My home is yours for the night." With that, she disappeared out the back door.

"I guess we might as well get some sleep," Marc said and picked up the pillow. "Dawn comes pretty early."

I headed for the shower. The cold water felt good trickling over my lightly burned skin. I washed my thick black hair twice with the lavender-scented shampoo that was on the wire rack hanging from the shower head. The fragrance reminded me of the flower market in Mumbai. On our way home from school, Adam and I would occasionally pinch a spray of lavender from one of the stalls to take back to Mother–at least when Adam was in trouble we would, which was most of the time. I'm thankful for the life I have now, but I missed India, my mother and father, and Adam. Especially Adam.

I toweled off with one of the thin bath towels Ga'ga gave us. I wrapped the damp terrycloth around my waist and grabbed my clothes. As I entered the bedroom, I announced to Marc, "It's all yours. Don't use up all the hot water."

"Very funny," he replied. His normally pale skin had turned from pink to bright red from the day's sun. "I don't think I'll be using *any* hot water tonight." He pressed a fingertip into his forearm, and it left a very white mark behind.

The room was small. A slight breeze crept in through the window, which Marc had opened. The wall opposite the single bed was painted with the gold and crimson of the Arizona state flag. A handmade quilt with a similar pattern covered the thin mattress.

While Marc was in the shower, I stood naked in front of the open bedroom window. The cool air evaporated what moisture was left on my brown skin, and the chill it left behind felt amazing. I thought of Bren and how much I missed her touch. I leaned out to look at the night sky. It too was amazing–more amazing than I ever remembered the stars in India. Maybe we'd be murdered in our sleep tonight, but I was temporarily lost in that moment.

Mark burst back into the room clutching his too-small towel around his waist. I quickly grabbed my underwear and pulled it on, somewhat embarrassed that he saw me standing naked at the window.

"Tighty-whities? Really? And your wife still sleeps with you? What are you, eight?"

I could feel my face flush at Marc's critique of my Fruit of the Loom underwear. The blush quickly froze and turned to disgust once I realized the cotton underpants were still soaked with sweat and quite uncomfortable. Marc tossed his towel over the doorknob. The stark contrast of the deep pink of his chest and arms against an otherworldly pale midsection was visually compelling.

"You're really burned," I said, stating the obvious. I looked away to give him a chance to pull on his shorts, but he didn't.

"Ya think?"

"Does it hurt?" Again, I glanced at his two-toned flesh.

"So much even the cold shower was painful."

"Do you want me to ask Ga'ga if she has some aloe or something?" I asked.

"That's OK. I think I'll just grab another beer and see if I can sleep it off."

"Here, let me get that," I offered. "At least I'm dressed–sort of."

I pushed past Marc and pulled a Heiny from the refrigerator. The feeling of damp underwear grew more revolting with each step.

I brought the beer back to Marc. He tried pressing the cold bottle against his reddened skin, but it just made him flinch. Eventually, he screwed off the cap and leaned heavily against the bedroom door still naked, trying to drink away the pain.

Marc set down the empty bottle, tossed the sunset quilt on the floor, and stretched out across the bed with his knees propped up to reduce contact with the rough cotton sheet. "Here," he said scooching closer to the cool wall. "There's enough room for both of us. Just try not to slap me in the night."

"That's OK," I replied. "I'll just lay the quilt out on the floor."

"Are we going to have this conversation again? I promise I won't molest you. Besides, you saw the size of the spiders crawling around here, didn't you? Or should I say *tarantulas*?"

"Tarantulas? Really? I guess you're right." I flipped off the lights and pulled back the sheet to lie down next to Marc. A few seconds later, I got back out of bed and slipped off the insufferable *tighty-whities*. I climbed back under the cover with my back to my sunburned bunkmate.

☼ ☼ ☼

The fragrance of lavender filled the night air as I sat on the hilltop, leaning on my elbows to look up at the night sky. Adam wrapped an arm around my shoulders, and we just gazed heavenward into the dance of starlight.

Suddenly, the sky burst with blinding brightness.

"What the hell!" An almost shrill male voice pierced the night air. "Ga'ga, what is this?" the man yelled.

It took a moment before I realized that my dream of India was interrupted by an angry Native American who wanted his bed back.

The old woman padded across the short hallway, brushing back the white hair from her eyes. I pulled the sheet up to cover my nakedness.

"Why are there two naked men in my bed?"

Marc realized his arm was draped over my shoulder–and that he was lying on another man's bed with no clothes on.

Ga'ga tenderly gave her grandson a kiss on his cheek. "Ba'ali, you're home early."

"Don't try to sweet-talk me, Ga'ga. There are two milgahn sleeping in my bed, and I want to know why."

The old woman peered into the bedroom and saw Marc lying naked on her grandson's bed with me huddled next to him. Marc grinned sheepishly and offered a small wave.

The old lady took her grandson's arm and pulled him from the absurd scene. "Come with me, Ba'ali. Let them get dressed." Ga'ga sat her grandson down next to her on the couch.

Marc and I threw on our shorts and staggered into the living room.

"Look, man," Marc began. "We didn't know..."

I interrupted, "We didn't know you were coming home so early...not that that really explains what we were doing in your bed." Marc and I looked at each other not knowing if we should run or fight or just wait to see if we could talk our way through this.

"Ga'ga?" The man turned to his grandmother. "You have one minute to explain."

"Ba'ali, their Jeep broke down out front. I kept them here until you got home so you could get them back on the road. I didn't expect you so early."

The grandson gave us a sideways look and grunted.

I jumped in, "I can explain about us being in bed naked. We just..."

"Don't bother." The young man stood and made his way to the kitchen to get a beer. "My brother and I have slept in that bed naked many nights. I don't care about that." When he opened the refrigerator, he let out an angry yelp. "But I care about this! Who drank all my beer?" He turned to face us. "I think we all know the answer to that."

"Look," Marc said, "we just want to get on the road and get out of here. We'll pay you for the beer and any, uh, damage we might have done."

An upraised hand indicated that the conversation was over. "I worked a twelve-hour shift. I'm tired, and I just want to get some sleep. I'm going to bed." He turned to his grandmother, "Ga'ga, get me a clean sheet. I need to get the stink of milgahn out of my bedroom." Then he pointed to us. "You two need to spend the rest of the night in your Jeep. I'll fix it when I get up in the morning–*if* I get up in the morning."

Ga'ga patted his arm. "That was wise of you, Ba'ali. Let's all get some sleep." She gave her grandson a hug. "I'll see these young men out."

The grandson pulled the bathroom door behind him, and Marc and I headed to the front door. As we stood on the makeshift porch, Ga'ga leaned through the doorway and grinned. "That went better than I expected," she said. The old woman reached out and handed me a bottle of Jergens lotion. Then the door closed behind us.

I looked at the bottle and then at Marc. "I think she wants me to put this on you."

Marc groaned and limped barefoot to the Jeep. I rubbed the lotion gently over his red chest and arms. "This isn't store-bought," I said, as a musky herbal scent filled the air.

Marc sighed and looked heavenward.

All we had with us were our shorts, but at least the Jeep key was in Marc's pocket. We put down the top, climbed in, and reclined the bucket seats. I gazed up at the stars and smelled lavender.

17

☼ ☼ ☼

The old woman's potion must have worked. Marc fell asleep shortly before dawn. I spent the rest of the night just drinking in the splendor of the bejeweled sky. The Milky Way stretched overhead like a sequined curtain. Meteors streaked across the scene every few minutes, some bright enough to silhouette the mountain peaks. This never-ending dance reprised nightly for an audience of all humanity for millennia–a choreography of billions of performers locked in an eternal ballet.

The first sounds of morning twilight punctuated the nighttime drone of crickets–the soothing calls of quails and doves, the occasional hoot of a spotted owl. Music to accompany the finale playing out overhead.

Adam would groan when I waxed poetic like this. His was a universe of physical, guttural obsession meant to satiate the human appetite of baser instincts. Or was it I who was debased? I was the one who retreated into a world of the cold, calculated physical evidence of science. No mystery. No drama. Only a fascination with the unknown-but-always-knowable truth. Was he the poet—the dreamer? Was I the one to tether him to an artificial reality, denying him the opportunity to pursue the passion of his dreams?

...Adam would groan when I waxed poetic.

This time, *I* had to pee. I climbed over the Jeep door trying not to wake Marc. Still barefoot, I landed on a thorn lying on the packed dirt. Marc stirred at my stifled yelp but seemed to go back to sleep. I made my way to the peeing bush with enough light now to make out a path. As I approached, two quails darted out from under the shrub. This was their home we were pissing on. Us humans, with marble and gilt bathrooms and a Starbucks on every corner, and we had to come here to piss on the simple patch of soil where they made their home. Heidegger came to mind as I stood holding my dick in my hand. "Man is not the lord of beings; Man is the shepherd of Being." How many beings had I defiled merely by my existence?

There was something in the air of this place that made my mind race. Race in several directions at once. Race with no goal in sight. I needed to just be—be more like Marc, more like Adam.

When I finished befouling the quails' humble abode, I bent to pull the broken thorn from my foot. The bloody mark it left behind reminded me, nature gets her revenge—she's had billions of years of practice.

I made my way carefully back to the Jeep. The sun was nearly up now, and the air was already growing warm. Marc brushed a honeybee from his nose and turned in my direction.

"Did I fall asleep?"

"For a little while," I said. "At least we aren't dead yet."

He laughed. "Yeah. At least there's that."

Ga'ga rounded the corner of the blue trailer carrying the woven clothes basket. She delivered our shirts and shoes along with some corn cakes stuffed with meat and said in a sing-song voice, "I hope you will strive to make this day the best in your life."

The old woman observed our puzzled looks. "It is a greeting the O'odham have started each day with for generations."

We expressed our gratitude.

"That was your grandson?" Marc asked.

"My Ba'ali, yes. You didn't meet under the best of situations." Her reply was as obvious as Marc's question. "I thought it would be better for you to spend the rest of the night outside. I hope you weren't too uncomfortable."

"No," I said. "It was amazingly beautiful out here. I'll have to thank Ba'ali for making this night possible." I laughed.

"He is *my* Ba'ali," she said, pointing to herself. "You call him by his name, Sea Horse."

Marc smirked. Then he raised an eyebrow and gave me a knowing look.

"Sea Horse?" I repeated. "Isn't that an unusual name for an, uh, Native American?"

"You can say Indian. It is just a name–not who we are. Just as Sea Horse is just a name. We aren't all that far from the great water–you know, the Pacific Ocean. Just another name. It was there that his mother became pregnant. His father wanted to call him Little Horse, but my daughter always dreamed of getting away from the desert. She loved the water, so they chose Sea Horse for his tribal name."

"Come, let's sit in the back under the mesquite tree." Ga'ga left the basket of clothes on the ground and headed toward the backyard. We pulled on our shirts and shoes and followed her.

"It's peaceful out here," Marc observed as we approached the squat patch of expanding shade. He set the grass basket next to the old lady and sat in one of the rusty steel patio chairs.

Ga'ga noticed I was studying the pattern woven with dark grass into the bottom of the laundry basket. "It is the maze of I'itoi," she said.

"It reminds me of the meditation maze my mother made from stones in our backyard garden in India," I replied, sifting through memories of my childhood. "More of a labyrinth, really. There was only one path. It's called the Chakravyuha." I saw Marc roll his eyes in anticipation of a lecture of some sort, so I obliged him. "The design was originally used as a military formation–the wheel puzzle. The tactic was to force the enemy into a tightening ring of battle so they'd always be engaging fresh soldiers along the way. Of course, it has to have seven rings to represent the seven chakras of life. You can't make something practical without tying it up with religion," I snorted. "It must have worked. They won the battle."

"Did you make that?" Marc asked her, eager to end my homily.

"No," the old woman laughed. "I bought it at Walmart." She anticipated our looks of surprise. "They sell them for twenty dollars in their *Authentic Indian Souvenirs* department." She grinned, exposing a gap behind her lower lip that a tooth once filled. "But that doesn't diminish the power of I'itoi," she added.

"I'itoi?" Marc repeated. "Is that a spirit or something?"

"Oh, I'itoi is more than a spirit. He is at the heart of all of us." The woman placed a finger on the small dark circle woven into the center of what looked like a wheel. She traced a path through the maze back to a stick figure at the outer edge and tapped it four times.

"This represents each of us," she said. "We spend our lives traveling through the maze seeking I'itoi."

"Sounds like a video game," Marc quipped. "Fighting your way through different levels of a dungeon so you can battle the boss."

This time, I rolled *my* eyes.

The woman went on to explain the legend of the O'odham god of creation, who secreted himself in Baboquivari Mountain after the people turned against him. She pointed to the jagged mountain peak north of us.

"Grandfather," I chuckled half aloud.

Marc looked surprised. "Since when do you speak Indian?"

I ignored the irony of his question. "The name of the mountain. It reminded me of my grandfather," I said. "*Babu* means grandfather in Hindi, and my mother's family name is Kuwari. That's the Hindu mountain god of gold and riches, but her family never saw any of it." I blinked away the image of their poor neighborhood in Punjab. "It's just a coincidence."

Ga'ga's eyes brightened. "The world is filled with coincidences." She smiled. "*Babo* is also how the O'odham say grandfather, but only on the mother's side. The mountain was given the name Quivari by the Hohokam long before the O'odham arrived. It is a sacred place for our people."

"Does anyone ever find I'itoi?" Marc asked, comprehending the philosophical implications.

Ga'ga laughed. "The conquistador Coronado never did. Five hundred years ago, he searched here for the gold that legend said was hidden in Quivira. He died a poor man."

"There's gold in these mountains?" Marc exclaimed. "You all should be rich!"

"It is one of the stories an ancient calendar stick tells of. The legend also says the gold was hidden because instead of bringing happiness, it brought disease and death at the hands of the Spanish conquerors. We are rich in himdag now because there was no gold to be found then."

"That sounds like something my mother would have told me," I commented.

"She must be a wise woman." Ga'ga grinned.

"So, what about I'itoi," Marc persisted. "Do you, like, go on quests to search for him?"

Ga'ga smiled. "There is only one path to I'itoi, but many obstacles along the way. If you give up the search, you will never find I'itoi." She leaned back in her chair and took a long sip of her iced tea. "But these are only legends. You didn't come here to listen to Indian legends," she concluded.

"Your grandson seemed pretty upset last night," Marc commented, changing the subject.

"My Ba'ali has a temper, but he is a good boy. Still, it gets him in trouble sometimes." She paused and looked into our eyes. "It gets his brother into trouble too."

Ga'ga had prepared a pitcher of cold water for us, and she poured us each a glass. Then she asked, "I know why you're here, but why did you come?"

Her question caught both of us off guard. Marc took it for just more mumbo-jumbo, but I understood what she meant, although I didn't know what that was.

"And you can stop telling that story about the stars. I know you came here for something," she said. "Something much more."

I looked over at Marc and shrugged. He nodded in assent.

"My brother-in-law," I began. "He's been charged with murder, but I don't think he did it."

"And you think my Ba'ali did?" Her question was simple and straightforward.

Marc leaned in, "We just know his truck was near where the explosion took place. We thought he might know something about what happened."

"Then you must ask him. He'll tell you one way or the other. He's a good boy. He won't lie."

"I'm not so sure that's a good idea," Marc said. "If the police show up with a warrant for Zacchaeus Redman, I doubt he'll take it very well."

"Maybe better than you think. That is not Zacchaeus Redman." She nodded toward the trailer.

Marc and I exchanged looks of surprise. I followed up, "But when you said Sea Horse was his tribal name, I assumed he had an, uh, Anglo name as well."

"He does," Ga'ga said, "but it's not Zacchaeus Redman."

"Then whose truck is that parked in front?" Marc asked.

"That truck belongs to my other Ba'ali. *His* name is Zacchaeus Redman, and that is why you are here."

Marc just scratched his head and stared at the truck.

She leaned in and spoke in almost a whisper, "There is something I must ask you to do for me."

Ga'ga went on to explain that her older grandson, Z, was being held on manslaughter charges in the jail in Sells, about half an hour west.

"You must talk with him. He is a great man who resists his destiny. He won't defend himself. You are here to do that for him."

"You say that with such certainty. How do you know?" I asked.

"I know, and I know that you do too."

With that, Ga'ga headed back to the kitchen.

Marc put his hand on my knee. "Do you know what she's talking about?"

I looked away for a moment. "She says I do."

Ga'ga returned holding a short carved walking stick. "Come with me," she said and headed toward the mountain ridge. Marc and I followed.

The frail-looking woman pushed through a patch of arrowgrass to a lightly worn trail. Without looking back, she pressed on at a pace that left us struggling to keep up. After what seemed like a mile or more, she stopped at the top of a ridge. When we arrived, we could see we were looking down into a valley. Not a valley really. More of a bowl.

"A crater?" Marc proposed.

"Yes, a crater. Maybe this is where your *meteor* landed," Ga'ga said in a mocking tone.

The woman turned to me. "You don't believe in signs, yet you always seek them." Then she faced the crater as if to address the chasm before us. "This was a sign," she said. "White men measure the world in time. But time is a river, flowing quickly in our youth and slowing to a trickle when we grow old. The O'odham measure time by when the river overflows its banks—great battles, severe droughts, broken treaties."

The old woman looked at me. "But you are not white."

Ga'ga held up the small staff she had carried with her. "This is how the O'odham record time. This calendar stick has been passed from generation to generation down to me." She took my hand and ran my finger over the marks carved into the smooth wood and stopped near the oldest notch.

"This carving," she said, "was made the day my grandmother's great-grandfather was born. The carving was not intended to honor his birth." She looked up and smiled. "We are born every day. This was the day the meteor fell to earth. The mark holds the story of when the sky flashed with a bright light, and rock and dirt rained on the small band of O'odham that lived near here. Two braves died when the earth shook." She turned to speak to us now. "The elders said it was a sign–a sign that the man born that day was to be a powerful magician–a great chief. But greatness passed over him and touched his eldest daughter instead." She gently slid my finger a few notches farther down the calendar stick.

Marc did the math. "Your, uh, great-great-great...uh...great-grandmother?"

"In your reckoning. She saw the coming of the milgahn."

"Europeans?" I inferred.

"Yes, she warned of the coming of the White Man. Most people treated her as just a crazy girl. Those who listened survived. At least some did." I saw a tear form in the old lady's eye.

"Legend says she had one child, but he did not share the visions of his mother. His son, my grandfather did, however. He was a great man of magic. The tribe made my father a chief hoping he was also blessed with the gift and could protect our people. He could not."

"But you have that gift, don't you?" Marc said, realizing the implications of the answer. "That's how you knew we were coming."

"Yes." Her hand guided mine to the most recent carving. "And that's how I know you won't harm either of my grandsons."

"And your daughter?" I asked. "The gift passed over her too?"

"Yes, to my great joy. Although a gift must be accepted, it is not always desired. I did not wish it for her."

Marc put the pieces together. "So, you think your older grandson has the gift?"

Ga'ga nodded. "He refuses to accept it, however. That is why you must bring your magic to him. You can save him, so he has a chance to save our people."

"My magic? I don't have any magic."

The old woman looked deep into my eyes. "I think you know you do," she said. Then she turned to walk back to the trailer.

Marc breathed the word we were both thinking–*Mnemosyne.*

18

☼ ☼ ☼

The words of Sea Horse proved to be prophetic. He didn't get up in the morning. Ga'ga prepared us a hot lunch of tortillas and beans. It was filling, and she had chilled another case of Heinekens. We made sure not to drink all the bottles.

The day was just as hot as the one before, but the darkened trailer managed to stay relatively comfortable. Marc and I retreated to the living room to wait for Sea Horse to stir, or possibly hoping he wouldn't.

We browsed through the remaining books on the makeshift bookcase.

"Philosophy. Poetry. Politics." Marc set a stack of books down. "Maybe I shouldn't be so quick to judge people."

"Ya think?" My response was less than articulate, but it got my point across.

Marc sat me next to him on the couch. "Do you think they knew? I mean, when they named him."

"Who?" I said, pulling back.

"Sea Horse. Don't you get it? *Sea Horse*? *Hippocampus*?"

I had to admit, the coincidence hadn't occurred to me. In ancient Greek, hippocampus translates to sea monster or seahorse. The name was given to the small organ in the brain because its shape resembles the snout and curled tail–and even the size of the enigmatic aquatic creature.

"Hippocampus," Marc pursued his line of reasoning–"That's the seat of memory. That's the key to Mnemosyne."

"And that's the name his parents compromised on thirty years ago." I stood to get another beer. "Coincidence. Just coincidence."

"And what about the old lady's fascination with you? It's like you two have this special bond between you."

"Delusion," I said as I screwed off the cap. "All just coincidence and delusion."

"Whatever," came Marc's typical response of concession.

We both relocated to the kitchen table when we heard Sea Horse starting to move about. The young man opened the bedroom door and strolled naked to the bathroom, towel in hand.

"What is it with sleeping naked in that bed?" Marc laughed. I just blushed.

☼ ☼ ☼

By mid-afternoon, Sea Horse had sprayed the red dirt out of the radiator vents and replaced the radiator hose–the upper one. Then he topped off the antifreeze and slammed the hood closed.

He gave us a condescending look and said, "You were lucky you didn't blow a head gasket. If you're going to wander around in the desert, learn to live like a snake." He took off back to the carport, where he kept his tools.

"What did that mean?" I asked.

Marc just hissed.

Ga'ga appeared from behind the shrub. "Now you are ready," she said. "I will take you to find what you're looking for, and you will take me to visit my other grandson." With that simple command, the old lady climbed into the back seat of the Jeep. "You may put the top up now. I like air conditioning."

I obediently lifted the canvas top, and Marc climbed in behind the wheel. "It looks like the road trip continues," he said as I got in on the passenger side.

We started to pull onto 86 when Marc slammed on the brakes.

"What the...?" I exclaimed, looking up. In front of us stood Sea Horse, arms spread, with his hands pressed against the hood.

The man came to my window and tapped hard. "Open the door," he demanded.

I complied. Sea Horse pushed the passenger seat forward and climbed in to sit next to his grandmother. "I don't trust these milgahn," he said. "They know no himdag. I'm going with you."

We headed west to Sells, halfway between Tucson and Gila Bend. With a population of less than three thousand, it's the largest city on the hundred-and-seventy-mile stretch of Highway 86. For the next few miles, we rode in silent appreciation of the air-conditioned cabin. Marc spoke first.

"We're going to the jail? What do we do when we get there?"

Sea Horse replied, "You take my Ga'ga to see my brother."

"Z?" I said, attempting to continue the conversation.

Sea Horse only grunted.

His grandmother leaned forward and explained, "Two men died in a fight at a bar five nights ago. My Ba'ali is said to have pushed them into a post, and the porch it supported fell and crushed the men. He's being held at the Tribal Detention Center."

"And they're holding him for that?" Marc interjected.

Sea Horse spoke more reasonably now. "You don't know my brother. He is proud and stubborn. This isn't the first time he has been in trouble with the law."

"Does he have a lawyer?" Marc asked.

"We don't need lawyers," Sea Horse answered. "The truth is our defense."

Ga'ga explained, "This is a tribal matter, at least for now. The elders will decide if my Ba'ali is to be freed or turned over to the authorities."

"Authorities," Sea Horse spat. "Whites who don't care about justice–only law."

In the mirror, I saw Ga'ga squeeze her grandson's knee. "I hope you can help defend him. He won't defend himself." She paused and said, "and then you can take what you came for."

"I hate victims who respect their executioners," Sea Horse said under his breath.

I recognized the quotation. "Sartre?" I commented.

"Don't sound so surprised. Indians read."

"I just didn't expect an, uh, Native American to know Western philosophers," I stammered.

"What? You think we sit around in wigwams getting drunk and saying 'How'?"

"That's not what I meant. I just..."

"That's exactly what you meant. Just because you're dark skinned, you still think like a milgahn."

Sea Horse's comment hit home. He was right. I was adrift between cultures. Not Asian–not Western.

Marc tried to lighten the tension. "Sartre, Kafka, Heidegger. Even that thick book about, uh..."

"The *Mahabharata,*" I provided the name for him.

"When did you study all these guys?"

"We have libraries–and the Internet."

Ga'ga said proudly, "My Ba'ali received a Master's degree from ASU. We are all very proud of him."

I caught Marc's look of surprise.

"And you work for the casino? How did that happen?" Marc attempted to continue the conversation.

"Just drive. No more talk," Sea Horse ordered. We rode the last few miles in silence.

When we reached Sells, Sea Horse guided us to the police station. "Park here," he directed. Marc stopped the Jeep, and we all got out and walked across the small parking lot to the stainless steel and glass doors of the newly built facility.

"Nice building," Marc said.

Sea Horse replied, "You were expecting a stockade?"

The guard at the front desk recognized Ga'ga immediately. "Welcome back, ma'am. You come to see your grandson?"

"Yes," she said. "And for him to meet these two men." She pointed to Marc and me.

"I'll call to have Z brought down. I'm afraid your visitors will have to be screened before I can let them in."

The sergeant picked up the phone and called for someone to escort the detainee to the visitors' area. "He'll be down in a few minutes. You can wait over there." He pointed to a cluster of upholstered chairs in the lobby. Then he looked at us and said, "You two wait here. I'll have someone take you to the screening room."

A few minutes later, Marc and I were escorted through a metal detector and ushered into a small, windowless room. "Sit there," the guard said, pointing to the padded chairs on the other side of a steel desk.

As the guard was leaving, a heavy-set older Native American man in jeans and a chambray shirt squeezed in and sat across from us. "I'm Detective Tomkin," he said as he flipped open a thick manila folder. He leaned back in the chair. "Who are you and why are you here?"

Marc and I introduced ourselves and presented the requested identification. I explained that we were neuroscientists from Fulton University working on a research project.

"And you want to conduct your research on Papago?" the detective asked accusingly.

"No sir," I said. "We had an invitation to stay with my brother-in-law, in Phoenix."

Marc broke in, "We wanted to experience life on a reservation, so we drove down here for the day."

"Yesterday, that is," I clarified. "Our Jeep broke down in front of Ga'ga's...Zacchaeus's grandmother's house, and she let us stay the night until her younger grandson came home to fix the vehicle." I glanced over at Marc looking for confirmation.

"Yeah, she...I mean *they* were great. They made us feel right at home. All himdag and everything." Marc's attempt to sound culturally aware did not impress Mr. Tomkin.

"Um," the detective grunted. "And have you *experienced* life on the rez?"

"I've learned more than I ever expected," I said absently.

"Now, tell me why you are really here."

Marc looked hard at me and said honestly, "Ga'ga says *he's* here to help her grandson."

The detective looked up slowly. "I hope that's true. Z can use all the help can get—and more than he'll accept."

Then he leaned hard on his elbows and said, "I've known Z from since he was little. He has a long history with the police. A troubled and violent history."

"What did he do?" Marc asked.

"Besides just killing two strangers?" the detective began. "Let me tell you." He opened the large file and began flipping through the yellowed pages. "Burglary, assault, stolen vehicle..." He was only a few pages back in the archive. "Then there was a reckless homicide charge in 2012 he got out of, assaulting an officer, arson, and...oh, yes, a murder conviction when he was fourteen."

The detective closed the folder. "You still think you can help him? Well, if you're just a couple of do-gooders trying to *uplift* the oppressed Native Americans, you've come to the wrong reservation."

The detective stood and picked up the file. "But if Ga'ga wants you to talk to Z, I won't stop you. I'd like to find a reason to turn him loose. You can see him after she and his brother leave." He opened the door and turned to us. "Wait here. Someone will get you when you can go in."

Marc was the first to speak. "And that's his people's *chosen one*? Now I'm having second thoughts about this."

"You? This was all your idea," I nearly raged. Then I leaned in, speaking in a loud whisper, "Burglary, assault, arson, MURDER! This is the guy we're going to help? And don't forget about that little thing of him blowing up Archie's office and his mistress." I sat back in the chair and folded my arms, staring hard at where a window should be.

After a long silence, Marc asked, "Do we tell him? What we're here for, that is."

"What do you think? Say, 'Hi, we're a couple of white guys...'" I ignored Marc's double-take for including myself in the description, "...looking for the man who murdered my brother-in-law's girlfriend. We think it's you, but we're not sure." I rolled my eyes. "Do you think that will do the trick?"

Marc breathed heavily. "I suppose you're right. We'll just say we want to use him as a research subject. These guys don't talk much. He probably won't even ask."

"And he'll never agree to it either," I commented.

It was another fifteen minutes before the guard returned to the interrogation room. "You can come with me," he said.

The guard led us to the visitation area. It was just a row of bar stools facing a plate-glass window constructed above a knee wall. Less restrictive than what you see in the movies, but still an effective barrier separating inmates from their visitors.

Sea Horse was ushering his grandmother back to the lounge when we arrived. He turned to us and said, "I told my brother not to talk to you." Then he followed Ga'ga out of the room.

The guard instructed us to sit on the two stools across from the very large, very somber looking Native American man on the other side of the glass wall.

"You have ten minutes," he said and stepped back.

"I'm David, and this is Marc," I began, leaning into the circular vent that served as a speaker.

"Save your breath," the deep voice rumbled from the other side. "My Ga'ga told me what you want–and what she wants." Z brushed his tangled locks of black hair off his shoulders and looked down at his large hands, which were folded in front of him. "You can work whatever magic on me you choose to. She still believes in the old ways."

Marc shot a surprised look in my direction.

"...after you get me out of here," the inmate added.

"But," I stammered, "how can we do that?"

Z just shrugged and raised a hand for the guard to take him back to his cell.

19

☼ ☼ ☼

Marc and I joined Ga'ga and Sea Horse in the visitors' lounge, and I told them what had Z said.

Sea Horse glared at us. "Then it's time you go back to where you came from."

Ga'ga clutched her grandson's arms. "They'll do no such thing," she scolded. "They have to get your brother out of jail."

Sea Horse shook himself free and stormed out of the building.

"We really want to help," I said, "but there's nothing we can do."

"Use your magic," came her sincere reply.

Marc explained, "We don't have Mnem....the device with us."

"And even if we did, we wouldn't be allowed to take it into the jail," I added.

"That is not the magic I speak of," she said and turned to join Sea Horse.

We assembled in the parking lot. Sea Horse avoided looking at us.

Ga'ga took command. "Come with me," she ordered and started walking to the other side of the street. Marc and I followed, with Sea Horse trailing behind.

The paved road was not busy, but we stood at the crosswalk and waited for the town's only stoplight to turn green. About half a block down the other side of the street, Ga'ga stopped us at the walk-up window of a Dairy Maid. "Four Bliss bars," she told the girl on the other side of the counter and pulled out a twenty-dollar bill from the woven bag she carried.

A minute later, Ga'ga explained, "My Ba'ali has always loved Bliss bars." She handed each of us one of the frozen treats. "It was the magic I worked on him to get him to do the right thing."

Sea Horse dropped his head, half in embarrassment but mostly to unwrap the chocolate-covered ice cream treat. Rolling his eyes upward, he said to her, "Thank you, Ga'ga. I will forever be your little Ba'ali."

We each held our Bliss bar by the stick and took a large bite of the already melting dessert. I recognized the universal message. Ice cream was also the magic my mother used to get me and Adam to do what was right.

"Now, it's nearly time for supper, and I'm hungry," Ga'ga said. "We will go down the street for something more nourishing to eat." With that, the old lady marched to the end of the block and turned left to lead us to the Red Pony Saloon.

The bar was large for a town this size. The sun hadn't set yet, so the interior was bright enough to reveal the patched plaster ceiling and stained concrete floor. I noticed the balcony above the back door and the makeshift post that held up one corner.

"This is the bar," I whispered to Marc. "The bar where the fight was."

Ga'ga led us to one of the wooden tables near the back.

"I need to use the toilet now," she said. "Order me a martini," she told her grandson and headed to a narrow hallway where signs for Braves and Squaws protruded above two doors.

Sea Horse waved the bartender over and ordered a vodka martini, straight up–onion, not olive, for his grandmother, and three Heinekens. He still wouldn't look either of us in the eye.

I leaned across the table. "I know you don't want us here, and I'm not sure we want to be here either," I began.

Sea Horse turned toward me and glared.

"...but maybe we can help your brother."

Marc gave me a sideways glance and said, "His brother-in-law has a lot of influence," not thinking about the implications of involving the man we came to defend.

The corners of Sea Horse's mouth curled. "I don't want your *influence* or your magic. I love my grandmother–and my brother, and I won't let you fool them with your slippery promises."

He spoke coolly now. "When she returns, we will eat. Then you will drive your Jeep back to Phoenix. I can get one of the casino cars from here, and we will go home–and never see you again."

Before Sea Horse had finished the last words of his implied threat, Ga'ga was standing next to our table, with the bar owner looking over her shoulder.

"This is Ben," she said. "Ben is the grandson of my sister. He will help us."

Ben looked at Sea Horse. "Sorry about your brother, cuz," he said.

Ga'ga peered up at the lanky young man. "My Ba'ali doesn't have much time. You need to work quickly."

Puzzled glances were exchanged around the table.

"I don't know what I can do," Ben said. "I didn't want to get Z thrown in jail, but two men died in my bar. There wasn't anything else I could do."

"We understand," Ga'ga said. "But my grandson could be charged with second-degree murder. You need to find a defense that will get him released."

Marc piped up, "For that, the charges would have to be reduced to involuntary manslaughter or, even better, self-defense."

"Then that's what you must prove." The small woman returned to her seat and lifted the martini glass the bartender had just delivered. "Wait," she addressed the bartender. "Bring us four cheesesteaks."

The rest of us sighed heavily while Ben pulled up a chair to join us.

"What happened?" I asked.

"It was Saturday night," Ben began. "We had a big crowd. They were getting pretty rowdy. I was helping clear tables when a fight broke out near the bar. I didn't see what happened until this Juhkam...you know," he said in response to my puzzled look, "a Mexican. He came flying across the room and slammed into that post there." Ben pointed to the four-by-four holding up the corner of the small balcony. "Half a dozen men were up there playing poker when the whole thing collapsed. They jumped off, and none of them was hurt bad, but the Mexican and I suppose it was his friend were crushed under the joist that came down."

Marc asked, "Did anyone see what happened?"

"I guess so," Ben said. "But none of them said nothing. After the ambulance arrived, the police came and tried to get a statement."

"So, who turned in my brother?" Sea Horse said, raising his voice.

"He did, himself."

Sea Horse just buried his head in his hands.

"My Ba'ali is an honest man. If they asked him who did it, he would tell them." Ga'ga looked both proud and disappointed at the same time.

"Maybe you can question some of the regulars," Marc suggested.

"You'd probably have to wait until Saturday night," Ben said.

Ga'ga raised her hand. "That will be too late. The council will have decided to hand him over to the State before then."

Our sandwiches arrived, but none of us was hungry anymore. We took a few bites, drank our beers, and decided to leave.

"I'll get this," Marc offered. "I can charge it to our expense account."

Sea Horse started to protest, but Ga'ga stopped him. "We'll be outside," she said.

I waited by the front door for Marc to pay the bill. The bartender rang up the check and slid open the cash drawer of the register. Marc pocketed the change and abruptly took a double-take to the opposite side of the register. "That's a...That's a surveillance monitor," he commented.

The bartender looked over at the dark screen and said, "Yeah, the boss had that hooked up a few months ago, but it stopped working, and he didn't bother to get it fixed."

Marc looked around and saw the two cameras mounted above the aging bar mirror. Tiny red lights blinked from the handles. He waved me over to the bar excitedly and said, “Call the others back in here.” Then he instructed the bartender, “Go get Ben.”

Soon, we were all gathered around the bar. Ben explained that he got the system in March from a gas station that was being torn down. He had it installed, but the video showed mostly static, so he just shut it off.

“Not completely,” Marc said pointing to the cameras. “They’re still running.”

“Yeah, I guess so,” Ben said. “I just turned off the monitor. I forgot about the cameras.”

Ga’ga spoke up, “Do you think you will find something?” she asked.

“At least we might be able to see what actually happened that night,” I proposed.

The bartender pointed out that even if the cameras were recording, the video was so bad we wouldn’t be able to make out the picture.

Sea Horse spoke up. “I can take care of that.”

“Really? But you’re a mechanic,” Marc blurted.

Sea Horse smiled and glanced at his grandmother. “Is that what she told you? Well, it’s close. I’m an electrical engineer. I manage the security system at the casino. I’ve fixed problems like this before.”

Sea Horse pulled up a stool and switched on the monitor. The screen filled with snow.

“Bring me a shot of everclear,” he demanded.

The bartender asked, “On the rocks?”

“It’s not for me,” he said gruffly. “I need it to clean the connections.”

While Sea Horse proceeded to pull off the cables connected to the monitor, a shot glass of colorless liquid was set before him.

In full technician mode now, he pulled a pocket knife from his jeans and began peeling back the insulation on some of the wires. He then dipped a corner of a cloth napkin in the alcohol and rubbed the wire ends and contacts briskly.

Sea Horse reconnected the wires and switched the monitor back on. A shadowy image rolled slowly over the screen.

"That's it?" Marc said. "We won't be able to make out much from that."

The threatening stare Marc received was enough to make him step back from the counter.

"Two corks," was all Sea Horse said.

The bartender disappeared into the kitchen and a minute later returned with the requisite stoppers and an open bottle of chilled Grenache. "I only found one, so I opened this," he said as he started filling wine glasses and setting them on the counter. I raised one of the glasses and whispered, "To success."

Sea Horse just grabbed the corks and proceeded to cut them lengthwise about halfway through. He took a sheet of aluminum foil from a dispenser next to the cash register and with his knife cut two strips about an inch wide. He then pried open one of the split pieces of cork and inserted a small square of the tin foil and laid a stripped section of wire through the center of the cork. Sea Horse stripped the other strand of the wire and laid it along the outer surface of the cork and wrapped the assembly with the rest of the aluminum strip. Our *casino mechanic* did the same thing with the other wire leading to the recorder and then secured the two corks tightly with insulated twist-ties.

Once again, Sea Horse flipped on the monitor. This time a steady image of the bar resolved on the screen. "Makeshift bypass capacitors," he said. Then he inserted the knife blade into the slot of a screw on the back of the surveillance station, and with a couple of small turns, the rolling picture came to a stop.

"That's genius," Marc said as a clear image of the four of us standing at the bar filled the screen.

I asked, "But even if the cameras were recording, would anything be saved from last weekend?"

Sea Horse returned the knife to his pocket. "It should. This size hard drive can store three months of recordings or more."

I handed a glass of wine to Ga'ga and refilled my own. The old lady took a sip and then poked a finger into her grandson's forearm. "Find that night," she said.

Images scrolled quickly over the screen as time receded into the previous week. When the date in the upper-right corner flashed May 16, Sea Horse froze the picture. A paramedic was kneeling next to a body lying amid the rubble of the collapsed balcony.

"There," Ga'ga ordered. "Back it up from there."

Sea Horse scrolled slowly back in time. The paramedic retreated from the scene, and soon the balcony reverted to its functional form. Ga'ga touched a finger on a figure standing near the bar. "That's him," she said, "facing two shorter men."

Sea Horse rolled the tape back a few minutes to replay the entire sequence of events. Z was seated at the bar when the two men approached him, one from either side. We could see Z stand, towering over the shorter of the two men, and raise his hand dismissively.

"Do you recognize either of those men?" I asked no one in particular.

"Just a Juhkam and a white guy who were here that night," the bartender replied, "but I never seen them in here before."

It looked like words were exchanged between Z and the shorter, dark-skinned man. We could see the very blond crew-cut youth circle behind Z.

"Stop," I said. "Can you zoom in?"

Sea Horse froze the frame and magnified the image enough to make out the outlines of the grainy figures. "The Mexican," I said. "What's that on his head?"

Marc squinted hard and looked up. "At first I thought it was a ballcap, but I think it's just his hair–tied back in a bun." He stared hard at me.

"...with a young skinhead," I finished his thought.

Ga'ga interrupted. "Look. In the other man's hand."

Sea Horse zoomed in on Z's mid-section.

"There," Marc said. "You can see it. He has a pistol stuck in your grandson's ribs."

The image was quite grainy, but we could see what looked like the barrel of a gun.

Ga'ga motioned to Sea Horse to continue.

In what was less than a minute of tape, we witnessed Z sweep the bar behind him with his right arm, driving a beer mug into the face of the blond assailant and knocking him off balance. The Juhkam lunged and wrapped his arms around Z's chest. The massive Native American lifted the man like he was a rag doll and tossed him, crosswise, into his taller accomplice, sending them both careening into the post that supported the balcony. In a matter of seconds, the platform and its occupants came crashing to the floor, crushing the two men.

Sea Horse stopped the tape, and we looked at one another in stunned silence. Eventually, Marc spoke. "It was self-defense. You can see that, right?"

We nodded in agreement.

"But the gun," Ben said. "The police didn't find a gun."

The bartender grabbed a nearby broom. He knelt to the floor and began dragging the handle across the cement beneath the narrow space under the bar.

"You think it might be under there?" Marc asked.

"Could be," he said looking up at us. "No one's swept under here for probably years."

An assortment of napkins, spoons, and bits of broken glass was mounded in the middle of the bar floor.

"Hey, here's the credit card I lost last year," the young man announced, proudly holding up the dusty square of plastic.

"Just focus," Sea Horse instructed while the rest of us pulled stools away from the bar so the sweeping could continue.

As the bartender dragged the broom handle under the last few feet of the bar, we heard the sound of metal scraping across the concrete floor, and a small black pistol spun to a stop in the middle of the room.

"A Glock," Sea Horse said. "They pulled a Glock on my brother."

I said, "I don't know what the disagreement was about, but that sure looked like self-defense to me."

Ga'ga added, "And it will look like self-defense to Detective Tomkin. We must get him to review the tape right away."

"And the gun," Marc said as he started to reach for the Glock.

Sea Horse lowered his foot on the dusty sidearm. "No. Leave it. That's evidence. Don't disturb it."

"But the bar," Ben protested. "I'll be getting customers coming in soon."

"Close now," Sea Horse ordered. "I will have the detective here in a few minutes–or would you rather be shut down for the weekend while you wait for a team to investigate the crime scene?"

Ben nodded and stepped to the door to flip a plastic sign to Closed.

"And you," Sea Horse pointed sternly at Marc and me. "You go back to where you came from."

Ga'ga squeezed his arm.

Her grandson continued, "...and come back in the morning with your magic."

20

☼ ☼ ☼

We slept in late after the previous day's excitement. I was too tired to protest sharing the bed with Marc. Besides, after last night's arrangement, sleeping together in a king-size bed in an air-conditioned room felt decadent.

The chime of an incoming text around ten thirty woke me. I rolled over and pulled my cell phone off the nightstand. Sea Horse had sent the time and location for us to meet. Before Marc and I left Sells, we agreed to return as soon as they could get Z released, assuming there was enough evidence now for the council to let him go.

I nudged Marc.

"Come on, buddy. It's time to play detective again."

Marc rolled over and buried his face in his pillow.

I slipped out of bed and reread the message. The police expected to process the paperwork by noon, and we were instructed to be in Sells at two. Since we had plenty of time to get there, I decided to let Marc sleep a bit longer. It had been too late to call Bren when we finally got a signal on the way back to Phoenix. I assumed she would be in meetings for at least another hour, so it was still too early to call her now, but I desperately needed to hear her voice. The past couple of days had been stressful.

Stressful. I rolled the word around in my mind. That didn't come close to describing how it felt, but I knew I didn't have the language to express the conflicting emotions I was experiencing–terrified one moment and exhilarated the next. Maybe this is how Adam felt when his platoon went on maneuvers. I laughed out loud–comparing Marc and me playing Hardy Boys with Adam facing IEDs in a combat zone. No, stressful was probably the best word I could come up with.

I sat at the desk in the studio and powered on my laptop to check the time in Amsterdam. When the screen flashed on, I saw Brenda had emailed me last night. The subject line read FIELD TRIP!

She wrote that environmentalists from the host country were taking a task force into the North Sea to observe how tidal changes attributed to global warming could be managed using floating platforms of hydrokinetic turbines. Something about how the massive pontoons dampened wave action and converted the kinetic energy into the power required to strategically deploy the tanker-size floating pods. She was delighted by the prospect of using similar systems in coastal areas like Miami and New Orleans, which are subject to tidal flooding. What's more, she was selected to join the expedition. That meant she would be without a cellular connection through the weekend.

I smiled at the irony of Bren not being able to contact *me* this time. I deserved the dig at the end of her email asking if I had been avoiding talking to her. I closed my laptop, pulled on a pair of shorts and a T-shirt, and grabbed my phone off the nightstand. Just as I stepped out of the room to get coffee, my cell phone buzzed. I plunged a hand deep into the pocket of my cargo shorts to retrieve it. The phone number wasn't one I recognized, but from the area code, I assumed the call was from the Chicago area. I was right about that, and I immediately recognized the voice.

"Jill," I said, "how did you get this number?"

With a laugh, she said finding phone numbers came with her job description. Then her tone turned serious.

"David," she said, "we're running out of time. This isn't a game, but you're already a player. You have to meet me in the Strathmore lounge. I'll be waiting for you." Before she hung up, she added, "Make sure you aren't followed."

Well, she can wait as long as she likes, I told myself as I headed to the hotel lobby. I'm not risking my career and my marriage to play her game. And this is indeed a game, but instead of being a player, I'm being played. Sounding so serious. That's just part of the act...I suppose. I realized that shred of doubt would be enough to compel the researcher in me to investigate. I returned to the room to leave a note for Marc and grab the keys to the Jeep.

The Strathmore was just ten minutes from where we were staying. I bypassed the valet and self-parked. Inside the luxury hotel, I made my way to the poolside lounge. Jill was sitting under a vine-covered pergola. As I approached her, she nodded and said, "I hoped you would come."

"You sounded confident that I would," I replied as I pulled a canvas chair into the shade.

"Confidence can sometimes conceal terror, and David, I'm actually terrified by what I know could happen."

Either she was laying it on much too thick to be convincing, or Jill was truly frightened. But of what?

I sat across the small café table from her. "Look, I don't know what you expect to..."

Jill interrupted me. "David, this story runs much deeper than I ever expected. Just hear me out. If you aren't as concerned as I am, you can walk away, and I won't bother you again."

I listened.

"You are in the middle of something bigger than a murder charge against your brother-in-law."

I leaned back and carefully considered the obviously distraught woman seated across from me.

"By now, I suppose you realize Archibald Trumble is not a nice person."

I smiled.

"He made his way to the top of the Phoenix social ladder climbing over the backs of many good people." She paused to assess my reaction. "And he didn't do it alone."

I raised an eyebrow but said nothing.

Jill reached across the table and said, "This won't be easy for you to hear, but the governor of this state–your father-in-law–has been complicit every step of the way."

I shifted uncomfortably in my seat.

"The section of border wall Archie is so proud of? It wasn't built just to keep out Mexicans."

I finally engaged in the conversation. "What do you mean?"

"I have a reliable source who tells me a network of tunnels was built under that section of the wall. It runs deep into Arizona to avoid border security detection. Your brother-in-law created a highly protected and lucrative passageway for smuggling drugs, arms, munitions, people–you name it. Anything that can increase his wealth."

I sat back and smirked. "You're trying to compete with all those conspiracy-theory sites, aren't you? Your paper lost its traditional readers, so you have to make shit up to survive." I pushed my chair back. "I've heard enough."

"I don't think so." Jill dropped a manila envelope on the table and pushed it toward me. "Take a look at these."

Curious, I eased myself down into the seat again and opened the package to thumb through the stack of documents and photos it contained.

"Have you been following the news? The big story here is that the Russian military s supporting the Mexican government. They saw a window of opportunity open and climbed right in. If the U.S. won't treat Mexico as an ally, they have to get protection from someone."

"You're right," I said. "I don't follow the news all that closely. Maybe I should."

"Of course you should. Everyone should!" Jill's passion was evident. "Everyone should care if they expect to have a say in what defines American values–if their vote will count in the next election."

"What, just because the Russians are hacking our elections? They've been doing that for years." I pointed out.

"Manipulating our elections was just the beginning. Now, they're arming Mexico for a border war." She pushed forward one of the photos from the stack of documents.

"You really believe that? Seriously?" I said. "What's next? You finally found Atlantis? That's the type of yellow journalism I'd expect from the looney rags, but from a *Chicago Star* reporter? Or should I say from DANG?"

"Not all conspiracy theories are false, you know."

"You mean fake, don't you?" I smirked at my intentional slam.

"You can scoff all you like. We know the Russians are shipping arms to Mexico. I just don't know what's so important it's worth going to war over."

"I promise," I said. "If I run into any Russian spies, I'll make sure you're the first to know."

As I turned to leave, Jill called after me. "Be careful, David. This is bigger than either of us can manage alone."

21

☼ ☼ ☼

It was almost noon when I got back to the room. Marc had just stepped out of the shower and was toweling off.

"See?" he said, proudly. "I *am* capable of getting up on my own."

"Yes, in time for lunch," I observed. "We need to get on the road. Get dressed, and we'll grab a burger on the way."

Marc tossed his long blond hair to one side and rubbed it vigorously with the towel. "So, where have you been?" he asked as he pulled on a pair of board shorts. I noticed that the burn line was already starting to fade. "Your note just said, 'Back soon.'"

I took a bottle of water from the small refrigerator and answered casually, "I met with Jill."

Marc turned and slid his tank top down from his face. "You what?"

"You heard me right. I met with Jill. She said she had something important to share with me."

"And did she?" he asked, slipping on one of his oversized Nikes.

"No. She just spouted some crazy theory about the Russians wanting to invade the U.S." I screwed off the plastic cap and took a sip of the spring water.

"Your brother-in-law is picking a fight with the mob, and now you're facing off with the Russians?" That's a bit out of our league, don't you think?"

"I don't think we're in any league. That's why we need to go home. Now."

"After we meet with Z, right? We promised."

I fingered the Jeep keys and tossed them on the side table. "I promised Bren I'd come back in one piece. That's the promise I plan to keep."

Marc tied off his other shoe and stood. "You don't mean that, do you? We've come this far. We found the guy we're looking for. His grandmother is counting on us. On you!"

I glanced at the morning paper, next to the set of keys. The headline read, "Russian arms arrive in Mexico." So, what if Jill was right? What could we do about it? Stop an international war? No, Marc nailed it. We were definitely out of our league.

Then there was Patsy to consider. What if we did hold the key to making things right for her? Bren would never forgive me if she even thought I walked away when there was a chance I could help. Was I just being selfish? Being a *wimp*?

I picked up the keys again and looked at Marc. "Alright, we'll do this one interview. Then we leave for Chicago. It doesn't matter what we do or don't find out."

I think Marc was surprised by my sudden change of mind, but he still took credit for it. "I'm glad I could talk some sense into

you." He tied an orange bandana around his forehead. "Let's go."
I grabbed my Antonio's cap and followed him to the Jeep.

Before we left Phoenix, I had Marc pull through a McDonald's as promised. Then we headed for I-10 toward Sells. This time we took the shorter route, through Maricopa County. Sea Horse texted us to meet at the casino he worked for. The Quivira Casino resort is in an Indian community called Ak Chin. We passed by it driving back the night before.

We ate our Big Macs while Marc drove. The radio signal was strong enough the entire route that Marc was able to blast the Phoenix progressive rock station. He left the top up on the Jeep, however, to minimize his exposure to the sun.

From a quick Google search before we left, I learned that the O'odham people identify themselves by the region they inhabit. The Tohono O'odham are the desert people, the Akimal O'odham live near the river. Ak Chin means *flood runoff,* so I suspected these people lived a hardscrabble existence. Now that we were passing through the community in daylight, I could see that the expensive new ranch-style stucco homes going up in perfectly laid out housing developments told a different story. Ak Chin was becoming one more Phoenix suburb.

It was nearly two o'clock when we pulled into the Quivira Casino parking lot. The temperature was well over one-hundred degrees, so we took our equipment with us to keep it cool. Once inside, we headed to the information desk. I was about to ask for the head of security when Sea Horse rounded the corner dressed in pressed denim jeans and an expensive white Western-style shirt.

"Surveillance cameras," he said, pointing to the silver domes in the ceiling. "I knew you were here."

I asked, "Is your Ga'ga joining us?"

"She is at home," Sea Horse said. "Women are not allowed to go where we will be. He led us to the bar, where Z occupied a corner table drinking what looked like a Coke.

"Brother," Sea Horse said, "time to go."

We followed the two men to a private level in the parking garage and climbed into the back seat of a dark-blue Mercedes SUV. "Company car," Sea Horse said.

"Where are we going?" Marc asked as he climbed into the back seat. His question was met with silence.

Sea Horse drove west about twenty minutes and pulled onto a desolate dirt road. Through the dust, I could make out the outline of a small domed building–more of a hut really. The SUV pulled to a stop, and we all climbed out of the vehicle. "Bring your gear," Sea Horse commanded as he grabbed a briefcase from the back. Z picked up a heavy white plastic ice chest and closed the hatch.

The ki looked like it had been abandoned for several years. The lower three or four feet was plastered over with crumbling adobe, and the upper two-thirds of the structure was covered with arrow weed. A low door of straight reeds lashed together with dried vines and draped with an animal hide seemed to be the only opening in the grass-and-mud exterior of the building.

Sea Horse pushed open the flimsy door and stepped inside. Z, being much taller, stooped to enter. Marc looked at me and shrugged, and we followed the brothers into the domed structure. A hole in the middle of the roof let in enough light that we could see the few items inside–some grass baskets, a few rolled blankets, a simple wooden chair. The small skylight was also the only source for ventilating the interior, which was even warmer than the desert heat outside. The two brothers seemed comfortable in the sweltering space, but Marc and I were already dripping with sweat.

Z set the ice chest on the dirt floor, in front of the wooden chair, and opened it to expose twenty pounds of crushed ice. He nodded for Marc and me to set up the laptop there. I had told Sea Horse we wouldn't need power for the session since we could rely on the computer's battery charge, and Marc always brings along a fully charged spare.

"This is the tribal sweat lodge," Sea Horse explained as he rolled out one of the patterned blankets on the packed-earth floor. "We won't be disturbed here."

Z added, "And this is where I want you to do your magic. If Ga'ga is right, we need to be here."

"It's really hot in here," Marc said.

Z smiled at his little brother. "Sweat lodge," he repeated.

"I think Marc's worried about the laptop," I said as I fanned myself with my ballcap. Sweat dripped from my eyebrows, clouding my vision. "It could overheat in here."

Sea Horse popped open the briefcase and pulled out a battery-operated plastic fan, which he clipped onto the cooler's plastic handle across from the laptop. "That's why I brought this." Then he informed us, "Magic is central to O'odham himdag. Some of it works, and much of it can be explained by scientific principles. Our magicians discovered many mysteries over the generations we have been here. Others were handed down from the Hohokam. The magicians practiced their rituals in sweat lodges like this one. Ga'ga believes you possess this magic. You will honor our ancestors by performing your experiment in here."

Z added, "Just so you know, I don't believe any of this spirit crap." He peeled off his white T-shirt and sat cross-legged on the wool blanket. He looked into my now-stinging eyes, "I'm doing this for Ga'ga, but you must play by my rules: ask me anything and I will answer truthfully, my brother stays with me and can stop you at any time, and only you may listen to the recordings when we are done. Now begin," Z commanded.

Marc wiped his brow with his bandana and adjusted the fan to blow the ice-chilled air across the laptop base. I had unpacked Nemy and positioned the sensors on our subject's head. Marc connected the wires to the computer. After running some tests, he said he was ready to start.

Marc took the chair, and I knelt next to Z. The air was slightly cooler closer to the earthen floor. "Have you ever been hypnotized?" I asked.

Z gave Sea Horse a knowing look and said, "I haven't, but we have seen magicians who seem to slip into trances."

I explained that I was going to ease him into a hypnotic state and ask him to visualize specific events. What he would see in his mind would appear on the computer screen. Z looked at his brother and grinned. Then he nodded.

After just a few minutes, Marc signaled that our subject was hypnotized and generating mental images.

I had Z picture some recent events so Marc could establish a baseline for the recordings–eating breakfast, brushing his teeth, driving to the sweat lodge.

Then I began with the first serious question: "Do you know someone called Angelo?"

Z nodded and said, "Yes."

"Remember the last time you spoke with Angelo," I suggested. The picture on the laptop began to reveal a black telephone with a rotary dial. A large hand came into view and lifted the receiver.

"What is Angelo saying?" I asked.

"He's telling me he needs a job done. He wants me to break into someone's house and steal something."

"What does he want you to steal?"

"He doesn't care, just so it's expensive. He says I need to get there right away. The alarm will be off. He says he'll pay."

"Now, remember doing what Angelo told you to do," I prompted.

We saw the door to Z's pickup open and watched as he started the truck. I instructed Z to skip ahead to when he arrived at his destination, and we witnessed his recollection of the events of that night.

After following a lighted footpath, Z's hand extended to the ground to lift a loose paving stone. The stone smashed through a small glass pane in what looked like a carved wooden door. The hand reached through the opening and then retreated as the door slowly opened. We were in what looked like a pantry or mudroom. The space was dark, but across the way images of kitchen appliances began to resolve. The scene shifted to a room with ornate period furniture. The walls were lined with painted shelves. Images of decorative pottery and bronze statuettes appeared on the screen as Z apparently scanned the shelves in search of valuables. A large hand reached out to examine a small jewel-encrusted box. Z's hand. The view shifted to a glass-top table, and the hand reached for a pearl necklace that was resting there. The string of pearls disappeared from view. Through the glass tabletop, we saw the outline of a person lying on the floor. The figure grew larger as Z apparently knelt next to the body. It was a woman. In the dim light, we couldn't make out her features, but she was well dressed and looked like she was in her fifties.

I cringed, and my hand shot up involuntarily to my lips at the sight of blood that trickled from the woman's forehead. Then I noticed that across from me, Sea Horse was scowling.

"Is this what you came to see?" he asked.

"I'm not sure," I said.

"Then get to the point for why you're here."

I tried to focus Z on the night of the explosion. "It's a Saturday night six weeks ago, March seventh. The cactus is blooming after a three-day rain, and the moon is nearly full. It's almost sunset. Remember where you are that evening."

A thin mattress on a metal frame appeared on the monitor. It looked like there were steel bars in the distance–prison bars.

"Remember driving your truck that night," I said.

The screen dimmed.

"Your truck," I repeated. "Where is your truck?"

Sea Horse stood abruptly. He held out his hand and ordered, "Stop." The stern-looking man loomed over his brother protectively.

"He does not know. But I do."

22

☼ ☼ ☼

Marc stopped recording as soon as Sea Horse ordered him to. The look in the younger brother's eyes was frightening.

I brought Z back to full awareness and removed the sensor cap from his head.

"Was it all right, brother? Did they get what they came for?"

"Maybe more," the younger man said. "They want to know where your pickup was a few weeks ago. I told them you don't know, but I do."

Sea Horse explained that Z was in jail that weekend for assaulting the tax assessor who paid Ga'ga an unannounced visit. Charges were dropped, but while Z was being held, Sea Horse answered a call that came in on his brother's mobile phone.

"I thought it might be the prosecutor. Instead, a man with a voice like wet cement said, 'Listen, don't talk,' ...so I did. He said he was Angelo, and he insisted you'd know what he was calling about. Brother, is that true?"

Z only grunted.

Sea Horse went on to tell us that Angelo instructed him to torch the Southwest Enterprise office trailer set up on the tribal burial grounds that the protesters now occupied. He said there would be two cars parked out front, but no one would be inside to get hurt.

"I was to arrive exactly at sunset. He said this would put an end to efforts to drill for oil on our sacred land."

"You believed him?" Z asked accusingly. His brother muttered something and hung his head.

Marc interrupted. "So, *you* were driving your brother's truck that night. It was you that pulled the Jerry can from the truck bed."

Sea Horse looked at Marc suspiciously. "I never said anything about a Jerry can. What do you know about that?"

Marc glanced nervously in my direction before answering. "How else would you go about torching a building, especially so it would set off a chain reaction like that?"

"The point is, I didn't start that fire."

I asked, "If you didn't, who did?"

"I don't know, but I need to find out. That's why I am telling you all this. I realized you think my brother did it, and I won't let him take the blame. With his record, no one would believe him. I am willing to say I was there that night, but I won't confess to a murder I didn't commit."

"Murder?" I said trying to sound surprised.

"I followed the news after that night. We all know about the woman who died in the explosion and the rich developer who is being blamed for her death." Sea Horse looked me squarely in my eyes. "Is that why you're here? To exonerate him?"

Sweat flowed freely from my face, pooling on the clay floor of the sweltering ki. "Yes," I admitted.

Sea Horse nodded his head in acknowledgment. "I know of this man. He is responsible for decades of exploitation of our people. If anyone deserves to be convicted of a serious crime, he does. I think you may know this to be true as well."

I raised an eyebrow involuntarily. I always suspected Archie was guilty of committing the crime he was being charged with.

"I stopped your questioning of my brother. I am the one you should be asking about that night. I saw what this device of yours can do. I want you to see for yourselves I am telling the truth. Resume your questioning–with me."

"OK," Marc said incredulously.

"This is what you will see. I pulled up to the trailer at sunset, just as Angelo had instructed. One car was there, not two. I did pull a gas can from the bed of the truck, and I carried it to the back of the trailer, but I felt uneasy about going through with the arson. I wanted to make sure no one would be hurt, so I set the can down to walk around the trailer and check. That's when I was knocked off my feet by the explosion. A ball of flame rolled past me and singed my hair, which was longer then. When I regained my senses, I threw the gas can back in the truck and took off down the dirt road."

I assured him, "Mnemosyne will show things just the way you remember them."

"It's ironic, don't you think, that I share my name with that of the organ that produces memories?"

Sea Horse smiled when he saw the look of surprise on Marc's face. "You thought I wouldn't know what my own name means? You don't understand how important a name is to an Indian."

Sea Horse unbuttoned his white shirt, now soaked in sweat, and slipped it off. Then he motioned for me to place the sensors on his head.

"I believe in technology," he said. "That's my job. But I also believe it is only one expression of the mysteries that surround us. You may continue using your technology, but instead of hypnotism, we will access my memories through himdag."

We could hear Z take a labored breath. He stood slowly and pulled four more bottles of water from the ice chest. "Here. You'll need these," he said as he passed them around.

Marc and I quickly drained the plastic bottles, which revived us somewhat. Sea Horse instructed us to remove our shirts and our shoes. He turned to me and said, "Your friend can continue to operate the equipment, but you must join in the ceremony."

Sea Horse took down a small grass basket that hung from the low ceiling of the ki and pulled out a cloth bundle about the size of a brick. He knelt on the blanket Z had been seated on and untied the leather thong that held the package closed. There he carefully unfolded the fabric to reveal a large handful of dried greenish-brown discs.

"Peyote cactus," he said. "This will unlock memories of what has been and maybe even of what is to come."

Marc gave me a thumbs-up and smiled. I could see the laptop screen from where I sat, although it was out of view of our subject.

"What do I do?" I asked drawing my bare feet under me.

Z smiled. "Chew and enjoy."

"But don't swallow," Sea Horse cautioned. "Just hold the dry button in your cheek." He took one of the green nuggets from the cloth and instructed me to do the same.

The taste was not pleasant, but tolerable. I bit down gently on the dried succulent and tucked the small orb in my left cheek to allow the juice to fill my mouth.

Sea Horse nodded to Marc. "You may begin. You must ask the questions now."

For the next several minutes Marc walked his subject through the events leading up to the explosion. We saw what Patsy had revealed but from a different perspective. The trailer came into view with the sun setting in the background. We saw a hand pull a red gas can from the bed of the truck and carry it past the parked car. The can was set next to the rear wheel of the trailer. Suddenly, a massive blue-white translucent ball came rushing toward the screen. The darkness that followed slowly resolved into the purple and orange of an evening sky. I could even make out a single star. Moments later, I could see the dirt road disappear beneath the cab of the truck.

"He was telling the truth," Marc said.

"At least the truth as he wants to remember it," I added.

I was feeling a bit light-headed from the peyote, as well as a bit nauseated. Its psychedelic effect seemed overrated, however. Sea Horse rocked gently forward and back on the blanket as I prepared to end the session. Before I could stand to remove the electrodes from his head, I noticed a new image appear. It was an old man wearing a loincloth and woven sandals. He was leaning on a large leather shield with one arm and motioning the viewer to draw closer with the other. I looked deep into the man's face and could see the lines of many years. Then he pointed to the field of rubble that stretched out from behind what must have been the trailer. Dry bones were scattered about–human bones. A strong wind blew across the field and swept up sand and dried grass and bits of bone as it passed. The old man began crying, and he fell to his knees and wept.

I motioned to Marc to keep recording. "Ask him who the man is and what he wants," I instructed. Sea Horse just rocked forward and back, humming a deep-throated tune.

The screen filled with debris. When it cleared, the old Indian and the field of bones were gone. In their place appeared a small village of domed structures similar to the one we were in. In a clearing, children, nearly naked, were playing a game with a leather ball. They seemed to be laughing and having a good time. Then streaks of fire started falling from above. The wood-and-grass structures burst into flames, and the children fell to the ground, dead.

The screen filled with gray smoke.

"What is happening?" I pleaded with Sea Horse to describe the scene, but he just continued to hum.

As the smoke cleared, I could see fields of green grass that extended in every direction. A broad river of blue-green water flowed through the middle. Native American women were in a clearing tossing blankets loaded with grain into the air, and the chaff drifted skyward. Then the river water slowed to a trickle, and the green fields turned yellow and then brown. The women sat on the blanket, and the chaff filled the screen.

"Are you getting this, Marc?" I asked excitedly. He didn't reply.

The chaff cleared, and in place of the green fields stood rows of large steel oil derricks. I could see them plunging into the dry, barren earth. At the foot of each rig stood four simple posts covered with a tattered cloth. Then I saw in the distant valley streaks of light rise from the desert floor. Scores of golden streams rose in gentle arcs like jets of water in a fountain. The trails of sparks rapidly grew in size as they ascended and then converged overhead in their descent. A blinding light filled the screen, and it seemed like a different, more intense heat had enveloped the space we were in. I sat transfixed, staring into the searing glare. When the light dimmed, all that was left were the post-and-cloth awnings. A gentle breeze seemed to sweep across the scene causing the tattered cloths to billow and then rise slowly, drifting upward and out of view.

I cried with unfathomable anguish.

23

I felt the refreshing drops of spring rain falling in Logan Square. Bren looked deep into my eyes while rivulets from her rain-soaked hair traced patterns across her face. We laughed, and I reached out to take her in my arms.

"I think he's back," I heard a deep voice say. Then I realized the dark, damp hair I was brushing back belonged to Sea Horse and not Brenda. I sat bolt upright, skulls nearly colliding. Z continued splashing my face with cool bottled water.

"Dude, you were really tripping," Marc exclaimed with a tone of admiration in his voice.

As my wits returned, I pointed to the monitor and said excitedly, "Did you get that?! Tell me you got that recorded."

The others exchanged questioning looks.

"Get what?" Marc said. "There wasn't anything to record after the laptop overheated. That was just after Sea Horse replayed his memory of the trailer explosion."

"But the old Indian...the wheat fields...the oil wells. I want to go over every scene in detail. This was an amazing breakthrough for our research!" I started to stand but realized my legs had no feeling in them.

Sea Horse said calmly, "The breakthrough is all you, my friend."

Z handed me the half-empty bottle of water to finish and pressed my red ballcap onto my head.

The group waited a few minutes for me to recover. Then Marc packed up Nemy, and the brothers helped me out of the ki. A slight breeze blew across our sweating chests, and the hundred-degree air outside seemed relatively refreshing.

Z passed out another round of water and then tossed the plastic ice chest into the hatch of the blue Mercedes. Sea Horse pulled out some white terry cloth towels and handed them to us along with our clothing. We mopped down and climbed into the SUV, with the air-conditioning already running and cranked up full.

We drove back to the Quivira Casino in silence. A combination of dehydration and awe consumed me, along with the peyote afterglow. After we returned to the garage, Sea Horse led us to the back entrance of the casino and up to his private apartment. "Sit," he commanded. Then he called room service and ordered rare steaks for all of us. "You need to recover."

"Recover? From what?" I asked.

"Your vision quest."

Z elaborated, "Most Indian boys experience this when we are eleven or twelve. At your age, it appears to be more intense." The brothers laughed, I think for the first time.

"Dude, those images were all in your head," Marc explained. "You'll have to hook up Nemy to yourself and record them if you want to play them back."

I realized that doing this was within the realm of possibility.

"Tell me, brother," Sea Horse said, addressing me this time, "what did you see?"

While we waited for our meals to arrive, I described in detail the scenes I had experienced. A dark expression came over Sea Horse's face when I told them about the fountain of sparks.

"What does that mean?" I asked.

"Only you can answer that," Z responded.

A knock on the door meant our steaks had arrived. We all ate hungrily and drank quarts of Perrier to rehydrate.

The two brothers explained that the O'odham have been tapping into their memories for countless generations with the assistance of peyote. Old men would hold their calendar sticks and retell in vivid detail the stories they had learned and virtually relive the events they had experienced. For the O'odham, the mind is not limited to the present. "We are able to enter the stream of time at any point, past or present or even in the future," Z explained. "Like the man in the maze, I'itoi, there are no right or wrong turns, only decision points. Sometimes we are able to decide, and sometimes our fate is decided for us. It is up to each of us to recognize when we encounter these events and to determine what actions we are able to take. Forever, we strive for the unreachable center. It is in striving, not arriving, that we persevere."

"You have the recordings you came for," Sea Horse said, "although not the ones you had expected. Perhaps now you know where else to look. I realize you can't present what you have as evidence in court, but it tells the truth–at least the part of the truth we have to share."

Sea Horse provided Marc and me each with a change of workout clothes and directed us to the open-air shower in his apartment. A canopy of palm trees shaded us from the afternoon sun as we stood naked on the smooth river stone floor and let the cooling spray of water flow over our bodies.

On the trip back to Phoenix, Marc and I reconstructed the events of that day–Z's alibi, Sea Horse's confession, my vision quest, and of course the relentless heat. That is one memory we both wished we could erase.

"So, what do you think was up with Z's story?" Marc started the conversation. "The two dudes he killed in the bar were Angelo's hitmen, and he talked with Angelo on Ga'ga's phone..."

"But it couldn't have been Angelo because Sea Horse took Angelo's call," I finished Marc's line of reasoning.

"...and Z talked to someone on a phone that's been disconnected for years," Marc added. "Unless..."

I quickly picked up the thread, "Unless it's not *who* but *when* we're talking about."

"Jumping in the river at a different point," Marc finished. "That conversation wasn't this year–it was before Ga'ga shut off the phone."

"That could have been five years ago or more. Why would Angelo be calling Z after five years?"

"And when Sea Horse took his call, why would he expect Z to know what he was calling about?" Marc wondered and then turned toward me. "And what was with that look on your face when he was remembering seeing that dead lady?"

My blood ran a bit cold when Marc said that. I wasn't sure what it was about seeing that scene that bothered me, but I felt like

I should. I changed the subject. "If Sea Horse didn't blow up the trailer, who did?"

"How do you blow up ten acres of land anyway?" Marc added.

We had lots of questions. Now we needed to find the answers. I realized we were talking as if we were going to keep investigating whatever it was we thought we were investigating.

"Hold it," I demanded. "We're done here, remember? We got Z out of jail and interviewed him the way we promised. It looks like Arch is guilty after all, and now there could be mobsters involved who won't be happy if they find out we're poking around in whatever it is they're up to. We're catching the next flight back to Chicago we can get."

Marc started to say something, but he stopped short. We drove the last twenty minutes just listening to the radio.

The national news came on about the time we arrived in Phoenix. A reporter was interviewing residents of Nogales, on the Mexico border. "We seen them clear as day, up there from the ridge," the voice of an older man said when asked about the arrival of Russian missiles in the Mexican state of Sonora. "A convoy of long-bed trucks carrying cargo the size of corn silos. They got 'em covered with camo nets, but we all know what they is." The newscaster went on to say the Secretary of State declared the actions by Russia as a clear provocation and a violation of U.S. sovereignty.

The Russians? I thought. Could it be possible Jill was right? Could we be standing on the brink of international war? Was there anything anyone could do to stop it?

It was getting dark by the time we got to the Festiva Inn. I was exhausted and just wanted to go to bed. Marc, on the other hand, was ready to party. Before we reached the door to our room, he was calling his nurse to set up a time to meet.

Marc showered and changed and was ready to head out by nine.

"Don't wait up for me, Dad," he said as he pulled the door closed behind him.

I got undressed and climbed into the large bed. Propped up against the oversized pillows, I took out my cell phone wishing I could talk to Bren. Instead, I settled for thumbing through pictures of our weekend in Galena. I marveled at how beautiful she is and how improbable it was that she married a man like me–the opposite of what anyone would have expected. Sometimes, I even wondered if that was the reason she consented to marry me. Maybe she was more like her sister than I wanted to recognize. Everyone thought Patsy took up with Archie just to piss off her father. Was that my role in our relationship? The poor Indian boy who could piss off Jack? Whether or not that was Brenda's motivation, I certainly fit the bill.

I stopped at the picture I took in the B&B of Brenda lying naked on the canopied bed, her skin smooth and white like polished alabaster. I pinched the image to enlarge her face, framed perfectly by her raven-black hair. Salaciously, I scrolled down to view her athletic breasts. She looked like she could be an Olympic swimmer–her perfectly formed nipples, taut with the tension of youth. I was aroused, and I knew what I would be doing next.

As a boy, I felt overwhelming shame every time I would masturbate, which was frequently. That never dissuaded me, of course. Adam taught me it was just part of growing up and being a man. "You can't get good at scoring goals if you don't practice a lot of free kicks," he would tell me and laugh.

As I grew older, the shame diminished, although maybe not the guilt. The joy of sexual climax was meant to be shared, preferably with someone you loved. My mother ingrained that idea in me, although we never talked about sex explicitly. Our father never talked about sex at all. Maybe that was why Adam's suicide hit him particularly hard. I wondered if he felt partly responsible for his oldest son's death because he would never acknowledge my brother's admitted homosexuality. I wondered the same thing about me.

When Adam came out to the family, we all pretended it was a phase—a reaction to losing his arm in Afghanistan. I think that might have been the hardest day of my brother's life—calling a family meeting and telling us he preferred the company of men. I smile now, thinking how he phrased it—*the company of men.* He never admitted he was homosexual or said the word queer or even gay. He just preferred the company of men. My mother actually seemed to understand. She was devastated, but I think that was more because she feared she would never have a grandchild from her eldest son. Our father just pretended it was a reaction to the tragic loss of what he thought defined his son's manhood. The IED left Adam less than a whole man, and he was projecting that on his sexuality. I, on the other hand, didn't know what to think. I loved my brother deeply. He was my hero. How, I thought, could my idol be like that? Like the kind of person I had been taught was less than a man?

I stepped into the bathroom, found the hotel lotion, and relieved my sexual tension thinking of Bren, but I was also thinking of Adam.

24

☼ ☼ ☼

I woke up early Saturday morning. Marc slipped in sometime in the night and was snoring heavily next to me. I headed to the hotel lobby and poured a cup of marginally drinkable coffee. My cell phone rang, and I answered to hear Archie's voice.

"David, glad I caught you. Patsy tells me you college boys are still trying to run down some leads on the murderer."

I responded with a noncommittal grunt.

"I got to tell you, it means a lot to me knowing I can count on family. Have you and that machine of yours found the guy yet?" he asked.

I let my brother-in-law know we had conducted a couple of interviews, but we didn't have any concrete evidence. Then Arch said something strange. "Don't think you can just jump in midstream."

I was sure that was meant to encourage me to keep going back and search from the start, but all I could think of was the cosmic timeline Sea Horse described. Are we forever jumping in midstream with no starting point and no end? Searching for an unattainable center? Searching for I'itoi?

As I sat at the dirty breakfast table, I wondered if going home now was just running away–running away from something I didn't think I could face, although I needed to. I slipped a hand into the pocket of my cargo shorts and pulled out the card Jill had given me. Could she help? She had the power to reach an audience of millions, but that was just with words. What could she say that would be powerful enough to restore balance? What could I tell her that might help? *We found the Native American who didn't blow up the trailer? His brother discovered a dead woman five years ago? I saw the end of the world in a vision?* No, none of this would help–not Patsy or Archie or the Tohono O'odham or the planet. Some things we can change and others are set by fate. Maybe the O'odham magicians were right, all we can do is try to discern the difference and seek new directions within the maze.

I choked down a stale blueberry muffin while I read the morning paper. It was ten a.m. when I headed back to the room. I had decided to book tickets to Chicago for that night. I followed the carpeted path to our suite. When I turned the corner, I could see Jill at the end of the hall, leaning against the door to our room. I started a retreat to the lobby when she saw me. Jill held up her hand like a trainer would, teaching a dog to stay. Then she marched over to me and grabbed my elbow.

"Come quickly," she said with unexpected urgency.

I was intrigued by her seeming sincerity and complied. We headed down another hall to the door that opened onto the pool area. Once outside, Jill found a table in the farthest corner, and we sat under a green and yellow umbrella.

Jill looked nervously about. Then she leaned in and said, "I found what I was looking for. The confirmation I need to run with this story."

I didn't know what she was talking about, and the confusion on my face must have been evident.

"You remember how I told you things were more complicated than you knew? Well, you're in the middle of something big, and I'm about to release a story to expose your brother-in-law. I wanted to warn you before I do that."

"You're trying to protect me?" I said skeptically.

"Yes, of course," she replied. "And to see if you have anything to add for the story. Archie Trumble is about to go down, along with the house-of-cards empire he built. I have the evidence now."

"How do you know this?" I asked.

"A leaker. Someone dropped off a thick envelope filled with numbers and dates. So far, they've all checked out. Evidence of fraud, racketeering, drug trafficking, maybe even attempted murder. After I confirm the remaining evidence, the story will make headlines across the country."

I couldn't tell if Jill was excited about having the scoop or in fear for her life. Probably both, I thought. And now that she had confided in me, that made me vulnerable as well.

"Do you know who leaked the documents?" I asked.

"No, but I'd say it's someone on the inside of state government and well connected."

"Why would someone pass along that kind of information?"

Jill shook her head. "It could be one or more of a hundred reasons, but you can bet it ultimately comes down to money and power. That's what it always comes down to."

I didn't have anything new for Jill's story, so she left hurriedly by the back gate.

"Well," I muttered, "if we try to leave the state now, Archie will suspect we had something to do with this."

I headed back to the room and woke Marc to tell him what Jill had planned. It took several minutes for him to comprehend the implications for us. He rubbed his eyes and said, "Archie's going to be really pissed. Do you think we should tell him?"

That thought had crossed my mind, but I suggested it might be in our best interests to let the events evolve and see what happened. Marc agreed. We spent the rest of the day in our cramped suite discussing what Archie's downfall would mean for Patsy and Jack and especially for us.

☼ ☼ ☼

The Sunday paper arrived with the headline we had been waiting for–"Local developer suspected of fraud." The sensational headline seemed understated after reading the list of charges leveled at Archibald Trumble by DANG reporter Jill Jackson.

Then it hit me, that's the same byline that appeared with the article about Mnemosyne. If Archie puts those things together, he might think I was the source who leaked the information. What if he called? I wanted to just pretend I wasn't there, but the smarter thing seemed to be to preempt any suspicions on his part. I picked up the phone and dialed Archie's private number.

"Yo, David," he answered. "I could tell by the number it was you."

I explained that I just read the headline and wanted to know if there was anything we could do.

"You read that crap?" he exploded. Then he offered a forced chuckle, "Ya think anyone else will see it?"

I sighed. "What do you think, Arch? So, what can Marc and I do?" I tried to sound genuinely concerned. "Do you know who leaked the story?" This time I was just fishing.

"Yeah, I think I do," he answered in a measured tone. "And you know how I feel about family sticking together, right?"

I felt blood rush to my head, and I could hear it pounding in my ears. After a moment, I said, "You think family had something to do with this?"

"Damn straight, I do," he yelled. "There's just one person who'd know some of this shit, and I plan to have a talk with him."

I wasn't positive, but it didn't sound like he meant me.

"Arch, I'll do what I can to help you and Patsy. Just say the word," I offered.

"I know you would, David. I know you would. I'll call you if anything comes to mind." He paused and said, "Just keep looking for the guy who murdered Lauren. If you can do that for me, I'll be real grateful." With that Archie hung up.

I told Marc what my brother-in-law had said.

"You're sure he wasn't talking about us?" Marc asked.

"Yes, I'm sure. Well, pretty sure," I replied. "But I think we need to concentrate on getting Archie what he's looking for. Let's go over what we know and see if we missed something. If his story about the car hitting that pig holds up, then he isn't the killer."

"And if Sea Horse's memories are reliable, he was just a witness. Then there's Patsy. But she has pictures of the explosion, so she couldn't have done it," Marc added.

"So, who else is there?" I asked, mostly to myself.

"What about this Angelo guy? Maybe he had his hitmen do it and planned to frame Z."

I agreed that sounded like the best possibility.

"What about Z's story?" Marc asked. "He talked with Angelo about doing a job, but that chick on the floor looked way too old to be Archie's squeeze."

A shudder ran through me when Marc mentioned the older woman we saw lying on the carpeted floor and with blood running down her forehead. That image had haunted me since that afternoon in the sweat lodge.

"Let's look at those recordings again," I suggested. Marc agreed and proceeded to set up the laptop.

Marc found the frames we were searching for on the recording and called me over. "This is it," he said. "This is where Z kneels down next to the body on the floor."

I had Marc zoom in on the face, and once again the shudder came over me. "I know that face. I'm just not sure how."

"Maybe it's someone famous. You know, you could have seen her on the news or something."

"No, I don't think that's it," I said. "It's something more personal." I closed my eyes and tried to imagine that face in some other setting, but I came up blank.

"Play the whole sequence again," I suggested.

Marc rolled the recording back several seconds to where Z was entering the room to search for some object of value to steal. That's when I thought I noticed something. "There," I said tentatively. "Zoom in on that shelf."

Marc did, and a framed portrait became clearer. I didn't recognize the face, but I thought I recognized the frame. The same pewter and velvet pattern was on the frame holding a picture of Patsy that Bren kept on her dresser. "See if you can boost the resolution of that photograph," I instructed. I knew it would take Marc some time, so I headed to the refrigerator and pulled out two Coronas. I handed one to Marc. "Here, I think we might need these."

By the time I was draining the last of the cold beer, Marc looked up proudly. "There you go," he said. Then he did a double take. "Oh my God! That's...that's Patsy!"

I leaned in to look. There was no mistaking it. The portrait was a copy of the one we had in our Logan Square brownstone.

"I knew those furnishings looked familiar," I said. "I've seen that room in Brenda's photo albums. That's the Stillwell estate the girls grew up in. That was before Jack moved the family to the governor's mansion, right after he was elected...and right after the girls' mother had died," I added excitedly. "Zoom in again on that woman's face."

Marc did, and this time I immediately recognized my mother-in-law. Z had been called to the scene of Evelyn Stillwell-Donovan's murder.

25

☼ ☼ ☼

"That's Brenda's mom?" Marc leaned in to examine the scene more closely.

I told him how when Jack was running for Arizona governor the first time, someone broke into the Donovan home and murdered the girls' mother. At least, that's the story the press reported and what Bren and Patsy were told. Brenda was sixteen at the time and about to start her senior year in high school. Jack had been trailing in the polls, but the sympathy vote pushed him to an easy victory.

"What do you suppose that means?" Marc wondered. "Do you think Jack killed his wife and called Z to take the blame?"

I didn't want to seriously consider Marc's speculation, but I knew that was the obvious conclusion. I just couldn't imagine Bren ever finding out. I never doubted that she loved her father, but I could tell that she and her mother had shared a special bond. I wondered what to do next. Tell Bren? Confront Jack?

Pretend I never knew? The last option was undoubtedly the most appealing.

I didn't have much time to think about it, however. My phone rang. It was Patsy. "Daddy's been in an accident," she sobbed.

Patsy was already at the hospital. I got the information for where to meet her. Bren was still on her field trip, and there was no way to contact her about this yet. I was glad for that.

Marc and I jumped into the Jeep, and he drove to Mesa University Hospital, about ten minutes away. Marc let me out at the emergency room door, and he went on to park. The receptionist told me only immediate family was allowed in urgent care, but she would let Patsy know I was there. I paced the short entryway until she arrived.

"David, I'm so glad you're here." Patsy threw her long arms around my neck and pulled me close. I could tell she was genuinely concerned for her father.

"How is he? What happened?" I stammered the run-together question. I immediately wondered if she wanted to talk about it.

"He stopped at the tobacconist to pick up cigars. He's done that every Sunday for years," she began. "Apparently a truck drove by as he was getting out of his limo and sideswiped the car. It took off the rear door and crushed Daddy against the fender." She began to sob heavily. From the description of the accident, it was surprising he was even alive.

I held Patsy in my arms and let her cry. The head nurse came over and said quietly, "Mr. Donovan is in critical condition. If he makes it through the night, he is likely to be in a coma for some time."

Marc stepped into the waiting room and found us clinging to each other in the middle of the floor. He started to say something, but I shook my head and raised a finger to my lips. Marc nodded and found a seat by the window. We both knew we would be there for quite a while.

Patsy eventually loosened her grip, and I led her to the chair next to Marc. She looked up at him and smiled. "Thank you for being here."

Marc actually blushed. "Can I get you something?' he asked. "Something to drink or something."

Patsy nodded. "Maybe a hot tea?" Marc headed to the canteen area to find a vending machine.

"Is Archie on his way?" I asked.

Patsy suddenly stiffened. "No, and I don't want him here either." She began crying again.

After several minutes, Patsy wiped her eyes and apologized for being *such a girl.* I smiled, but I didn't argue with her. Then she began to explain that the last person Jack had spoken to was Archie. She overheard the phone call from the pool changing room and said Archie sounded furious and was cursing at her father. Patsy heard only one side of the conversation, but she thought Arch was accusing Jack of framing him. Then she heard him threaten her father and hang up. That was at ten in the morning. By noon, an ambulance was bringing Governor Jack Donovan to the emergency room hemorrhaging from multiple contusions, broken bones, a ruptured spleen, and a punctured lung. The paramedics didn't expect him to survive the ride, but he did, and he was still hanging on in intensive care. A state trooper had been posted at the entrance to the private room he was moved to. The authorizes hadn't ruled out foul play, and they were searching for leads.

The head nurse came over again, this time smiling. "I think we have him stabilized," she said. "You may both go in, but for just a few minutes."

I followed Patsy into Jack's room. He was tented and wrapped with gauze over much of his body. He had already received nine units of blood, and he was now on a saline drip.

Patsy put her hand to her mouth when she saw her father. Then she pulled me close. "He looks so..." She reached out to hold him, but it was difficult to find a place on his body that didn't appear injured.

We stayed in the room until the nurse returned and asked us to wait in the lounge. The team had to change some of Jack's bandages and conduct more tests.

I asked Marc to get Patsy another hot tea, and I set out to find the head physician. The nurse on duty told me Dr. Mandel was in charge of the case. He was head of the Neurology Department, and she would send him over as soon as she could find him. I went back to sit with Patsy and tell Marc he probably should go back to the hotel. We were going to be there for quite a while. He said he had planned to spend the afternoon with the nurse he picked up when he arrived in Phoenix. That was just a few blocks away, so he offered to walk there. Marc handed me the Jeep key and left the hospital.

It was three fifteen when Dr. Mandel met with Patsy and me. He ushered us into a small conference room and explained the extent of Jack's injuries. The prospects of him surviving were looking better, but there was no way to tell if the coma was temporary or even if he had already suffered permanent brain damage.

Patsy asked, "What do you mean you can't tell if he's suffered brain damage? Aren't there tests for that?"

The doctor shook his head and explained that the EEG had detected cognitive activity, but we wouldn't know how regular his thought patterns were or what memory loss he might have suffered.

Patsy looked over at me. "He can tell," she said. "David has this gadget that reads memories."

Dr. Mandel sat up and raised his eyebrows. "Does he now?"

I explained our research using Mnemosyne and how we were able to view what our subjects were remembering. I said I didn't know if the technique would work on someone in a coma, but I would be willing to give it a try.

Dr. Mandel smiled smugly and said, "I don't think we need to stoop to any experimental mind reading." He assured us his team was providing the best care available in Arizona. Then he excused himself saying he needed to check on Jack again.

We returned to the waiting area. Patsy asked me how soon her sister could be there. I explained that Bren was doing field research, and we couldn't reach her until tomorrow, but I promised to leave a message for her so she would know about their father's condition as soon as she returned.

I sat with Patsy the next couple of hours and finally convinced her to go with me to get something to eat in the cafeteria. When we returned, the head nurse let us know that the hospital had arranged for a private room down the hall so Patsy could stay the night.

Patsy thanked the nurse for making the arrangements, and then she thanked me for being so good to the family. She said there was nothing I could do at the hospital and told me I should go back to the hotel. She'd call if anything changed. I agreed and headed to the Festiva Inn.

While I walked to the Jeep, I left messages on Bren's cell phone and at the front desk of the hotel where she was staying to call me as soon as she got back. I hoped it sounded like I just wanted to talk with her–which I did, and not get her worked up about the tragedy. I would tell her about that over the phone.

26

☼ ☼ ☼

Marc wasn't back when I got to the hotel. I expected he was still out with his nurse. I just sat on the overstuffed chair in the living area. It was dusk, and I didn't bother to put on the lights. The room quickly grew as dark as my mood. I felt utterly helpless. Bren's father could be dying. Patsy's husband was facing murder charges. The O'odham were about to lose their sacred lands. My research project was in jeopardy. And if Jill was right, the Russians were preparing to launch an attack on the United States. I was involved with tragedies large and small, and there was nothing I could do about any of them. Then I thought about the tragedy I couldn't resolve that haunted me most. I thought about Adam, and I started to cry.

I don't know how long I sat there in the dark before Marc returned. He opened the door to the darkened room and figured I was asleep, so he didn't flip on the light. As he tiptoed toward the bedroom door, he realized I was sitting in the living room still sobbing.

"David?" he said softly. "Did your father-in-law... Is he...?"

"No," I said, choking back the tears. "He's stable."

"Then what's wrong?" Marc clicked on the light in the bedroom to fill the living area with a soft glow.

I shook my head. "It's just...just that there's nothing I can do. I can't fix things."

Marc sat on the ottoman at the foot of the overstuffed chair. He was being uncharacteristically sympathetic. "Tell me what's going on," he said.

I tried blaming it on Jack's accident and almost losing our research grant, but I knew that wasn't the problem. Marc knew it too.

"You miss Brenda. Is that it?" he asked.

That's when I realized that not having Bren there was a large part of my feeling depressed. I missed her, of course, but we'd been apart for only a week. It wasn't so much that I missed her than it was that I feared losing her. With some coaxing from Marc, I admitted as much.

"Why do you think you might lose her?" he asked. "You two are perfect together."

"No," I tried to joke, "she's perfect, and we're together. That's what bothers me. Bren is smart and sophisticated and beautiful, and she's stuck with this dorky Indian boy. Someday she's going to realize she deserves better, and I'm the one standing in the way of her having what she deserves."

"Dude, what brought all this up?" Marc said leaning in close. "Sure, you're lucky to have a lady like that, but she's lucky to have you too, you know."

"Me? Really? Look at me. I'm short and pudgy and I have a face that looks like a moon pie. I don't know how to act around her family and friends. We can't even have our own family."

Marc was overwhelmed by my sudden outpouring of self-loathing, but he persisted. "Dude, you have some serious self-image issues. You think a relationship is about what you look like? How cool you act? No, man, it's this mysterious thing that never makes any sense. It just works when it's right, and I'm telling you, you and Bren are right. I think you know that, so why are you working so hard to tear apart what you have?"

He might as well have slapped me in the face. Why, indeed? I did have everything–the woman of my dreams, the career I always imagined. Was I trying to sabotage my own happiness? At that moment, I realized why I felt I didn't deserve to be happy. It was because I never embraced my brother's happiness. Adam had discovered what he needed to make him complete, and I didn't celebrate that with him. Instead, I pulled back, questioning his worth as a man–and my own.

"I killed my brother," I blurted out choking back tears.

Marc now looked more astonished than consoling. All he could do was ask what I meant, so I told him. I told him how Adam came out to our family and how my father brushed it off as a phase and how I was never able to look at him the same way after that. I was ashamed of my own brother, my best friend and my hero. If I had accepted him as the type of man he had to be, he might still be alive.

Marc was dumbfounded. Eventually, he managed to say, "You don't know that."

"What? That my brother wouldn't have committed suicide if I had accepted him for who he was? But I didn't, so what else am I supposed to think?"

Marc sighed. "OK, so you should have reacted another way. Maybe it would have made a difference, but you didn't. You can carry the guilt for your brother's death the rest of your life and punish yourself, or you can learn from it and move on. Do you think he'd want you to feel like this?"

"You don't understand. It's different for Hindu boys. You think in terms of male and female, but in Indian culture, there's a third gender. The middle gender–effeminate men or masculine women. That role is generally accepted, but only as subservient to real men."

"Is that it? You stopped thinking of your brother as a real man?"

"Yes, I guess so. If he *preferred the company of other men*, that made him their bitch–just a male prostitute." I thought of my brother as a whore! I was practically wailing now.

"And he was your idol, right? You wanted to be just like him. Is that it? You feel like you're less than a man too–you're just everyone's bitch?"

"Yes, that's it–that's it exactly! That's what I'm afraid Bren will discover if she hasn't already–that I'm not man enough for her." I wasn't sobbing now. A kind of rage had overwhelmed me.

"So, you're afraid you *prefer the company of men* too?"

What Marc said caught me by surprise. I had never considered that, but what if it was true? What if by turning my back on my brother I was rejecting myself? "I don't know," I howled. "I just don't know!"

"Well, I suggest you find out!" Now Marc sounded agitated.

"What do you mean?" I said suspecting I knew the answer.

"You think you might be queer. Have you ever had sex with a man?" Marc asked bluntly.

I realized I didn't know how to answer that question. Hindu boys are expected to experiment sexually with other boys. It's referred to as *masti*–basically, messing around. The practice is frowned upon and not discussed among polite company, but it's considered a normal part of coming of age–something boys grow out of. My friends and I had joined in circle jerks a few times, but that was the extent of it.

Marc could tell from the look in my eyes that I was uncertain. He leaned in and grabbed my hand and pressed it against his cock. "There," he said, "that's what another man feels like. Don't fight it. You need to know if you're missing something in your life."

At first, I resisted, but I knew he was right. How could I be the man Brenda needed if I didn't know what kind of man I was? And how could I have accepted who Adam was if I couldn't accept that part of myself? I allowed my hand to explore Marc's rapidly stiffening penis.

Marc stood and lifted me from the chair. Then he slid his shorts to the floor and returned my hand to his crotch. "I'm enjoying this," he said with a grin. "I can't help but enjoy someone feeling me up. I don't care who it is. The question is, are you?" He wrapped an arm around me and pulled me close.

I looked into Marc's eyes and without shame felt the firmness of his testicles between my thumb and fingers, and I brushed the palm of my hand along the length of his cock. It was exciting.

Marc pressed his own hand against my erect penis and smiled. "So, at least you find it stimulating. That's a start." Then he squeezed my dick and added, "And I see I underestimated Indian cocks." He chuckled.

I clutched Marc firmly now, thrilling in the sensation of the tip of his penis pressed against my flesh. I could feel his body shudder.

Marc slipped his left hand down the waistband of my cargo shorts and began rubbing his palm gently over my groin, pulling me ever tighter to his chest with his other arm.

We kissed, and I pulled away. Then we kissed again. Marc led me to the bedroom where he unbuttoned my polo and slipped it over my head. Then he undid the button on my shorts and slowly unzipped them so they dropped to the floor. Marc slid down my Fruit of the Loom briefs, and I voluntarily stepped out of them. Then he pulled me down onto the crisp white sheets and held our bodies tight.

I placed my hand on Marc's upper arm. "Flex for me," I insisted. Adam used to have me wrap my fingers around his flexed biceps, and he would ask me if his workouts were making his arms bigger. I remembered how it thrilled me to know my muscular brother was watching out for me and sharing with me his physicality. Marc obliged, and I squeezed his arm and thought of Adam.

Marc brushed his hand across my erect penis. "I can tell you're enjoying this," he said with a laugh. "Why shouldn't you? You're a man, and you're getting your rocks off. That's what men do. Do you want to keep going?" I wanted to say no, but that would have been a lie. I nodded in assent.

Marc smiled and slid to the foot of the bed. His long blond hair caressed my face and then trailed softly down my chest as he positioned himself between my knees. I felt the hair on my arms stand as erect as my penis, and goosebumps made me quiver. Marc cupped my cock and balls in his large hands, and the warmth of his mouth engulfed me. I felt the tip of my penis brush against the back of his throat while his moist lips clamped hungrily around the base. Marc's tongue darted up and down the length of the shaft, and I moaned with ecstasy. With his left hand, Marc began massaging my balls, and he slipped the tip of a finger into my anus. I arched my back in resistance and then sank heavily onto the probing digit. Marc's other hand moved gently up my belly and then along my chest. He brushed his thumb across my hardening nipple, and I sighed deeply.

Marc's mouth slid slowly up and down on my penis, and I was consumed by sensual pleasure. I began to imagine I was holding Brenda, and the thought relaxed and excited me at the same time. Bren had given me hundreds of blowjobs claiming that aroused her. I certainly never protested, and I almost always would climax, but the feeling of pleasure was never like this. Marc had aroused every erotic spot in my body, and I squirmed with irrational delight.

Marc rolled his eyes upward, and I could tell he was smiling. He continued rhythmically sliding his tongue and lips over my throbbing cock and massaging my ass with his finger. My body arched with uncontrollable spasms, and a voice I scarcely recognized as my own rasped, "I'm going to come! O god, I'm going to come!" Marc responded with increased pressure and applied suction that made me feel like the semen was being ripped from the depths of my groin. I let out a cry of such primal intensity I was sure everyone in the Festiva Inn could hear–and I didn't care.

Marc sat up with drops of my come oozing from the corners of his mouth. He grinned broadly, and his eyes danced with satisfaction. "Was that all right?" he asked rhetorically. The answer was obvious to us both. I just smiled. Marc had fulfilled in me fantasies I never realized I had. Depths of pleasure I never knew existed. I lay there a few moments and found myself thinking of Brenda. It wasn't shame I felt, but desire–the desire to share with the woman I love the ecstasy Marc had awakened in me. Then my thoughts shifted to Adam. Was this what he felt? Was this what convinced him he preferred the company of men? Had he just indulged himself in a bit of masti, or was he born to a third sex–a middle sex? Did such a thing even exist, or is pleasure indifferent to sexuality? I needed to know what Adam knew. I needed to prove to myself that I understood what he was going through, even if I didn't share the same feelings.

"Fuck me," I said softly to Marc. "I need you to fuck me."

Marc seemed to understand. His expression was serious as he nodded slightly. He opened the night table drawer and pulled out a Trojan and a tube of lube. I rolled onto my belly, still wet with come. A moment later I felt the warmth of Marc lubricating my ass. He slid his finger in and out gently several times, massaging me until I no longer winced from the sensation. Marc's hair brushed against my face as he knelt over me. He wrapped me in his arms, and I felt the soft, smooth skin of the tip of his penis press against me, ultimately forcing its way deep inside–into my body and into my soul. Marc rocked back and forth tenderly, not with the animal passion I expected. It was as though he was the physician come to heal me–to release my pain. I let my thoughts drift to Adam, pretending he was the one experiencing this moment of compassion. I whispered, "Forgive me, brother. We're not all that different after all. Forgive me." I sobbed softly.

Marc withdrew before relieving himself. Without saying a word, he rolled onto his back beside me and pulled my head close to his chest while tears streamed down my cheeks.

27

☼ ☼ ☼

I don't know when I actually fell asleep, but it was late in the morning when I woke up. Marc was still in bed next to me, snoring. I tried to recall the events of last night, and then I tried to forget. My body stirred with the ache of physical exhaustion, not in pain but with deep satisfaction. It was true then. I had fucked my graduate assistant. The act seemed wrong in every way, and yet it seemed completely right. A kind of numbness overcame me, and I had to force myself to climb out of bed and shower.

I allowed the warm water to flow over my body for several minutes. I thought I should be trying to wash away my shame, but instead of shame, I felt something akin to enlightenment. I slid my hand slowly over my chest recalling the pleasure I had felt the night before. I imagined Bren standing beside me as I lathered. My hand found its way to my groin, and I closed my eyes and sighed. This was the depth of pleasure I wanted to share with my wife, and I wanted her to share with me. We were in love. I never doubted that, but we didn't experience the kind of passion that stokes the fire of that love. That was more my fault than hers. Or maybe it was no one's fault. Maybe we just play out the roles we've been raised to believe we are destined for.

I was sitting at the writing desk reading clinical studies when Marc stepped out of the bedroom area still naked. He paused a moment and said, "Are you OK? With last night, I mean."

I looked up slowly. I had been thinking about this moment and what I would say. Then I shook my head slightly and replied, "I don't know. I don't know what I am."

Marc grabbed a towel he had left draped over the chair and wrapped it around his waist. Then he sat next to me. "I know it might be different for you than for me," he said. "I just like sex. A lot. I enjoy it every chance I get. Maybe that makes me a slut, but I do what I like, and I don't worry about what anyone else thinks."

"You're right about that," I said. "I'm different than you. Sex is intimate for me. Something I want with just one person. Don't get me wrong–last night was amazing. I felt things I never dreamed anyone could experience. I just don't know yet what that means for me."

"You mean you don't know if you're gay or not. I get it. You were with a man, and you enjoyed it. That doesn't mean you're gay you know. In fact, I'm not sure I even know what being gay means." Marc looked away for a moment. "You have to understand, I'm good at sex–really good. I should be. I've had enough experience. I shared my experience with you, and you learned things I discovered long ago. That's all."

"So, you're my carnal Yoda. Is that what you're saying?"

Marc laughed. "Yeah, I like that. Maybe I should print up business cards." Then he turned serious. "So, what were you thinking about when we were...you know..."

"Fucking?" I said the word we both were avoiding. "Other than that my entire body might explode, I guess I was thinking of Brenda and how much I wanted to share what I was experiencing with her."

"Then that's your answer, dude. You like chicks. Well, so do I, but in a different way, I guess. I like the way they feel and smell and their smooth skin pressed against mine...and fucking them of course. But I like it because it feels good. You like it because you're committed to some sort of bond. I envy you for that. Sometimes I wish I could do that too. Maybe I need you to be my relationship Yoda."

The thought of that made me smile, but it was my own relationship I was worried about. How would I tell Brenda? Would I even tell her? I didn't want to keep secrets from her, but this was bigger than just smoking a cigar in the car–this could change our relationship forever. If I was afraid of losing Bren before, I was terrified by the thought now.

Marc left to shower. When he returned, I said, "I think you better go back home."

My pronouncement stunned Marc. The best explanation I could give was that we would have to work together. We both realized that made no sense, but it seemed to be the only way for me to face Brenda.

Marc protested, but he finally conceded that I had made up my mind. He packed his things, and I scheduled his flight back to Chicago.

My phone chimed to announce I had received a text. It was Bren. She must have gotten my message.

JUST GOT BACK FROM FANTASTIC WEEKEND! CALL ME!!!

I considered for a moment what to say. Then I pulled up her number.

"David! I missed you so much. How are things going?"

How should I answer that question? How do I tell her that her father was in a coma, he might have killed her mother, and I had sex with my assistant? I stalled. "You go first," I said. "I want to hear about your *fantastic* weekend."

Bren proceeded to tell me about riding an icebreaker into the North Atlantic surf and spending two nights on a small island in the North Sea at the Borkum research center. She talked about seeing a narwhal and actually stepping onto the floating platform designed by the Dutch. Bren was nearly ecstatic speculating about the possibilities for this new technology. After a few minutes, she paused.

"David? You aren't saying much. Is everything all right?"

I sighed and told her that her father had been in an accident and he was in critical but stable condition at Mesa Hospital. I finished by saying, "I think you need to come to Phoenix."

There was a moment of silence. Then Bren said, "I'll be there as soon as I can get a flight."

I let her know Patsy was upset, and I suggested she call her. Bren agreed. Before she hung up, I said, "I love you. I hope you know that I always will." The words sounded strange, and I could tell Brenda was trying to parse their meaning, but she was too distressed to give it a second thought. I let her call her sister and make arrangements to fly back.

After the call, I sat thinking of all the things I wanted to say to my wife and couldn't. I picked up the cap I got in Galena and ran my finger across the brim. "Never forget," I said aloud. Now all I wished for was to be able to forget.

Marc entered the room. I let him know I booked a four-thirty flight for him to O'Hare. Since the Jeep was reserved in his name, I told him to return it, and I would rent a car locally. He just shook his head, grabbed his bag, and stormed out. Marc muttered the word *dick* before he slammed the door behind him.

Is that what I was–just a dick? Is that what it means to be a man? Is that why men are dicks? I cheated on my wife, who I love very much. I jeopardized my career by having sexual relations with my assistant. I was close to getting both my brother-in-law and my father-in-law convicted of murder. Instead of a relationship Yoda, I was a master dick.

I promised Patsy I'd visit the hospital before noon to give her a chance to get some lunch, so I arranged for a rental car to pick me up. A driver would bring the car around in about an hour, which gave me time to clean up and then relive last night. Instead of the total liberation I was sure I had felt, now only a sense of shame overwhelmed me. The person I needed to tell was the one person I couldn't talk to. I feared I might never be able to talk honestly to my wife again.

I turned on the TV to try to crowd out my thoughts. The Channel 5 news was reporting on the protesters that had been camped out at the site of the Southwest Enterprise explosion since the day after their sacred land was desecrated. The governor–my father-in-law–had earlier announced that the National Guard would be activated to remove them. It was Memorial Day weekend, and scores of people sympathetic to the cause of the Native Americans had converged on the Tohono O'odham Reservation and were massing on the makeshift campsite. Camera crews were close in pursuit.

A live feed broadcast by the U.S. Border Patrol provided overhead coverage from a white surveillance blimp tethered above the border wall. The newscast played an excerpt from the county sheriff announcing over a bullhorn that bulldozers would be brought in to clear the land of squatters who had not vacated by the next weekend. Then the cameras cut to an interview with a small Native American woman. It was Ga'ga. She was dressed in what must have been her most elaborate ceremonial costume, complete with multiple layers of woven fabric and several silver and jade necklaces. The old woman looked directly into the camera and spoke calmly, "We will stay until he comes." The interviewer followed up by asking who was coming. Ga'ga simply said, "He knows."

The hotel receptionist at the front desk called to tell me my car had arrived. I clicked off the TV and pulled on my Antonio's cap. Then I headed to the lobby to go get the Chevy Impala I reserved. The young woman who picked me up drove us to the rental agency, about a mile away, where I signed for the vehicle. I pulled the cap down on my forehead to shade my eyes from the midday sun and drove to Mesa Hospital.

It wasn't until I saw my reflection in the glass doors of the hospital that I realized I was still wearing the red cap. I look like a delivery boy, I thought. The dark circles under my eyes added to my disheveled appearance.

Patsy was in the waiting area near her father's room when I arrived. When she saw me, she said, "David, you look terrible. You must have had a worse night than I did."

I just smiled and forced myself to appear pleasant for her sake. "Yeah, I didn't sleep much. I'm sure you didn't either."

Patsy smiled and reached into her purse to pull out a bottle of blue pills. "Not so bad after a few of these." Then she told me there was no discernible change in Jack's condition, which was probably a good sign at this point.

I told her to get something to eat, and I'd stay near Jack. Before Patsy reached the elevator, she turned and said, "Bren called. Thank you for asking her to do that. She said she booked a flight for tomorrow afternoon and to let you know to pick her up at six thirty."

Before I could reply, the elevator door closed, and I was left by myself in the waiting room. A man I suspected of killing his wife lay in a coma just a few yards away. How ironic, I thought, that I was standing watch over the person who probably murdered Brenda's mother. The thought sickened me. Then I thought about how I would have to be the one to tell her–me, the man who cheated on her with another man. The sickening thought turned physical, and I dashed for the toilet in the empty room across the hall. The nurse heard me vomiting and rushed over to see if one of her patients was in trouble. She discovered it was just a visitor hurling his guts out.

"Sir, if you're ill, I'm going to have to ask you to leave," she said as I turned to see her standing behind me, bits of vomit clinging to my lower lip. I picked up my cap, which had fallen to the floor and quickly rinsed my mouth in the small sink. I explained that I was just overcome by fatigue and stress, but the nurse looked skeptical. She instructed me to get a bottle of water from the drink cart and continued to watch me until I returned to the waiting area.

I took a seat on the short vinyl couch, still feeling queasy. The headline of the newspaper lying on the end table caught my attention. "Governor's accident might have been deliberate." I read the first few paragraphs. The police chief announced that the department was considering the possibility that the hit-and-run of Jack Donovan might not have been accidental. The list of his enemies included members of the Papago Indian tribe and

Milwaukee mobsters. And Patsy suspects Archie, I thought. Any of those possibilities put me in the middle of something bigger than I could even comprehend.

Patsy returned and handed me a cup of coffee. I let her know I wasn't feeling well, and I thought I should go back to my hotel. I apologized for leaving her alone. She said she understood, but I could tell she needed family around. At least Bren would be there the next day. A wave of nausea rushed through me at that thought, and I quickly excused myself and left the hospital. The blast of hot air outside only added to the sick feeling. I stepped off the curb to make my way across the parking garage when a silver Lexus quickly pulled in front of me. It was Jill. She rolled down the passenger window and leaned in my direction. "Get in," she said.

I stepped toward the car door and began to argue with her. She interrupted me in a tone that left no option to disagree. "Get in now! I'll explain on the way."

I didn't trust her, but for a moment I thought she might actually have been looking out for me. I reluctantly settled into the passenger seat. Before I had the door closed, Jill was speeding out of the parking garage.

"What's going on?" I asked. "Are you trying to get us killed?"

"Not me," she said. "Someone else." She looked nervously in the rearview mirror.

"I don't know what more you expect to get from me for your story, but this sure isn't the way to do it."

Jill seemed to be driving aimlessly.

"Where are we going? Or maybe I should ask why?" We were on I-17 now, heading north. Traffic was light since it was the holiday.

"You met with the Indian, didn't you?" She didn't wait for a reply. "You made some people very unhappy. The Milwaukee mob. The Indian killed two of their soldiers, and their code says they have to take that person's life in exchange. They could have done that while he was in prison, but you helped get him released."

"It was self-defense. The tapes proved that." I knew I had done the right thing, and I refused to accept what she was saying.

"You're in way over your head, college boy," Jill almost cracked a smile. "These guys play for keeps."

"How do you know all this?" I asked, not admitting that what she was saying was true.

"I have an informant. A reliable informant. He's been passing me information for two years now. It's mostly information the mob wants leaked, but it makes for good investigative reporting."

"And good ratings, no doubt," I said sarcastically.

"Yes, that too," Jill admitted. "The man actually works for your brother-in-law. He got a position with Southwest Enterprise, and he's been reporting on the company's activities ever since."

"Ted?" I said surprised.

Jill seemed even more astonished. "You know Ted?"

"Yes, I do. And Arch has known what he's been up to all along. He's been playing him." I could see Jill was pondering the implications of that revelation.

"How do you know Ted?"

"I ran him through a session with Mnemosyne." I immediately realized I shouldn't have said that. If Jill reported on our administering the memory technique outside of the trials, we were sure to lose IRB approval.

"He knows about your research?" There was a look of concern on Jill's face. "I don't know why Ted didn't tell me about that."

"It could be because Archie was blackmailing him. He knew Ted was skimming, and he threatened to tell the mob."

"Well, that's probably a good thing. If Angelo found out about your memory...thing, he'd be trying to get his hands on it."

"Nemy!" I exclaimed. "She's at the hotel. What if someone tries to steal her?"

"That's definitely a possibility. We can head back there. As far as I know, Angelo's soldiers don't know about me so they won't be looking for my car, but they're probably waiting for you to return."

I told her I just picked up a rental, and I doubted anyone would notice a tan Chevrolet. But if she was right about someone waiting for me, I couldn't be seen going to my room. I agreed to her plan.

We drove in silence a few minutes. Then Jill asked, "Where's that cute assistant of yours?"

"Marc?" I looked at my watch. "He's probably on a plane back to Chicago right now. Why?"

"You realize he's part of this too, don't you? It's not just you who might be in danger. You better let him know."

I pulled out my cell phone and tapped a message to Marc. I had to think for a minute how to start.

SORRY I WAS A DICK. JUST WORKING THROUGH THINGS. WITH JILL NOW. SHE SAYS THE BAD GUYS ARE PISSED BECAUSE WE HELPED Z. WE COULD BE IN DANGER. BE CAREFUL.

Jill took an exit ramp off I-17 and headed back toward the city. About ten minutes later, she pulled into the parking lot of a theater across the street from the Festiva Inn and parked around back. "Give me your key card and wait here," she said. "They'll probably have someone near the lobby watching for you, but they won't pay any attention to me."

"The device is in an old backpack, next to the desk. Bring my laptop too," I instructed.

It was dusk, and I watched the orange glow of sunset fill the sky to the west as I waited for Jill to return. I reached for my phone and began texting Bren. I REALLY MISS YOU. THINGS ARE GETTING PRETTY STRANGE AND I WANT YOU HERE. I just hoped she would still want to be with me.

Jill had been gone fifteen minutes, and I started to wonder what happened. What if they *did* pay attention to her? What would they do, toss her in the trunk of a limo and drive off? That only happens in gangster movies, I told myself. Then I considered the possibility that movies get their plots from actual events. A feeling of panic briefly swept over me. The image of fists pummeling me that afternoon Adam had to rescue me in the park flashed through my mind–how I just curled up in a ball and didn't fight back. How I never fight back. Marc was right. It was time for me to man up.

From the car window, I could see the Festiva Inn. A heavyset man leaning against a lamppost near the entrance was thumbing through his cell phone. Could that be one of them, I wondered? Did the mob really have someone waiting for me? I had to find out if Jill was all right, but how would I get past the lookout?

I glanced at a dumpster by the back door of the theater. A large white pizza box was sitting on the ground nearby. Someone was too lazy to lift the lid, I thought, but that might be my way past the mob's goon.

I pulled my Antonio's cap down so the brim covered my eyes and got out of the car. After I locked the Lexus, I casually walked to the dumpster to pick up the pizza box. There were a couple of slices inside, and they were still warm. I can do this I tried convincing myself and walked deliberately toward the Festiva Inn.

Bougainvillea bushes bordering the sidewalk concealed my approach. I emerged from between two shrubs just as a beat-up Saturn station wagon pulled to the curb. The driver got out and headed toward the theater. Perfect, I thought as I stepped out from behind the car and walked as confidently as I could toward the hotel doors. I kept my head down, pretending I was reading a delivery address on the pizza box.

The man standing guard looked up briefly, but he didn't seem to pay any attention to me. My plan was to avoid eye contact with the desk clerk and walk directly to the hallway my room was in. If anyone noticed, they'd think I was delivering a pizza–I hoped.

As I reached for the handle of the glass front door, I saw Jill rounding the hallway corner. She was carrying my computer case, and she had my backpack slung over her shoulder. I froze.

Then I heard a deep voice behind me rumble, "Hey, pizza boy."

Without looking up, I shrugged and mumbled, "Delivery."

"Stop," the man ordered before I could pull the door open. A drop of sweat fell from my forehead. From the corner of my eye, I saw his hand move toward his pocket. Jill had reached the foyer by now, and she noticed him too. The man pulled out his wallet and waved a bill in my direction. "I'll give you a fifty for that pizza, kid. I've been standing here over an hour, and I'm getting hungry."

Before I could react, Jill pushed her way through the glass doors, brushing past me as she headed directly toward the burly man. I dipped inside before the door closed and walked toward the back hallway. As I turned the corner, I saw Jill pressed up against the grinning mobster. I dropped the pizza box on the pool deck and snuck out through the back gate. From there, I cautiously made my way back to the theater parking lot. Jill was waiting by her car when I arrived. I could tell she was pissed.

"Oh," I said sheepishly, fingering my pocket. "I have the key."

I beeped the locks open and handed the fob to Jill. She just glared at me and opened the back door to deposit my computer and backpack.

"What the hell were you thinking?" she admonished after we pulled the doors closed. "You could have gotten us both killed!" She turned away and started the Lexus.

We drove around in silence for several minutes. Eventually, I said weakly, "I'm sorry. I was...worried about you." I could see the hint of a smile form on her lips. "Thanks for...well, for saving my life, I guess."

"That's right," she said forcefully. "I probably did save your life."

"How did you do it?" I asked hesitantly.

A grin spread across her face. "I told him I knew a better way for him to spend that fifty." She seemed to forget about how I nearly blew our cover as she recalled the look on the thug's face.

"But what if..." I didn't have to finish the sentence.

"If he took me up on my offer?" she laughed. "I knew he couldn't leave his post or he'd be the one getting killed."

She headed north.

"Now where are we going?" I asked.

"My place."

28

☼ ☼ ☼

Jill ordered an all-meat pizza for supper. "We'll have someone else deliver this one," she said with a smirk.

While we waited, Jill explained how the Milwaukee mob was now an extension of the Russian Brotherhood, a group that had been steadily amassing billions and gaining international influence after the fall of the Soviet Union. She said the mob had promoted building the wall between the United States and Mexico because it was helping to break down the alliance our two countries had enjoyed. She suspected the Russians were hoping to gain a foothold in the Western Hemisphere by playing up tensions between our nations and providing Mexico with a reliable trade partner and protection from U.S. aggression. The recent deployment of Russian advisors and arms to Mexico seemed to bear out those suspicions. When I asked her why she was focusing on the murder trial of a local business tycoon, she said Archie was a much bigger player in the whole scheme–maybe bigger than even he realized.

After we finished the pizza and downed a six-pack of St. Pauli Girl, Jill worked through her emails and caught up on the current news cycle.

Just before ten, Jill said, "It's been a long day. I'm going to turn in." Then she retired to the bedroom for the night.

I hadn't gotten much sleep, so I was happy to turn in early. I slept on the studio couch that night. At least it was more comfortable than the Festiva Inn sofa.

☼ ☼ ☼

In the morning, I woke up before Jill did. I showered and dressed as quietly as I could. Jill was still sleeping, so I slipped down to the lobby for a cup of coffee and to check my cell phone. There were no messages, either from Marc or from Bren. I wouldn't blame him for still being angry, and I expected Bren soon would be. I tried texting Marc again, but he was probably sleeping in, so I wasn't surprised that he didn't reply.

It was eight thirty when I went back to the room. Jill was up and already dressed. She was sitting at the writing desk scrolling through the day's news when I walked in.

"How much do you know about your Indian?" she asked before I had closed the door.

"He's not *my* Indian, you know. He calls himself Z." I was slightly insulted by her degrading use of the word *Indian*–the same word that applied to me.

"Ted told me Angelo put out a contract on him, but he didn't know why. Did the Indian...Z say why he was targeted?"

I told her I didn't think Z knew why the two thugs approached him, but given his reputation, it could have been for any number of reasons.

"And was one of those reasons why you hunted him down?" Her investigative instincts were kicking in.

"We thought so," I told her, "but it turned out we were wrong."

"Did your little machine tell you that?" She nodded toward the backpack Nemy was in.

"Yes, in a way." I paused. "We thought Z might have been the murderer Archie is looking for. It turns out he isn't."

"Do you know who is?" she persisted.

I told her I didn't know, but I was starting to think my brother-in-law had been guilty all along. She just smiled. I was growing weary of the interrogation.

"How long do you think I need to be locked up here?" I asked.

"Is that how you feel—like a prisoner? Nobody is keeping you here except maybe Angelo's hitmen and your realization that they might actually be after you."

"You've been following their gang probably for years. You know how they operate. Seeing that they really are out to get me, what do you think they want?"

"It's not so much what they want. Things would be easier if you had something to give up in exchange. But their type live by a strict code of honor. The eye-for-an-eye rule of order."

"So, I gave their reputation a black eye, is that it? I mean it isn't like I actually did anything against any of them." I suspected Jill could hear the growing tension in my voice.

"That's a valid point, and you can take some comfort in knowing that they also live by a code of fairness—at least fairness as defined by them. Retribution is typically measured based on the severity of the offense. They're more likely to break a few fingers than kill you."

"That's comforting," I snorted. "Somehow, I still think you're the one playing me, and not them."

"Think what you like. All I can tell you is that I'm concerned for your safety. After last night, I would think you'd understand why." Jill got up and headed for the door. "Breakfast?"

I nodded. At least I'd get out of the hotel. I made sure to bring Nemy along.

We took the elevator down to the lobby and walked to a coffee shop next door. Jill claimed a café table away from the entrance, and I retrieved our pastries and drinks.

Jill needed to drive into town to meet someone at the newsroom of the *Arizona Chronicle*, a sister publication of the *Chicago Star*. She said they received a tape from a local TV station, and the clip might support the story Jill was working on. I convinced her to let me pick up my car at Mesa Hospital, but I promised to be careful and return to her room and stay there until we figured out what to do next. When we got to the hospital parking garage, Jill circled the area cautiously before she let me get out.

I spent the morning just driving around town before heading back to Jill's hotel. It was two thirty, and I had just fixed myself a cup of tea when a text message flashed on my cell phone. It was from Marc. A part of me didn't want to hear from him, but my concern that he was OK was even stronger.

PICK ME UP, is all it said.

Pick him up? In Chicago? How was I supposed to do that?

IN TROUBLE. KELSEY'S ON ROUNDS. DON'T KNOW WHO ELSE TO ASK.

That didn't sound like he was good with where we were. I texted back, CALL ME.

A few minutes passed before his reply came. CAN'T. MEET ME AT TONTO MON.

I texted him a few times to get more information, but Marc didn't reply. What did he mean he was in trouble? Did the hitmen follow him to O'Hare? It would make sense that the Milwaukee mob would have soldiers there too.

I logged onto my laptop. What was Tonto, and why did Marc ask me to meet him there Monday? This was already Tuesday. Was I supposed to pick him up someplace next week? I searched for Tonto. Hits came up for *The Lone Ranger* and Jay Silverheels. That couldn't be right. I tried adding Chicago. The only thing new was a reptile house at Brookfield Zoo. Does he want me to meet him at the zoo? Why next week? I looked at his text again. Maybe it wasn't Monday. I typed in TONTO MON. The hit at the top of the page grabbed my attention. *Tonto National Monument.* It's a national park–in Arizona.

I pulled out my phone and tapped in the location in Maps. The park was more than two hours east of Phoenix, near Roosevelt Lake, a vast recreational reservoir on the Salt River. Did he want me to meet him there? It was almost three in the afternoon. I wouldn't be able to drive there and back before Bren's plane arrived. I decided to ask Patsy if she could meet her sister at the airport. As much as I wanted to see my wife, the thought of confronting her with the inevitable made me queasy. An uncomfortable two-hour ride with Marc might not be much better, but I realized he wouldn't have called me if it wasn't urgent.

Patsy agreed to pick up Bren at Sky Harbor. She was concerned when I said I needed to get Marc out of some trouble, but I tried to pass it off as one of his boyish pranks. We decided to meet for supper when I got back. Knowing Patsy would be with us the first couple of hours helped settle my stomach. I left a note for Jill saying I had to run an errand and then meet up with Bren. She'd think it was crazy for me to go out alone, but I really didn't want her poking around into something I wasn't even sure about.

The Beeline Highway east out of the city veered several miles north to get around Brown's Peak before the route turned south toward my destination. I considered the irony of the name, at least for this trip. The road is a new divided highway that didn't seem warranted considering the few cars and trucks I encountered. As I climbed higher into the foothills of the Superstition Mountains, I felt some relief from the relentless heat of Phoenix. I even rolled down the window for a few minutes but soon retreated to the comfort of air conditioning. About halfway to Tonto Monument, the Beeline ended, and I headed south on Highway 188. A few miles down this stretch of winding road was a small town and past that occasional turn-offs for campsites. Only a few campers passed me, headed back to the city after an extended Memorial Day weekend at the lake.

Several miles down the road I saw the first highway sign for Tonto National Monument. It was another ninety miles. My thoughts drifted to Brenda and our inevitable conversation about...that night. I'd given up any notion of not telling her. If I thought there was a chance she'd never find out, the idea was tempting, but she *would* find out eventually. She always did. No, I had to come up with a strategy that would save our marriage. Every script I rehearsed wound up with the opposite outcome. *I was drunk.... He seduced me.... We were conducting research.... I was with him, but I thought about you.*

At least the last one was true. I was thinking of Bren—not about how guilty I should be feeling but of all the times we held each other, we kissed, we fucked. It was as though our entire romantic relationship had been distilled into a single moment of intense pleasure, as though an entire universe of delight spread before me at that moment I climaxed. It was more than physical thrill—it was transcendent. Marc had been my sensual guide to a new level of Eros the way Sea Horse had led me on my spirit quest.

I laughed. Only I could turn the most tragic event of my life into a poetic experience. Adam would have punched me if he was here. But he wasn't here. He'd never be here. I loved my brother with the same intensity that I loved my wife. Now I stood to lose them both. Tears started to cloud my vision. I had to think about something else—about Marc. I checked my cell phone, but I hadn't seen any bars for several miles. What if he wasn't even at the park? Did I misinterpret his text? Maybe he was in Chicago at the zoo. Or maybe he was in serious trouble. The price I'd pay for that night with Marc might pale compared to what he could be facing if there were actually hitmen after him. At least I knew he was alive. Thoughts tumbled through my head like the shrubs that blew along the highway as I passed. Or what if....? He never texted back. Why hadn't I heard back from him if he was really in trouble? My foot gradually sank deeper into the accelerator, and I tried turning up the only radio station I could find in an attempt to drown out darker thoughts.

The country songs gave way to the local news. The number of protesters supporting the O'odham resistance was steadily growing, and the acting governor was threatening to deploy National Guard units this coming weekend. That was taking place a few hundred miles away, but I felt like I was in the middle of it. The wall Archie built on one side, the troops the Governor's

Office was sending on the other, Ga'ga and Sea Horse and Z caught in the middle. Was Jill right? Was I in over my head?

A few small billboards dotted the roadside now, advertising local businesses in Tonto Basin just ahead. I saw a cellular bar flicker on and decided to try calling Marc again once the signal got stronger. I drove another ten minutes before I had a solid bar. RV parks dotted the roadside as I approached the small but sprawling resort community. I pulled in at the only gas station and bought a cold bottle of tea. The temperature had risen to over a hundred now that I was in the valley again, and I was glad to get back to the air-conditioned car. I tried calling Marc, but I wasn't surprised he didn't answer. Then I texted him and waited for a reply. After I finished drinking the tea, I got back on the road. At this rate, I'd be there in half an hour.

The highway soon traced the edge of the massive reservoir. Theodore Roosevelt Lake captured most of the water passing through the Salt River—water that had irrigated village farms belonging to the O'odham people for hundreds of years. Now the water was diverted for commercial crops and for filling swimming pools in wealthy Arizona neighborhoods. The O'odham farms had dried up generations ago.

It was after four o'clock when I came to the turnoff for Tonto Monument. Saguaro cactuses stood like sentries at the entrance. The road led to ancient cliff dwellings. These sacred ancestral homes of some Sonoran Desert tribe are now a tourist attraction managed by the National Park Service. A mile down the access road sat a modern visitor center. To the west, primitive adobe ruins loomed under a brow of natural stone. I parked and stepped into what looked like a combination museum and gift shop. The fair-haired ranger behind the cash register asked, "Are you looking for your friend?"

I nodded, and he pointed toward the bathroom doors. "We were hoping you'd show up," he said.

I stepped past a tall display of locally made pottery and saw Marc sitting on a steel bench with his head in his hands. He looked up when I said his name. My heart sank. Instead of the vibrant, boyish California blond I knew, slumped a gaunt and haggard man I barely recognized. Marc's long hair was ratted, and one eye was blackened. His face and arms were red and blistered with peeling skin. Traces of dried blood were spattered across the tan tank top and plaid board shorts he was wearing.

"You look terrible," I said involuntarily. "What happened?"

"I'll tell you in the car," he replied, wincing as he stood. Marc stopped to refill the plastic water bottle he was holding. The ranger saw we were leaving and said, "I wanted to call an ambulance, but he told me you'd be here to pick him up. That must have been some fall he took." He called after Marc, who was limping slowly toward the exit, "Good luck, man. I hope you recover soon." Marc nodded and grimaced.

I opened the passenger door, and Marc got in, still clutching his side. I climbed in behind the wheel and turned the air on full for our drive back to the city.

I let Marc finish his bottle of water before trying to find out what happened.

"You fell?"

Marc just shook his head. "That's what I told the guy." Marc's voice was raspy and forced. He looked at me and smiled, "I guess you were serious about the bad guys being pissed." He started to chuckle but just flinched.

"You're not in Chicago." I realized the obviousness of my statement. "You missed the flight back?"

"No," he shook his head. I just canceled the ticket. "Kelsey wanted me to shack up, so I went there instead. Oh, and I didn't turn in the Jeep either."

"Don't tell me. Angelo's boys tailed you?"

"They must have," Marc wheezed. "When I parked near Kelsey's place, two guys pulled up behind me. The bigger one forced me to get in the back of their SUV with him, and the other guy drove us up into the mountains."

"They dropped you at the ranger station?"

Marc shook his head again. "No. Not there. About twenty miles up the road, past a turnoff that led to the lake."

"Are you all right to talk? You sound awful," I said.

Marc waved me off. "I'm OK. Maybe stop for some ice cream?" For a moment I thought of Adam and how he'd try to get our parents to stop for ice cream. We were approaching Tonto Basin, and I pulled into the convenience store I passed on the way down. I realized it had probably been twenty-four hours since Marc had last eaten, so I grabbed some deli meat and yogurt from the cooler and added a box of donuts to a growing pile on the counter that included a six-pack of Coronas, a bottle of Motrin, and, of course, ice cream.

As soon as we were back on the road, Marc devoured his two Klondike bars and washed them down with cold beer. Then he took a handful of pills and drained the beer bottle.

"So, what did they want? What happened?"

"The guy who drove did all the talking. He said two of his buddies had been killed, and they needed to even the score."

"They planned to kill you?!" I nearly drove off the road when I turned to Marc in horror. Then I remembered last night and wondered if the same fate might have awaited me.

"No, I don't think so. They were just upset that we helped the two Indian brothers get away."

I looked Marc up and down. "This is what happens when they're upset? What exactly did they do?"

"It was late at night, and nobody was on the highway. We turned off onto a dirt road and drove a long way to the edge of a bluff. The driver got out and pulled me from the back seat. The big guy had zip-tied my hands behind my back." Marc stretched out his arms to show me the abrasions around both his wrists. "The driver backed me up to the cliff edge, where I could see the reflection of a crescent moon in the water below. The other guy kept poking at me and laughing, calling me 'college boy.'"

"Did you think they were going to, you know, push you over?"

"Yeah, they actually joked about that. Instead, they decided to just beat me up and leave me there. They wanted me to *tell my friend* we should mind our own business."

"They really beat you up?"

"Not real bad. Just a black eye and bloody nose, and I think they might have broken a rib."

I just bit my lip and shook my head slowly.

"Before they left, the big guy pulled my wallet from my shorts pocket, and the driver took my phone. My wallet got thrown into the reservoir, but the little guy just pitched my iPhone in the bushes. He laughed and said a lot of good it would do me since the nearest cell tower was fifty miles away. I guess he was right about that because I couldn't get a signal."

"So how were you able to text me?" I asked.

"I picked up a bar when I got closer to the park. Not enough to call, but it seemed like texts were getting through. Then the battery died."

"How did you get to the ranger station?" I was afraid I already knew the answer.

"I walked."

"All night?! You could have been eaten by...something," I gasped.

"Tell me about it," Marc chuckled. "The moon was barely a sliver, so it was nearly pitch black out. I could hear the coyotes in the distance, and it sounded like a pig or something heavy tried to charge me when I was walking through a valley. I carried a big stick with me, but I don't know how much good that would have done."

"At least you lived to talk about it."

"Yeah, but that wasn't the worst part."

My eyebrows arched in disbelief.

"It was late morning by the time I made it to the highway. It must have been ninety already."

"And you didn't have any water?"

"One bottle. The big guy tossed one out the window as they drove away. That lasted me until morning, and I held onto it in case I came across a spring or something." Mark grasped the empty plastic bottle next to him and squeezed it.

"I started walking west. I thought I might be able to catch a ride, but the couple of trucks I saw were headed the other direction. There was a sign that said the national park was ten miles ahead, so I knew I could make it that far, although in that heat I was starting to wonder."

By now we were near the turnoff for the Beeline. Marc stopped to drink two more beers and shove down a couple of donuts before he fell asleep. I let him rest.

29

☼ ☼ ☼

It was almost six before I had a signal on my phone. I called Patsy to let her know we were still more than an hour away. She was already at Sky Harbor and said Bren's plane had just landed. We agreed to meet someplace quiet for supper where we could talk. Patsy said she'd text me an address.

We were moving with traffic, and the Beeline was pretty busy by the time we reached Phoenix. I decided to wake Marc so we could discuss what to do next. He groaned and started to stretch when he was overcome by the pain in his side. Marc let out a yelp.

"Alright, we're taking you to a hospital," I said.

Marc rubbed his eyes. "No, we can't do that. Maybe those goons let me live–this time, but if they don't get their revenge with the Indians, they'll want to take it out on us."

I remembered what Jill said, and I knew Marc was right.

"Then we can at least stop at a drug store. We need to wrap your rib cage."

"And get lots of Solarcaine," Marc added, gingerly touching his blistered flesh. "Wait, I have a better idea," he said. "Drop me off at Kelsey's where I can get real medical attention and some stronger painkillers. You go meet up with Brenda and her sister. I don't think you want me tagging along for that anyway."

I started to argue, but I realized he was right. I didn't want Marc to be there. Not tonight.

"OK," I agreed. "But you said that's where you were when you were...abducted. Can you call to see if you can meet somewhere?"

Marc used my phone and reached Kelsey at home. He arranged to be picked up at a Starbucks a few blocks away.

"Look, Marc," I said. "About the other night..."

"Forget it. It never happened." He turned his head and looked out the window.

"I can't forget it. I don't think I want to forget it. That was a turning point in my life."

"That was two guys getting each other off. That's all," he snapped.

I waited in silence for the light to turn green. This might not be the best time to talk about us, but we needed to talk about what to do next.

"Jill picked up Nemy from the hotel," I informed him. "One of the mobsters was waiting for me there. It's probably not safe for either of us to do anything *typical* until this blows over."

"So, what? You plan to take your wife to your new girlfriend's hotel for the week?" Marc turned to me. "Have you even thought this through?"

He was right. I hadn't thought it through. Where was I going to go? How much was I going to tell Brenda?

"Well, I probably shouldn't stay at Archie's. Angelo's boys might expect me to go there, and for all I know, it could even have been Arch who arranged for the hit." I took a deep breath. "But at least Brenda will be safe there."

"Whatever, man," Marc said. "We don't have a lot of options here. I can't even catch a flight until I get my ID replaced. I'll just try to clean up my shit, and you clean up yours."

Marc directed me to the neighborhood Starbucks, and I dropped him off there. I tried to convince him to let me stay until Kelsey arrived since I was worried he could be dehydrated and might need someone to watch him, but he insisted I go to dinner with my wife. I gave him fifty dollars to tide him over. "Call me," I said before I drove away.

Patsy texted directions to a fancy French bistro in North Scottsdale. It was almost eight when I arrived. Even though I didn't expect anyone to recognize my new rental car, I parked behind the stucco building. The restaurant was dark and intimate, and I quickly spotted Bren at a table by the window. She looked up and saw me and nearly leaped from her chair to throw her arms around me.

"Oh, David, I'm so glad you're here. I missed you so much," she said between kisses.

"The pizza scarf!" I exclaimed, pointing to the satin sash Bren had wrapped around her waist.

"I've worn it every day, one way or another," she said. Then she tapped the brim of my Antonio's cap.

"Me too," I said.

"Never forget!" we exclaimed with exploding fingers. Patsy looked on and just shook her head.

I pulled Bren close and rocked her in my arms. For one moment, I felt the tensions of that day and the entire week flow from my body. I didn't want to let go. Bren pushed back and studied my face. "David, what's wrong. You look...worried."

It was as though she could read me in a matter of seconds, but she had always had that ability. "I'm sorry you had to come back from your trip early," I said. "Especially under these circumstances."

Bren looked over at her sister and led me to their table. I took Patsy's hand and held it for a moment. "Has his condition changed?" I asked as I took a seat.

She shook her head. "Brenda's flight arrived early, so we stopped by the hospital before meeting you here. They say he's stable and in no pain. We just have to be patient." I knew Patsy would have told her sister about the accident, but I wasn't sure if she mentioned she suspected Archie was behind it. I didn't ask any more questions.

Bren wondered where Marc was and what kind of trouble he'd gotten into. I think she expected that I needed to bail him out of jail. I wasn't prepared to tell her the truth–not yet, so I told them he'd been hiking in the mountains and fell. He was banged up pretty bad, and he needed me to pick him up. I said I dropped him off for some personal care from the nurse he'd been dating.

"*Personal* care," Patsy repeated. "He might not be the only one banged up tonight," she laughed. Brenda just blushed and giggled. It was nice to see her smile.

The girls had ordered an assortment of small plates, which arrived just before I did. We shared a bottle of Beaujolais, and Patsy and I prodded Brenda to talk about her week. I could tell she felt conflicted bubbling over with enthusiasm about the conference and worrying about her father's health.

The conversation turned back to Jack's condition. I could see tears form in Brenda's eyes. "How could someone just run into Daddy like that and then drive off? Do you think they were drunk?" I could honestly say I didn't know.

It was after nine o'clock by the time we finished our second bottle of wine. "Do you want to go back to stay with your father?" I asked.

Brenda shook her head. "The nurse said she'd call us if there was any change. "I've been up twenty hours, and I'm not even sure what day this is. I think I'll just try to get some sleep."

Patsy said, "She's right. We don't have any idea how long Daddy will be like this. They said it could be months–even years before he comes out of his coma. We just have to be there for him when he does. You two are staying at our guest house. I won't take no for an answer." The possibility of the mob finding me there made me hesitate, but the thought of not being with my wife outweighed my concern. Bren and I nodded in agreement.

I told the girls I could pick up my things in the morning, and we should just get some sleep. I'd explain later why going back to the Festiva Inn might not be a good idea.

It was a half-hour drive to the Trumble estate. Patsy arrived first with Bren's luggage in her car, and we were right behind her. Archie's security guard let us in, and Jesus met us at the door. He took Brenda's bags to the foyer and parked our cars.

Archie strolled in from the patio with a glass of what looked like whiskey in his hand. It obviously wasn't his first of the night. He bowed ironically to Patsy and said, "My lady doth return. Apparently, she needs a roof over her head tonight." He then turned to Brenda and me. "And look, she brings her courtiers with her. What a fine lady I have." He bowed even lower this time.

"Archie, you're drunk," Patsy stated the obvious.

"Maybe I am–hic. Maybe I am," he said staggering back toward the pool. Under his breath, he muttered, "And maybe I have a right to be." Then he turned on his heel and took a step toward Patsy. "You read the story in the papers didn't you?" Arch leaned heavily on his wife's shoulder. "Or maybe you didn't have to. Maybe your father told you about it before the story was leaked."

Patsy brushed his arm away. "I'm going to bed now. Brenda and David will be staying in the guest house while our father is in the hospital." She turned to Jesus. "Please take my sister's things to their room, and bring a robe and a change of clothes for my brother-in-law."

Jesus picked up the bags and disappeared through the patio door.

Archie turned his attention to me. "And you, the brainy one in the family. What have you done for me lately, huh?"

I told Arch how Marc and I tracked down a suspect, but the person turned out to be innocent. We didn't have any other leads.

"So that's it, huh? Give it the ol' college try and go home?" He stepped closer and looked up into my face. "Well, the way things are going, the only home I'll have is federal prison." Then he leaned in close. "Don't you get it? If I go down, the entire family goes down." Archie pivoted and stumbled back to a chaise lounge by the pool to pour himself another drink.

Patsy led us to the guest house, on the other side of the patio. Brenda had spent several weeks there the first year we were married. Her pregnancy was difficult, and her doctor ordered bed rest for the last trimester. I needed to start my senior research project, so I stayed in Massachusetts. We were optimistic about everything working out. Bren decided that if the baby was a girl, we'd name her Eve in honor of her mother. We lost the baby while we were apart, and that thought has haunted me ever since. As soon as we entered the comfortable living room, I could see those memories rushing back into Brenda's mind.

"You know your way around," Patsy said. Just press the intercom button if you need anything."

Jesus had finished turning down the bed, and he wished us a good night. Patsy was close behind. "The intercom," she repeated, pointing to the device on the wall near the door. "For anything." She smiled and closed the door behind her.

I turned down the lights, and we both collapsed on the brocade love seat. Brenda kicked off her shoes and curled up next to me. She looked into my eyes. "It was exciting being in the middle of all those scientists and activists trying to save the planet," she said, "but I still thought about you...and us every day."

I gave her a squeeze. "So did I," I said. "So did I."

Jesus had set out two wine glasses and a chilled bottle of Prosecco on the coffee table. We sipped wine and held each other in the dark, and I didn't want that moment to end.

I thought Bren was about to fall asleep when suddenly she sat up and said, "Tell me what's wrong."

I didn't need to ask how she knew something was wrong. It was part of her nature to know. I just didn't know where to begin or when to end, but I knew I had to tell her something. I considered that her father's condition was foremost on her mind, so I decided to start there.

"I talked to your father's doctor," I said. "He told me there was no way of knowing the level of Jack's consciousness."

"Yes, that's what the head nurse told us."

"I'm not so sure," I said. "I told him about our research and that I had the equipment with me to actually look into your father's memories. I said we'd never tried using Mnemosyne on a coma patient, but I thought it might work, and it certainly couldn't hurt."

Brenda looked at me expectantly. "What did he say?"

"Basically, no way. Not at *his* hospital." I sighed.

"Sometimes, people in this state can be very narrow-minded," she said wistfully. "I suppose it doesn't matter in the long run if we know or not. We're still going to treat him like he hears and understands us."

I grinned a tight smile at her optimism.

Then she looked at me through squinted eyes and with her head cocked. I knew that meant she wasn't satisfied with my answer. "There's more, isn't there?"

I leaned my head back and signed. "Yes," I said. "There's more. Much more. But I don't think you should worry about it now." I realized immediately that was the wrong thing to say.

"And I think that's something I should decide for myself. Tell me. What are you holding back?"

I refilled our wine glasses and told Bren about finding Z and about his memories that Nemy revealed. "I think he saw your mother the night she was murdered."

Brenda finished the last swallow of her wine and considered what I said for several seconds. "You think Daddy killed her, don't you?"

"I never said that," I protested. "We didn't have any way to tell who killed your mother." I softened my tone. "All I know is someone called a Native American to break into your house the night she died."

She finished my thought. "And that person tried to set him up to cover up their crime." She set her champagne glass down and said with resolution, "Then we have to ask Daddy."

Brenda and I both slept well that night. There was something comforting about lying in bed with our limbs entwined for the first time in more than a week. We got up and dressed and made our way to the patio. The morning air was still comfortably cool. Patsy was sitting by the pool sipping iced coffee and thumbing through the online news. She wore a broad-brimmed, black woven hat and a sheer black short robe over a modest black bikini. The look was quite chic.

"David. Sister!" She rose to greet us. "Join me for breakfast poolside." Patsy raised a finger, and Jesus stepped out from the shadows to take our orders.

"Have you read the news?" she asked pointing to a feed on her tablet. "Nearly a hundred people have gathered to support the Papago Indians, and they're camped out at Archie's worksite."

I looked closer at the news photo. "Isn't that where..."

"Where the office trailer was blown up?" she finished. "That's precisely where it is." Patsy smiled broadly.

Jesus returned with two more coffees and retreated to fetch our food.

"Our father was going to call in the National Guard to have them removed, but I guess he can't do that now," she added. I wasn't sure which side she was supporting.

Brenda changed the subject to interviewing Jack. She mentioned my suggestion to use Nemy to assess his cognitive presence. Patsy was delighted with the idea, especially after she remembered how the doctor had forbidden it.

"So, we should go this morning?" Brenda proposed. That's when I realized I hadn't told her the entire story. She didn't know that by showing my face at the hospital, I could be putting the whole family in danger. I had to think of something quick.

"We can't if your father's doctor is there," I stammered. "He'd have me thrown out."

Patsy's response was instantaneous. "Not if he doesn't know it's you."

Bren and I thought for a moment, and then we smiled.

Patsy enlisted Jesus to put her plan into action. She ordered a wheelchair, a baggy Panama suit, and her makeup kit. Bren helped me dress in the white suit, and Patsy applied the makeup to age me. A wig of wavy white hair completed the disguise. Pretty convincing, I thought, when I looked in the mirror. I'm now Uncle Angus, Jack's older half-brother. The girls hadn't seen their uncle in well over a decade, after the Christmas party when he tried to molest one of the servers in the coat closet. The family settled with the catering company and distanced themselves from Angus after that.

Jesus brought around the limo, put the wheelchair in the trunk, and helped us into our seats. We were headed to Mesa Hospital for a family reunion with brother Jack.

At the hospital, Jesus helped me into the wheelchair and tucked a shawl over my legs. Nemy was concealed in a bag attached to the back of the chair, and Patsy carried my laptop case. Jesus wheeled me to the elevator, and the girls took me to the third floor, where Jack was located. Introductions at the nurses' station were brief, and we got past the trooper stationed at Jack's door by telling him the device in the backpack was my heart monitor. Everyone at the hospital knew the family members by now, so they admitted Angus without a second thought.

Bren wheeled me to the head of the bed, facing Jack. She sat in the only chair in the room, and Patsy perched on the edge of the bed, next to their father. Brenda cautiously removed the headgear from the backpack and slipped it into my jacket pocket. Jack's head was still wrapped in bandages, which made attaching the neurosensors a bit tricky. I stood feebly and leaned over the bed. In a moment of feigned anguish, I hovered close to Angus's brother's face. One by one, I pulled the sensors from my pocket and gently slid them into place under the bandages. The connecting wires ran beneath the bedsheet to the backpack, which Bren had placed between my feet. Patsy held the computer on her lap. She logged onto the hospital's Wi-Fi and scrolled through Facebook posts until everything was set up.

Marc and I had never considered conducting research on a comatose patient, so I wasn't prepared for how to go about it. Various studies have shown that even in a coma, someone can be induced into hypnosis. The technique has been demonstrated to be effective as therapy, and I saw no harm in trying it now. I whispered close to Jack's ear the words I typically used for my trial subjects. I sensed that his breathing eventually slowed slightly, and the heart-rate monitor confirmed my observation. He was in a stable state so no alarms would be set off at the nurses' station.

When everything was set up, I plugged the laptop into the USB port on Nemy's control unit, which was secreted in the backpack. Immediately, images began to appear on the screen. At first, they were jumbled like an abstractionist painting. I repeatedly whispered in Jack's ear the scenes I wanted him to focus on. The image slowly resolved into what the girls recognized as the garden in the backyard of their childhood home. I asked Jack to visualize other scenes from his past that I was familiar with. Patsy giggled while she watched her father walk her down the church aisle at her wedding. Brenda smiled when she saw herself in her high-school prom dress. Both girls gasped silently when images of their mother appeared, and sadness filled their eyes.

Brenda stood and put an arm around her sister's shoulders. Then she leaned in and told Patsy there were more things she wanted to ask their father to remember–things that might be painful, but she needed to learn the truth. Patsy looked bewildered, but she nodded her approval. Brenda placed her other hand on my arm as the cue for me to proceed. I began asking Jack about the night Evelyn died.

Jack's breathing tensed with the first memory. It was of Evelyn, standing in another room of their house, possibly the foyer. Then Jack's view shifted to someone sitting in a leather chair next to a dark-colored desk.

"That's Daddy's study," Bren exclaimed in a whisper.

"And that's...that's Larry," Patsy added.

Suddenly the view was elevated as though someone was raising a camera. Evelyn's face steadily grew larger until it filled the screen.

"He must be walking over to Mother," Patsy observed.

Evelyn Donovan was not an especially pretty woman, but her poise and grace made her a stunning figure. Now, however, she looked worn and angry. She was holding a piece of paper and waving it close to Jack.

"Is that a receipt for something?" Bren wondered.

Patsy responded, "No, I think it's a check."

I asked Jack to concentrate on what was in his wife's hand, and Patsy's observation seemed to be correct. The more Jack focused on the slip of paper, the clearer the numbers became.

"That looks like a lot of numbers," Patsy commented.

The screen now showed Evelyn waving the check in Jack's face, almost striking him with it. We could tell she was shouting something as she grasped the piece of paper as if to tear it. That's when a man's hand appeared in the scene. It was apparently Jack's hand, and it pulled down on Evelyn's right arm.

The image on the screen morphed into a swirl of shapes and dark colors.

"What's happening?" Patsy gasped.

I continued to whisper in Jack's ear, mostly to calm him and to focus his thoughts.

After a few moments, the image resolved back to the face of the girls' mother. It loomed larger as Jack apparently came closer. The background was a pattern of blue paisley.

"That's the foyer carpet," Patsy said.

Around the now-still face, a pool of red was forming.

"Blood!" Brenda screamed.

Instantly the door opened, and the state trooper poked his head in to see what had caused the commotion.

Patsy forced a smile and a little laugh when she saw the officer. "Oh, it's all right," she said. We're showing Daddy some old family videos."

"You realize your father is in a coma, don't you?" the officer replied.

Patsy rose from the bed and walked toward the guard. "And you realize that just because someone is in a coma doesn't mean they can't hear and think and feel, don't you?" Her face grew stern. "This is our father. If you don't mind, we'd like to spend some family time with him." Then she closed the door in the officer's face.

"You don't think Daddy...?" Brenda couldn't bring herself to finish the thought.

"Someone did," Patsy said coldly. "We just always thought it was a burglar."

Throughout the commotion, I tried to keep Jack calm and focused. Working with a comatose subject was new ground for me, and I didn't know how concerned to be.

When we glanced back at the laptop screen again, we could see Evelyn's face full on. The image rocked gently side to side.

"I think he's cradling her in his arms," I said. A tear formed in Brenda's eye.

Patsy wanted to know more. "Find out what he did next," she instructed.

I whispered more suggestions in Jack's ear. Eventually, we saw Larry's face on the screen again. A hand reached for the telephone–Jack's hand. Larry grabbed the receiver and hung up the phone. It seemed that a heated conversation ensued. Larry was pointing, possibly in the direction of the foyer, stabbing vigorously with his finger. He took the slip of paper from Jack's hand, looked at it, and shook his head. Larry's arms reached out, apparently to Jack's shoulders. From the rapid change in perspective, Larry must have been pushing Jack down so he was seated. Larry's left hand reached into his jacket breast pocket and pulled out a pen while his right hand waved the check close to Jack's face. Through Jack's eyes, we could see the check clearly. It was for half a million dollars. Jack's hand turned over the check, and we saw him write his signature on the back. A dark spot formed on the yellow paper. It was a tear.

The view shifted back up to Larry, who lifted the telephone receiver again and dialed a number. He spoke for only a minute and then hung up.

Brenda said, "I think I want to go home, now."

31

☼ ☼ ☼

The two-hour ride back to Archie's estate was mostly silent. Jesus deposited us at the main door and then parked the limo. We moved to the cool, dark confines of the library and took seats around the dark-pine coffee table.

Patsy suddenly took charge of her emotions and our agenda. "Let's get real, here," she began. "Daddy isn't who we always thought he was."

Her sister protested, "He's still the same person. The man who raised us and loved us, and the man I still love." She choked back a sob. "He just did something...something awful."

"You saw it with your own eyes," Patsy said. "He killed our mother."

"But..."

Patsy cut Bren short. "Maybe he didn't mean to, but he did. I don't know if I can forgive him for that. I don't know if I want to."

She clutched Brenda's hands. "He lied to us. He lied to the world."

I wanted to be able to offer a more acceptable alternative, but all I could come up with was reminding the girls that Nemy only shows what someone remembers, not the actual event. Patsy just rolled her eyes. "Do you really think he remembers something worse than what happened?" I admitted that wasn't a likely response for human nature, but it was possible.

Patsy continued reviewing the situation. "Apparently, our mother was about to tear up a check written out to Jack–probably a donation she promised for his reelection campaign."

"Daddy did say at the funeral he was going to continue campaigning to *honor his wife's wishes before she died*." Brenda recalled the funeral, with all the cameras and reporters and interviews. Everyone said that's what propelled Jack to a narrow victory–that and a last-minute infusion of cash.

"Why was Larry there?" Bren wondered. "What does he have to do with this?"

"Obviously, he didn't want Daddy calling for help," Patsy snapped. "At least not until that check was signed."

Brenda tightened her jaw. "It couldn't have been Larry who called for an ambulance. The 911 call came in the morning when the housekeeper found Mother dead on the floor. That means..."

"Instead of calling for help, he called someone else and left Mother to die," Patsy finished the thought.

Brenda fell into her sister's arms, and the two rocked gently with Bren sobbing and Patsy staring resolutely at an unseen spot on the ceiling.

It was then that I realized I knew who Larry had called–Angelo. That's where Z's instructions came from. Despite the enormity of their tragedy, I decided to confide in my wife and her sister.

"I know who it was," I began, and then proceeded to recount the events of the past week. The girls sat silent, as if in shock. There was a look of disbelief on Patsy's face.

"You mean to tell us that this past week you tracked down a potential murderer, were held hostage in his grandmother's trailer, got some crazed Indian out of jail, went on some psychedelic spirit quest, rescued Marc from a kidnapping, and now you're hiding out from the mob?"

When Patsy put it that way, it did sound absurd. I froze, mouth half open, and just nodded.

Brenda looked up at me with concern and admiration in her eyes. She threw her arms around me and said, "I had no idea." Then she held me tight for several minutes. She still had no idea of the unforgivable thing I had done. Our tears mingled on my chest–hers of relief that I was all right and mine of terror that she wouldn't be.

"What do we do next?" I eventually said.

Patsy was composed again. "First, we have to make sure you're safe from the mob–hell, that we're all safe from the mob. I know what Pauly is capable of, and Angelo will carry out his orders no matter how senseless they might seem."

"We're safe here, aren't we?" Brenda said. "You told me Archie was used to pushing back against the mob. He's been doing that for years, right?"'

"Yes, but there's something I didn't tell you." Patsy looked at her sister and then glanced up at me. "I think Archie might have ordered someone to run down Daddy."

Brenda sat back in dismay. "Why? Why would he...?"

"Because of that." Patsy's gaze focused on Sunday's newspaper, which was lying on the coffee table. I opened it and showed the headline for the article exposing Archie's fraudulent dealings. "Arch thinks our father leaked the story."

"If that's true, then we're not safe here either," Brenda said.

"I agree with you," Patsy replied. "And David thinks my darling husband actually set off the explosion to murder his mistress. That's why we have to leave, and soon. I knew Archie would be meeting with his team of lawyers most of today, but he could come back at any minute. We need to go before he returns."

Since my rental car was our least conspicuous vehicle, we asked Jesus to bring the Impala around. Patsy and Bren put together an overnight bag, and we told him I was taking them to the spa for the day. We were a few miles from the DC Ranch community when I pulled into a Target parking lot in North Scottsdale so we could figure out what to do next.

We concluded I couldn't go to my hotel, and we couldn't go back to Archie's estate. That's when Bren thought to ask where I'd been staying. Marc warned me I'd have to face telling my wife I spent the night in Jill's hotel room. Given the seriousness of all the events swirling in our heads, Bren accepted my explanation with only slight suspicion.

We bought some basics at Target–food and drinks so we wouldn't need to stop, and toiletries and a change of clothes for me. We planned to keep a low profile. Patsy thought of some friends she might turn to, but she didn't trust any of them enough not to tell Archie. Then I thought of the one place we could truly be safe. I took out my cell phone and called Sea Horse.

Two hours later we pulled into the Quivira Casino. Sea Horse's valet, Leon, met us in the private garage and escorted us to a suite on the top floor of one of the two resort towers. The furnishings were opulent by my standards, although I'm sure this was nothing special for the Donovans. We were to be casino guests for as long as we needed.

Sea Horse met us in our suite. He seemed accustomed to this sort of intrigue. He instructed Leon to drop off my rental car at Sky Harbor and return with an SUV rented in his name from a different agency. He had me hand my credit card to Leon and tell him what my zip code was so the valet could use my card in Phoenix to fill the tank. Sea Horse also had us disconnect cell service from our phones and turn them off. He said he'd have three prepaid phones delivered to the room for us to use. He also had a laptop brought up so we wouldn't accidentally log on to our personal accounts. We agreed to meet in his apartment later in the day to talk. Before he left, Sea Horse dropped three bundles of twenty-dollar bills on the side table. "This is for pocket money. Just don't use it to break the bank at the roulette table." He laughed at his inside joke.

We ordered a late lunch to be brought up to our suite. While we waited, Patsy commented, "You realize he's not just their security technician, don't you?"

I knew she must be right. With the clout Sea Horse had at the casino and the perks he was able to dole out, he wasn't just a techie geek. "At least that's a big step up from what his grandmother calls him—the casino mechanic."

I flipped open the laptop and logged onto the secure Wi-Fi account Sea Horse directed us to use. "Should I check the news?" I asked.

Patsy and Bren gathered around. Patsy wanted to find out if there was anything about Archie. All I came up with was the exposé published three days ago. Bren asked to check on news about the environment conference. Patsy and I both gave her a questioning look, but I proceeded to browse for related stories. Then I searched for articles about the Russian mob. There was something posted by a financial journal on the second page. "Russian bank purchases majority of Southwest Gas."

"Isn't that one of Archie's companies?" I asked. Patsy nodded.

The article was published late last month. It stated that the Russian bank, headed by a wealthy Soviet-era oligarch, submitted an application to the Federal Trade Commission to purchase a majority interest in the small U.S. energy company. The senior senator from Arizona and head of the Commerce Committee went on record recommending that the deal get scrubbed because of allegations that the bank has ties to the Russian mob.

"That's the senator Daddy is facing in the primaries next spring," Patsy noted.

"None of this feels right," Brenda said.

I decided to check out Larry to see what we could come up with on his background. It turns out that Larry Berman is a fairly common name. With a few refinements to the search, we learned he was a decorated veteran of the Gulf War, where he served as a demolitions expert. Larry graduated from the same university as the girls' youngest uncle, Andrew. Patsy remembered the Christmas Uncle Andy brought Larry home with him on winter break. The family promised to help Larry start his legal career, and he wound up becoming the Donovans' personal lawyer. There didn't seem to be anything newsworthy about him after that, not even a Facebook page.

"I suppose he hasn't needed any other clients since the family retained him and Jack entered public office," Patsy said.

A knock at the door announced lunch had arrived. The bellhop rolled the cart to the center of the dining room and laid out our salads and sandwiches. Three cell phones had been placed on a tray. That reminded me that I needed to let Jill know where I was. She didn't answer, so I left a short message telling her I was OK and lying low.

Shortly before four, there was another knock at the door. Leon had returned to escort us to Sea Horse's apartment.

The space was modest in comparison to our penthouse suite. Sea Horse greeted us barefoot, wearing jeans and a white T-shirt. The TV was on in the living room. I saw scenes from the sit-in at the Southwest Enterprise site. On second look, I realized the broadcast was a live feed. Sea Horse was monitoring the activity there. He explained, "Your brother-in-law was in for the long haul. He had a generator set up at the construction site just to power a portable satellite dish so he could make calls and connect to the Internet." He gestured toward the monitor in the background. "I helped provision the compound when I heard my brother planned to stage a protest–along with my grandmother. It was mostly for her. While I was at Edagith, I set up a monitor feed so I could keep an eye on what's going on."

"Edagith?" Brenda asked.

"That's the tribal name for the plateau where our ancestors are buried," he explained. "It means *ownership*. Ironic, don't you think?"

We found seats in the small living area. Sea Horse took the overstuffed chair and wrapped his bare feet under him while we talked. I started by thanking our host for taking us in.

"You can't thank me for doing what you asked," he said. "You are family now. At least that's what Ga'ga thinks."

I could tell from the looks on the faces of the sisters that they were trying to understand what that meant.

"Didn't he tell you?" Sea Horse continued. "He is the ordained savior of our people." He spat the last words.

I wasn't sure if I should apologize or merely accept the old woman's fantasy. "Look," I said. "I don't know what she's talking about. Besides, I thought that honor went to your brother."

"Z? He's not even good at saving himself. He's family, and I look out for him when I can, but he finds trouble in its burrow sleeping."

"But he decided to stage a protest," I said in Z's defense.

"There are times I think he tries to get arrested. Maybe jail is his safe place."

Sea Horse reached to the table between us and pushed forward a plate of shriveled, brown objects for us to eat. I eyed them suspiciously.

He grinned. "They're dates. Maybe you'd rather have something more–potent."

He continued, "My brother has a good heart, but little sense. You know he has killed five men?" Even Patsy seemed shocked to hear that. "The two men who attacked him in the bar, of course, but there were others. The first when he was only fourteen. It was called an accident, but he spent a year in juvie for it. You think he will lead our people? With what? His bare fists and arrows? This is no longer the nineteenth century. There are other ways to beat the milgahn." Sea Horse looked around his apartment pointedly.

"I need to tell you that you and your brother might be in danger." I thought I was revealing a dark truth, but Sea Horse let out a hearty laugh.

"From Angelo? You think I worry about that snake?"

"Then you know?" I said.

"Of course I know. From the minute he spoke on my brother's phone I knew. It's my job to know."

"You knew Angelo gave the order to burn down the trailer, and you went along with it?" I said incredulously.

Sea Horse glared hard at me and said deliberately. "And I knew if Z refused to do a job for him, it wouldn't go well for my brother." He leaned back in the chair and tossed his head casually. "Pauly and his Milwaukee mob are watopi—maggots that feed off decay. They've been an annoyance for years trying to move in on my cash buffalo, but they know better than to keep trying."

I didn't ask why.

"But I see they have you cowering here in my casino." Sea Horse stood and looked down on me. "Quite the savior."

Patsy spoke up. "You have it all figured out, don't you? I get it. Your people have been lied to and stolen from for hundreds of years, and you found a way to live in both worlds. You resent that your brother didn't sell out the way you did."

I didn't know what stoked her fire, but she seemed outraged by Sea Horse's comments.

"This, coming from you?" Sea Horse growled. "You, born into a world of privilege that you turned your back on to make a life with the fattest worm of all?"

Patsy sat back in her seat. "I see you've done your homework," she said. "And you're absolutely right. I was a stupid kid trying to prove nobody owned me, and now I can't escape from the prison I committed myself to."

"At least you have learned," Sea Horse said almost apologetically. "What about your brother-in-law? What has he learned?" He turned to face me.

"You are said to have *the gift*. If that's true, what would you do with it? Abandon your own people to help? You don't even know who your people are. No, you're Indian like me, living among strangers and pretending you belong–no, pretending you're better because you accept what is expected of you even when it hurts the ones you care about."

I was dumbstruck. It was as though he was looking through my dark flesh into an even darker heart.

I protested, "We all make choices just to survive. That is human and does not respect the color of our skin." The words sounded false even to my ears.

Brenda rose to her feet and pressed a finger into our host's chest. "You're wrong. You think everyone is as jaded as you've become. Well, there are some truly decent people in this world, and David is one of them." She stood behind me and placed her hands on my shoulders. I was afraid to look into her eyes for fear that she might see he was right.

"I need to attend to my casino patrons," Sea Horse huffed. "You are welcome to stay here as my guests until you feel safe enough to return to your lives." He brusquely excused himself and left the room.

Bren was physically shaking. "What nerve," she said and returned to her seat.

Patsy just looked out the window. "He's right, you know. I thought I was rebelling when I married Archie, but I just threw off a gilded collar for an iron shackle." She sipped her drink. "At least I never had to step into the real world."

Bren had a pained expression on her face. "He's gotten to both of you with his hollow talk about sacrifice and honesty. Don't you see? He's trying to make himself feel better about his own self-serving choices."

"Whether he's right or wrong," I said, "we still have the mob after us, and I don't know how to fight back."

Brenda offered, "I'd suggest we talk to Daddy and tell him to make it go away, but he can't help us now, even if I trusted him to."

"The same goes for Archie," Patsy added.

"Maybe Sea Horse is right about one thing," I said. "Maybe we're powerless to defend ourselves, but we might be able to help defend *them*." I pointed to the images of the crowd assembled at Edagith. "We just need a plan."

32

☼ ☼ ☼

We didn't have a plan, but we decided to join the band of protestors. Late the next morning, we found the Escalade Leon picked up for me in Phoenix and set out on the three-hour drive south to Edagith. Bren wore her pizza scarf tied loosely around her neck, and I wore my Antonio's cap to shade my eyes from the afternoon sun. Patsy had the foresight to get two large coolers from the casino and fill them with ice and beverages. We loaded the back of the SUV with bags of food for the protestors since we assumed supplies would be running short.

I stopped in Sells and filled the gas tank. I decided to use the phone Sea Horse had given me to text Marc. FAMILY TRIP TO VISIT GA'GA was all it said. This might be our last chance to let anyone know, I thought.

Patsy commented that the road trip had the feel of a family vacation, even though we were running for our lives. Bren and I laughed if only to ease the tension. I knew Bren loved adventure and she actually enjoyed roughing it. For me, daily life in India was essentially roughing it, and that had been enough. I was surprised, however, to see how well Patsy was adjusting to life on the lam.

The desert heat was relentless, even though evening approached when we arrived in San Miguel, a village a few miles north of our destination. I was glad we had supplies because the town consisted of only a handful of small ranches. Social life, if there was any, probably revolved around the Catholic mission a mile south. Edagith and the U.S.-Mexico border were five miles beyond that, at the tip of the Baboquivari Mountains.

We gradually climbed in elevation and arrived at the Southwest Enterprise construction site late that afternoon. As we approached Edagith, we could make out an armed guard sitting uncomfortably in a lawn chair next to the road. "What if they won't let us in?" I asked.

Patsy leaned over my shoulder. "Don't worry. He'll let us in. Just let me do the talking."

I slowed the Escalade to a stop in front of the guard, who was now standing with his left hand outstretched and his right hand hovering above his sidearm. He motioned for me to roll down the window. "You folks will have to turn around," he ordered pointing back down the road.

Patsy leaned forward, elbowing me toward the console. "No, I'm afraid we won't," she said sweetly, with her chin resting firmly on her folded hands.

"Ma'am, this is a restricted area–private property," the guard replied indifferently.

"You're absolutely right," she purred, "and you're doing a superb job protecting it. I'll make sure to tell my *husband* to give you a bonus. Maybe I can even get him to install an air-conditioned guard house for you," she laughed.

The security guard looked confused. His right hand inched closer to his holster. Patsy extended a business card, which she had already withdrawn from her purse. The guard looked at it carefully and then up at her.

"That's right. I'm *Mrs.* Archibald Trumble." She batted her eyes as she snatched the card from the guard's hand. "Would you like me to call my husband to verify that his wife has arrived to photograph what's happening on his property?" She raised the Nikon camera strapped around her neck. "He'd like to know how much damage these squatters have done and why they're still here," she said coldly.

"Of course not, Mrs. Trumble," the guard stammered. "Your husband has...uh...mentioned you, more than once."

"I'm sure he has," she said as she pressed her finger on the switch to raise the window. I drove the SUV up the crushed-gravel trail that passed for an entrance road. In the valley below us, a tall concrete wall separating the U.S. from Mexico marched across the horizon. It was underscored by a well-worn road probably used by Border Patrol vehicles. To the west, I could make out a small cement block building and beyond it the green of scrub brush growing along the broad wash of what in springtime is the San Pedro River. Remnants of the mangled office trailer stood feebly on the desert plateau that was now littered with chunks of concrete and twisted metal shards. A few construction vehicles were parked near the center of the plateau–a couple of backhoes and a massive bulldozer.

Bren raised the visor and pointed to something overhead. Floating above us was the white dirigible I had seen on the news.

It's smaller than it looked on TV, I thought. I knew the blimp contained surveillance devices, but I hadn't noticed the Jumbotron screens attached to the sides of the balloon. Giant words scrolled across the body of the airship, mostly in Spanish. Then pixelated images filled the screens–pictures of bruised and battered detainees and brown-skinned children looking soulfully at handcuffed parents. The montage included video clips of raids by ICE agents. Loudspeakers blared messages in Spanish and then in English, warning migrants to stay clear of the border.

"It looks like a Vegas billboard," Bren remarked.

"Maybe for the Abu Ghraib Hotel," Patsy added.

A fleet of pickup trucks and SUVs were parked in a large circle ahead of us. The headlights all faced outward. Immediately, a battery of rifles was pointed in our direction. A large man, silhouetted against the setting sun, stepped into the bed of one of the pickup trucks and eyed us suspiciously. I could tell by his size and hulking figure it was Z.

Slowly, I pushed the van door open with my foot, keeping my hands in plain sight while I stepped out of the vehicle. "Z," I shouted. "It's me. David."

The man shaded his eyes from the sun for a better look. I could see him toss his head back and sigh. Then he hopped out of the pickup to the red dirt and gave a casual wave to indicate I could approach the group.

"Why have you come?" he asked when we were within speaking distance.

"I didn't have any place better to be." My attempt to lighten the mood fell flat. "Seriously, the mob is after me. They're after you and your brother too," I said.

Z didn't look overly concerned. "Then this is a good place to be." This time he laughed. "Who did you bring?"

"My wife and her sister are in the SUV," I said waving for them to come out. "We want to stand with you."

A small group of men joined Z to assess the newcomers. They were mostly dark-skinned, but there were a few fair-haired Millennials among them. I speculated that most of them were college drop-outs desperate to be socially relevant.

"We came with supplies, courtesy of your brother." I motioned to a couple of the posse to help unload the groceries.

"I hope you brought sunscreen," Z said. "These college kids are starting to broil." He laughed again.

Z greeted Patsy and Bren while I helped unload the Cadillac. He saw that Patsy had a Nikon draped around her neck. "You have a camera. That's good. We need the world to see what we've done."

I set a large box of sandwiches on one of the ice chests the college boys had carried to the center of the ring of vehicles. Nylon tents and Winnebagos were scattered around the campsite providing small oases of shade where the other protesters were huddled. I realized there were several women among them, Native American and white. Then an old woman emerged from one of the domed tents. It was Ga'ga. She held out her arms for me to come to her and called out, "My astronomer has come home."

I smiled self-consciously and waved Bren and Patsy over to introduce them. "How can we help?" I asked.

"Come. Sit under the watto." She motioned to us to follow her to a canvas tarpaulin stretched over an aluminum frame. Before we sat on the blankets that were spread beneath the heavy canopy, Ga'ga pulled me close and said, "Did you happen to bring tea?" She gestured toward the ice chest. I nodded and strode to the cooler to extract a cold bottle of Snapple while the sisters sat on either side of the tiny woman.

"This is your wife," Ga'ga said, taking Brenda's hand. "She is passionate...for what is right." Then she turned to Patsy and looked deep into her eyes. "This one has a good heart. They are strong, together."

"I know," I said. "They are very strong."

Brenda smiled. "We saw you on the news. You are the strong one."

Ga'ga squeezed her hand. "It is not strength that compels us to act when we have no other choice." She paused. "That is why you are here, isn't it?"

The three of us exchanged sheepish looks and nodded.

The old woman continued, "Sometimes we must be forced to face our destiny."

Z had just walked over to join us. "Is this old woman spouting words of wisdom again?" His tone bordered on disrespect.

"Are you so certain she isn't right?" I was surprised by my own directness.

Z grunted. "Hmm. She flatters you with some mystical blessing, and suddenly you've gone Indian."

I chuckled at the irony of my choosing to *go Indian.* Here I *am* Indian, the only real Indian in the group, and yet I had chosen to be anything but Indian–East or West.

Ga'ga turned to the girls. "My Ba'ali knows. Someday he will accept."

"If you came to help," Z interrupted, "you'll have to do more than sit under a watto talking story. Come, I'll show you what we face."

Z led me up a small rise. We sat on the tailgate of his beat-up Dodge pickup, which served as a lookout near the ridge. North of us, I could make out the cross on the bell tower of the San Miguel Chapel. To the east, we could see a military outpost. Desert-tan camouflage netting was stretched out to conceal a bivouac of olive-drab semi-permanent tents. Humvees surrounded the encampment, and a row of earth movers formed the forward flank.

"The National Guard is staging an attack from the valley. They're waiting for the recruits to play soldier for the weekend."

"That soon?" I said. "That gives us just a couple of days."

"The reporters have all left, and now it's up to the lawyers to tear up the laws that hold back the politicians."

"Will you fight?" I asked.

"We have been fighting all our lives, and for generations before us. We will have to fight, but maybe in ways you don't understand."

I tried to parse what he meant. Then my mind raced to the protests led by Mahatma Gandhi. He fought, and he won. He was a true Indian. I am nothing like Gandhi.

I considered the life of the stern, husky Native American sitting next to me and what it must have been like. He grew up being told he was destined to lead his people, and he couldn't even get his own life on track.

"How did you get a name like that?" I asked casually.

"Zacchaeus?" he answered, still scanning the horizon. "The missionaries chose it for my parents to christen me. They believed in the milgahn's magic."

The idea of Z having been baptized Catholic surprised me.

"No," I said. "Redman. That must have come from the Anglos as well. You could have adopted your native name like your brother did. Why didn't you do that instead of live with a name that's, well, practically a racial slur?"

Z turned to face me now. "Is that what you see? Just the color of my skin?" His natural scowl deepened as he looked back toward the mountains.

After an uncomfortable period of silence, he continued. "My great-grandfather's name was Hiram Redman. He was a good man. His was a good name. Our father told us to be proud of that name because that is who we are. Not for the color of our skin, but for the blood that runs through our bodies. The blood spilled by so many of our ancestors. The blood that gives us life." He turned toward me again. "You, brother, are a *red man*, too," he said. "We are all *red man*."

I thought about Z's words. *We are all red man.* For Adam, that was literally true. When my brother announced he had changed his name from Adamya, he told me he had researched his new name's meaning. He said he didn't want a name that meant *booger picker* or maybe something worse.

Adam is a Hebrew name. Even in India, we know the Jewish myth about the first human, made of soil and cast out of paradise by a vengeful god. The Hebrew word *adam* literally means *man*. But the name is also derived from *dom*, the Hebrew word for *red* as well as for *blood*.

My brother thought it was cool that his ancient Sanskrit name, Adamya, is also the Jewish word for soil–the stuff God made the first Adam from. "See, my Indian name means *dirt*," Adamya joked. "Not that I can't be a dirty boy!" he said with an evil grin. "I'll be going from a *dirty boy* to a *red-blooded man*," he stated with a touch of pride in his voice.

If Z was right–we are all red man–then Adam was the original red man.

A warm breeze blew across us as I pondered the thought.

A horn honked from our circle of campers and pickup trucks. It was a signal to return. We scrambled down the hill and rushed back to the encampment. The college boys were pointing toward the balloon, which they had taken to calling the Gila Ghost. It floated directly above the border wall, to the south. A gigantic image of the acting governor flashed on the screen. He delivered a message to the hundred-or-so protesters gathered at Edagith, his voice blaring over the loudspeakers.

> This message is directed to the Native Americans camped illegally on property to be appropriated by the U.S. Government and to the agitators who have joined you. Legal proceedings have been cleared by the United States District Court in Phoenix to allow for your removal from this parcel of land by any means necessary. You are impeding development in the interest of national security, and you will be arrested and jailed if you do not vacate the premises by midnight tomorrow, May thirtieth. I have authorized deputizing good Arizona citizens who have volunteered to assist in your removal. You will be advised of your terms of surrender by newly appointed Arizona legal counsel, Larry Berman.

"Larry," Brenda gasped.

"That snake," Patsy hissed.

We stared at the surveillance balloon in disbelief while Jack's lawyer read the court order. Mandatory jail sentences would be meted out to anyone who did not comply. The disputed territory would then be annexed by the United States Government in the interest of national defense and administered by the Department of Homeland Security.

"They can't do that," Brenda shouted.

"They can," Z replied calmly. "They've been doing that for three hundred years."

The last rays of sun wrapped the expansive horizon in a blanket of ochre and gold. Z and I sat cross-legged on the crest of the hill that marked the edge of Edagith, silently absorbing the natural grandeur.

My eyes focused on the Arizona state flag that hung limply from an aluminum pole erected next to the Border Patrol outpost, in the valley west of us. It mimicked the colors of the transcendent sunset. Without looking away, I said, "I saw the flag pattern on the quilt in your bedroom at Ga'ga's. Why would you want to keep a symbol of white oppression on your bed?"

"A symbol can mean many things. The milgahn say it is their state flag–the declaration that they own the land." He looked into my eyes. "No one can own the land. The land decides who it allows to stay and who must leave."

"So, what does the symbol mean to you?"

Z smiled broadly and gazed into the sunset. Then he pointed to the cup of deep orange retreating behind a distant mountain range. "All things return to the center," he said. "See how the rays of light reach out and fade into the darkening blue? They have reached their limit and must return to their source."

"The sun? Is that what we do? Think we're breaking free and always returning to where we started?" I pondered the words of Hindu philosophy I had learned in India. Was Z describing a cosmic form of reincarnation? He made no reply.

The sky grew darker, and the sun's rays formed a golden halo around the shrinking slice of orange.

"For the O'odham, the sun is the gateway to the next life. We grow old, and the paths we strike out on grow shorter until we finally arrive at the center."

"That's the man in the maze? I'itoi?"

Z nodded. "You know the legend?" He seemed surprised.

"Yes, your grandmother told Marc and me about it. She traced the pattern on her laundry basket with her finger."

Z smiled. "There are many paths we may choose, but only one destination."

I thought about the paths I had chosen in my life. The number of times I reached an end and had to start over. But if life is a maze, we never start over. We might have to retreat and set out in a new direction, but we ultimately arrive at the center.

I sighed. "Then why do we struggle so hard? We wind up in the same place anyway."

Z continued his westward gaze. "The destination remains unchanged. We do not." Then he stood and walked back to the campsite alone.

I stayed to see the last rays of sunlight extinguished by the mountain ridge. Had I changed?

A hint of coolness was in the twilight air by the time I returned to the group. Brenda and Patsy were sitting on either side of Ga'ga. I could tell the old lady had been imparting her wisdom to them. The girls looked like children sitting at their mother's feet. I thought of how their real mother had been taken from them and wondered how I would react to learning that my father was a murderer. *Murderer*. The word seemed unforgivingly harsh. Yet, I knew the girls still loved their father, even though they might never forgive him. Would Bren be able to forgive me even if she still loved me? Would I find the courage to share with her the path I took even if it was a dead end? Could she accept my retreat and rejoin me on our journey through the maze of our lives?

A burst of laughter broke the evening silence. I saw Ga'ga rock back and forth, one hand covering her mouth and the other clutching her breasts. I could only guess that the girls had told her something embarrassing about me. Their sudden silence when they saw me approach confirmed my suspicion.

"David," Patsy said, "we were just talking about you."

"So I gathered," I replied. "Anything I need to contradict?"

Ga'ga interrupted the polite laughter. "They know."

I pulled up, my lips pursed in disapproval. "Do they? And what is it that they know?" My question came out more like a reproach.

Ga'ga stood. "I need to tend to our socially conscious guests. Their hearts are in the right place, but they don't understand why they are here." With that, she left to attend to the college protesters.

An awkward silence fell over the two sisters and me. I wasn't sure if the title *sisters* seemed more appropriate than thinking of Bren as my wife because of my feelings of guilt, or because I recognized their renewed bond of sisterhood.

"David, is it true?" Bren asked.

"The old woman seems to think you're some kind of medicine man or something," Patsy added.

"Do you think she's right?" Bren looked at me expectantly.

"I think she's seen one too many movies with the wise old Indian theme, and she's playing out the role," I answered, only half joking.

"Peyote? I can't believe you actually tried peyote," Patsy said with admiration in her voice.

"David, you know that could cost you your grant," Bren reprimanded.

I took a deep breath. I realized I'd have to address the issue. "Yes, I participated in a ceremonial peyote ritual."

Patsy leaned forward. "So...?"

"I saw things, alright? Things I didn't expect. It seemed so real, but it wasn't."

"How can you be so sure?" Bren laid down the challenge. She was always the one open to spiritual enlightenment, while I remained rooted in objective reality.

I related the experience I had in the ki. How I saw the old Indian and the children crying for their mothers and the fountain of sparks. Most haunting was the fountain of sparks.

"You studied Jung," Brenda persisted. "What if you were tapping into some collective unconscious?"

"What, like elephants rediscovering ancestral migration routes?" I caught myself snorting at the thought.

"Or rabbits that freeze when the shadow of a hawk passes over, even if they've never seen a bird of prey." Brenda was passionate about nature and its intrinsic capacity for self-preservation.

Patsy brought a sense of reason to the conversation. "We all know the Native Americans have generally been fucked by the

Whites from the day Europeans set foot on this continent. It's no surprise you heard their pleas for justice when you were tripping."

"Yes, I've done plenty of research on psychedelic drugs, but it's not the same as really going there."

I wanted to change the subject. "Now that we're here, what do you think we should do?" I asked.

"Oh," Patsy offered, "maybe get the mob off our backs, then get my husband thrown in jail, wait for Daddy to recover before we press for murder charges, and, oh yeah, get the land back for the old lady. I think that should just about do it."

I let Patsy vent her frustration, but everything she said sounded entirely reasonable.

"Maybe we should focus on the mob thing," Brenda offered.

"That sounds like a good idea to me. What do you think it will take to get them to leave us alone?" My question was directed at Patsy since this was more a part of her world.

"If you're not standing in the way of one of their money laundering schemes or shake-downs, they just need to even the score. Maybe humiliating Marc will satisfy them."

"Marc." His name passed my lips involuntarily. "I almost forgot how much danger he might be in."

Bren interjected. "I still don't understand why you sent him off on his own like that. The two of you have been through so much together."

An uneasy silence followed as I stared at the ground. I heard the soft crush of sand as a pair of worn cowboy boots penetrated my view. Z stood there without speaking and extended a large hand gripping four cold bottles of Heineken that we brought from the casino.

"David told us it was your favorite," Patsy said as she dislodged a bottle suspended from between his fingers.

"Thanks," Z said as he turned over a plastic crate next to Bren and sat. Twilight was giving way to darkness, and we could hear the sound of frogs in the distance.

"We need a plan," Patsy said.

Z gestured toward the ring of trucks and campers facing the encampment perimeter. "We've already gathered the station wagons in a circle." Then he laughed at his appropriation of the movie cliché.

"We could plead for a pardon from the governor," I offered in a feeble attempt at humor.

Bren shot me a look that was either shock or hurt–anything but amusement.

I took her hand and said softly, "That was a stupid thing to say. I'm sorry. I know this is harder for you than anyone."

She returned a tight smile and then stared at our shadows in the sand, cast from the light of the hovering surveillance balloon.

I looked up over my shoulder and paused. "Maybe we could turn their propaganda machine against them," I thought aloud.

Almost in unison, all heads swiveled to follow my gaze.

"The blimp?" Patsy said. "That's brilliant!"

Z mentioned that his cousins had already tried shooting the Gila Ghost out of the sky just to silence the drone of propaganda. He suggested that instead, we substitute O'odham videos supporting the resistance in place of ICE scenes of forced deportations.

Bren just frowned. "There's one detail you haven't considered. How do you propose we get a message on there? Call in a request to wish us *Happy Anniversary*?"

The shocked look was on my face now. How could I have forgotten our second anniversary? I even had something special arranged with the concierge in Amsterdam, since I expected Bren would still be in Europe. "Oh, my god. I didn't...I just...."

The light overhead reflected in Bren's dark eyes, which sparkled with silent laughter. "The look of horror on your face was the best present you could have given me," she said with a broad grin and then pulled me close to her.

Z interrupted. "I might know how," he said.

"How?" I asked, raising my hand before realizing the culturally stereotypical connotation.

This time Z laughed. "You aren't very good at this sensitivity business, are you?" He put his meaty palm on my shoulder. "That's all right, brother. Us Injuns have to stick together." Then Z explained how Sea Horse had tapped into the communications network Archie had set up for the mobile office. "My brother is kind of a genius when it comes to hacking accounts." He stopped short when he saw the expressions on our faces. "He can. I didn't say that he does. But if you get a message for him to display on that floating pollywog, I wager he'll be able to do it."

"What would we say?" Patsy wondered aloud.

"I have an idea about that," I offered. "We let our friend Larry do the talking for us."

"David? Is there something you haven't told me?" Brenda asked. I knew she meant about Larry, but Marc's face immediately came to mind. What made the moment even more uncomfortable was that Marc's help was essential for the plan to work.

I turned to Z. "Can we get calls back to Sea Horse and to Phoenix?"

"As long as the generator your brother-in-law left here is running, yes. My brother is probably watching us on a remote camera right now."

"Yeah, we saw the live video when we were in his apartment," I commented. If we can get a feed to him, we need him to forward it to the Jumbotron overhead."

Z immediately rose to go back to the encampment. "I'll call him to find out what he'd need us to do."

"What are you planning, David?" Brenda asked.

"I'm planning to get Larry to confess over a live broadcast," I said.

"Confess to what exactly?" Patsy said a bit skeptically.

That was one question I didn't have an answer for. "We'll have to let him tell us that, but I expect there will be plenty." I just hoped I was right.

Now I had to contact Marc to see if he could make the impossible happen. My phone showed two bars, so the mobile cell tower must have been doing its job. I promised Brenda and Patsy I'd explain after I made the call.

Since Marc wouldn't recognize my number, I anticipated he'd be hesitant to answer. The phone rang four times before I heard a tentative, "Ya?" It turned out that he and Kelsey were with Jill because they were worried about the hitmen returning. I told him that was good because we'd need all three of them to execute the plan.

It took a while to convince Marc he could make this work. Then I talked with Jill and explained what she had to do. She sounded eager to be involved. Jill said the producer she was working with at the local TV station offered to let her use the KPZY broadcast booth after hours any evening she wanted to run with a story.

We agreed to coordinate our efforts for ten o'clock the next night. That would provide enough time for Sea Horse to hack into the broadcast system and Marc and Jill to arrange what they needed to do.

"What was that all about?" Patsy asked.

Her sister offered to explain. "Well, it sounds like your brilliant brother-in-law plans to kidnap a state official, drug him, and force a confession out of him to broadcast over a hacked government agency network." She turned to me. "Does that sound about right?"

I had to admit her assessment of the scheme was basically correct, and it sounded insane when reduced to a single sentence. But it was the only scheme we had to work with.

Z returned and told us about his call to Sea Horse. "He says we're all crazy...and he's willing to help."

We sat in a circle and mapped our plan of attack in the sand.

Sea Horse would let us know when he had a link with the Border Patrol surveillance computer. He assured Z he could hack in by the next evening. Jill was going to call Larry and tell him to meet with her at the local TV station so he could respond to a bombshell report she would claim was ready for broadcast. Marc would get Kelsey to procure samples of the experimental truth serum drug cyclophaxolone.

"So," Bren summarized, "we get Larry to confess his crimes on live TV. How exactly is that going to help us?"

I wasn't sure of the answer to that either. I just sensed that he needed to incriminate himself to set things right.

Ga'ga approached us carrying a round grass basket piled with sandwiches and drinks. Z just nodded and reached out to take the catered meal.

"You need to eat. Then sleep," she said leaving as silently as she arrived.

We all agreed and soon turned in for the night.

34

☼ ☼ ☼

Bren and Patsy spent the night stretched out in the back of the Escalade while I tried to find a comfortable position reclined in the passenger seat. The refreshing night air and the steady drone of crickets and frogs made it possible for us to get some rest. I woke up when the first rays of sunlight crept over the dashboard. The air smelled of coffee and roasted meat.

I left the vehicle as quietly as I could, trying not to wake the girls, and joined the small crowd gathering around the Coleman stove being used to fry up a kind of beef-jerky-and-eggs morning meal.

Z handed me a paper cup filled with strong coffee. He acknowledged my presence with more of a grunt than a greeting. "We need to get to work," he said. I nodded in agreement.

Z gestured to his grandmother, who was spooning the breakfast hash onto a plate for one of the college boys. "She wants to talk to you," he said. "Alone." Then he left to inspect the small cache of weapons stored in the back of his pickup.

From behind the cook stove, Ga'ga looked deep into my eyes and gestured toward the watto as she set down the spoon. I followed her to the colorful blankets laid out on the sand. She sat facing the sunrise and tapped the ground for me to join her. The horizontal rays of sunlight concealed the deep furrows in her face. At that moment, I saw the strength and determination of a much younger woman. I knelt beside her.

"War is coming," she said.

"War? With the vigilantes?"

Ga'ga looked deep into my eyes. "You know," she said. "You know." She placed her hand on my shoulder as she stood and returned to the cook stove.

That old woman is just crazy, I thought. That or trying to live up to the stereotype. "You know," she says like I'm in on some cosmic conspiracy. But I don't even know shit about my own life, let alone the future of the world. *You know*–ha.

I got up to check on the girls. As I approached the Escalade, images of sparks flashed through my mind. Vermillion and gold arcs slowly sketched across the sky. Just like the sunset, I thought, but these were not the tranquil colors mimicked in the flag; they were the colors of blood and bile–terrifying and tragic. Could the old lady be right? Did I know? I only had a sensation from the vision in the sweat lodge, but it had frightened me, and I still wasn't sure why. I felt compelled to learn more, but how? The vision, I thought. I needed to return to the experience that shook me to my core that afternoon. I needed to resume the trance. There was no peyote for me to resort to–at least none that I knew of, but the mystical Hindu teachings I was raised with could provide another path to the same destination. Was this the center

I needed to return to? Was this the path to I'itoi? I had to find out.

Instead of going back to the SUV, I pressed my cap down on my head and climbed the rise to the spot where Z and I watched last night's sunset. The morning was already turning warm, and I stripped off the T-shirt I slept in. The early sun warmed my back as I sat and stared into the fading gray of the horizon. From my religious upbringing and research in neuroscience, I had become convinced that the line between meditation and hypnosis is a thin one. I had practiced self-hypnosis for my research. Maybe I could use that to recreate a trancelike experience. Maybe I could reimagine the sparks to understand their meaning. War? What if Ga'ga was right? I don't believe in mystical events, but I am open to the possibility that the human mind has an extraordinary capacity for intuiting possible scenarios—processing a multitude of seemingly unrelated data and merging that into a storyline with calculable probability.

Calculable. What a geek word. Adam would make fun of me when I used words like that. He said they were just camouflage for being a dumbass. I suppose he was right. How can probability be calculable? Something either happens or it doesn't. Probability can only be measured after an event has happened—or not. It has no predictive value.

My thoughts began to merge with the gray horizon as I slipped into a state of semi-consciousness. I was focused now on the question I was trying to answer. What was the meaning of the trails of sparks? If my intuitive mind had constructed the image once, the same neuropathways must still be present to arrive at the same conclusion—the same destination, but this time I could seek a different path to get there.

I felt myself slipping deeper into oneness with—with something. Something I had never been able to identify rationally. Cultures have described this meditative state as a trance, an out-of-body experience, an astral plane, or just tripping. Whatever these visions shared by humanity throughout time might be, I never found a satisfactory explanation for what I had personally experienced, and that admission of ignorance disturbed me.

I sensed the moment my rational thought gave way to the altered state I was seeking. I could see in the distance the sparks arcing through the sky. The faces of the old man and the crying mothers and the children reappeared just as before. I followed my pre-hypnotic suggestion to approach these apparitions to explore their meaning more fully. If my mind had created them from the collective of my experience, I would be able to penetrate deeper into the thoughts that produced them.

I stepped into the stream of thought that I believed would carry me to the vision of my spirit quest. The images reappeared, but they remained silent. I could only recreate the memory of the vision—not the vision itself. I imagined myself pounding on closed doors and getting no answer. A sense of deep sadness overwhelmed me, and I forced myself to return to consciousness. The old woman was wrong, I did *not* know.

After I returned to full awareness, I could feel the naturally brown skin of my shoulders turning pink, and I pulled my T-shirt back on. When I reached the Escalade, I discovered that the girls had already left. I found them seated with Ga'ga and Z near the cook stove. They each had a plate of hash and were sipping coffee under the watto.

"There you are," Bren exclaimed. "We thought you might have headed up a scouting party."

"Something like that," I replied.

"Did you find what you were searching for?" Ga'ga asked.

I kicked at the sand and shook my head. An expression of sadness consumed the old woman's face, and she stood and returned to her pup tent.

Z grunted. "More spirit crap?" I knew he could see the answer in my pained expression.

"Maybe we can concentrate on doing something other than just talk," he said. "My brother needs access to the terminal they use to communicate with the balloon."

Patsy spoke up, "I thought that's what *he* was supposed to be doing."

Z returned a harsh look. "He can break into their network, but not until someone breaks into their guard station."

"We can't do that!" I gasped. "That's a federal offense. He can't be serious."

"He's serious. But *we* won't be breaking in—I will." Z got up to leave. He turned halfway to face us and added, "You can cover me, or you can talk to spirits with my grandmother."

35

☼ ☼ ☼

I called Marc for a status on his and Jill's parts in our scheme. Jill was right–Larry was eager to meet with her to find out what dirt on him she was planning to release. He agreed to show up at the KPZY station at nine thirty that evening. Local broadcasts would be over then, and the studio would be empty. Kelsey managed to crib the truth serum and even offered to help administer the drug. They would be ready for a 10:00 p.m. broadcast. At least that was the plan.

Z organized a raiding party of O'odham braves who had proven their expertise in traditional combat. Most of them had been champions in the annual Wapkial Ha'tas festival. The tribe keeps the traditional arts of horsemanship and combat alive to honor himdag. Now, however, these champions intended to employ their skills in real battle. Z insisted that only traditional weapons would be used in the raid. His reasoned that if the band of raiders were caught, they'd be more likely to generate public support this way. He was probably correct about that, and he was almost certainly right that they would be caught.

By noon, a few dozen hastily deputized militiamen had assembled in the valley west of us, and more were arriving in a steady stream. This redneck army was attempting to secure the perimeter of our stronghold, leaving the tribal defenders literally with their backs against the wall–the wall Archie had built to keep the immigrants out, which now served to keep the rightful inhabitants in.

From the rise to the east, we could see what looked like hundreds of people gathered in a tent city on the other side of the border. Z told us they were mostly O'odham separated from family members when the border divided their nation in two. Until the wall was constructed, tribe members could move freely from the Mexican side to the U.S. and back, but now families were permanently divided. There were also many Mexicans hoping for an opportunity to migrate to the U.S. for work or to join family members, either legally or otherwise.

The U.S. Border Patrol had ceased their rounds along the stretch of contested land soon after the uprising began partly to protect their agents but more to forestall a public relations incident. Their outpost across the valley was also minimally staffed, reportedly to reduce tension. All that remained on duty were two guards to maintain the surveillance balloon and the steady stream of propaganda it spewed out–a situation Z planned to exploit to gain access to the communications server they used.

The National Guard hadn't mobilized yet, but supplies were already arriving to fortify their encampment.

I borrowed the pair of binoculars one of the college boys brought with him and climbed into the bed of Z's pickup. I pushed the brim of my cap back and pressed the spyglasses to my eyes. From there I could distinguish the faces in the valley below. On the Mexican side of the wall, children played soccer and mothers held infants in their arms. On the American side, all the faces seemed to look similar. They were nearly all men approaching middle age, mostly heavy set, and they were of obvious European descent. Then I focused on the face of a man sitting on the hood of a white F-150 pickup. "That's Ted," I exclaimed.

Patsy, who was standing near the tailgate, looked up. "Who?" she asked. "Not the Ted you interviewed."

I nodded without looking away from the scene. Patsy jumped into the truck bed and pulled the binoculars from my hands. She peered intently into the crowd of vigilantes.

"There's a dozen of them–maybe more," she said.

"Who?" I asked.

"Archie's men. Most of those *deputies* work for his trucking firm. He must have planted them there to make sure he keeps control of the property."

We returned to the camp stove for hot coffee before we separated into smaller groups to prepare for the impending invasion. We could only hope that we would be the ones to attack first.

Z worked with the braves most of the day, honing their combat skills and rehearsing their battle plan. At dusk, they would circle around the back of the outpost. Z was confident this part would go smoothly because some of these men had been running this route undetected for years to smuggle relatives and contraband into Tucson and north. The scouts were familiar with the guards' daily routine, and the raiding party would attack at nine thirty that evening, just after the night crew settled in. The rest of us, observing from the ridge, were to create a diversion that would draw out one of the guards.

The braves knew from experience that firing their rifles into the air triggered an alarm from the surveillance balloon, and one guard would emerge from the shack to visually inspect the Gila Ghost. The government agents never seemed concerned since the blimp was suspended at an altitude high enough that the likelihood of a bullet reaching it was low, and even if one did, damage to the skin could easily be patched. The raiders would rush the building when the guard reentered. Once inside, they planned to hold the guards hostage and take control of the network server. Sea Horse briefed Z on what he would need to do for him to hack in. They would have about half an hour before Jill would be ready to broadcast Larry's confession–if he confessed.

I stood staring at the horizon when Bren placed her hand on my shoulder. "I know how hard this has been on you," she said gently.

"Me? What about you and Patsy? With Archie and your father–everything you believed in changing."

"But I can see the stress of this week weighing on you. Something isn't right." She looked away for a moment. "Did something happen between you and Marc?"

My body stiffened. "How...how did you know?" I sensed the same fear I felt as the sparks arced through the sky. I wanted to tell her when the time was right. I wanted to be able to confess what I had done, not have her discover my infidelity on her own.

"You and Marc have been more than colleagues from the day you two met. I understand."

"You do?" Could this actually be happening–the moment I had been dreading resolved so easily? Suspicion now replaced my fear.

"Of course I do," she laughed. "I understand how boys have to have a best friend. You pretend Marc annoys you with his California-blond swagger, but you didn't have a best friend when we moved here, and that's what he's become for you." She smiled. "I'm right, aren't I?"

I just stood there dumbfounded.

"Did you two have a fight? I can see it in your eyes every time you mention his name."

A fight? Is that what she thought we had? I knew I should have been relieved, but I was more disappointed that she didn't know. I was prepared for the pain of exorcising this demon that haunted me. Now I had to name it and hide it away even deeper in my soul.

I wrapped my arms around my wife and held her close. "I love you," was all I said.

We returned to the watto to find shade. Patsy was taking photographs of the camp and each of the protestors. She joked about winning a Pulitzer.

Z saw me and came over. "We must prepare," he said. Then he looked at Bren. "You, go help the women mix war paint."

She smiled broadly at the large man. "You realize that's wrong on so many levels, don't you?" Then she laughed and joined Ga'ga and the other *squaws*.

Z marched us back to our observation point. Morning shadows gathered around our feet. A light breeze lifted the flag gently from the silver pole next to the Border Patrol outpost.

"What do we need to prepare?" I asked.

Z continued to gaze into the distance and tapped his chest. "The spirit."

"I thought you didn't believe in all that *spirit crap*."

Z's dark eyes shifted in my direction. "Sit," he commanded.

I settled onto the still-cool sand in Vajrasana position. It occurred to me how difficult it was to separate the traditions of my Hindu upbringing–my own himdag–from the most basic of actions such as sitting. Ironically, Z had assumed the same position.

His voice sounded like stream water flowing over pebbles when he spoke. "I did not say I don't believe in the spirits. I simply doubt they believe in us."

I pondered his observation for a moment. "That sounds like something your grandmother would say," I quipped. Z didn't smile.

"You are curious about our myth of I'itoi," he began. "The spirit hides for a reason. Maybe he mocks us, making us waste our lives searching for him. Then what? We all die. We come to the same destination in the end."

A thin cloud drifted past the morning sun as he spoke. The sadness in Z's voice was palpable. I let him continue with his thoughts.

"My Ga'ga believes the spirits watch over us." He turned to me. "If they are watching, they are laughing. We make the same mistakes. We feel the same pain over and over. It makes no difference."

I reflected on the Hindu teachings I was raised with. Z shared the same sense of inevitability–the endless cycles of repetition I had strived to divorce myself from.

He continued. "My brother believes in the power of knowledge, much like you. He's a modern, rational Indian." Z smirked. "He is a brilliant man who can do anything he sets his mind to." Z closed his eyes for a moment. "Sometimes I wish I could view the world through his eyes."

We sat in silence as we watched a roadrunner chase down a lizard.

"I had a brother," I said. Z did not respond. "I was the rational one and he–he was the fatalist."

Z spoke without looking away from the horizon. "You loved your brother, as I love mine."

"Yes," I said. "He died, and I couldn't save him."

Now Z looked into my eyes. "Can we save anyone?"

I thought about his words. "I could have tried," I said. "I should have tried." I felt a tear roll down my cheek.

"My brother has tried to save me," Z said. "Save me from what he calls my *self-destructive behaviors.* He tries to pull me into his modern world, and Ga'ga tries to bind me to the past."

I felt that he was talking about me–stuck between two worlds, not committed to either one. Wandering aimlessly through the maze, turning randomly at each dead end.

"The milgahn came and taught my people about redemption. It is important for them to find a path to absolve them of the evil they do."

"Yes," I agreed. "They are confident in their own righteousness. Maybe we all are."

"Your brother... He took his life?"

"Yes. He shot himself. He couldn't be the man everyone expected him to be. The man he knew I expected him to be." Another tear ran down my cheek. "The thought haunts me every day."

Z looked away and swallowed hard. "Only your memory haunts you if you believe he didn't love you. Maybe that memory seeks to offer you a path to your own redemption."

I nodded as I considered Z's words. Was I torturing myself to feel worthy of forgiveness? Would Adam have wanted that? I knew the answer, and for a moment it comforted me.

"What about the memory of all the suffering your people have gone through? Do you ever feel guilty for that?" I asked.

"Guilt is an illusion of the milgahn. It lets them substitute how they feel for what they do. A man cannot change the past–only the future. That is why we are here today, to change the future."

I realized then what Z meant by preparing our spirits. We were facing battle–maybe death. What if our spirits carry the pain of unresolved guilt with us when we die? I knew Adam would have forgiven me. It was arrogant for me to even think I was responsible for what he did. He would only have blamed me for believing I was. My sense of guilt was just using self-pity as a path to redemption. It was *my* spirit that haunted me, not his. I felt Z's arm drape across my shoulders as he pulled me close to him, and we sat in silence watching buzzards circle overhead.

"I am ready now," Z said abruptly, pulling me up as he stood. "It's time for battle."

36

The day passed quickly. A stockpile of traditional combat gear was assembled, mostly by the women in the camp. The members of the raiding party spent as much time preparing their battledress as they did practicing their skills. That made me think of Adam and when he got me to play *Call of Duty* with him. We put as much effort into outfitting our characters as we did playing the game. Was this just a game to these men? Did they realize they could be sent to prison or even killed? Did they even care?

I talked to Jill, and everything was ready in Phoenix for the interrogation. She and Marc were probably in more danger than we were on the battle line, I thought.

Z and his nine O'odham volunteers prepared for the raid on the Border Patrol outpost. The men were in their twenties or early thirties except for Brown Eagle, a repeat Wapkial Ha'tas champion in his late forties. They all went by their native names—

Cloud Bow, Running Wind, even Rat Skin, and they were dressed in traditional war-party garb. That consisted principally of a buckskin loincloth, laced sandals, and elaborately beaded neck gear. Those without natural tattoos had painted colorful markings on their cheeks or across their noses. Despite their attempts to look ferocious, few of them failed to apply a liberal coat of sunscreen since most of these *braves* were not accustomed to exposing their bodies to the desert sun. The women were finishing the last of the battle headdresses. These were mostly simple knots of feathers–mountain jay for stealth, owl and hawk for clear vision, and eagle for swiftness. Tufts of mountain lion and coyote fur were added to impart their prowess of strength and cunning. Each man would bind his headpiece above his left ear before setting out on the raid. Until then, they practiced the arts of their ancestors.

After an early lunch of quail stew, the group assembled under the shade of the watto, which served as the ceremonial meeting place. Ga'ga recited the legend of Se'he, or Elder Brother as he is better known today–the same I'itoi secreted at the center of life's maze. She held the calendar stick as she retold the tales of how he was created as the defender of humankind and how he claimed the title of Elder Brother for himself. But humanity rejected him, and Se'he sought the destruction of his creation.

Ga'ga sang the song of deliverance, and the raiders danced in a circle to the beat of the basket drums and rattles that played a steady rhythm.

It was after noon before the celebration ended. Exhilaration and anxiety mingled with the heavy scent of sweat and suntan lotion. The braves collected their headdresses and weapons of war–either bow and arrows or shield and club–and proceeded to find a spot for the smudging ceremony. Each man took a spray of creosote leaves bundled by the women and found a rock where he could privately offer up the smoke of the burning leaves as an oblation to the spirits of his ancestors. Each warrior was to place the bundle of twigs on his chosen alter, speak a prayer of blessing, and light the dry leaves. A strong-smelling smoke rose from different parts of the encampment as the offerings were consumed by flames. The warriors used the knot of feathers to wave the gray smoke across their bodies and over their weapons to invoke the powers of the spirits. Afterward, the braves sought out private places of solitude for reflection and purification. There, they would remain until dusk.

Our phone calls to the outside world were few and brief, but Sea Horse and Marc and Jill were prepared for our offensive.

The gathering militia, which now included an assortment of redneck ranchers and wannabe cowboys, had grown to several dozen deputized volunteers. Many had arrived from neighboring states, and a few even flew in from across the country for the opportunity to put down the Pima Revolt, as the media had dubbed the protest. The phrase harkened back to an eighteenth-century rebellion of the same name, which resulted in the Spanish expelling the Jesuit missionaries from the colonial territories for inflaming the uprising.

As the sun slipped behind Baboquivari Mountain, the myth of I'itoi came to my mind. I found it ironic that the mountain home of Elder Brother had been excluded from the Tohono O'odham Nation's boundaries. I'itoi's lair is the most sacred site for these modest people, and it is no longer theirs. Each evening, the sun returns to its resting place, now beyond the borders of the O'odham. Is it possible to deny anyone the opportunity to look back and consider the maze of their life, or do the obstacles we face merely strengthen our resolve to do so?

The Gila Ghost broadcast a steady stream of anti-immigrant propaganda. Intermixed with the repeated clips of ICE raids and deportations were newly recorded messages directed at the dissenters. A clock was displayed from time to time, counting down the hours until the deadline for voluntary evacuation. By this time tomorrow, a monotone voice announced, National Guard troops would be staged for a direct assault on our camp.

After a while, no one paid much attention to the scrolling billboard on the side of the balloon. That changed with the announcement that everyone on the occupied land would be required to pass through a makeshift gate for processing after their surrender to the authorities. To ensure none of the protesters would attempt to evade prosecution, remote unmanned rovers had been deployed overnight to embed sensors around the plateau. Anyone passing within two yards of one of these sensors would trigger an alarm and dispatch an aerial drone to *apprehend* them.

"Apprehend?" I remarked to some college students standing near me.

Nathan, one of the few African-American protesters, who had served in Afghanistan explained, "That means they'll hunt you down and then blow you away."

Bren gasped. "They can't do that...can they?"

Patsy took her hand. "I wouldn't chance it. I've seen them do worse."

"What about the raiding party?" I said. "They have to set out soon if Z is going to take the guard station."

"And Marc and Jill. What will they do when Larry shows up and there's no way to broadcast his confession?" Brenda asked. "If he's as dangerous as you seem to think he is, they could be..."

I closed my eyes and turned my face skyward. "I don't know."

The braves were huddled around Z now, considering their options. After what sounded like an intense argument, Z walked toward us deliberately. "I don't think we can get past the electronic sentries," he said somberly. "We might be trapped here."

Ga'ga, who was standing on the ridge, could see the graveness in her Ba'ali's face. She came over and looked at me. "You know," she said. "You know."

I snapped, "You keep saying that, but I *don't* know. I don't know what to do or how to help. All I know is that we're stuck here, and my friends could be in danger."

Z turned to his grandmother. "I love you, Ga'ga, but your magic is of no help to us now." He turned angrily and started to walk away. After a few paces, he looked back and spat, "It never has been." Then he stormed off to sit beneath the watto.

"David," Bren implored, "can't you think of anything?"

Now I was trapped. Everyone seemed to be looking to me to find a way out of this. I felt like the badger being backed into its hole. What was worse, I knew I was partly responsible for things getting this far.

I shook my head. "There's nothing we can do. Even their best tracker can't get past the sensors."

I walked to the ridge alone and watched as the vigilantes seemed to be setting up for a massive tailgate party. The air was festive and terrifying. A small breeze brushed over the sand at my feet. It was as though a voice was speaking to me–not the disembodied voice of conscience or self-reflection. It was a specific voice. A familiar voice. Jill's voice. I heard her repeat the words she spoke at the Strathmore, "A network of tunnels was built under that section of the wall."

That was it! My memory had rummaged through my unconscious and found a possible solution. The raiding party wouldn't pass over the ring of sensors–they'd pass *under* it.

I rushed to the watto and dropped to my knees facing Z. "Go under," I said breathlessly.

He glared at me and then turned his head. The commotion attracted others to gather around us. Bren pushed her way to my side.

"David, what is it?" she said. "Are you all right?"

I looked up at her, beaming. "We might all be all right," I said.

I called the rest of the braves to join us and explained that Archie had built a tunnel under the wall–a tunnel that ran deep into the interior of Arizona to evade detection.

The band of marauders immediately realized how this could work to their advantage.

Patsy spoke up. "I don't doubt it," she said. "That would explain a lot about why Archie was so concerned about holding onto this property."

One of the college boys asked, "How do we find the entrance to a tunnel that was designed to evade detection?"

Looks were exchanged among the group, but no one had an answer. Not until Brown Eagle, the eldest of the party stepped forward and said, "I might know."

Brown Eagle had worked with the grading crew that initially cleared the land for Southwest Enterprise, a fact he would have preferred not to disclose. "Come with me," he directed. He guided us past the bulldozer and backhoes Archie's crew left behind. We made our way east to an overlook about a hundred yards from the wall. The Border Patrol road was well below us, tucked between the fence and the sheer cliff we were standing on.

Brown Eagle swept his arm across the horizon. "My foreman had me build up this mound instead of leveling it off like we did in other places along the road. I thought that was strange, but I did what he told me."

"That means we could be standing over the tunnel right now," a college boy exclaimed.

"There's one way to find out," Z said, and he started to lead the team of braves down the steep slope.

"Wait," said Nathan. "I've done this sort of thing before when we searched for Bin Laden. "Let me come with you."

The braves exchanged looks. They had planned on including only O'odham in their party. Z didn't hesitate, however. "Come. We might need you," he said.

The eleven men, most wearing only thin sandals and a loincloth, made their way down the sheer rock face. The cliff was far enough from the fence that it would be out of sensor range, and the angle of the ridge provided cover from observation by the Gila Ghost.

"Arch sure picked a good spot to avoid detection," Patsy remarked.

After about twenty minutes of searching around the boulders that littered the base of the cliff, we saw someone waving his arms. It was Nathan. He found the entrance to Archie's secret tunnel. We might have a chance after all.

37

☼ ☼ ☼

We were running out of time for the 10:00 p.m. broadcast. The O'odham warriors had discovered the entrance to the tunnel, but they didn't know where it would end. From Jill's description, that could be a mile or more from the border. Z was confident they could quickly assess the terrain once they came out of the tunnel and then find their way to the guard shack, but they wouldn't know until they emerged how long it would take to reach their target. Fortunately, now the band didn't have to wait for sundown to head out. Ga'ga had the college boys run back to the camp to collect the braves' battle gear so it would be ready for them as soon as they made it back up the cliff. That would save some time.

It was still nearly dusk before the raiding party was outfitted and ready to head back down the escarpment to make their way to their objective. Z had left one of the braves in the tunnel to conduct reconnaissance. The remaining ten warriors, now bearing bows or clubs, climbed down the sheer wall of rock to the cave entrance and then disappeared into the crevasse that concealed the opening.

The rest of us returned to the campsite while it was still light enough to see the path. Patsy paused when we passed the earth moving equipment. "I always wanted to drive one of those," she joked.

"Seriously?" Bren laughed. "I still remember the stories about when you rode Daddy's golf cart into the swimming pool."

"I was six," came her sister's only excuse.

I was glad the girls were together for this...this ordeal. At least they had each other as the world seemed to collapse around us.

When we got back to the camp, Ga'ga took most of the women and a few of the college boys with her to gather firewood for the evening. The rest of us waited anxiously on the ridge. We had no way of knowing what was happening until the raiders captured the outpost–*if* they captured the outpost.

Our objective was to create a distraction at precisely twenty-one thirty hours–terminology the two Army veterans in the band insisted on. That would give Sea Horse half an hour to hack into the Border Patrol server. It also meant Z and the members of the raiding party he took with him had to hold off any counter-offensive for that long. From the valley, headlights of the vehicles that faced us began to blink on as the militia attempted to contain our makeshift tribe. Their lights only served to distract them from discovering the attack that was already underway and literally underfoot.

Illumination from the surveillance balloon was a more significant concern. The scouts knew that before the sensors were planted to confine the Edagith protesters, motion detectors had been concentrated only along the border. If the raiding party emerged from the tunnel north of the new perimeter, the risk of their discovery was negligible. The flickering glow from the Jumbotron posed a greater threat of exposing their movement across the open stretches, which would probably be sparsely protected by mesquite and creosote shrubs. Still, the braves were confident they could avoid detection, at least until they were ready to attack. We prayed they were right.

The drone of propaganda from the Gila Ghost was routinely interrupted by diatribes hurled toward our camp by megaphone-wielding vigilantes. In return, the O'odham used their own bullhorn to fill the evening air with tribal songs and recitations. This verbal exchange little resembled discourse, but it was a distraction of sorts. Not the distraction we had planned, but perhaps enough to serve as cover for the advancing warriors.

The Native Americans and their supporters who remained in our camp prepared to create the scheduled diversion. It was nearly nine when Ga'ga returned to the ridge with the group she led to scrounge for firewood. Their arms were laden with twigs and small branches and even dried-out saguaro cactus skeletons. They deposited their loads on a pyre and ignited a blaze that could easily be seen from the valley.

The assembly held hands and sang songs around the roaring fire, mostly to annoy the militia. Half an hour later, three men climbed into the bed of the surveillance pickup truck, armed with rifles to fire into the night sky. At the stroke of twenty-one thirty, a volley of shots rang out. It was quickly answered by gunfire from the Arizona deputies caught up in the thrill of an imminent kill. This was the signal for Z's party to prepare to attack, although we had no idea if they had reached their objective.

On cue, one of the Border Patrol guards stepped out from the fortified hut. We could see the slash of light that emanated through the portal where the door was left ajar. We knew the agent would use night-vision glasses to scour the horizon and examine the surveillance balloon, which would take just a few minutes. When he returned from his inspection, the band of marauders planned to overpower the guards and commandeer the outpost. All we could do is wait and hope.

I concentrated the binoculars on the small block building. A minute later I could see the slice of light vanish. The door had closed. We just didn't know yet which side Z was on. We waited nearly breathless for a phone call. Only silence followed. None of the vigilantes noticed the altercation we assumed had taken place, and they continued hurling racial slurs in our direction. I encouraged one of the college boys to pick up the megaphone and say something to distract our harassers. Reluctantly, he climbed into the bed of the truck and started to recite the Declaration of Independence. Who else would have memorized the Declaration of Independence? I thought, but I was glad he had.

When he reached the part about "whenever any form of Government becomes destructive of these ends, it is the right of the people to alter or to abolish it and to institute new government," my cell phone rang. Z called from the Border Patrol's phone to say he was in position. Two braves were with him, including Nathan, who turned out to have been a signals officer in the Army. The rest of the war party members were returning to camp via the tunnel. As far as Z knew, the guards had surrendered before they could raise an alarm, which gave the defenders some time. He was going to force the agents staffing the broadcast system to leave an open channel for Sea Horse to hack into. I used Patsy's phone to talk with Z's brother and relay messages between the two of them. We hoped that diverting our conversations this way would delay any government attempts to disrupt our communications.

With the forced cooperation of the attending border guards, Sea Horse established a direct link with the Gila Ghost. They were ready to stream whatever it was Jill and Marc could provide from the KPZY broadcast booth. It was up to them now to supply the damning confession we anticipated Larry would provide.

We waited for Marc's call. The scheduled time of 10:00 p.m. passed. "I'll give them ten minutes," I said to no one in particular. "If we don't hear from Marc by then, I'll call to see what's gone wrong." I realized we didn't have a backup plan.

The minutes dragged by, and we began to worry about what would become of Z and his squad. The sound of an approaching helicopter faintly penetrated the night air. They knew! An alert must have gone out silently. It would be only minutes before reinforcements arrived.

I was about to call Marc when my phone rang. "We're in!" he nearly shouted. "And *he's* talking. Patch us through."

Sea Horse quickly established the link. The images of captured detainees on the Gila Ghost blinked off, and the face of a red-haired woman filled the display.

"This is Jill Jackson, reporting live from Phoenix, Arizona with this breaking report. I am interviewing Larry Berman, recently appointed legal counsel for the State of Arizona." The camera then focused on the distinguished but sedated figure of the Donovan family lawyer." Mr. Berman, say hello to the millions of viewers watching right now."

"Hello," Larry responded in a monotone voice.

The camera swung awkwardly back to Jill. "You might notice that Mr. Berman is outfitted with neuroreceptors attached to a skull cap and he has been hypnotized. That in addition to being under the influence of an experimental truth serum. I realize these are extraordinary circumstances for an interview," she leaned into the camera, "but Mr. Berman has an extraordinary story to tell."

"We are conducting this interview with the aid of a breakthrough technology that allows us to see images of the events Mr. Berman will recall for us. Here to explain more about how this works, we have Marcus Anders, research assistant at Fulton University for the Mnemosyne project."

Jill's hands reached out to aim the camera at Marc. He looked uncharacteristically nervous.

"Hi." Marc raised his hand in a small gesture. "Like Jill said, I'm the research assistant for the Mnemosyne project. With Nemy..." Jill aimed the camera at the ordinary-looking laptop, "whatever the subject is recalling from memory is displayed on the monitor as though it was happening in real time."

Jill swung the camera back to herself. "We also have medical assistance from nurse Kelsey Franklin." This time the panels on the blimp were filled with the image of an athletic-looking African-American man.

I blurted out, "Nurse Kelsey is male?!" The two sisters simultaneously turned to look at me as though I were some misogynistic Neanderthal.

"Mr. Franklin, Mr. Anders, and I are bringing you this live broadcast at great risk to our lives and certainly to our careers. We accept these risks and take responsibility for what you are about to see and hear. Many of the questions I will pose to Mr. Berman are backed up by thorough investigative research. We don't know what other revelations might come from this interview if any. Since our time is limited, possibly abruptly, I'll start by asking Mr. Berman to recall the events he witnessed six years ago, the evening of May 24, 2014–the day Evelyn Stillwell-Donovan, environmental advocate and wife of Arizona gubernatorial candidate Jack Donovan, died."

I looked toward the valley and saw the head of every hastily appointed deputy staring up to watch the live broadcast.

Marc switched the view to display Larry's memories on the monitor. We could hear him repeat the hypnotic suggestion to his subject. From where we stood, we saw the dark display on the sides of the balloon flicker on with the golds and wood tones of the entry to the Stillwell mansion. Three-quarter images of a middle-aged couple appeared.

"Please tell us where you are and who these two people are," Jill instructed.

Larry's reply was clearly audible.

The scene of the couple quarreling played out in much the same way as their daughters and I had witnessed while probing Jack's memories, but this time from a vantage point that included them both.

Jill interrupted when Jack snatched the slip of paper from Evelyn's hand. "Can you recall what they are arguing about?" Marc rephrased the question off camera.

"Evelyn's campaign contribution. She threatened to withdraw her check for half a million dollars and destroy Jack's chance in the election," Larry explained.

This time, we could see clearly what happened the moment before the girls' mother fell and hit her head on the side table. Evelyn reached for the check, and Jack grabbed her arm, pulling her off balance.

We were distracted by the sound of the helicopter, now circling almost directly overhead. One of the college boys said it looked like a Chinook. By the time our attention returned to the dirigible, Jack's face had filled the frame. He looked panic-stricken and was holding the receiver of the phone that was on the desk next to where Larry was standing. Jill asked, "What is Mr. Donovan doing?"

Larry replied, "Calling for an ambulance." Then we saw Larry's hand force the receiver back down onto the telephone cradle.

"And what are you telling Mr. Donovan?"

"I'll take care of it, Jack. I have friends I can call. Just endorse the check and leave it with me. Then go to your office until I phone you." Larry seemed to be reliving the scene.

The helicopter dropped close to the ground, between the vigilantes and the Border Patrol hut.

On the Jumbotron, we could see Larry lifting the phone receiver. Jill inquired about the conversation, which Larry reenacted literally from memory. When Jill asked who Angelo was, Larry explained that he's a lieutenant in the Milwaukee mob. He went on to reveal that the new Russian mob bosses were in his direct chain of command in the Russian SVR, the successor of the Soviet-era KGB.

Jill instructed Larry to remember the day he was recruited by the Russian spy agency. The scene shifted to a desert with towers of flames rising in the background. These, Larry said, were the oil rigs his Army explosives team had been deployed to extinguish during Desert Storm. The man standing before him was dressed in camo fatigues. The conversation Larry recalled revealed that he was being blackmailed by the Russian agent after he was caught smuggling out protected artifacts.

Jill pursued this line of questioning to find out that the Russians had been supporting the erection of the border wall to drive a wedge between the U.S. and Mexican governments. They were exploiting the rift so they could establish themselves as Mexico's ally and protector. That would give them control of the massive gas and oil field recently detected under the Sonoran Desert and a military foothold in the Western Hemisphere. If possible, they would provoke a military conflict between the two countries, providing Mexico's government with missiles for retaliation.

"The sparks in the sky," I gasped. "Those are missiles being fired at the United States!"

The helicopter kicked up a cloud of sand when it landed. The Chinook's blade continued to turn while it disgorged a team of half a dozen National Guard soldiers. We assumed this was their equivalent of an elite force. One of the platoon members used a bullhorn to announce that the occupants of the Border Patrol outpost had ten minutes to surrender. I hastily called Z to tell him to accept their offer. We had Larry's confession, and there was no reason now to continue occupying the site. As I was dialing, I heard the protesters' bullhorn switch on behind me.

We all turned to see Ga'ga standing in the bed of Z's pickup. "Shame," she said in an uncharacteristically firm voice. The sound must have carried over the roar of the helicopter blades and the interview that continued to be broadcast over the border loudspeakers because the vigilantes all turned to look in our direction. Even the families on the Mexico side of the border seemed to direct their attention to the old woman standing in the bed of a pickup truck.

"You claim what is not yours to take. You challenge what you do not understand. You deny what you know to be true." Her voice grew stronger as she spoke. "The time has come," she continued, "for the goodness that is in all of us to right the wrongs we see, even the wrongs we did not inflict."

Our band of protesters stood on the crest nodding in agreement with the O'odham magician's impassioned plea for reason. The militia camped below us just froze in place.

Then the sound of a single rifle shot pierced the blare of competing sounds. The next moment the megaphone clanked on the steel bed of the truck, and the frail woman slumped out of sight. Ga'ga had been shot.

A voice came over the cell phone I was holding unconsciously now. "I heard gunfire," Z said. "Is anyone hurt?"

"Your Ga'ga," I stammered into my hand as I turned to run to the truck. "I'm going to her." I slipped the phone into my pocket as I rushed to the pickup. Some of the women had already gathered around their magician, and I could see her tiny body curled up in the bed of the truck. I jumped up on the tailgate and knelt next to her heavily bleeding body. Ga'ga pulled me close and whispered to me. Then she fell silent. I pressed my fingers to her neck. I felt no pulse. I pulled the phone from my pocket. "I'm sorry, Z. I think she's...dead," I said softly. There was silence at the other end.

Patsy was the first to join me. She saw from my eyes that it was too late. Bren soon followed. I shook my head slowly. Tears began to form. I looked up at my wife. "She said, 'You know.'" At that moment, I thought maybe I did.

As I clutched the old woman's hand in mine, a chill came over me. It wasn't the chill of night air but a sensation of impending doom. Ga'ga had been responsible for opening my eyes to...to something. I couldn't say what that was, but it had changed me. I lifted her head to my lap. This pure soul, open to the mysteries of the universe, now a victim of senseless hate. I threw back my head and let out a primal howl as though invoking the spirits that had turned a blind eye to her pleas–to the pleas of these humble people and the pleas of all humanity.

In that instant, I saw the answer to my unspoken prayer. The spirits of my vision returned. Somehow, I had revived the hallucinogenic trance I experienced in the sweat lodge. The old women reaching out to their children, the braves who sacrificed their lives in battle, the magicians helpless to save their people. The apparitions ascended from the barren soil like the smoke from the ceremonial offerings of creosote. This time I embraced the visions as firmly as I could, holding on to their mystical powers like a child clings to a favorite blanket. Once again, the streaks of vermillion and gold sparks arced across the sky. But this time they seemed to fade and vanish in midair. Was I observing the future, or what the future *might* be?

I assumed I was experiencing another vision, but I felt more aware of my surroundings than when I was under the influence of peyote. I felt aware of the present in a way I didn't before. Now hundreds–no, thousands of spirits were rising from the soil around me. I could see the ghosts of souls as they ascended, massing as a surreal army above us.

But it wasn't just the celestial choir that radiated overhead–the Gila Ghost was aglow with the specters as their images filled the Jumbotron screens.

Brenda caught my arm and gestured broadly across the landscape. "Are these the figures in your vision? Is this what you saw?"

It was then that I realized this wasn't my personal vision–the experience was being shared by everyone on the plateau. And it was being broadcast on the Jumbotron, a vision shared with the entire planet. But how? How was this happening?

The apparitions from my peyote-induced dream were streaming from the Edagith burial grounds. Gauzy spirits of men and women, young and old drifted upward and hovered above the heads of onlookers–faces of ocher etched in a miasma of translucent blue, like William Blake's illustrations depicting heaven and hell. The spirits were anything but hellish, however. They possessed an impassioned sincerity that moved me to tears, and the figures seemed to be gathering above the outpost. This wasn't my vision. It was Z's!

Warriors who had fallen in battle, women toiling to grind grain, children clamoring for a meal–each one crying out, not for vengeance but for mercy. The broken promises and lies that had been endured for centuries were expressed in the faces of generations of O'odham, and their murmur was translated by their tears.

One figure stood out among the scores of others. Its luminescence radiated above the horizon like the rising of a full moon. The cacophony that had filled the night air was silenced, and only the voice of an old woman could be heard. It was Ga'ga.

She smiled broadly, but a sadness emanated from her as she spoke.

"The magic has passed," our celestial magician announced. "It now falls on Gray Feather to lead our people."

The voice was small but powerful, amplified over the loudspeakers standing like heralds at the gates of the cinderblock building. The spirit's words were clear and easily heard from the plateau and across the border. The light of campfires on the Mexican side silhouetted the shapes of scores of people kneeling devoutly before the specter. I couldn't be sure, but it seemed that each person heard her words in their own language–Spanish to the Mexicans, Papago to the O'odham, and I wasn't even sure if I was hearing her message in English or Hindi or even Sanskrit.

"Our people have suffered for generations, but so have countless others. We all set out on the same path. We all come to the same end. Each one chooses to help others on the journey or to set up barriers along the way. It has always been this way, and it always will be this way. You must choose how you travel the path."

I wondered if it was not just the words that adapted to each listener but also the message. The phantoms coalesced around the form that was Ga'ga. A small rectangle of light appeared beneath the apparition and silhouetted three figures that emerged from the outpost door. Z looked up, arms raised high above his head as though he supported the heavens. In an instant, the gleaming mass above him concentrated into a single point of blinding light that shot up into the night sky like a meteor departing this atmosphere.

The soldiers who faced the occupied headquarters tentatively raised their assault rifles and pointed them at the three braves standing transfixed before them. It was clear no one was sure what to do next. Then one of the vigilantes in the valley turned to face the military squadron. He raised his automatic weapon and pointed it directly at the platoon leader. "Let them go!" he yelled.

Another of the vigilantes joined him in taking an offensive posture.

One by one, the rest of militia turned and concentrated their rifles on the handful of bewildered soldiers. One of the truckers shouted defiantly, "He speaks for all of us." I thought it might be Ted.

The elite force slowly laid their weapons at their feet. They seemed relieved to have an excuse to do so. Z walked forward through their ranks and toward the plateau, where he watched in amazement as the militia trained their firearms on the National Guard soldiers.

The sound of a diesel engine rumbled across the stony soil behind us. Two beams of light flared on, and we could see the massive bulldozer roll toward us a few feet and then turn slowly toward the south. As the cab came into view, I saw who was at the controls. Patsy had commandeered the earth mover and was heading directly toward the barrier that divided this native tribe and separated the peoples of two nations. She was going to tear down Archie's wall.

The bulldozer quickly gained speed as it descended the stony slope and reached the perimeter road. In a matter of seconds, the massive steel bucket crashed into the thirty-foot slab of reinforced concrete. The yellow bulldozer recoiled violently from the impact. The machine backed up several feet as Patsy extended the bucket. The engine revved and the bulldozer lunged forward, pushing its way through the middle of the wall. Patsy dragged the bucket back and forth several times until only a pile of rubble separated the two nations. The band of gray that stretched across the valley was now interrupted by the blackness of the night sky visible through a gaping hole.

Patsy stepped out of the cab and climbed up onto the lip of the bucket. She aimed her camera into the darkness to document the stream of people about to cross north into Arizona. Migrant workers scrambled over the concrete chunks first. Then entire families started across, with fathers holding the hands of their children and mothers carrying infants in their arms. Several O'odham joined the immigrants, some reuniting with family members for the first time in a generation.

On the other side of us, we could see the vigilantes talking excitedly with each other as though trying to explain what they had witnessed and why they reacted the way they did.

Z picked up a bullhorn and switched it on. Every head turned in the direction of the squelch. "I am Gray Feather," he began. "We must stop this...this inhumanity," he implored. "The milgahn have stolen our lands and murdered our people, and we have forgiven them. It is not just, but our people have long honored compassion over justice. It is not fair, but life is seldom fair. I have broken the law, and I am not ashamed of the actions I have taken today–I am proud of the sacrifice these braves who joined me have made. I take responsibility for what I have done, and now I turn myself over to these men and women who are obliged to take me into custody." He set down the bullhorn and walked resolutely toward the National Guard soldiers, arms apart and his hands held peacefully above him.

A member of the militia, presumably their leader, raised his rifle high above his head, suspending it between his upraised palms. Then he slowly lowered his outstretched arms in front of him and knelt so his weapon rested on the ground. One by one the rest of the vigilantes did the same, and they marched in unison down the small rise and turned themselves in to the military force as well.

Brenda squeezed my hand. "That means we can all just–go?"

38

The road was as dark as our mood as we drove back to the Quivira Casino. Despite the thoughts that swirled through our minds, the three hours passed mostly in silence. Patsy turned quiet after she mentioned Archie. Bren seemed to be struggling with conflicting emotions about her father and what he did to their mother. I just thought about Marc and how I would tell my wife I cheated on her.

We arrived at the casino unannounced, knowing we might be targets of the Milwaukee mob or the U.S. federal government or both. It was about two in the morning when I texted Sea Horse to let him know we were approaching the garage. He replied he'd have Leon meet us at his private parking area and bring us up to his apartment.

"You survived," Sea Horse said when he greeted us at the door.

I nodded. "Barely, I guess. So did your brother, but I'm so sorry about..."

The young man raised a hand to stop me in mid-sentence. "My Ga'ga died a hero to her people. Her spirit will rest peacefully."

"Not just her people," Brenda added. "Perhaps the entire world."

Sea Horse smiled. "She has touched many lives," he said. "Especially my brother's...and mine."

"I don't think Z...I mean Gray Feather, is in any danger right now," I said trying to offer a comforting note.

"My brother has always been in danger," Sea Horse said smiling. "He seeks danger, and now it looks like it has claimed him in a way he never expected." He looked away for a moment. "...and in the way he worked hardest to avoid."

Our host gestured for us to sit and then poured us shots of whiskey. We raised our glasses in a toast–a toast to the liberation of a people and to the old woman who knew.

After a moment of silence, I asked, "Are we safe here tonight?"

Sea Horse nodded. "The mob won't bother you from now on," he said matter-of-factly.

"You...did something?" Patsy remarked.

"You might say I have some influence over their activities," Sea Horse said cryptically. "I made arrangements for your protection."

The sisters and I looked at each other and then thanked him without asking any more questions.

"That goes for your friend and the reporter as well," Sea Horse added.

"And what about you?" Patsy said. "You took quite a risk doing what you did."

"It was the path I had to take. There is no risk when you do what you must." Then he told us to get some sleep, and we would talk in the morning about what our next move would be.

Bren and I said goodnight and headed to the adjoining tower where Sea Horse had arranged for a suite for us. I closed the door to our room, and we wrapped our arms around each other. For several minutes we swayed silently, finally safe in each other's company. Then Bren started to cry.

"David, I was so worried about Daddy I didn't stop to think about the danger you might be in. I'm so sorry," she sobbed. "I could have lost you."

I realized that same thought had been consuming me for the past week, but more because of what I had done.

I led her to the edge of the bed, where we sat, and I leaned back to look at her. She was so beautiful. I knew I didn't deserve her love before, and even less so now.

"I realize how much you've been through these past few days too," I said. "What you're still going through." I sat upright and took her hands. "I wanted to wait for the right time to tell you something, but there will never be a right time, so I'll tell you now."

She looked up at me with her dark eyes, "David, what is it? The way you said that, you have me even more worried."

"I'm the one who is worried," I said. "Worried that you won't be able to forgive me for what I've done."

Her look turned to one of dread.

"I was...unfaithful." The word came out awkwardly, but I couldn't think of any other way to say it. "I had sex with someone while you were away," I blurted out. Tears began to sting my eyes.

Bren pulled her hands away and sat stunned for a moment as her eyes pierced through me as if to peer into my soul. She looked away as she slowly stood and took a few paces toward the door. She turned. "With that reporter?"

I leaped up and pressed my fist against my lips. "No, no," I said emphatically. "Not her." I took a trembling step toward my wife, but she held up her hand to stop me.

"Then...who?" The last word oozed from her lips like poison.

I hung my head and answered softly, "Marc."

Bren's look of hurt turned to one of shock. "Marc?" She turned away. "How long has this been going on?" she asked. "Are you...?"

"No, no. It's not that." I approached her as close as I dared to. "It's not that I'm...gay."

She looked at me and just rolled her eyes.

"I was thinking about my brother and how I betrayed him. I thought somehow that being with Marc would make things right—make us even."

"You realize that doesn't make any sense, don't you? You cheated on me to defend your brother's honor or something?" I could see that now she was growing angry. "The fact is, I was gone for a week, and you had sex with your boy toy."

"I can't explain it," I began.

"Then don't try. I'm going to spend the night with my sister. I don't want to see you until I've gone back to Chicago and figure out what to do then." She stormed out of the room and slammed the door behind her. I slumped to the bed and cried.

☼ ☼ ☼

I must have fallen asleep from exhaustion. When I woke up, the room was bright with sunlight. I walked to Patsy's room to see if there was anything I could say or do to make things right between Bren and me. I rapped lightly on the door, but there was no answer. The housekeeper down the hall turned and said, "They left early this morning." Then she continued on her rounds.

I don't recall how I made my way to the casino, but someone there approached me and told me the boss wanted to see me. She ushered me to Sea Horse's office.

When I stepped inside, Sea Horse motioned for me to sit on the leather couch next to his desk.

"Boss?"

"Sometimes they call me that," he replied without looking up. Then he stood. "You know by now your wife left with her sister early this morning. I had a limo take them to the airport."

I nodded. Then Sea Horse sat next to me and put his hand on my shoulder. "I don't know what you did, but she was upset, and it was obviously with you."

"I cheated on her," I said. "I slept with a man." I was surprised by my own frankness. Somehow, I trusted this man with my darkest secret.

He looked away for a moment. Then he asked, "Do you love her?"

I nodded and felt a tear run down my cheek. "Yes, desperately."

Sea Horse stood and leaned close to look into my eyes. "Do you love this man?"

I shook my head. "Not like that."

"What do you plan to do?" he asked.

"There's nothing I can do," I sniffed. "The damage is done."

"So, your wife isn't worth fighting for," he said casually. "That's a shame."

"No, no! It's not that," I protested.

He turned to me sharply. "Then fight for her," he nearly commanded. "You stood up to the mob, and you won. You faced down political corruption, and you won. You challenged a gang of vigilantes and even the entire U.S. military, and you won. You don't think you can win back the love of your wife?"

My face was buried in my hands now. "It's not that I can't. It's that I don't deserve to."

"Come with me." Sea Horse pulled me from the couch and marched me to the garage. We walked to the Mercedes SUV, and he told me to get in.

"Ga'ga called you a magician," he said as he climbed in behind the wheel and started the vehicle. "So, magician, confront this spirit that defeats you...and win."

I could tell we were returning to the sweat lodge. The sun was nearing its peak, and the thermometer on the dash registered 115 degrees.

After driving several minutes, we pulled up to the domed structure, and Sea Horse led me past the rawhide flap. It was hotter inside the ki than out. "Strip," he ordered. "You could die in here if you don't sweat. And this time you will find your answers without your tools or your science or your pathetic logic. Not even the peyote that ushered you into the other world. You will find the spirit you seek from among those you already know."

I pulled off my T-shirt, which was already soaked with sweat and let my shorts drop to the ground. Sea Horse had done the same and was now sitting cross-legged on the patterned blanket, wearing only a pair of black silk boxer shorts.

"I said strip. That means everything. You must bear yourself before the spirits."

I slid off my Fruit of the Loom briefs. Sweat now coated every inch of my bare skin. That provided only a little relief as it evaporated in the desert heat.

"How do you propose I call these spirits," I said sarcastically as I stood naked before the man I resented for helping my wife leave me.

"You're the magician. You figure it out."

"And what do I ask them if they come?"

"Again, that's all on you. Your own spirit knows what it lacks. Let it guide you." Sea Horse scooted across the floor so his back was near the flap of hide that blocked the entrance, or in this case, my exit. Then he said, "Your people know how to meditate. You invented it. So, meditate." He sounded more like a scolding schoolmarm now.

I dropped to my knees and slipped from the butterfly to the lotus position–forms I had been schooled in since my youth. I took a deep breath and felt my lips move to form an unenunciated *om.* The mantra echoed from my memory as a starting point to drown out conscious thought, yet the act itself was calculated. I smiled at the irony. My soft groan must have become audible because I could see Sea Horse smile as well. Maybe the sound was pressed from my lungs by the stifling heat. *Om.* I could hear the buzz of traffic that passed near our Mumbai community. *Om.* Like the hum of locust before their voices crescendo in the scream of their autumn chant. *Om.* It was the wail of my mother when they buried her twenty-five-year-old son.

It was the spirit of Adamya that haunted me. I had admitted that to myself long ago. He took his life, and I was partly to blame for not stopping him, or at least for not being there for him as the darkness overwhelmed him. I had gone on to live a life far grander than I ever imagined, while Adam gave up the dreams he felt he would never realize. It wasn't fair. He had been the strong one. He was my hero, and he...

"Is that it, little brother?"

The unspoken voice made the sweat that poured from my body feel like ice water. I wanted to believe Sea Horse had uttered the words, but I knew the voice belonged to Adam.

"You're angry with me because I let you down?"

I was aware this wasn't real, but I desperately wanted to hear my brother's voice, so I indulged the hallucination. I wasn't sure if my words were spoken aloud or only formed in my mind.

"Adamya? Brother, I am so..."

I could see him now as he held a finger aside his nose, the sign we used as boys to warn that father might be listening. Then he said, "Sorry? Sorry for what? You think there's something you could have done to change things? To give me back my arm? To make it all right for me to be...queer? You always were a bit of an arrogant prick." Then he laughed.

"I could have been there for you. I could at least have accepted that you..."

"What? That I'm a fag? I'm not sure I was even able to accept that."

I felt myself groan with an anguish I had long contained.

"It's OK, little brother. I forgive you. Not that there's anything to forgive, but if that makes you feel better, then that's good enough for me."

"But I miss you. I envied you. I practically worshiped you."

"And I was supposed to live up to that? That's not fair, you know. I had my own shit to deal with."

I felt tears mingling with the sweat on my cheeks. The salty sweetness dampened my parched lips.

"Devi, you were the strong one. Always setting goals and moving forward. Making your dreams come true. I just drifted like a lotus leaf, swept along by the current–caught up at every bend and eddy." He laughed again. "Listen to me. I'm talking the kind of flowery shit I used to poke fun of you for."

I could see his eyes clearly now. They darted away for a moment, then fixed hard on me. "I loved that flowery shit, but I'd never let you know that. Maybe I was the one passing myself off as an idol. I really dug how you almost worshiped me. You, all confident and determined, thinking I was someone to look up to when I was the one who didn't know where to turn or what to do."

I could feel myself slipping onto a parallel plane, aware that I was observing myself. My more rational side asked, "How is this happening? You can't be here."

"You have to ask that?" Adam said. "You know the answer, and I'm pretty sure you know you know."

"That...that you're just a manifestation of my imagination? I'm just imagining you're here?"

"Oh, I don't think it's all that simple. I'm here, all right. But ask yourself, how did I get here?"

"My memories of you? You're just a projection of my memories. Is that it?"

"We're all just a projection of our memories when you get down to it, right? I mean, you're only who you remember you are. You know better than anyone, memories and reality can be hugely different. But without memories, we'd just be like stones, unaware of the path we're on or the rains that fall on us."

"But I don't even know what path I'm on. It's all so...so random."

"Don't give me that shit," Adam said. "I'm in your head, remember? I know you call it I'itoi now, but that's no different than what we were taught as kids."

I reflected on our religious instruction. "The Mandukya Upanishad?"

"I knew you'd remember. I never made it past the first state of awareness. I was lost in the world of the physical. You, on the other hand, were all brainy—a dreamer. Maybe that was what you admired about me. I was brute physicality, the essence of the childhood you grew out of too fast. When I needed to move on, I couldn't break through the maze."

"It was just a dead end. All you needed to do was turn around."

"And go back? That's what I was running from. But you, you knew the dreaming mind long before you invented that contraption. You were far down that path, and someday you'll find the true consciousness Mom and Dad always preached about."

I remembered how we were taught to strive for the fourth state—dreamless sleep. "Turiya?"

"Turiya, I'itoi, whatever you want to call it. I didn't want to find it, even if I knew how. I was the coward. But you're on your way, brother. Go find I'itoi and look him in the eye and scream, 'I made it, you fucking bastard! You tried to hide from me, but now I'm at the center, and no one is sending me back!'"

"But if they were right, I don't want to find turiya. I don't want to stop dreaming."

"Just do it, brother. Stop remembering. Stop calculating every move. Just be. You'll find the path, so long as you don't step on your own dick."

"That means I need to let you go. I can't do that."

"You can, brother, and you have to. I love you, man. More than you'll ever know. But you're stuck at this dead end, and it's time for you to move on."

"I love you too, Adamya. I always will."

"Oh, and that stunt you pulled with your little research companion? That was pretty lame. You weren't helping anybody with that shit. Time to move on, brother, just like I have to move on."

I did sleep. When I awakened, I was in Sea Horse's bed.

"It's about time you woke up," he said. "I was about to get you to a hospital." He poured a tall glass of water and made me drink it all.

"How long have I been asleep?" I asked in a raspy voice even I scarcely recognized.

"Over a day now," he said. "You passed out in the sweat lodge. I got you back here and soaked you in a cool bath. That's what my Ga'ga did for me after my first spirit journey. You started to regain consciousness a few times, so I wasn't too worried."

Sea Horse took the glass I had quickly drained and refilled it.

"Ga'ga was right about you," he said as I took slower sips now. "You are a magician. I'm proud of you, little brother."

The words of Adam echoed in my head, and I grinned.

"You find that funny? Some people believe traders from India sailed to this continent thousands of years ago. The voyagers brought with them their own himdag and passed it on to the O'odham. Those could have been your ancestors."

"What, the Hohokam? Do you believe that?" I asked.

"It doesn't matter what I believe or what I don't believe. Either it is true, or it is not. The important thing is that we consider the possibility and learn from it."

Sea Horse's words struck me. Our obligation in this world is to learn from our experiences. That is at the heart of the teachings of Lord Shiva. That is the lesson of I'itoi. I looked upon my new brother in a different light now. Maybe we shared more than just the events of the past week. Perhaps we shared a memory that transcends time.

I realized I didn't even know his birth name. "What did your parents call you before you adopted your tribal name?" I asked.

Sea Horse looked away for a moment. I think he might have blushed. Under his breath, he muttered, "Clarence."

I tried to stifle the laugh that involuntarily passed my lips. "I'm sorry," I chuckled. "You will always be Sea Horse to me, my brother." I propped myself up on an elbow and leaned forward. "My name is Devi."

He smiled and clenched my hand ceremoniously.

"You were muttering some crazy shit, and all without the peyote. Where did your journey take you?"

"My brother came to me," I said. "He told me I needed to sleep."

Sea Horse's expression didn't change. "Apparently, he was right."

"How's Z?" I asked.

"Oh, he'll be OK. He's in jail again, but that's typical for my brother." Sea Horse rolled his eyes. "A lot of good people set up a legal fund for him, and he has a real lawyer."

"And your Ga'ga—did you...?"

"There was a big ceremony on the plateau before everyone left. She is resting now at Edagith with our elders."

I saw a tear form in Sea Horse's eye before he looked away.

"Then demolition of the burial ground was stopped?"

"Not just at Edagith, brother. Work on the entire wall stopped." I saw Sea Horse animated, maybe for the first time. "The whole world saw what we saw that night, and the government was pressured into halting construction until the entire immigration policy is reviewed."

"And the sparks in the sky I saw...the Russian missiles?"

"They're gone too. The president of Mexico ordered the Russians to leave and to take their weapons with them. He said Mexico is committed to peace, and he unilaterally disarmed the country."

"All because of what was broadcast on the Gila Ghost?"

"All because of that. It's like the entire world opened their eyes for the first time in a long time." Sea Horse was practically grinning. "Oh, and your friends in Phoenix? They were held and released after their bail was posted." He looked away.

"And who would have done that for them?" I asked suspecting I knew the answer.

A guilty smile formed on the man's lips. "Certainly not your family lawyer. He's behind bars now. He's been charged with the murder of your brother-in-law's secretary and as an accomplice to manslaughter for the death of your wife's mother."

"Sounds like I should have stayed passed out longer. Who knows what else might have been accomplished?" I coughed deeply enough for Sea Horse to look concerned.

"That thought crossed my mind," he said after I resumed breathing normally.

"And you?" I continued. "I'm sure you pissed off the mob. Do you have anything to worry about?"

"We've come to an understanding," he said.

I could tell the arrangement didn't bode well for my new brother. "What does that involve?"

"I'll be leaving the casino."

"Oh, man, I'm so sorry."

"Don't be," Sea Horse said sternly. "I think this could be a main turning point in my life. I decided to take a position on the council as Indian Affairs advocate." Then he added smiling. "We're going to really stick it to those motherfuckers!"

Sea Horse took the empty glass from my hand and set it on the side table. "I'll call to get you something to eat. Is there anything special you'd like?" he asked.

"The kitchen wouldn't happen to serve rattlesnake stew, would it?" I tried to laugh, but I didn't have the energy for that.

"You'll have to settle for prime rib."

Sea Horse placed the order, and I sank back into the white comforter he had laid me on. When he hung up, he let me know that Bren had called. He told her that I had a rough night and I was sleeping it off, which was true in a way.

"Did she sound...angry?" I asked.

"With you? Because you slept with that twinky assistant of yours?"

"Yeah, that."

"I think she's more concerned that you're all right."

Sea Horse paused. "Marc also called me. He said he was worried about you, and he thought I would know what to do."

I snorted and turned my head. Sea Horse pulled up a chair and sat next to me.

"You can't pretend it didn't happen," he said. "Not to your wife. Not to Marc. And especially not to yourself."

"Then all I can do is live with the consequences," I sniffed.

"You can own it as a stop along your journey. Just another path to explore and then move on." Sea Horse's tone was forceful but sympathetic. He grasped my arm and squeezed it firmly.

"Another dead end. Is that all we have to look forward to? Running into dead ends and starting over?"

Sea Horse stood. "You never start over," he said almost as an order. "You remember, and you learn." He stepped away to the window and pulled back the heavy curtain.

Remember and learn. Is that what Adam was telling me? Our memories are just foggy projections of how things might have happened–of what they might become?

"She really loves you, you know," Sea Horse said. "I could tell she wants you to come to her–to resume the path you both are on."

"I hope you're right. I don't think I could continue the journey alone."

Sea Horse turned to face me. "It isn't for us to decide where the journey takes us. We all find I'itoi eventually." He seemed to be peering into my soul now. "But only a few recognize him when they arrive."

40

☼ ☼ ☼

"Devi, dear. Would you pour me another martini please?"

Bren slouched on the iron bench in our Logan Square patio garden. The afternoon sun was hot even for July in Chicago. She opened the gauzy white jacket she was wearing over a scarlet halter and navy-blue hot pants.

"I see you're dressed appropriately for the holiday," I commented and tipped the brim of my red Antonio's cap.

"It's Independence Day," she exclaimed as she flung the pizza scarf draped around her neck over her shoulder. "I'd say we have something to celebrate this year."

I nodded in agreement and handed her a glass of chilled cranberry juice. "I think this calls for a toast." I made myself a *real* cosmo. "Here's to a freer country that our daughter can be proud to grow up in," I said as we clinked glasses.

"It's not fair that I'm doing all the work and you're the one who gets to drink alcohol." She made a pouty face and took a sip of juice as I sprawled out next to her.

Bren straightened herself and stared into my eyes. "And just how do you know it's a girl?"

"She has to be," I answered. "I need another woman in my life."

Brenda slapped my hand. Then she clutched it, and her tone changed.

"And how do you know..." The sadness of our first pregnancy suddenly gripped her.

I pulled her close. "I just know." I placed my hand on my wife's still-trim belly. "I know someday we'll have a daughter, and we'll name her Eve, and she'll be as strong and passionate as you are and as her grandmother was. Someday, somehow it will be the three of us." I grinned. "Then four. Then, who knows, half a dozen or more."

Bren smiled and pushed me away. "You better not," she warned. "I have ways to keep that from happening." She crossed her slender legs tightly and took a sip of her virgin cosmopolitan.

I grasped her other hand and said, "Whether it's a dozen kids or just the two of us, I'm so very much looking forward to taking this journey with you. And I'm so very much in love with you I could..."

"Die?" she threw down.

"Well, I don't know that I'd go *that* far."

Her slap was more earnest this time.

I rested an elbow on the glass table and admired the woman sitting in the sunshine that was filtering through the leaves. I was the luckiest man alive, I thought.

Brenda's cell phone rang. It was Patsy, and the two sisters talked and giggled for several minutes while I refilled our drinks.

"How's she doing?" I asked after she hung up.

"Patsy? A lot better now that she's officially separated from Arch. She called to say that she and Jill landed a book deal to publish a coffee-table volume about that night on Edagith Plateau. Her publisher is talking Pulitzer for photo-journalism!"

"That's fantastic," I said as I sat next to my wife. "She deserves a break. Has she visited your father?"

"Every day. He's under house arrest until the trial."

"I'm just glad he's out of the hospital, and the three of you worked things out." I paused reflectively. "I know what it's like carrying the guilt of feeling you're responsible for the death of someone you love."

Brenda stood and took my hand to pull me up. "We all live with memories we'd rather forget," she said softly. "That's part of being alive I suppose."

We held each other tight for a moment.

Bren brightened. "When is Marc coming over? Is he going to bring Kelsey with him this time?"

"He said they'd be here around six for a cookout, but it has to be soy burgers. They've gone vegan."

"Of course they have. We wouldn't want our California golden boy any other way," she laughed. I knew Bren had forgiven me, but more importantly, I was starting to believe she trusted me again.

"We can talk about plans for the new business after supper," I said.

"Not until we set off a few firecrackers," Bren insisted.

The Mnemosyne program was canceled, and Marc and I had been dismissed from Fulton University–too much bad press according to Dean Krause. But we were given a substantial severance package and uncontested rights to the invention and subsequent research. Now, we planned to develop memory therapy as a tool to help PTSD sufferers deal with their traumatic experiences. Brenda lost her job with the EPA for basically the same reason, and she intended to devote her efforts to environmental activism on behalf of the Evelyn Stillwell-Donovan Foundation.

Bren said, “Patsy found a house for us in North Scottsdale we might be interested in. She told me it’s big enough to operate a clinic from.”

“That wouldn’t happen to be a nine-bedroom DC Ranch estate, would it?”

Brenda smiled. “It’s paid for, and Patsy doesn’t want to live there. She moved into one of those trendy artist grottos with bare brick walls and exposed pipes running across the ceiling. And she can’t sell the place until Archie’s court case is settled. That could be years—rent free. Or were you planning to move to the reservation as resident medicine man?”

I laughed. “That job belongs to Z...I mean Gray Feather now.” Then I said with all seriousness, “But I want us to take Nemy there to help when we can.”

Brenda looked up at me. “I want that too,” she said.

I pulled her close, and we swayed in the afternoon breeze. “Mrs. Donovan-Patel, I love you.”

“Never forget,” we said in unison and laughed.

“Just remember that when we’re old,” she added.

“Oh, I’ll remember. I’ll remember, and I’ll cherish every memory.”

NEVER FORGET

Bones brittle.
Knuckles gnarl.
Blood flows frozen to the toes.

Thoughts of you–
soft, supple, warm
revive me when my reason fails.
Thank God that reason fails.

I wrote these words as a tribute to my brother–the kind of flowery shit Adam said he loved, and to remind me that we shape our memories and carry them with us always. Oh, and to make sure I don't forget another anniversary.

The memory I just shared with you was only last May, but I know it is a memory that will never fade with time, although it might be embellished by experience. I have far to go on my path to find I'itoi, but knowing I'm not on that path alone makes all the difference.

We are all *red man.* Never forget.

☼ ☼ ☼

THE END

ACKNOWLEDGEMENTS

It hardly seems like almost two years have passed from the time I brushed off the dream that inspired *REDMAN* until the story was published. I sincerely thank the people who kept me motivated during those long months.

To my early readers, Cheryl and Emily, I thank you for saying you actually enjoyed reading the very rough drafts you had to struggle through. To my nephew, Kristofer, I appreciated the tough questions you asked about the characters. To my long-time friend from my Navy days, Kevin, thank you for the incredible job of editing you did. I might have argued with a few of your comments, but I ultimately agreed with all of them. You are an amazing talent.

There are a few people who stuck by me through the insufferable months of writing *REDMAN*. My neighbors and close friends, author Greg Koren and Amy, thank you for believing I could actually write a novel. To my editor from the first word to the last, Suzanne Charles, I wouldn't have made it to "The End" without your encouragement. Thank you, Suz, for enduring my bouts with self-doubt and the countless revisions I sent you. You talked me back from the cliff edge more than once.

I owe my deepest debt of gratitude to Garry and Damian for putting up with my late-night sessions with rewrites when I could have been fixing leaky faucets and patching plaster. Damian, you blazed the trail when you published *Fool to the World* last year. I'm just walking in your shadow.

A special thank you goes to author Abby Bardi, who told me more than twenty years ago she wouldn't speak to me again if I didn't publish something. Abby, your words have haunted me for two decades. Can we talk now?

REDMAN

MAN IN THE MAZE

Made in the USA
Middletown, DE
18 January 2018